FIC TURTLE- DOVE
Turtledove, Harry
Powerless

WITHDRAWN

JUL 0 8 2025

Powerless

POWERLESS

Harry Turtledove

FAIRHOPE PUBLIC LIBRARY
501 FAIRHOPE AVE.
FAIRHOPE, AL 36532

CAEZIK
SF & FANTASY

ARC MANOR
ROCKVILLE, MARYLAND

*

SHAHID MAHMUD
PUBLISHER

www.caeziksf.com

For Greg Benford, who suggested I turn it into a novel.

Powerless copyright © 2025 by Harry Turtledove. All rights reserved. This book may not be copied or reproduced, in whole or in part, by any means, electronic, mechanical, or otherwise without written permission except short excerpts in a review, critical analysis, or academic work.

Chapters 1 and 2 appeared in somewhat different form in the September/October 2018 issue of *The Magazine of Fantasy & Science Fiction*.

This is a work of fiction.

Cover art by Dany V.

ISBN: 978-1-64710-149-7

First Edition. First Printing. July 2025.
1 2 3 4 5 6 7 8 9 10

Caezik,. Phoenix Pick and Galaxy's Edge are imprints of Arc Manor

www.CaezikSF.com

chapter

Charlie Simpkins kissed his daughter, Sally, who was eleven; his son, Nikita, who was thirteen; and his wife, Lucille, who was thirty-eight. He walked out of the one-bedroom apartment they lived in. As Lucille closed the door behind him, he lit another in the day's endless stream of cheap, nasty Progress cigarettes.

Down the stairs he went, and out of the apartment building's front entrance onto Gresham Street. In the San Fernando Valley's smoky air, sunrises were usually worth seeing. Today's was no exception: a symphony of apricots and salmons and scarlets. For a few minutes, anyway, that the air made him cough as much as his cigarettes did seemed beside the point.

He had to walk three blocks to the bus stop at the corner of De Soto. He watched his step all the way. You needed to. The sidewalk was made of cheap concrete, full of pits and cracks. Somebody'd pocketed the difference between what he promised and what he delivered. What could you do? It happened all the time.

A new billboard, red as the sunrise, was mounted on the frame across the street from the bus stop. A brawny young worker strode into the future, a sledge hammer clenched in his right fist. TRUE COMMUNISM IS COMING! shouted gold letters beside him. Charlie noticed the billboard because it was new. Having noticed it, he forgot about it. He'd seen too many, for too long. Half a dozen, of all different sizes, lay between the stop and the shop where he worked.

Another man came up, and then a gray-haired woman. Charlie exchanged nods and a few words with each. Like him, they were regulars at the stop. Strangers made regulars clam up. You never could tell if they were NBI informers. Of course, you never could tell if a regular was, either. But you had to talk to *somebody*.

Here came the bus, south down De Soto. Charlie glanced at his watch. It was ten minutes late. Well, usually it was twenty minutes late, so that could have been worse. Black diesel smoke belched from its tailpipe, adding to the sweetness of the air. The engine sounded old and tired. The bus looked old and tired. So did all the buses on the line. He hoped it wouldn't break down before it took him to Sherman Way.

It wheezed to a stop, brake shoes grinding against worn-out drums. The driver got out of his seat and yanked the door open; the compressed-air mechanism that was supposed to do the job was dead. Charlie dropped a quarter into the fare box and found a seat. He fired up a fresh Progress.

No one already on the bus paid him any special attention. A man with thick glasses read the *Los Angeles Times*. A woman methodically went through *The Daily Worker*. A young man wearing a Stars cap took a nip from a pint. Charlie thought it was too early to start getting loaded. You really weren't supposed to do it on the bus, either. He didn't say anything. If the guy needed hooch to get his heart started, then he did, that was all.

A few of the slots above the dirty windows advertised local shops. Most held propaganda posters. Charlie noticed a smaller version of the TRUE COMMUNISM IS COMING! billboard. Some of the others were new to him, too. He sighed to himself, longing for a slug of the young man's rotgut. Plainly a new campaign was in the offing. If the thought of that didn't drive you to drink, nothing ever would.

The bus jounced along. Its shocks had seen better years, and De Soto was as beat-up as any street in the Valley—as any street in the West Coast People's Democratic Republic, odds were. Potholes alternated with blacktop mushroom tops that did too good a job of filling holes.

Just south of Roscoe, a labor gang was working on the paving. The men in the drab denim uniforms worked no faster or more carefully than they had to. Watching them made Charlie shiver. He'd done a month in a labor gang a few years earlier, when the guy he punched in the nose in a barroom brawl turned out to have Central Committee connections. At that, he'd got off easy. The month cleared the books for him. His dossier didn't get permanently tagged with *antisocial element*.

Most of the zeks in the labor gang, though, would be men who violated Penal Code Article 203; you drew up to three years for systematically evading honest labor—which often meant whatever the Party wanted it to mean. The gang was supposed to turn slackers into productive workers. To make sure it did, a bored-looking guard with a Tommy gun kept an eye on them.

People got on the bus. People got off. At Sherman Way, Charlie was a person who got off. The fruit-and-vegetable shop he ran lay two and a half blocks west of De Soto. Sure as hell, a new propaganda campaign was on. Just about all the shops—the druggist's, the pet store, the flower shop, of course the WCPDR-run liquor store, even the dentist's office—sported fresh posters in their windows. What SOLIDARITY WITH THE PROLETARIAT had to do with pulling teeth, Charlie didn't know, but Dr. Fried took no chances with the powers that be.

A fat Mexican with a bandit's mustache ran the junk shop next to Charlie's place. Gomez called it a hardware store, but it sold a little of this, a little of that, some old, some new, none of the stuff expensive. Junk, in other words.

Gomez was taping a POWER SPRINGS FROM THE BARREL OF A GUN poster to the inside of his window when Charlie walked by. Charlie rapped on the glass. "How's it going, Manuel?" he asked. Gomez cupped a hand behind his ear to show he couldn't hear. Charlie repeated himself, louder and with exaggerated mouthing.

One more piece of tape finished the job of securing the poster. Then Gomez gave a thumbs-up, showing everything was okay. He came outside to survey his handiwork and asked, "What did they give you this time?"

"I dunno. I'll find out as soon as I open up." Charlie looked along Sherman Way, both west and east. Hardly anyone was on the street—it was still early. All the same, he lowered his voice as he went on, "Whatever it is, it's bound to be the same old bullshit."

He'd just put his life in Manuel Gomez's hands. If the junk-shop man felt like reporting him, Lucille would wonder why he didn't come home tonight. But it wasn't as if Gomez didn't grouse to him every now and again, too. You tried to think you were a man, not just an infinitesimal tooth on a tiny gear on a small part of the gigantic mechanism that was the West Coast People's Democratic Republic. Yes, you tried, but it wasn't always easy.

Charlie got away with it this time. Gomez rolled his eyes and chuckled sourly. He also glanced up and down the street before murmuring, "Boy, you sure hit that nail right on the head." He set a beefy hand on Charlie's shoulder for a moment before ducking back inside his shop as if embarrassed to agree. Well, he probably was.

As soon as Charlie unlocked his own front door, he smiled. He liked the odors the shop trapped: the earthy aroma of potatoes, vegetables' green smells, and the sweetness rising from peaches and apricots. The odors were always wonderful, but never quite the same from one day to the next.

His smile disappeared when he saw the cardboard tube under the mail slot. The address label on the tube bore the CPWCPDR's oil-well-and-logger's-axe emblem. Sighing, Charlie picked it up and popped off the pot-metal round on one end. Which stupid slogan would the Party inflict on him for the campaign?

He extracted the poster from the tube and unrolled it, holding it at top and bottom so he could take it all in at once. Laborers from industry and agriculture, their faces all identically grim and determined, marched in military ranks. They held the tools of their trades in the same aggressive position, as if they were weapons. Above them, in big sans-serif letters, were the words WORKERS OF THE WORLD, UNITE!

"Son of a bitch!" Charlie said, there where no one could overhear him, and then, "Oh, my aching back!" Why did they stick *him* with the oldest, stalest chestnut on the tree? Was it just luck of the draw? Or did somebody on the West Valley Central Committee have it in for him?

He looked at the poster. He half turned to look at the window where he was supposed to stick it. He could see just where it should go. Marks from pieces of tape that went up in earlier campaigns did a perfect *X marks the spot*.

"Stick it," he murmured in surprisingly thoughtful tones, and looked at the poster again. It wasn't as if he personally gave a damn whether the workers of the world united or not. He'd been taught to care in school, but in school they taught you all kinds of garbage you forgot about as soon as you escaped.

Why would you bother putting up a poster you didn't give a damn about? In a way, that question answered itself: you were liable to get in trouble if you didn't. Up till now, Charlie had always gone along with the way things worked. Up till now, it hadn't occurred to him that he might not. Maybe more of the things they'd taught him in school had stuck than he suspected.

Or maybe it was just that, as somebody or other said once upon a time, you didn't need to be a weatherman to know which way the wind blew. What would happen when a fat cat from the Central Committee hopped into his Packard—no riding smelly, rattletrap buses for people like that—and drove down Sherman Way to see how the campaign was going? What would happen when he noticed (and the SOB *would* notice) one of the buildings didn't have a poster prominently displayed?

Nothing good, not to the guy who didn't prominently display it.

Yes, that was obvious. All at once, Charlie didn't give a rat's ass. He took pride—oh, not enormous pride, but pride even so—in giving his customers a square deal. He didn't shortchange them or drop his thumb on the scale while he was weighing their spuds. You had to look at yourself in the mirror.

He looked out through the plate glass at the dingy, potholed street. An old man in ragged overalls pedaled past on a bicycle. A truck that farted smoke as badly as the bus he'd ridden clattered by. Its bed was full of worn-out tires; no doubt it was heading for the recapping outfit up the street.

Had the Central Committee, and the Party in which the Central Committee was a gear, given the neighborhood a square deal? As if to answer the question, a pretty young woman who looked as if she might be the secretary for somebody important stooped, graceful as a ballerina from the Bolshoi, to pick up a cigarette butt and stash it in a tobacco pouch.

Saying yes all the time was easy. The path of least resistance always was. But what did it get you? It got you … this. Charlie wished he'd spotted the butt the pretty girl cadged. He would have grabbed it himself.

What would happen if you said no? Charlie eyed the poster one more time. Then he crumpled it into a ball and tossed it into the wastebasket behind the counter. The mailing tube followed it in.

Whistling under his breath, he switched the sign on the door from CLOSED to OPEN. One more worker in the world was on the job.

A woman came in and bought apricots. A man came in and wanted to buy apples. Charlie spread his hands. "Can't sell you what I don't have."

"*Why* don't you have any?" The man sounded indignant, which probably meant he was a Party member, used to getting whatever he wanted whenever he wanted it.

But Charlie just spread his hands wider. "Because the shipment hasn't come in," he answered, and left it right there. He didn't know this would-be customer. With a regular, he would have rolled his eyes and gone *What can you do?* But a regular, of course, would have known as well as Charlie that you couldn't do one damn thing.

"Somebody will hear about this," the man declared, and stomped out of the shop in a huff. Party member or not, he didn't notice there was no propaganda poster in the front window. Neither had the woman who left with the sack of apricots.

So there, Charlie thought. Propaganda campaigns, as far as he could see, mattered only to the apparatchiks who ordered them. And, as far as he could see, those functionaries only ordered them so they would look good to *their* bosses. Ordinary folks ignored them as much as they could and privately giggled at what was too funny or too stupid to ignore.

Vissarion Gomez, Manuel's son, walked up the street. He helped Manuel at the junk shop. He also ate up a good part of whatever money they made. Five minutes later, he came back munching on a hot dog he'd bought from the stand at the corner. He looked into Charlie's shop and started to wave. He wasn't a bad kid, just hungry all the time.

The wave dissolved in a double take that should have gone on the silver screen. Vissarion opened the door and looked around to make sure Charlie was alone before he said anything. Then he went, "Hey, Mr. Simpkins, how come you don't got no poster up?"

Unlike the Party honcho, he could see what wasn't right in front of him. Charlie shrugged an elaborate shrug. "I just don't."

"They forgot to give you one? Some o' them jokers, they don't got all o' their shit in one bag, know what I'm sayin'?"

"Do I ever," Charlie said. "But they didn't forget."

"They didn't?" Vissarion needed a few seconds to process that—and to take another bite of the hot dog. "Then how come it ain't taped to the window like everybody else's?"

Charlie shrugged again. "Because it isn't." He had trouble finding a better reason than that even for himself. *Because I'm too sick and tired of all the nonsense to stomach it one more second* might have come closest.

Vissarion Gomez stared at him. He stared at the spot on the window where the poster should have gone. He popped the rest of the hot dog into his mouth. Around it, he said, "Your funeral, man." He walked out. The door clicked shut behind him, an oddly final sound.

He was much too likely to be right. But nobody else said anything else about the glass where the poster should have been for the rest of the day. People came in. They bought things. Sometimes, like the Party guy early in the morning, they pissed and moaned about what Charlie didn't have. It wasn't as if he'd never pissed and moaned in ill-stocked shops himself. They left, happy or otherwise.

He'd have bet he wouldn't have noticed a missing poster in one of those other shops, either. Nobody noticed stuff like that when it was there; why should anybody notice it when it wasn't? Propaganda pervaded the West Coast People's Democratic Republic, as it pervaded every fraternal socialist state. They were built on five-year plans and bullshit.

Everybody knew it. People made sour jokes about it, things like *We pretend to work and they pretend to pay us*. But nobody did anything. How could you, when doing something was liable to mean a tenner in a corrective-labor camp? Even an act—or rather, an un-act—so small as omitting a poster might be construed as counterrevolutionary if a commissar or a police lieutenant happened to get up on the wrong side of the bed.

Charlie understood all that. He didn't feel particularly heroic about chucking WORKERS OF THE WORLD, UNITE! into the trash can. He was just sick and tired of giving lies a helping hand. The lies, no doubt, would go on all the same, but they could go on without him.

Toward closing time, Manuel Gomez ambled over from the junk shop. As Vissarion had before, he looked at the place where the poster wasn't. "The kid told me what you done," he said, "but I couldn't hardly believe it till I seen it for myself."

"I didn't do anything," Charlie said: the exact and literal truth, not that that would do him any good.

"That's what I'm talkin' about," Gomez said. "How come you didn't?"

"I didn't, that's all." Charlie'd known Manuel for fifteen years. He didn't think the junk-shop man or his son were informers. But you didn't say everything that was in your mind to anybody but your most trusted friends and your loved ones … and sometimes not to them. Often not to them.

Gomez could read between the lines; it was a knack people who lived in socialist countries picked up quickly if they wanted to go on living. "You got big ones, buddy," he said, not without admiration. After a pause, he added, "Just makes 'em easier to drape over a doorknob, though."

"It'll be okay," Charlie said without conviction.

"It will if you ask for a new poster—tell 'em you squashed some squash on the old one or somethin'," Gomez said.

Charlie thought about it. The junk-shop man stood a decent chance of being right. All the same, he shook his head. "I don't think I'm gonna do that."

"What's with you, man? You got a death wish, or what?" Manuel sounded concerned in a clinical way, as if a neighbor's cat were shitting blood. "You go and buck the Party, you ain't just a flyweight up against a heavyweight. You're a goddamn *fly* up against a heavyweight, and he'll swat your sorry ass and not even notice he done it."

Gomez stood a decent chance—a much better than decent chance, in fact—of being right about that, too. But Charlie shook his head again. He was sick to death of lies. Lying to the Central Committee about why the poster would go in the window late disgusted him as much as taping it up there to begin with would have. "I'm just gonna roll with it," he said.

"Vissarion told me what he told you. He ain't wrong. You're a good guy, Charlie. You don't wanna get messed up on account of somethin' that ain't worth it, hear what I'm sayin'?"

"I hear you. Thanks." Charlie left it there. He could have said he thought the truth was worth it, but the less he said about anything, the better off he'd be. He suspected he wouldn't be *well* off no matter how little he said, but even so…. Sure as hell, sometimes you just got tired.

Manuel Gomez read his determination. Gomez's jowls wobbled when he shook his head. "Good luck, buddy. I got the feeling you're gonna need it." As his son had before him, he walked out. The click of the latch behind him sounded even more as if it came from a closing cell door than it had when Vissarion left.

"How'd it go?" Lucille Simpkins asked when Charlie got back to the apartment.

"Another day," Charlie answered. "Some people got bent out of shape 'cause I didn't have any apples. Like I didn't have apples on purpose. C'mon! How stupid is that?"

"Pretty stupid." His wife eyed him. "You look beat-up, like. It really must have got under your skin."

"Could be. How about you fix me a bourbon onna rocks?" Charlie wasn't going to tell her about not putting up the poster, not yet and maybe not ever. But he knew she saw the strain of that on his face, even if she couldn't name it.

"I can do that," Lucille said. They'd been married for eighteen years. She could read his tone as well as—probably better than—he could read hers. Then again, she didn't need to be a National Bureau of Investigation interrogator to realize he had more on his mind than he felt like talking about. A good thing, too; an NBI man wouldn't have made him the drink.

A stiff knock of bourbon (well, corn whiskey aged in barrels—only the upper echelons of the nomenklatura got the genuine article from Old Dominion province of the Southeastern Confederated People's Republic) improved his attitude, or at least dulled the edge of his worry. If one was good, wouldn't two be better?

Lucille raised an eyebrow when he held out the glass for a refill. "I need it," he said. "Two drinks aren't enough to make me start knocking you around."

"That's nice," she said warily, but she did pour him more booze. She had her reasons for sounding anxious. Plenty of men beat their wives once they'd had a few drinks after getting home from work. Plenty of men stopped at a saloon on the way home from office or shop or factory, got back already toasted, and wasted no time laying into the alleged love of their life. It was a sport for them, like playing poker or watching the Coast League on TV if they were lucky enough to have a TV to watch.

Charlie didn't get drunk very often. He'd never smacked Lucille in all the time they'd been together. Manuel Gomez would have called him a petty-bourgeois sentimentalist, or more likely just laughed his ass off.

Not caring to dwell on that, Charlie asked, "What are we gonna eat tonight?"

"Noodles and cottage cheese," his wife said.

"Maybe I *should* beat you," Charlie said. "Not even some sausage that tastes like it's half ground-up inner tube?"

"I'm sorry. I *am* sorry," Lucille said. "But butcher shops were closed today. They had the NO MEAT signs in their front windows."

"Crap. Right next to the SOCIALISM IS PROSPERITY! posters, too, I bet," Charlie said.

Lucille nodded. "That's about the size of it. They're everywhere. Which one did they give you for the shop?"

"WORKERS OF THE WORLD, UNITE!" Those two slugs of bourbon let Charlie's mouth come out with what he'd meant to keep quiet about: "Only I didn't put the stupid goddamn thing up."

"You didn't?" his wife exclaimed. "What did you do with it, then?"

"Threw it in the trash," he answered, not without pride.

Lucille gaped. She looked around to make sure Nikita and Sally couldn't hear. They couldn't; they were back in the bedroom, wrestling with homework. "You didn't!" she said again. After a long look at him, her shoulders slumped. "You did. How could you do anything so stupid?"

No, Charlie wasn't a man who thumped his wife whenever she got out of line. If he were, she would have got a fat lip or a black eye then and there. Instead, Charlie shrugged as wearily as he had while he was talking with Manuel Gomez.

"I just got sick of lying," he said, keeping his voice low so the kids wouldn't overhear. "I know it's garbage. You know it's garbage. Even the people who give us the propaganda posters to stick in our windows know it's garbage. I can't stand it any more."

"Can you stand a visit from the NBI?" Lucille asked. "You're going to get one."

"One missing poster isn't enough to get the Nibbies all excited." Charlie didn't sound sure of that, even to himself.

"They get excited about whatever they feel like getting excited about," Lucille said, which was much too likely to be true. "But suppose they *don't* care. How much good does that do you? You think you won't see a black-and-white? You think they won't haul you back to the station on Vanowen for some questions?"

The cops at the West Valley station did not have a reputation for lovingkindness. Few Los Angeles policemen—few policemen anywhere in the WCPDR—did. Even so, Charlie said, "I'd rather see them than the Nibbies."

"You would? Why?" His wife looked amazed—and dubious.

"Because I've got a decent chance of being able to pay off the heat. The NBI ...." Charlie shook his head. Unlike ordinary local cops, agents of the state got paid well enough to make them tough to bribe. Also, some actually believed in the inevitability of the glorious proletarian revolution and the rise of true Communism. Cops—the ordinary guys in blue serge and Sam Browne belts—liked telling other people what to do and beating them up if they didn't do it more than most folks, but they didn't pretend they were up on some lofty pedestal. Most of the time they didn't, anyhow.

"Maybe." Lucille still wasn't convinced, not by the way she said that.

"Let's worry about it later, okay?" Charlie said. "How long till supper? I'm starved." *The condemned man ate a hearty meal* ran through his mind. By what would do for a miracle in this age of scientific socialism, he managed not to say it out loud.

Sometimes the axe fell on you right away. Sometimes it dropped in slow motion. Whenever somebody walked into the fruits-and-vegetables shop over the next couple of days, Charlie's stomach knotted like a fist. He braced himself for trouble. He braced himself for a fight, or at least for a shouting match.

And nothing happened. Over and over, nothing happened. People came in. They bought what they needed if he had it. They muttered and fumed and walked away if he didn't. Nobody seemed to notice that his front window was missing its WORKERS OF THE WORLD, UNITE! poster or some other sign of full-bore socialist solidarity.

Suppose they gave a propaganda campaign and nobody cared. Suppose they gave one and nobody even knew it was on, Charlie thought dizzily.

He began to think—to hope, anyway—he'd honest to Pete flouted the authorities.

Lucille didn't believe it, not for a second. "They're stupid, but they aren't blind," she whispered to him in bed after the kids had fallen asleep—the only even halfway safe time to say such things.

"They've been blind so far," Charlie whispered back. Lucille just shrugged, which got across what she thought without using any more dangerous words at all.

She proved right, of course. Part of Charlie had known from the beginning that she would. Even the part that hadn't known it had feared she would.

Mary Ann Hannegan ran an apartment-rental office a few doors up Sherman Way from Charlie's shop. She was a tall, very fair woman who wore her graying blond hair almost mannishly short. Back in her twenties, she must have been one hot number. Now, in her fifties, she looked hard and tough. The Marlboros she puffed through one after another did nothing to ease the impression.

As soon as she walked through the doorway, Charlie knew things had hit the fan. As the fancy cigarettes showed, she was a Party block chairman and an associate member of the West Valley Central Committee. "Good morning, Comrade," she said briskly, leaving him in no doubt that she wasn't here for asparagus or an artichoke.

"Hello," he said. "What can I do for you, uh, Comrade?" The title didn't come so naturally to his lips as it did to hers.

She blew a stream of smoke at him as if, like power, it sprang from the barrel of a gun. "Somebody told me you'd been slacking in the new campaign," she said, and blew another stream of submachine gun–like smoke at the place where the poster wasn't. "I didn't want to believe that. It reflects on the block's revolutionary spirit. It reflects on *me*. But I can't help seeing it's true."

"Yeah, well …." Charlie shuffled his feet and looked faintly contrite, as if she'd caught him looking at dirty pictures.

"You can still fix it, you know," she said. "Put up the poster, stop acting like a stubborn fool, and we'll look the other way. We're reasonable people, Comrade. We know we're dealing with human beings. Anybody will slip up once in a while. Don't be stupid. Going along is the easy way, the sensible way." She ground out a Marlboro under the sole of a sensible shoe at the same time as she was lighting another one—she smoked the way Charlie did.

And it wasn't as if she were wrong. Going along *was* the easy way. It was the sensible way, too, if you thought being sensible meant not giving the regime any excuse to land on you with both feet. They taught you to be sensible like that from the moment you were born. They didn't wait till you started school. You were well on your way by then.

Charlie had always been sensible like that. He was no braver than the next guy. But sometimes it got too obvious that what they told you and what you saw with your own eyes didn't match up. What were you supposed to do then? Pretend you didn't see? Plenty of people had no trouble with that. For a long time, Charlie hadn't, either. Now .... Now he lacked the gift of unseeing, the gift that came so naturally to so many.

Mary Ann Hannegan watched him with eyes keen and pitiless as a sniper's. He hadn't told her no. But he also hadn't fallen all over himself blubbering gratitude at possibly escaping the Party's shit list. That was what you were supposed to do under such circumstances.

She blew out another stream of smoke. Softly, she said, "You think you know how bad it will be, don't you, Comrade? I'm here to tell you, though, you don't have any idea. Remember that when you find out."

"Comrade Hannegan—" Charlie broke off. What could he say? If he taped up a poster, he went back into the fold like a good little sheep. If he didn't, he was fair game instead.

Did he want to go on getting sheared and eventually butchered at the Party's convenience? Or did he want to make things difficult for the powers that be? If that wasn't the question, what was?

The block leader shook her head like a judge handing down a guilty verdict. *Yeah, just like that,* Charlie thought. She told him, "Comrade, a wise and progressive writer once said, 'The world breaks everyone and afterward many are strong at the broken places. But those that will not break it kills.' Do you understand what he meant?"

"Oh, I think I just might," Charlie answered.

"Well, then," Mary Ann Hannegan said, as if it were a complete sentence. To her, no doubt it was. She would have played this game before with other backsliders. She knew the rules, and could make up some of them as she went along. Charlie had to guess and try to play at the same time.

He said, "Can I show you some apricots? They're from an orchard in Sylmar, and sweet as sugar."

Her nostrils flared. She wasn't used to being flouted, and she didn't like it. "Let's try this one more time," she said. "If you won't think of yourself, think of all the things that can happen to your family."

So it got there that fast, did it? Charlie'd known it would sooner or later, but he'd expected later. He gave her a look almost as hostile as the one she was giving him. "Comrade, all I want is for people to leave me alone," he said quietly. "I'll leave everybody else alone, too, promise."

"That is … not sufficient." The pause told Charlie she was casting about for the exact phrase she wanted.

"No? Can I please ask you one question, then?" he said.

"Go ahead, if you must." Mary Ann Hannegan made it sound more like a warning than an offer.

"Thanks." Charlie pretended not to hear that. "What I want to know is, if you've got to threaten somebody's family to make him do what the Party says he has to, how can you stand working for the Party to begin with?"

The question had any number of possible answers. The chance to tell other people what to do. Those nice cigarettes she smoked. A bigger, newer apartment. A better car, and one you got without spending years on the waiting list. Holidays sledding in the Rocky Mountain People's Republic, or lolling on a tropical beach in the Mexican Soviet Socialist Republic. If your thoughts ran that way, being in the vanguard of history.

Mary Ann Hannegan gave him none of them. She just shook her head, once, in a final way, trampled another butt underfoot, and stalked from the shop.

Charlie's courage and resolve dribbled out of him as if he were a cracked pot. He had to grab the counter to stay upright; his legs didn't want to support him. No matter what he did, he was in for it now. The only question left was how bad *it* would be.

Four days later, the letter came. It had no stamp; it was in a highly official envelope that warned against unauthorized use on penalty of a $300 fine. Lucille handed it to Charlie without a word when he got home from the fruit-and-vegetable shop.

"Oh, joy," he said. "The other shoe has dropped. That didn't take long, did it?"

"Are you going to open it?" his wife asked.

"I don't know. Am I?" Charlie wanted to see what was inside about as much as he wanted a root canal. Sometimes a rotting tooth left you no choice. Sometimes an official envelope didn't, either. He pulled out the sheet of paper inside and read it.

"Well?" Lucille inquired when he didn't say anything right away.

He'd needed a little while to wade through the turgid, contorted prose the letter used. But that wasn't the only reason he'd stayed quiet; if he'd spoken up right away, anything he said would have been used against him. Even with the breather, he paused to light a Progress and take a deep, soothing drag before finding words: "Starting Monday, I'm not the manager at the shop any more. They're putting in a new guy."

"Do you still have a job?" Lucille sounded terrified. Plainly, she was picturing an Article 203 around his neck. She'd have a hard time living down the shame if he drew another stretch in a labor gang fixing potholes on De Soto or pulling garbage out of the Los Angeles River's concrete channel after a rain.

But he managed a jerky nod. "They're sending me to a warehouse in Studio City. My monthly salary gets cut fifty bucks, too."

"That's terrible!" she exclaimed.

Charlie shrugged. It wasn't great, no, but in the workers' paradise the workers didn't have all that much to buy. He said, "I'll tell you what's terrible. This is more than twice as far away as the old place. I'll have to take two buses to get there and two more to get back. So it'll take three times as long coming and going."

"Wouldn't it have been simpler just to tape up the damn poster?" Lucille didn't try to hide her bitterness.

"I don't know." Charlie didn't try to hide his weariness. He had the vague feeling that if more people didn't automatically do what the authorities told them to, the West Coast People's Democratic Republic might not be a place where things like his punitive transfer and pay cut happened every day.

"Will they give you your old job back if you tell them you *will* tape up the damn poster?" his wife asked.

15

"I don't know," Charlie repeated. But that wasn't enough. He went on, "I don't want to tape it up. That's the size of things, hon. If you aren't happy about it, you better figure out what you want to do next."

Lucille looked at him as if she'd never seen him before. In a certain sense, she probably hadn't. Charlie looked at her with what he hoped was disguised terror. If she took Nikita and Sally and filed for divorce on the grounds that she didn't want to stay married to a politically unreliable man, the WCPDR's legal system would be stacked in her favor. No doubt she'd keep the apartment. He'd be out on the street, and lucky if he didn't lose even the warehouse job along with the place to stay.

Was she making that same calculation? Of course she was. How could she not? Anyone in her shoes would have. Without a word, she turned and walked into the small, cramped kitchen. She came back with the bottle of not-quite-bourbon and two mismatched glasses. After pouring stiff drinks for both of them, she raised her glass (once upon a time, it had held grape jelly). "Here's to getting by," she said, and drank.

Something in Charlie's chest loosened as he drank with her. He hadn't noticed it was there till it suddenly wasn't any more. Maybe because it wasn't, the whiskey didn't seem to scorch so much going down the pipe. "Jesus, but I love you!" he said.

"You're a jerk, Charlie. I've known you were a jerk for years," Lucille said, more fondly than not. "But you're my jerk, and I'm stuck with you, so what am I going to do but stick with you?"

She wasn't stuck with him, not if she didn't want to be. If he was going to start dissenting from things like propaganda campaigns, she had to be a jerk herself if she wanted to stay stuck with him. That she did want to made him think he might have done a few things right in his life after all. "Thanks," he whispered, and for once the huskiness in his voice didn't come from the harsh corn liquor.

"For what?" she said. Sentiment—what he would have called mush when he was a kid—came almost as unnaturally to her as it did to him. She went into the kitchen again. This time, she started banging pots and pans around. No matter what else happened, she had to put supper together.

chapter

Monday morning, Charlie rode his usual bus south from Gresham. The driver gave him a curious look when he didn't get off at Sherman Way. "New job," he said with a shrug, and stayed aboard down past the agricultural college, all the way down to Ventura Boulevard. He left the bus there. It went west on Ventura. He needed to go east, and crossed the street to wait for the bus heading that way.

It was late. *Of course it is*, Charlie thought gloomily. He looked around for places that sold coffee and donuts. He'd do the same thing when he got to the warehouse. A motor didn't run without fuel.

A tall, skinny, gray-haired man waited in front of the warehouse. Charlie saw that it was plastered with a fine selection of posters from the new campaign. He sighed to himself but didn't let what he was thinking show on his face. That proved wise. The gray-haired man said, "You Comrade Simpkins?"

"That's me. They mostly call me Charlie."

"Well, Comrade Simpkins, I'm Comrade Muldberg," the gray-haired man said, ignoring the overture. "I'm responsible for his warehouse, and for meeting all the required norms. I've heard you've got an antisocial attitude. I hope that's not true. But if it is, you'll be sorry. Nobody here wants any interference with our smooth operation. You understand me?"

"I sure do, Comrade." Charlie nodded. Again, his face and voice gave away nothing: a skill useful for staying out of trouble. He went on, "Just tell me what to do, and I'll do it."

That gave Muldberg—whose first name Charlie still hadn't learned—nowhere to let his anger light. He muttered to himself and spat a stream of tobacco juice a couple of inches to one side of Charlie's left shoe. "Come on, then," he growled.

Charlie lugged sacks of beans and potatoes and crates of fruit and nuts out to the floor where truck drivers could take them to shops all through the Valley. He recognized a couple of the drivers, but didn't let on. They probably recognized him, too. They also didn't show it; disgrace might be contagious.

They had dollies to help move the sacks and crates. Charlie didn't. When he asked Comrade Muldberg if he could use one, the skinny man shook his head. "We don't have those here," he said curtly.

"How come?" Charlie asked.

"Because we damn well don't," Muldberg snapped. "Now quit malingering, or I'll write you up."

By the way he said it, he was just looking for the chance. Charlie went back to work without another word. None of the other haulers spoke to him all day long. They had to know he hadn't won a promotion to get here. From the sidelong glances they sent his way, they were scared to come anywhere near him. By quitting time, his shoulders ached and his back was sore. He took more than an hour to get home.

"How was it?" Lucille asked.

"For Chrissake, fix me a bourbon," Charlie explained.

Before he headed for the bus stop the next morning, he dug their old baby stroller out of the back of the closet. It had gathered dust there for years. He didn't know why they'd never chucked it, but they hadn't. "What are you going to do with that?" Lucille wondered.

"Ride it," Charlie said. His wife shut up.

On the bus, he folded the stroller so it fit between his knees and the seatback in front of him. "What you got that thing with you for?" the driver asked, as Lucille had before him.

"Never can tell when I might run across a baby," Charlie answered cheerfully. Like Lucille before him, the driver asked no more questions.

Comrade Muldberg scowled when Charlie wheeled the stroller into the warehouse. "You can't bring that stupid thing in here," he said.

"But it's a work aid, Comrade. It will make me look like a Stakhanovite," Charlie said. He might be sick to death of the Party's jargon, but he happily used it when it worked to his advantage. *The devil can cite Scripture for his purpose.* Somebody'd said that. He'd read it in school. He couldn't remember who, though.

The stroller had carried first Nikita and then Sally. Now he loaded it with produce so he could move the stuff out onto the warehouse floor without using his back and his arms so much. Sure enough, with it he could easily surpass his work norms, for all the world as if he *were* a hero of socialist labor.

Comrade Muldberg scowled worse than ever. But, since Charlie was doing more than required, the warehouse boss couldn't very well tell him to stop.

Muldberg's scowl made the other guys in the warehouse see Charlie with different eyes. "You ain't so dumb, are you?" a big black man murmured as they passed each other.

"If I weren't dumb, would I be here?" Charlie replied, also softly. The black guy's shoulders shook with swallowed laughter.

A wiry fellow who looked like a sneak thief said, "Fuck, man, you got old Emmett shitting rivets."

"Emmett?" Charlie echoed.

"Muldberg," the wiry fellow said, so Charlie learned the boss's first name at last.

Before the week was out, more workers started bringing in strollers and foldup shopping carts and other contraptions with wheels. One even begged, borrowed, or (most likely) stole a genuine dolly. The work went much smoother and faster for everybody after that. Once they'd finished what they needed to do, the men had time to talk and smoke and take it easy.

Comrade Muldberg summoned Charlie to his office first thing in the morning on the Wednesday of the following week. He had a soft chair behind the desk for himself and a hard chair in front of it for summonees. On the wall in back of his head was taped a copy of the WORKERS OF THE WORLD, UNITE! poster that had got Charlie into hot water to begin with.

"You were the one who began bringing wheeled devices into this warehouse," Muldberg said. From another man, or even in a different tone of voice, that would have been praise. From Emmett Muldberg, it sounded more like a denunciation.

Charlie chose to ignore the way it sounded. "That's right, Comrade," he said, nodding and smiling. "Aren't you glad I've made the whole place more efficient?" He was sure people had won Standout of Socialist Labor pins for less, but he didn't care if they stuck one on him or not.

A good thing, too, because they weren't going to. In the same deadly tone he'd started with, Muldberg continued, "As your previous history demonstrates, Comrade, you are a disruptive element."

"I don't see how," Charlie said. Some of his surprise was real, some artfully assumed. "All I was trying to do was take the strain off my back. Not getting any younger, you know."

By the look on Muldberg's face, he wouldn't get any older if the warehouse boss had anything to do with it. "You have made a mockery of work norms here," Muldberg said. "You have made a mockery of warehouse work norms all over the county, all over the state, all over the West Coast People's Democratic Republic!"

"Issue everybody dollies or carts, then. Come up with some new work norms," Charlie said—reasonably, he thought.

Again, Comrade Muldberg might as well not have heard him. "Starting tomorrow, wheeled conveyances of any kind will be banned from the warehouse floor."

"Even the ones the guys on the trucks use?" Charlie asked.

Muldberg gave him a look that should have turned him to the low-grade concrete that went into so many cheap apartment blocks, a look that said he wasn't worth turning to stone. "Shop-floor lawyers usually get what they deserve," he said. "I'll enjoy giving it to you."

"I just don't understand why the guys in warehouses haven't had dollies all along. They would have got more done, and they wouldn't have needed to go to the doctor so much with blown-out backs and things," Charlie said.

"They haven't had them because that's not how warehouse policy is written," Emmett Muldberg replied, as if to an idiot. "Writing policy isn't for the likes of you, Comrade Simpkins. It's for the experts at the Secretariat for Agricultural Development."

"Yeah, what do I know? I'm just a worker."

"That's right. High time you—" Muldberg broke off, alarm and hatred chasing each other across his bony face. The regime boasted that it rested on the broad backs of the proletariat. When it came to dealing with actual workers, though, the bosses called the shots. But they risked trouble when they showed what they really thought of the people they ordered around. Charlie would have had Muldberg in his back pocket if he'd come out with something like *High time you remember it*. The warehouse boss pointed to the door. "Get out of here!"

Charlie got. He went to work ... with the old stroller. Before long, Comrade Muldberg posted carbons of a typed notice banning wheeled vehicles of any kind all over the warehouse. Charlie didn't say a thing. For one thing, he'd got the word. For another, he was already on Muldberg's shit list. The other workers groused furiously. "What's up with that bullshit, Comrade?" shouted the big black man, whose name was Dornel.

"It's not bullshit," Muldberg said. "It's an authorized work directive in the spirit of socialist labor, is what it is."

"Sure sounds like bullshit to me," Dornel said. Several others growled agreement.

"I don't care what it sounds like to you, Comrade Banks. If you want to find out what the consequences of disobedience are, be my guest," Muldberg replied. That could mean anything from a reprimand in his personnel file to a visit from the NBI and an all-expenses-paid trip to a corrective-labor camp. Dornel zipped his lip. So did the others.

Later that day, the guy who looked like a sneak thief—he went by Eddie—sidled up to Charlie and murmured, "Well, man, it was fun while it lasted."

"Yeah." Charlie nodded. "It was, wasn't it?"

Thursday morning, nobody showed up with anything that had wheels. Fear of Comrade Muldberg made cowards of them all. Muldberg stared around the warehouse with baleful satisfaction. "That's more like it, Comrades," he said. "And I want to remind you all that next Tuesday is an election day. In the spirit of freedom and democracy and progress toward true Communism, be sure to cast your ballot at your local polling place." He didn't tell them they'd catch it if they didn't. He knew they knew that.

People bitched all day long. A bald man named Dave said, "Voting'll do us about as much good as combing my hair'll do me." He ran a hand over his shiny scalp. Charlie grinned and nodded. Somebody—he didn't see who—whistled softly. Dave was sailing close to the wind. If anyone squealed, he might be in deep.

You could vote for progress toward true Communism, or for what the Communist Party of the West Coast People's Democratic Republic called progress toward true Communism. You couldn't vote against it, though. That was what the CPWCPDR called the spirit of freedom and democracy.

Taking two buses back home meant Charlie didn't get to his polling place till almost eight o'clock. It stayed open till ten, so that wasn't a problem ... for the authorities. It meant Charlie would be starved by the time he walked into his apartment, but he wouldn't be the only one today.

A clerk had him sign in and gave him a ballot, then waved him to a voting booth. The ballot had a number on it. They could trace it back to him if they wanted to. The voting booth didn't have a curtain, either. Chances were good someone was keeping an eye on him.

Along with the CPWCPDR candidates, Democrats, Progressives, and Republicans also appeared on the ballot—in smaller type, to remind you that, while they were still legal, they weren't exactly approved of. To Charlie, they were like the head on a glass of beer. They looked nice, but they didn't add any weight. And they tasted just like the lager below.

He looked at the ballot for a minute or so. Then he folded it up without marking it at all and stuck it in the ballot box. That was the strongest way he had to tell the powers that be that he didn't want to play their game. Voting for one of the unapproved parties would have gone along with the system, and he didn't want to. Besides, the Party was counting the votes. Honestly?

The next morning, the *Times* trumpeted that CPWCPDR candidates all over California had triumphed with majorities ranging from ninety-three to ninety-nine percent. Charlie wondered who the poor shlub who'd got only ninety-three percent was. He might be too embarrassed to show his face in Sacramento.

When he got to the warehouse, Eddie handed him a petition. It asked Comrade Muldberg's superiors to permit the workers to use dollies on the floor. Eight or ten men had already signed it. Charlie scribbled his name, too.

"It won't do any good, you know," he said. "It'll just get all of our tits in the wringer."

Eddie smiled crookedly. "How will we know the difference?"

Since Charlie hadn't been there long enough yet to know who Emmett Muldberg's superiors were or how to get the petition to any of them, he just shrugged. He and the others on the floor worked no harder or faster than they had to. Muldberg looked as if he longed for a cat o' nine tails to spur them on. He might have been happier had they kept their strollers and carts. Or he might not have. He was not a man made for happiness.

Friday morning, Eddie whispered to Charlie, "We managed to pass it on."

"Good," Charlie said, and wondered how big a liar he was.

He found out Monday. Comrade Muldberg assembled the workers. "You bastards think you can screw me over, do you? I've got news for you. The Party knows I'm a good, loyal, solid proletarian," he ground out. "The Party knows how to take care of wreckers, too. The deviationists who tried to undercut me will pay the price, and you can count on that."

Charlie made sure he met his norm that day, no matter how much his back and shoulders regretted it. He wasn't the only one, either. He did the same thing Tuesday and Wednesday. He wondered whether, if he kept at it for a while, his muscles and joints would get used to the work.

But he discovered that not giving Muldberg any more excuses to come down on him didn't spare him from the Party's wrath. Or maybe the punishment landed because of the blank ballot. When he came home Wednesday night, he found Lucille trying to console Nikita. His son seemed inconsolable. "What's the matter?" Charlie asked.

"They threw me out of the Falcons today," Nikita said. "They threw me out because of you. They said they didn't want an unreliable reactionary's son. All the kids at school were laughing at me."

"Ah, shit," Charlie said wearily. Getting expelled from the CPW-CPDR's youth organization was no laughing matter. The black mark would stay in Nikita's file forever. It would certainly hurt him if he tried to get into college. It might go on hurting him when he looked for work five years from now, or fifteen, or thirty-five.

Not for the first time, Lucille asked, "Wouldn't it have been easier just to stick that stupid poster up and get along the way you always did?"

"I don't know. Would it? How can you want to clap hands for a bunch of people who go and hurt the son for what the father did?" Charlie said.

He hadn't really said anything bad about the powers that be in front of Nikita before. The boy stared at him. "You *are* an unreliable reactionary," he said.

"Maybe I am. Who knows?" Charlie said. "But if I am, they just went and showed you why I am. So welcome to the club, kiddo. It's bigger than you think, I bet."

Once they started doing things to you, you wanted to hit back, even if tiny blows were all you could strike. Monthly political meetings were mandatory. They had to be mandatory; they were so deadly dull, no one would have shown up if they were voluntary.

This one, at the recreation center down the street from Charlie's apartment building, seemed no different from any other. Vince Gionfriddo, the block chairman, rapped loudly for order. They read and approved the minutes of the previous meeting. They presented a pin to a former block supervisor who was retiring after years of spying on her neighbors. They went through old business, which involved such inspiring topics as a drive to get secondhand books for the rec-center library.

"New business?" Gionfriddo asked. Most of the time, there was none. They would drink watery coffee or watery punch, eat a few cookies, move to adjourn, and go home. Tonight, Charlie raised his hand. The block chairman was a bookkeeper, but got his sums wrong and recognized him. "Comrade Simpkins?"

"Thanks, Comrade Chairman." As Charlie stood up, people sent him curious looks. The recording secretary sent him a dirty look—she had to transcribe what he said. "I want to complain about inefficiency at my work site," he began—yes, he knew how the jargon was supposed to sound. And he went on to lay out how the warehouse had no dollies and refused to let the workers on the floor bring in anything with wheels to make the job easier. "This flies in the face of all CPW-CPDR principles," he finished, and sat down.

Complaining to the authorities flew in the face of all CPWCP-DR principles. Vince Gionfriddo looked gobsmacked. The recording secretary—her name was Elsa Payne—looked as if she'd been asked to put several paragraphs from a pornographic novel into the minutes. "This warehouse is not in our block, is it?" the chairman floundered.

"No, Comrade Chairman," Charlie said, thinking *No, you idiot.* "It's down on Ventura Boulevard."

"Then why don't you take it up with your supervisor there?"

"Who do you think is doing all this stupid stuff?" Charlie didn't say *You fucking lardhead*, but he came close.

Gionfriddo coughed. "Then you should refer the difficulty to his superiors."

"You know what, Comrade Chairman? We tried that," Charlie said. "It just landed us in more trouble."

Someone did move to adjourn then. The motion passed with only five votes against. Charlie was surprised anyone but Lucille and him opposed it. As they walked home, his wife said, "That won't do you any good, you know."

"Nothing's gonna do me any good now. As soon as I didn't stick up that stupid, worthless poster, I knew nothing'd do me any good," Charlie replied. "But you know what? I don't give a rat's ass any more. If they're gonna screw me anyhow, I may as well have some fun of my own, right?"

He thought Lucille gave him an odd look. He wasn't sure, because the streetlight they were walking under had burned out two years earlier and never been replaced. She said, "They haven't even started with you yet."

"Yeah, well, I haven't started with them yet, either," Charlie said. "Besides, like I told Nikita, I can't be the only guy who's fed up with how things are. Can I?"

"Maybe not, but do you really want to find the others? That means jail or a labor camp," Lucille said. Charlie didn't want to give her the last word, but he was damned if he could find a clever comeback.

He'd just sat down to eat his lunch—a cheese sandwich, an orange that came from a sack Lucille'd got in trade for a sweater now too

25

small on Sally, and a slice of pound cake she'd baked herself—at work when a blocky man in an ill-fitting suit he'd never seen before strode up to him and said, "You are Comrade Charles Raymond Simpkins." It wasn't a question.

"That's right," Charlie agreed. "Who are you?" He knew—he knew too well—but showing you were scared only made things worse.

"Rasmussen. NBI." The blocky man flashed a badge. "I need to talk to you."

At least he didn't say *You're under arrest*. Since he didn't, Charlie replied, "Can I eat while we talk? They only give me twenty minutes. Workers' paradise, you know?"

Rasmussen scribbled in a notebook. "I see you *do* have the habit of dissident speech," he said. "This lends credence to the account we've received of your subversive remarks at the block political assembly last week."

"What subversive remarks?"

"You deny making them?" Rasmussen's scowl suggested that wasn't such a great idea.

But Charlie shook his head. "Nah. I deny they were subversive. All I did was tell the truth. Ask anybody here on the floor if what I said was a lie. Hell, ask Comrade Muldberg. He should be the guy with the problem, not me."

"You are insubordinate and deviationist. He is a member in good standing of the CPWCPDR," the NBI man said.

"And so? I bet he doesn't shit angels when he sits on the pot."

"He is a socially reliable element. Your every word shows you to be anything but."

Charlie started peeling the orange. "He's still a jackass. He's making us work a lot less efficiently than we could."

"That's not for you to decide," Rasmussen said.

"Why not? I'm the guy doing the work. Shouldn't I have a say in how to do it best?" Charlie split the orange in two. "Want a segment?"

"No," Rasmussen said gruffly, as if joining the NBI had required him to swear off oranges forever. He eyed Charlie like a man finding dog shit on the sole of his shoe. "If I had my way, you'd be heading for Manzanar right now."

As deliberately as he could, Charlie ate the orange segment. Not showing fear came harder now. Manzanar, in the desert on the far side of the Sierras, had the nastiest name of any corrective-labor camp in the WCPDR. "How come you don't have your way?" he asked, doing his none too good best to seem casual.

"Because my lieutenant doesn't think you're worth getting excited about. Powerless, he calls you." Rasmussen sounded disgusted. "You ask me, every damn *svoloch* around ought to get put away."

The Russian word for *scum* showed he was part of the group that ran things. Charlie was too busy chewing to say anything right away, which had to be just as well. Once or twice a generation, the West Coast People's Democratic Republic, like any self-respecting socialist state, purged itself of unreliable elements. Right now, luckily, things on the political front were quiet.

"I tried to work better, like I told you—work better and explain what was going on here," Charlie muttered after he choked down the citrus pulp.

"Oh, horseshit." The NBI man curled his lip. "If you'd taped up that poster, you'd still be a functional part of society."

"I've already heard that too damn often from my wife. I don't need to hear it from you, too," Charlie said.

"You shoulda listened to her," Rasmussen said. "If you put the poster up now—I mean, if you left it up when you went back to the shop—we might rehabilitate you yet."

"Even if I did, my name would stay on a list, wouldn't it?"

The NBI man opened his mouth. He was going to lie. Something in his eyes told Charlie so as clearly as if he had LIAR! written on his forehead in glowing neon. He must have seen that on Charlie's face. Shaking his almost neckless head, he stumped away.

It was time for Charlie to go back to work. He didn't get the chance to eat Lucille's good pound cake. He felt he'd won at least a small victory. Next to Manzanar, the warehouse didn't look half bad. "Powerless, am I?" he muttered. "Huh!"

Charlie remembered what he'd said to his son about there having to be other people who didn't fancy the way things had—or hadn't—worked for so long. He started looking for them. He knew he had to be careful. Plenty who made dissident noises would be trolling for suckers for the NBI.

Day by day, he learned what going against the regime meant. The biggest thing it meant was hopelessness. As long as the men with the guns obeyed the men and women who gave the orders, the West Coast People's Democratic Republic would be what it was: state without end, amen. The leaders might talk about the arrival of true Communism and the withering away of the state, but they ruled as if they and their successors, like the dead leaders who appeared only on coins and postage stamps and monuments these days, were in for the long haul.

But there were smaller humiliations, too. Comrade Muldberg was reassigned … and replaced by Comrade Horton Wilder, an even worse hard-liner. Wheels remained forbidden. Charlie's tobacco ration was cut by two-thirds for no visible reason. That meant either stretching the time between cigarettes till his jitters got bad or cadging butts off the sidewalk and the warehouse floor like that pretty girl in front of the shop he'd run.

When Sally turned twelve, she was refused entry into the Kittens, the girls' organization that paralleled the Falcons. "They said you were an unreliable," she told Charlie. "Why are you an unreliable?"

"I'm not an unreliable," he said. "They are."

"There are more of them," she said, which was much too true.

A few days later, he said, "Hey, Eddie, know where I can get me some smokes?"

"Drugstore's right around the corner, man," his ferret-faced co-worker replied.

"No, no, no." Charlie lowered his voice. "Off-ration smokes, I mean."

Eddie's eyes flicked left and right. No one else was close by. Charlie'd made sure of that beforehand. "You wanna deal on the left, huh? It'll cost ya."

"I know," Charlie said. Everybody knew that. The black market was where you got stuff you couldn't lay your hands on through regular channels, and where some of the goodies meant for the nomenklatura and Party apparatchiks trickled down to the proletariat. You paid for scarcity, and you paid for risk.

"Cigarettes?" Eddie paused. The pause stretched. Charlie reached into a pants pocket and pulled out a five. You paid for knowledge, too. Eddie made the bill disappear. "Thursday after work, go up to

Moorpark"—a couple of blocks north of Ventura—"to the alley behind the laundry. Tell the guy Dmitri sent you."

"Which guy?"

"You'll know." Eddie sidled away. Horton Wilder's beady little eyes bored into his back. Charlie got busy. As long as the boss was watching you, you worked hard. But the bastard couldn't do that all the time. The regime couldn't do it all the time, no matter how hard it tried. In the spaces when it was looking somewhere else, that was when freedom happened.

Thursday afternoon, Charlie walked down the alley behind the shops on Moorpark. It was getting dark. The alley stank of garbage and stale piss. A large guy came out of a doorway and blocked Charlie's path. "Who the fuck're you?" he growled.

"Dmitri sent me," Charlie said, hoping Eddie hadn't set him up for a thumping.

"Oh, yeah?" The bruiser looked him over. He must have passed muster, because the big man asked, "What you lookin' for?"

"Smokes."

"Hang on a sec." The guy ducked into the laundry. He came back with a couple of cartons. "I got Camels—buck a pack—and Winstons for a buck an' a half."

Charlie pulled out another fin. "Lemme have five packs of Camels." Most of the time, only people with pull got their hands on the famous old brands; he remembered Mary Ann Hannegan's Marlboros. These would help stretch the crappy cigarettes he could still get on his cut ration. He had a folded paper bag he'd lifted from the warehouse. He stuck the packs into it so nobody on the bus ride home would see he had them.

"You ain't so dumb." The small-time capitalist gave grudging approval.

"Who says? I'm dealing on the left, aren't I?" Charlie answered. The bruiser grunted what might have been a chuckle. Charlie turned around and headed for his bus stop. He was coming out of the alley when another fellow with an urgent look on his face hurried in. They avoided making eye contact.

"What's in the bag?" Lucille asked when he got home. He showed her the Camels. When he told her what he'd forked over for them, she sighed and said, "Get used to more cabbage and potatoes."

"Happy day." Charlie tossed her two of the packs. Since all this was his fault, it seemed the least he could do.

Some of the warehouse workers drank beer or shots at a class-four tavern near the warehouse after their shift ended. After they decided Charlie wasn't an informer, they started inviting him along. He only went once in a while. Even a class-four joint, the cheapest and most basic kind, took money he could ill afford to spend out of his wallet.

One day, Comrade Wilder was a bigger pain in the ass than usual, which was really saying something. When Eddie and Dornel headed for the Valley Relic after clocking out, Charlie went with them.

Of course, you paid more for beer at even a class-four tavern than at a liquor store, but Charlie worried less after he'd had a couple. Less, but not none. "My wife'll be sore at me for coming home late," he predicted.

Eddie scoffed. "Pop the bitch in the snoot. That'll shut her up."

He didn't know Lucille. Charlie suspected it was more likely to make her stick a knife in him while he was asleep. He just took another pull at his overpriced suds. He didn't want Eddie laughing any more.

When he lit a coffin nail, it was one of the cheap, nasty Progresses that were part of his diminished ration. In a place like the Valley Relic, you didn't want to show anything that suggested money in your pockets.

One of the tables had a poker game going. Dornel bought in. Pretty soon, some of his wealth got redistributed to the other players. Two guys shot pool at a table whose felt was almost as bald as Dave. Charlie wasn't a terrible pool player. Eyeing them, he soon decided he wasn't good enough.

Men talked about sports, about women, about drinking. Not many of them sounded happy. But then, happy people didn't come to dives like this. They had better places to spend their time.

After a while, Charlie heard somebody bitching about how his family needed to move because a junior commissar had a yen for their apartment. His ears pricked up. Maybe the complainer was a government plant with a line out to snag dissidents. But you couldn't win if you didn't bet. (Then again, sometimes you couldn't win even if you did bet, as Dornel was proving.)

If Charlie hadn't already had a few beers in him, he would have sat tight, then gone home so Lucille could yell at him. As things were, he slid off his stool and ambled over to the table where the guy who was grousing sat with a couple of other men nearing middle age.

"Heard what you said," Charlie remarked. "Can I sit down with you? I've got a story like that. Christ, most people have a story like that."

The complainer eyed him. The fellow was about thirty-five, lean, with a sour expression Charlie recognized from the inside out. "Every NBI man has a story like that," he said coldly. "Every single one."

"Yup." Charlie nodded. "Ain't life grand? Come to that, how do I know it doesn't take one to know one?"

Had the guy got huffy, he would have walked away and seen what happened next. But the sour-faced man's mouth twisted. "You don't," he said. "So, yeah, siddown, and we'll feel each other out, like."

"You aren't my type, thweetie," Charlie lisped, which made the complainer snort. It was funny, and then again it wasn't. Quite a few men who liked men wound up in places like Manzanar as "degenerate elements" or "social undesirables." Charlie hooked a chair from another table with his foot and planted himself. He told how he'd wound up on the regime's wrong side by not posting the poster for the propaganda campaign.

The guy who'd been bitching nodded. "That bites, all right … if it's true."

"Believe me or don't. I don't give a shit," Charlie answered. "For all I know, you're trying to suck me in." He hadn't done anything but tell the truth. That, of course, was part of the problem. If the NBI decided to drop on him, the truth would be no defense. That it was the truth might even make things worse.

"Maybe I am. Maybe you are. Maybe neither one of us is. Wouldn't that be a kick in the nuts?" Without waiting for a reply, the sour-faced man got into a low-voiced colloquy with his friends. One of them nodded; the other just shrugged. The complainer gave his attention back to Charlie. "You wanna be here at seven tomorrow night, maybe you can talk to somebody else."

"Who?"

"Somebody."

Stalemate. Charlie knew Lucille would give him a hard time for coming back late tonight. She'd give it to him in quadruplicate if he did it two nights running. Or the NBI might give it to him way worse than that. But the NBI could grab him any old time. He was already on their list. If neither he nor this guy was trying to suck the other in ... that *would* be a kick in the nuts. Or it could be, anyhow.

"Well, hell. Maybe I will," he said.

Lucille gave him grief, all right. She gave him more when he warned her he'd be late again the next day. "You keep messing with this stuff, you'll be sorry," she said.

"I'm already sorry," Charlie said. "But I'd be sorrier if I didn't." At least she believed it was politics. He would have been in for a worse kind of tough time had she thought he was running around on her.

He walked into the Valley Relic at seven on the dot. There at the table where he'd been before was the sour-faced guy. With him sat an older, Jewish-looking man with a white fringe and a bald dome. They had beers in front of them. Charlie got himself a Brew 102 and sat down with them.

"I'm Ervin," the old bald guy said in a voice all sandpapery from a million cigarettes. "Frank tells me you've joined the opposition."

"My name's Charlie." The night before, Charlie hadn't even learned Frank's handle. He took a sip from his beer. It was local, and no better than it had to be. "What do you mean, the opposition? You're, like, a Democrat or something?"

Ervin laughed harshly. The bare bulb in the fixture above his head turned his scalp all shiny. "I hope I'm not that stupid," he said. "The little parties, they're the parsley on the plate when you get a fancy dinner. They look pretty, but they get tossed with the rest of the garbage."

Charlie drank again. "Foam on the beer," he said, remembering his own thought in the voting booth.

"There you go." Ervin nodded. "You see how things work, all right."

"So what kind of opposition are you, then? What are you after? How do you aim to get it?"

"You ask a lot of questions." Frank made that sound like an denunciation. In the West Coast People's Democratic Republic, it often was.

But Ervin said, "He's got a right to know. If I really had my druthers, I'd like to see elections where the people you're voting for don't all sing the same song."

"Good fucking luck!" Charlie said. The CPWCPDR was convinced that it alone knew the pathway to true Communism, and that that was the only possible pathway for the WCPDR to travel.

"Tell me about it. They've killed some fine men who wouldn't settle for anything less than that," Ervin said. Sounding faintly embarrassed, he went on, "I'm not ready to be a martyr. Not yet, maybe not ever."

"So you're willing to settle? What'll you settle for?" Charlie asked.

Frank spoke before Ervin could: "For starters, how about a country where some asshole with connections can't throw a guy out of his apartment just 'cause he wants it?"

"That would be a good start," Ervin agreed. "We aren't there yet. But Frank's got the hang of it. Some room in the system so ordinary people can go about their ordinary business without getting in trouble with the state would make a fair start. The fraternal socialist states have differences, too."

Charlie found himself nodding. "I was just out of high school when the Russians finally cracked down on the NESSR." The General Secretary of the Northeastern Soviet Socialist Republic's Party had turned Long Island into a corrective-labor camp for people he called deviationists, and had worked or frozen hundreds of thousands more to exhaustion or death in the forests of Maine. The USSR intervened to stop a full-scale revolt before it really got started, and to install a more pliable apparatchik in the General Secretary's seat.

"'With an iron fist, we shall lead mankind to happiness.'" Ervin's lip curled as he quoted the deposed NESSR boss's slogan. "It doesn't work like that, you know. The best thing they can do for us, most of the time, is leave us the fuck alone, give us as much room inside the system as we can take."

"Sounds good to me," Frank said. "Or it would, if they'd do it."

"Sounds good to me, too," Charlie said. "Most of the time, I don't care about political crap at all. Like you said, I just want to get on with things. And it wasn't the iron fist that got me, not at first. It was all the shoveling I had to do."

Ervin hoisted a bushy eyebrow. "Shoveling?"

"To get rid of the bullshit they kept dumping on me."

"Oh. Yeah." The old man chuckled hoarsely. "There's a lot of it, sure as hell."

"But we're powerless. I mean, totally powerless. So how do we go about getting rid of it?" Charlie remembered too well what the NBI lieutenant had called him. Not till he asked the question that way, though, did he realize he'd joined whatever shadowy opposition Ervin belonged to. And if Ervin and Frank were provocateurs, they or their muscular friends could drop on him any time they chose.

Of course, they could do that anyway. In the WCPDR, as in the other fraternal socialist republics that filled the world, the secret police could do whatever it pleased. That was one more piece of the problem.

Ervin turned lighting a Progress into a small production. After blowing a stream of smoke at the light bulb above his head, he said, "How? The powerless have more power than you think, Charlie. We don't have much to lose. They can't take much away from us because we don't. So be as difficult as you can. Ask questions in public, where they've got to give you some kind of answer. If you get a chance, check the laws. A lot of the time, they sound good—it's just how the bastards use 'em that screws ordinary people. If you quote what they really say, you scare the crap out of the apparatchiks."

"Isn't that stuff, like, secret?"

"Nah." Ervin waved his hand. "Any library has the WCPDR law codes. They're in with the collected works of the past Party chairmen and General Secretaries, so they'll have half an inch of dust on 'em, but they're there. It's boring shit, but it helps you play the game."

"How about that?" Charlie got to his feet. He shook hands with Ervin and with Frank. "Thanks. Thanks to both of you. Now I'm heading home. My wife'll be on my ass any which way."

"Yeah, you gotta play that game, too." Ervin chuckled again.

Before Charlie left, he asked, "Think there's any chance?"

"For my druthers? Maybe one day, but I don't think soon," Ervin answered. "For some wiggle room? Mostly you lose. Once in a while, though, you don't. Trying's better than not trying, or that's how I see it."

"Uh-huh." With half a wave, Charlie headed for the door.

"You're smiling." By the way Lucille said it, she was accusing him of something nasty. And well she might have been, for she continued, "We're going to the mandatory political meeting, and you're smiling. What's wrong with you?"

"Not a thing," Charlie said, smiling still.

His wife eyed him for a moment—only for a moment, since she had to make sure she didn't trip on the crumbling, tree-root–heaved sidewalk. "You're going to do something again, aren't you?"

"We're going to the meeting, like you said. That's stupid to begin with. How can I make it any worse?"

"I don't know. I'm just afraid I'll find out," Lucille said.

The folding chairs in the rec center numbed Charlie's butt and made it hurt at the same time. That should have been impossible, but those chairs proved it wasn't. He'd taken Lucille farther forward than they usually sat, though the chairs didn't change. The ones behind the table on the platform up front, like the warehouse boss's office chair, were nicer. They, after all, parked the important cans of the people who told other people what to do.

As the rec center filled, Charlie heard more grumbling than usual. No one had said anything official, but the scuttlebutt was that they were going to tear down the apartment building next to his and replace it with a center for Party members in the Northwest Valley. What would happen to the families living in the building now? Again, no one had said anything official, but the scuttlebutt was that they'd be stuck with finding new places to stay and with their moving expenses.

Odds were some wouldn't be able to find new places fast enough to keep the police happy. Vagrancy raps would land adults in jail or, if the authorities felt grumpy, in labor camps. Kids would go into one state orphanage or another. The orphanages doubled as finishing schools for most of the WCPDR's second-story men, flimflam artists, and other yeggs.

But Party members would have a shiny new place to drink coffee—good coffee, no doubt, with real cream if they wanted it—and smoke expensive cigarettes and discuss Marx and Engels and try to get laid. When you evaluated social benefits against costs, how could you overlook something so important?

Right on time, the block chairman banged for order. Vince Gionfriddo had to bang twice, which didn't happen very often. Sure enough, the people about to get tossed from their apartments weren't very happy. Neither were their neighbors. But obedience was a longtime habit; everybody also knew what could happen to anyone who got out of line. Little by little, things quieted down. The meeting droned ahead.

When they got to new business, the block chairman tried to make the important item seem as trivial as he could: "The West Valley Central Committee of the CPWCPDR has generously approved the block committee's request for authorization to begin the dismantling of a superfluous structure so as to facilitate the construction of a new and socially advantageous edifice. Any questions or comments? If not, we will proceed to the next order of business."

He started to do just that. People in the crowd shouted for recognition, though. They knew which structure had been tagged superfluous and which edifice would take its place. Quite a few of them lived in the allegedly superfluous structure, in fact. Even if they went against the Party's desires, they were going to get their two cents' worth in.

Vince Gionfriddo sat in his form-fitting, padded chair and let their abuse wash over him. That was part of his job. Even if he didn't enjoy it, he did it well. He confirmed that, yes, the apartment building next to Charlie's was the one chosen for demolition, and no, people thrown out on the street wouldn't get anything for being thrown out. "As always, the needs of the Party and the protection of our glorious socialist revolution take precedence," he declared.

That brought fresh complaints, as he must have known it would. Elsa Payne scribbled busily. Was she just transcribing for the minutes, or was she taking names for later action by the police or NBI? Charlie didn't know, but he thought he could make a fair guess.

He waited till things had started slowing again before he stuck up his hand. The weary chairman incautiously pointed his way. "Thank you, Comrade Block Chairman," Charlie said, and the apparatchik pulled a face when he realized whom he'd recognized. Loudly, Charlie continued, "Comrade Block Chairman, have you and the block committee and the West Valley Central Committee considered Article 1101, Section 9, Subsection 16 of the organic law of the West Coast People's Democratic Republic?"

"What's in it, Comrade Simpkins?" Gionfriddo had the air of a cobra meeting a hungry mongoose.

Charlie fished a scrap of paper out of his pants pocket so he could be sure he was quoting accurately. "Along with a bunch of other stuff, Comrade Block Chairman, it says 'nor shall private property be taken for public use without just compensation.' That's the *law*, Comrade, just the way they printed it in San Francisco all those years ago."

The meeting had been quieting down. It heated up again in a hurry. Shouts of "The law!" and "Follow the law!" filled the recreation room, even if the people doing the shouting had never heard of the law in question till a moment before.

"We haven't got the money for all those apartments!" Vince Gionfriddo blurted in horror, which might have been the most truth he'd ever come out with at one of these meetings.

"Comrade, in that case I move that you don't tear down the building and that you put the Party center somewhere else," Charlie said. Half a dozen people bawled seconds. The block chairman had to allow a vote if he wanted to get away without a new suit of tar and feathers. No one who wasn't sitting up on the platform voted against it.

"I will convey the sense of the popular will to the West Valley Central Committee," Gionfriddo said, putting the best face on things he could. The slitted glance he sent Charlie said he would also convey the name of the man who'd ignited the popular will. Well, it wasn't as if Charlie hadn't already known he'd do that.

People carried Charlie out of the meeting on their shoulders. If not for the honor of the thing, he would rather have walked. They didn't put him down till he was halfway back to his own building. They thought he was the greatest thing since Marxism-Leninism-Stalinism.

When they did put him down, Lucille whispered in his ear: "You're gonna catch it again."

"Yeah, yeah." He nodded impatiently. "But the clowns won't be able to throw a buildingful of people out on the street with diddly-squat. I hope they won't, anyway."

"I hope they won't throw *us* out on the street," Lucille said.

"If they do, they have to compensate us. That's the *law*." Charlie never would have known it if he hadn't poked around in the dusty old books the way Ervin suggested. The other interesting question was whether the people who ran things gave a damn about the law. The way the WCPDR worked argued against it. But maybe they just hadn't had their noses rubbed in it for a long, long time. Charlie hoped so.

Not one but two official envelopes arrived five days after the mandatory political meeting. One was addressed to Charlie, the other to Lucille. His wife handed him his as soon as he got back from the warehouse that evening. She also showed him the one with her name on it.

They looked at each other in mutual apprehension. Then they both said "You go first" at the same time.

Laughing—nervously, but laughing—Charlie opened his envelope and read the letter inside. "Well, it could be worse," he said when he got done.

"Why? What's in it?" his wife asked.

"It says that they found some clerical errors in the application we submitted for a car all those years ago. Because of that, they're kicking us back down to the bottom of the waiting list again. So we're not three or four years away any more. We're eleven or twelve years away."

"You're right. It could be worse." Lucille eyed him. "Do you believe them when they say they found mistakes in our paperwork?"

"Sure. The mistake was, the stinking thing had our names on it," Charlie answered. "Now, what are they telling us in the one to you?"

Lucille extracted her letter. "It's the same as yours, only it's about our application for a TV set," she reported. "We're back to the bottom of the list for that, too."

"Hey, the waiting time for those isn't as long as it is for cars," Charlie said. "We may get one in eight years or so—or they may kick us down again when we start coming close."

"It isn't fair. It isn't right," Lucille said.

"Of course it isn't. But you know what, babe? I'm just not gonna get all hot and bothered about it, 'cause that's what the SOBs want me to do. Before they sent us these letters, when were we gonna buy the car and the TV? On the twelfth of Never, that's when. So now we'll buy 'em on the twenty-ninth of Never. What's the big deal?"

"That's a good way to look at things," Lucille said. "Who would've thought you had it in you?"

"Hey, watch how you talk to a dissident. I gotta think long-range."

"Why? Because if you don't, you'll give up?"

"That's just why, only I'll like you better if you don't remind me of it."

"How much better?"

He patted her on the behind. "How about that?" She shrugged, but she was smiling. Charlie smiled back. If the kids fell asleep promptly, if he and Lucille could stay awake .... Well, it was one more thing to hope for.

A few evenings later, he ran into Ervin at the Valley Relic. "What you been up to?" the old man rasped. Charlie told how he'd disrupted the political meeting. Ervin clapped his hands. "That was you? I heard about it. Good job! You made 'em look like a buncha shlemiels."

"They are a buncha shlemiels," Charlie said. "That's the problem."

"They're a buncha shlemiels with power. *That's* the problem. Gotta loosen 'em up if we're ever gonna get anywhere."

"You said that before. But are we ever gonna get anywhere?" Charlie asked. "Loosening 'em up is good, yeah, but will we ever see the Party wither away, like?" He dropped his voice; he knew his words were dangerous. And, even in talking about the end of the regime, he spoke its language.

"I have good days and bad days. When I heard what you done, that was a good day. Others ... not so much. Like I told you the last time we talked, maybe we'll see it sooner than we think, maybe we won't see it for a thousand years. But we'll see it." Ervin sounded serenely confident.

Of course, apparatchiks talking about the coming of true Communism sounded the same way. All you could do was all you could do. Right now, all Charlie could do was order fresh drinks for them both. So he did that.

chapter

Charlie probably hated hauling potatoes worse than any other job in the produce warehouse. In bulk, the spuds came in burlap bags that weighed about ninety pounds. One person could tote one bag; work norms required one person to do so. But, after doing so for any length of time, one person felt it in the arms and the shoulders and the back. To add insult to injury, the burlap scratched up forearms and palms.

Somehow, Horton Wilder gave Charlie spud-hauling duty more and more often these days. Had that started happening right after he kept the Party headquarters from going up on his block? Looking back, he was pretty sure it had.

But what could you do? Like a man plagued by a gnat, the West Coast People's Democratic Republic worked hard to squash anything that annoyed it. If it couldn't immediately flatten the person disturbing it, it would make him as miserable as it could. Charlie had too much pride to complain—that and an acute understanding that letting the state know he was miserable would make things worse, not better.

So he lugged sack after sack of potatoes from the back of the warehouse to the front in grim silence. If he didn't move any too fast, well, neither did anyone else. Wilder exhorted his crews to show true Stakhanovite socialist spirit. Since he did exactly no heavy lifting himself, the workers tuned him out. If the potatoes didn't get out front right away, they would eventually.

Then the warehouse supervisor startled Charlie. He'd just set down a bag and was wondering whether he could pause in the back room long enough for a cigarette when Wilder said, "Simpkins! Yes, *you*, Comrade Simpkins! Come here. Somebody needs to see you."

"Me?" Charlie knew he sounded apprehensive. He damn well was. Like prisoners all over the world, workers in the workers' paradise knew breaks in routine weren't likely to mean good news.

Sure as hell, Eddie whispered, "What did you go and do now?"

"Beats me," Charlie answered out of the side of his mouth. Then he raised his voice to call back to the warehouse supervisor: "Coming, Comrade Wilder!" Maybe whatever this was wouldn't be as bad as busting his back on the potatoes. Maybe. He wished he could believe it.

"Took you long enough," Wilder grumbled when Charlie finally presented himself. "Well, follow me." He led his dissident worker over to the office he used. The door was closed. Instead of opening it, he waved Charlie forward. "Go on in."

Charlie had visions of a team of security men with submachine guns waiting inside to fill him full of holes. The rational part of his mind told him how silly that was. They could dispose of him much less dramatically if they wanted to. But the fear wouldn't quite go away.

His hesitation lasted no more than a heartbeat. Every time you let them see you scared, they won. "Okey-doke," he said, and turned the knob.

No NBI goons waited inside, only a tall, fair, short-haired woman who blew another stream of Marlboro smoke at him. "Good afternoon, Comrade Simpkins," Mary Ann Hannegan said. "Close the door, why don't you?"

"You sure?"

Her nod was as crisp and decisive as everything she did or said. "I'm not going to seduce you, and Wilder doesn't need to hear what we're going to talk about. So close it." She didn't bother giving the warehouse supervisor his title.

"You're the boss." Charlie nudged the door with his foot. It clicked shut.

"Yes, I am," Mary Ann Hannegan agreed placidly. Those blue, blue eyes narrowed, as if she were centering him in the crosshairs of a sniper scope. "You think you're hot shit because you managed to stop that Party development, don't you?"

"No, Comrade Hannegan." The surprise in his voice must have shown her he meant it, because her eyes lost some of that marksman's stare. He went on, "I was just trying to keep a bunch of people from getting their lives turned inside out, and maybe some of 'em from ending up out on the street, that's all."

"You know what? I believe you. You know what else? It doesn't matter, not even a nickel's worth. Most people here"—by which she could only mean *most people whose views count*—"still think you're nothing but a small-time pest. I'm not so sure any more." Now she eyed him like an entomologist examining a nondescript cricket and wondering where to stick in the specimen pin.

"I told you once before, Comrade Hannegan—all I want to do is live my life quietly and not bother anybody." Charlie didn't add *and not be bothered, either*, but the words hung in the air whether he said them or not.

"Yes, you told me." Mary Ann Hannegan shook her head. "Too much counterrevolutionary sentiment around these days. Much too much."

Charlie didn't think wanting to be left alone was a counterrevolutionary sentiment, but he didn't tell her so. Either she'd assume he was lying, which was bad, or she'd think he meant it, which might be worse. You had no business telling the state it had no business looking at you, looking into you.

He just stood there. She hadn't invited him to sit down, and he didn't presume to without an invitation. She stared at him like a woman from the nomenklatura deciding which cut of round steak to tell the butcher to grind into hamburger. Yeah, just like that.

When he didn't say anything, she shook her head in what might have been real regret. "You used to be a sensible fellow. I don't know what tipped you over the edge, but you aren't better off on account of it. You'll see."

"I'm already seeing," he answered, and some of his bitterness came out.

"You haven't even started. I was hoping to redeem you, but… ." Mary Ann Hannegan shook her head again. "Officially, this meeting never happened. If Wilder asks you, we talked about the weather."

"Oh, he'll love that!" Charlie said.

She looked at him. "Do you want to land in trouble with him, or do you want to land in trouble with me?"

None of the above? But Charlie knew he didn't have that choice. The WCPDR didn't give you choices like that. It would have been a roomier, more comfortable place to live if it had.

Someone had left behind a copy of *The Daily Worker* on the first of the two buses Charlie rode to get home. Most evenings, he wouldn't have picked it up. It was even less readable than the *Times*. The paper it was printed on was too scratchy to make a good ass wipe, though you could roll pretty fair cigarettes with it.

After an afternoon full of unpleasant politics, though (not telling Horton Wilder what his meeting was about went as well as he'd known it would), he decided that, if they'd thrown him in the water, he'd better try to swim. So he opened up *The Worker* and studied it. He couldn't get in trouble for that. Reading it made him look like a good Communist even if he wasn't.

A story near the bottom of the front page caught his eye. It announced that Alex Eichenlode, who had been Party Secretary for Eastern Washington, was named a full member of the national Politburo in Sacramento. Folks in bustling California made jokes about eastern Washington, how it had more cows than people and how outsiders had trouble telling the one from the other.

So it was a surprise that someone from that part of the West Coast People's Democratic Republic would reach the Politburo at all. And Eichenlode, the story said, was only forty-four. *A comer*, Charlie thought, and kept reading.

Apparently, Eichenlode had made his reputation by cleaning up Spokane and cleaning it out. Reading between the lines, Charlie gathered the problem hadn't been corruption so much as fossilized bureaucracy. All over the WCPDR, people waited years to get things they needed or wanted. In Spokane, they'd waited forever and got nothing … till Alex Eichenlode came along.

"Workers and peasants know their requirements better than the administrative system does," he was quoted as saying. "They should not be repressed for stating them, and should be accommodated in obtaining them wherever this is at all possible."

After Charlie saw that, he looked to the newspaper's masthead again. Yes, it really was *The Daily Worker*, with the familiar red star between the Y and the W. You could say things like that and get them printed in the country's official paper? You could say them and get promoted to the Politburo instead of sent to Manzanar?

"What's the world coming to?" Charlie muttered. That one story inspired him to go through the rest of *The Worker*, but nothing else in there was even a quarter as interesting.

All the same, he didn't chuck the paper in the trash while he waited for his second bus. He didn't throw it out or leave it behind when he got off the second bus, either. He carried it back to his apartment. He couldn't remember the last time he'd done anything like that.

"How did it go?" Lucille asked when he came inside.

"Not so hot," Charlie said. "Comrade Hannegan read me the riot act at work, so who knows what's gonna happen with that? But there's a really interesting piece in *The Daily Worker*." He brandished the newspaper.

His wife's expression said she thought he was talking for the benefit of any bugs the NBI might have planted in the flat. "Is there?" she replied, her voice as neutral as she could make it.

"There really is." He showed her the article about the new Politburo member who'd cleaned up Spokane and who made noises about being willing to let people do as they pleased … within limits, of course.

She read it. Then she said, "I don't know, Charlie. How much difference can any one person make?"

That was a better question than Charlie wished it were. Shrugging, he said, "Maybe more of a difference than no people would make. Comrade Hannegan said there was a lot of counterrevolutionary sentiment around. Some loosening up might make it go away."

"Or it might make some fools stick their necks out so they can get their stupid heads chopped off." Lucille eyed him. "Don't be that kind of fool."

He sighed. "My neck's already out. If they want to bring the axe down, they can." He waited for her to contradict him. When she didn't, he sighed again and changed the subject: "What's for supper?"

"Noodles and cottage cheese. That's what we had ration coupons for—and what the store had."

"Oh, boy." Charlie almost added *Welcome to the workers' paradise*, but he didn't. He was the kind of fool who got the government sore at him, yes. But he thought the apartment was likely bugged, too. He wasn't the kind of fool who gave the NBI ammunition for free.

"It's food," Lucille said. Charlie nodded. It would fill their bellies, and the kids'. They'd get through another day. Tomorrow … might be noodles and cottage cheese again, or cabbage and cottage cheese, or cabbage and noodles. Whatever it was, Charlie didn't want to hear about it ahead of time.

Horton Wilder kept riding Charlie and wanting to know what Mary Ann Hannegan had had to talk about with him. Charlie was tempted to tell the warehouse boss she'd been after a denunciation. Wilder might well believe that; it was the kind of thing he'd do himself.

But getting Comrade Hannegan angrier at him than she already was didn't look like a smart move. Finally, after shrugs and evasions grew threadbare, Charlie said, "Why don't you call her and ask her yourself?"

"Because I'm asking you," Comrade Wilder snapped. Charlie just stood there. Wilder turned red. "I can write you up for insubordination. You know that, don't you? You'd better know that!"

"Before you do, Comrade, you *should* call Comrade Hannegan," Charlie said.

Stalemate. Horton Wilder shot Charlie a glare full of fear and hatred. The warehouse supervisor couldn't be sure where he stood with this particular worker. Was Charlie in Mary Ann Hannegan's good graces? Was he reporting to her about what went on at the warehouse? "Get out of here!" Wilder barked, and Charlie got.

That evening, he didn't go straight home. He needed to loosen up first, so he headed for the Valley Relic. The booze it served was a sorry excuse for bourbon, but even a sorry excuse improved on no bourbon at all.

Frank was there. Charlie had the feeling Frank was there just about every night. Charlie raised his glass to him. "Ervin gonna be around?" he asked.

"Who knows?" the other malcontent answered with a shrug. "Ervin shows up when he feels like showing up—kinda like you." He lit a Progress and blew smoke at the ceiling. "Anything I can do for you?"

"I need to pick his brain a little, that's all." Like anyone with an ounce of sense in the West Coast People's Democratic Republic, Charlie showed no cards he didn't have to. Frank shrugged again, acknowledging someone else who understood the rules of the game.

Ervin ambled in half an hour later. Even a class-four tavern had its stars and celebrities. At the Valley Relic, Ervin was one of them. People vied for the chance to buy him a beer. When he let Charlie do it, Charlie basked for a moment in reflected prestige.

He also got to sit by Ervin, which was why he'd laid out four bits. "So how's it going?" Ervin said. "You still giving 'em hell?"

"Seems like it's their turn for a while," Charlie answered.

"Yeah, that happens. There's more o' them than there are of us, an' they can hit harder'n we can. Bastards," Ervin said, almost without rancor, and lit a Progress of his own. When it made him cough, he stared at it reproachfully through the bottoms of his bifocals.

As casually as he could, Charlie asked, "Ever hear of an apparatchik called Alex Eichenlode?"

"The new guy on the Politburo, you mean?" Ervin said, and Charlie nodded. Ervin took another drag on his cigarette. He didn't cough this time. He went on, "Yeah, I heard of him. He's one of the funny folks who show a halfway decent human being can get ahead in the Party every once in a while. Hard to believe, I know, but damned if he didn't make it all the way to Sacramento."

"How about that?" Charlie said, and then, more casually still, "Think he can get any higher?"

"Like really running things, you mean?" Ervin said. Charlie nodded again. Ervin didn't; in fact, he shook his head. "Not likely. My guess is, Premier Newman got him sent to Sacramento so he could keep an eye on him and clip his feathers if he had to. Tony Newman's a hard-nosed son of a bitch, but nobody ever called him a jerk."

Charlie nodded one more time, less happily now. What Ervin said matched what he'd seen himself only too well. Tony Newman had led the WCPDR for a dozen years. As long as he kept the Soviet Union happy, as long as he didn't go crazy the way the boss of the Northeastern Soviet Socialist Republic had, he might stay Premier for another twenty years. After all, how often did apparatchiks lose elections? That poor fellow who'd got only ninety-three percent in the recent voting was on the low end of the scale.

Almost in a whisper, Charlie said, "What if the West Coast People's Democratic Republic really had some democracy for the people?"

"Yeah. What if?" Ervin stubbed out his Progress and lit another one. "Like I told you before, don't hold your breath waiting for anything like that. You'll end up mighty blue if you do."

"Uh-huh," Charlie said. He might be blue as in sad; he might be blue as in needing air; he might be both.

"They could loosen the screws a little bit, though," Ervin went on. "It wouldn't cost 'em anything. We'd have more fun if they did. Maybe Eichenlode can manage that much … unless Newman uses pushing the idea for an excuse to cut his throat."

"Somebody told me"—Charlie wasn't about to name names—"there was a lot of counterrevolutionary sentiment around. You know—people like you and me."

Ervin laughed harshly. "People like you and me are drinking shitty booze and smoking crappy cigarettes in a class-four joint while we bitch about how rotten everything is. We're about as dangerous as a couple of feather dusters. Only a dumb asshole like Horton Wilder would think any different."

Charlie didn't correct him. After all, Horton Wilder was a dumb asshole. Mary Ann Hannegan might be an asshole, but Charlie knew how far from dumb she was.

He bought Ervin another beer, drank another bourbon himself, and headed for the bus stop. Buses ran less often after dark, so he got back to the apartment even later than he would have otherwise. Lucille yelled at him. He'd been sure she would. He let it roll off his back. He'd found out what he needed to know. When the WCPDR made that so hard, doing it was worth some yelling.

Instead of buying the *Times* every day to read on the way to work, Charlie started putting his quarter in *The Daily Worker* machine more often than not. The *Times* carried a wider variety of news. When he did buy it, he got it mostly for the sports. If the Stars could win the Coast League title and the All-American Socialist Workers' Baseball Cup, he'd be a happy man.

But *The Daily Worker* focused like a burning glass on ideology and politics. Charlie hadn't meant to get involved in ideology and politics, but what you meant to do and what happened often had little to do with each other. He'd made the politicos notice him; now he had to pay attention to them.

Alex Eichenlode's name showed up in the *Worker* every now and then. The young hotshot from eastern Washington proposed a measure to eliminate the annual tax everyone paid on radios, and another to grant full freedom of movement and employment to people who kept their noses clean for five years after being released from a labor camp.

The Politburo voted down both proposals. Neither garnered more than a handful of supporting votes. Tony Newman commented that the one about giving more rights to people who got out of labor camps was destructive of order and state security. *The Daily Worker* made sure readers saw the Premier's comment, separating it in a box.

A politician the Premier rebuked like that often vanished from the radar not long afterwards. But Eichenlode didn't get sent back to Spokane with his tail between his legs or end up starring in a show trial. He stayed on the Politburo and kept proposing modest reforms that kept getting voted down. A few more apparatchiks started backing his measures, but nowhere near enough to push them through.

And, by the hints Charlie gleaned from *The Worker*, he realized Premier Newman had more pressing worries than an ineffective would-be do-gooder. Every few years, the General Secretary of the Communist Party of the Soviet Union toured his American satellites. The Russians had been doing that ever since the Northeastern Soviet Socialist Republic went haywire. They wanted to stop trouble before it started if they could.

Charlie, on the other hand, wanted to make as much trouble as he could. He wrote Alex Eichenlode a letter detailing what he'd gone through since he didn't tape the WORKERS OF THE WORLD, UNITE! poster in his front window. He was no newspaperman or novelist, but he could write a letter that made sense.

If I get in this much trouble for not doing something I'm supposed to do because I want to, why should I want to do it? he finished. He put *Respectfully* before his signature. He wouldn't have for most CPWCPDR officials, but he had hopes for Eichenlode. *Fool that I am*, he thought.

When he put a stamp on the envelope, he chose one with a harvester loading grain into a truck. There were lots of stamps like that, glorifying collectivized agriculture. "Happy tractors," people called them, at least when no informers or NBI men could hear them.

He dropped the letter in a mailbox on the corner where he waited between buses. Not until that evening, when he couldn't do anything about it, did he tell Lucille he'd written and mailed it.

She looked at him. "You really *are* trying to get it in the neck, aren't you?" she said after a brief pause.

"I … hope not," Charlie said slowly. "With any of the other … people"—he didn't quite say *clowns*—"up in Sacramento, I wouldn't've wasted my time. But Eichenlode, Eichenlode's different. Honest to God, I think he is."

"Yeah, and rain makes applesauce," his wife replied. Charlie's cheeks heated, not least because she had such a good chance to be right. She went on, "Besides, if he's as wonderful as you say he is, what do you want to bet the snoops see all his mail before he does?"

She had a good chance to be right about that, too. Charlie said what he could: "Eichenlode's moving up. If they aren't careful with him, he's liable to pay them back in spades one day soon."

"Maybe." By the way Lucille said it, she didn't believe it for a second. She aimed a forefinger at Charlie's head as if it were the barrel of a .45. "Just remember, Comrade Simpkins, this big shot in Sacramento may be moving up, but you damn well aren't. If the NBI decides to give you the treatment, you'll get it. Boy, will you ever!"

"Thanks, hon. You always know how to cheer me up," Charlie said. The laugh he surprised from Lucille was as much of a victory as he got that night.

Next morning, he spent the long bus ride down to Ventura Boulevard and the shorter one along it worrying about whether he should have sent the letter. When he and his fellow warehouse workers complained that Emmett Muldberg wouldn't let them use things with wheels to haul produce around, they got him removed, all right. And Horton Wilder was a worse hardass, and they still broke their backs lugging sacks and boxes.

He was worrying too late, of course. You couldn't unsend a letter once you'd sent it. Some poem he'd read in school bubbled up inside his head. *The Moving Finger writes, and having writ, / Moves on: nor all your Piety nor Wit / Shall lure it back to cancel half a Line, / Nor all your Tears wash out a Word of it.*

The Moving Letter's writ, and, once it's writ, / Moves on. Charlie shook his head. A letter was one thing. He'd never make a poet, let alone one as good as … as … . "Shit!" he said, loud enough to make the middle-aged woman across the aisle send him a wary look. For the life of him, he couldn't come up with the name of the guy who'd done those verses.

That turned out to be the least of his worries. When he walked into the warehouse, Dornel sidled up to him and spoke in a prison-yard whisper: "Watch yourself today, man. Wilder's really on the rag."

"Thanks." Charlie's lips didn't move any more than the big black man's had. Wilder stood scowling by the clock as he punched in. Since he wasn't late—he was, by God, four minutes early—he nodded and said, "Morning, Comrade."

"Don't you give me any trouble, Simpkins," the warehouse boss snapped.

"Okay, okay." Charlie stepped back in a hurry, as if from a mean dog baring its teeth. Sure as hell, Dornel wasn't kidding.

Everything went downhill from there. When Eddie called in sick, Horton Wilder slammed down the phone and said, "Little rat's probably too hung over to see straight." Knowing Eddie, Charlie didn't think that was a bad guess. But he also didn't think it was anything a supervisor ought to say about a worker without proof.

Whatever he thought, he kept his mouth shut about it. He did his job. He kept his head down. He tried not to give Comrade Wilder any excuse to notice him. It didn't work. Wilder noticed things today whether they were there or not. Wasn't hell bad enough without a demon throwing pitchforks at you? To Horton Wilder, evidently not.

A lot of warehouse workers headed for the Valley Relic or other watering holes when they finally got to clock out. Dornel sent Charlie a curious look when he just went off to the bus stop. "Don't you need some R and R, man?" he said. "Wilder's been on everybody's ass today, but yours worse'n most. What did you do to piss him off?"

"I'm breathing," Charlie answered. Dornel chuckled, for all the world as if he were joking. He went on, "What I need is, I need to stay in good with Lucille. She thinks I go to that place too often as is."

"Pop her one," Dornel said, as Eddie had before him.

"Not a good plan," Charlie told him. Dornel's face called him a softy. Dornel had never met Lucille. He also had no idea how much her standing by Charlie meant to him. Charlie crossed the street and leaned against the metal pole for the bus-stop sign. Sooner or later, a bus *would* stop.

A week went by, then another one. Alex Eichenlode kept putting forward small reforms. The Politburo kept rejecting them. In a speech before a hall full of mid-level apparatchiks, Premier Newman declared, "We will root out reactionary dissidence and counterrevolutionary tendencies wherever we find them!"

Both the *Los Angeles Times* and *The Daily Worker* reported that the assembled Party functionaries applauded thunderously. To Charlie, that said somebody'd told the papers—and likely others he didn't read—just how to report on the speech. When you paid attention, you noticed plenty of things like that.

He wondered whether Mary Ann Hannegan had been in the hall. A speech from Tony Newman sounded like the kind of thing she'd love … or do a good job of pretending to love, especially when people who could push her higher were around to notice.

Horton Wilder stayed on the warpath, too. Charlie understood that the West Coast People's Democratic Republic wouldn't let dissidents off easy. He would have understood it even if Tony Newman hadn't spelled it out. But the warehouse supervisor used his position of petty power for all it was worth and then some.

One night after Charlie did go to the Valley Relic for bourbon and to piss and moan a bit, Lucille thrust an envelope in his face as soon as he got home. "It's for you," she said. They didn't open each other's mail: that was a longstanding family rule.

Charlie took the envelope. It seemed ordinary enough. Whoever'd written his name and address had spiky but legible handwriting. Then Charlie noticed the return address: *Eichenlode*, it said in the same script. The happy tractor that franked the envelope had been canceled in Sacramento.

"My God!" he said. "He answered me!"

"What does he say?" Lucille asked—a good question if ever there was one.

"Stay tuned for the next exciting episode," Charlie said, as if he were an announcer signing off a radio serial. People who had TVs said the announcers there did the same thing, but he wouldn't need to worry about getting one for years now.

He opened the envelope, unfolded the paper—Politburo stationery, no less!—and read the letter. It wasn't typed by a secretary (no AE/cr or anything like that) or even by Eichenlode himself. It was in the same spiky script and bright blue ink as the address.

"Dear Comrade Simpkins," he read, "Thank you for bringing your situation to my attention. I have looked into it, and find you state the facts accurately. I will do what I can to correct it. I must tell you, though, I do not know how much that will be. Entrenched bureaucracy is a continuing problem in the West Coast People's Democratic Republic, as it is in other socialist states. In my view, more openness and freedom are not only permissible but desirable. You should understand, though, that while I speak as a Politburo member, I am not one who sets policy. I wish you all good fortune. Sincerely—" Charlie didn't bother with the signature.

"Wow!" Lucille's eyes were wide. "A Politburo member wrote to you. To you! He said you had a real beef, too."

"And he said he wasn't sure he could do anything about it." If Charlie hadn't been cynical before, his run-in with the Party and the government since he tossed the WORKERS OF THE WORLD, UNITE! poster would have turned him that way. But, like most people in the WCPDR, he'd already got a head start by then.

His wife also came back to earth in a hurry. "If he does try to do something, will it help you or hurt you?"

"Good question. I mean, I like having an angel on my side, but if he's on the outs with Tony Newman ... ." Charlie let his voice trail off. As much as any man could in the American satellites, Premier Newman called the shots in the WCPDR. You opposed him at your peril.

That was all the truer if you were a big shot yourself. Charlie knew he was no more than an administrative annoyance to the state and the Party. Alex Eichenlode, though, might be gunning for Newman's job. Or Newman might think so, which would be just as bad.

"Maybe when the General Secretary comes, he'll see that Newman isn't ... everything he's looking for." Once more, Lucille plainly changed what she'd been about to say to something milder and safer in case the NBI really did happen to be listening in. People made those swerves in speech all the time. Unless you were looking for them, you hardly noticed.

"Could be." But Charlie didn't believe it. Yuri Zhuravlev had been running the USSR longer than Tony Newman had been in charge of the WCPDR. You didn't stay on top of the strongest socialist state in the world by being a nice guy or by making changes in the way things worked unless you absolutely had to.

"Nikita! Sally! Come see the letter your dad got!" Lucille called. Charlie wished she hadn't, but he couldn't do anything about it now. The kids were glad for any excuse not to do homework for a while. They hustled out of the bedroom. Nikita held the letter while he and Sally read it together.

"Is it really from the guy on the Politburo?" Nikita asked in hushed tones.

"It really is," Charlie answered, glad for the chance to have his son impressed with him, not angry at him, for a change.

"Can I take it to school and show it to people? I bet they let me into the Falcons then!" Nikita said.

"That's … not a good idea. I'm sorry, but it isn't." Charlie heard the regret in his own voice. Telling your kids no was one of the hardest things you had to do. "The letter isn't a promise of anything. Comrade Eichenlode may help. Or I may end up in even more trouble than I am already. So don't say anything about it till we know how things look. Okay? It's important."

"Okay." Nikita wasn't happy, but he nodded. He was old enough to have started getting an idea of how things worked.

Sally wasn't. "It's not fair," she said.

"I don't think it is, either, hon, but it's true anyway. So keep quiet about the letter for now. You promise?" Charlie said.

Sally sighed. "Promise." She crossed her heart to seal the deal. Such Christian relics lingered even though religion was long discouraged. Charlie looked at Nikita. His son nodded, too.

After the kids went back to wrestling with math and history, Lucille said, "I'm sorry I didn't work that through. You handled it fine, though."

Such praise from her didn't come every day, or every week. "Thanks, babe," Charlie said, and kissed her. "I wasn't even kidding with them. Who knows if it means anything? Would be nice, sure, but who the hell knows?"

chapter

Charlie sat on the bench at the corner of De Soto and Ventura Boulevard, swearing under his breath. The bus that had brought him down De Soto was late, so he'd missed the one he usually took along Ventura to the produce warehouse. The next bus on that route should have got to this corner ten minutes ago, but it was running behind, too. He'd be late to work.

He wouldn't have felt so put upon if this weren't the third time the miserable, decrepit buses had left him in the lurch over the past two weeks. Some people at the warehouse might have got away with that. Some people at the warehouse, in fact, got away with a lot more than that. But Horton Wilder eyed Charlie like a man trying to decide if he'd want the chicken he'd kill tonight roasted or stewed.

Another ten minutes crawled by before the eastbound bus finally wheezed up. "You're late," Charlie snapped as he handed the driver his transfer.

"Yeah, well ... ." The driver shrugged. He didn't care. He'd have some excuse to feed his supervisors if they got enough complaints to talk to him about it. Chances were, they wouldn't.

Still muttering, Charlie sat down. As long as you were politically reliable, you could damn near get away with murder. *Damn* near. *People like me, though ... .* Charlie didn't finish that gloomy thought.

The bus got rolling with a horrible clatter of gears. Charlie glared at the driver's back. No, he didn't care about a thing. *You shiftless bastard*, Charlie thought, and then snorted. He hadn't made the joke on purpose, but liked it when he noticed.

He was still smiling a little as he got off and walked up to the warehouse. Any trace of good humor, though, disappeared as soon as he came through the front door. Showing up late was bad enough. Showing up late and happy had to be four times worse.

"Oh, man," Eddie said as Charlie headed for the time clock to punch in.

"Fucking buses," Charlie answered.

Eddie just shook his head and said, "Oh, man," again. That couldn't be a good sign.

As Charlie stuck his card in the slot for the time stamp that would tell the world—and his boss—exactly how late he was, he glanced around to see whether Horton Wilder was lying in wait for him. He didn't spot the warehouse manager, and felt relieved not to.

As soon as the clock chimed and stamped, though, Wilder's cold snarl came from no more than six inches behind his left ear: "*So* good of you to join us today, Comrade Simpkins."

Charlie didn't jump. Looking back later, he was proud he didn't, not that staying still helped him one bit. Only after he pulled out his card and stuck it back in its proper slot in the fiberboard case on the wall next to the time clock did he turn around and answer, "I'm sorry, Comrade. The buses did me in."

"Excuses don't pave the road to true Communism, Comrade. Results do. The results I've had from you lately have been less than satisfactory." Yes indeed, the look in Wilder's eye said Charlie was a plump, steaming, perfectly cooked drumstick.

"I'll stay late to make up the time if you want me to. Or I'll work like a Stakhanovite to make my norm any which way." Party jargon tasted like manure in Charlie's mouth these days, but he spouted it anyway. If that didn't prove how desperate he was, nothing ever would.

Horton Wilder's smile showed uncommonly long, uncommonly sharp teeth. Maybe Charlie was imagining things, but he didn't think so. Wilder said, "Get to work now that you're here. I'll decide later what to do about you."

"Okay," Charlie said, but he was talking to the manager's back. Wilder disappeared into his office, closing—almost slamming—the door behind him. A moment later, Charlie heard his voice through the thick wood. He was on the phone with … somebody, though Charlie couldn't make out what he was saying. Of course a warehouse manager boasted a telephone, even if most ordinary people didn't.

Shoulder slumping, Charlie turned away. Nobody stood close by, enjoying his reaming out. People liked him well enough not to do that, anyway. It was something: something, but not nearly enough.

He found Eddie, who'd smoke a cigarette down to a butt as small as he could keep in his mouth without a holder. "What needs doing?" he asked.

Eddie let the butt fall to the rough concrete floor and ground it out under his heel. "Wish that was Wilder's ugly mug," he remarked. Charlie grunted. Eddie went on, "We're full of beans, that's what. No, I mean it—they came in graveyard shift. Navies, pintos, I don't know what the hell all else. We gotta move 'em so the truckers who'll get 'em out to the stores can get at 'em easier."

"Beans," Charlie echoed without enthusiasm. They weren't as bad as spuds. They came in sixty-pound sacks, not ninety-, and most of the time the burlap was of a less abrasive grade. But hauling those sacks around was nobody's idea of fun. He sighed. "Okay, beans."

"You gonna bust your hump to show the boss what a good boy you are?" Eddie asked, rough sympathy in his voice.

"I better." Charlie sighed again. "Not like I can tell him I wasn't late. I damn well was. It wasn't my fault, but a lot he cares about that."

"Listen, if they decide they're gonna cut your nuts, they'll cut 'em whether you make like a good boy or not," Eddie said. He was much too likely to be right, too.

Though Charlie knew that so well his own nuts wanted to crawl up out of their sack, he made himself shrug and sound light as he answered, "Guess I'll give it a shot anyway. Maybe I'll get through to when the heat comes off. Maybe the goddamn buses'll start running on time."

"Tell me another one!" But Eddie punched him on the upper arm. "Luck, man. You deserve to catch a break if anybody ever did."

"Yeah. If," Charlie said. The way Eddie laughed said he knew Charlie wasn't kidding.

Beans. Sacks of beans. Endless sacks of beans. Charlie hated the work they had him doing, but sometimes he could lose himself in the sheer animal physicality of it. Hours flew by then, and he'd clock out wondering where they'd gone. This wasn't one of those days. Every little thing made him glance back toward Horton Wilder's closed door. *If they decide they're gonna cut your nuts ... .* He wished to the God he seldom remembered Eddie hadn't put it quite like that.

But nothing happened all morning long, or for the first couple of hours after lunch. He began to hope the manager'd got it out of his system with yelling. As his hopes rose, the sacks seemed lighter.

Then, a little past three, Wilder's sharp voice pierced the workers' chatter like an antitank round smashing through steel: "Comrade Simpkins! Come to my office right now!"

"Luck," Dornel said as Charlie dropped his last sack of beans on the pile.

"Thanks." Charlie headed back to the office. Horton Wilder waited outside. If that wasn't a smirk of anticipation on the manager's face, Charlie'd never seen one. *Never let them know you're hurt* went through his mind. As calmly as he could, he said, "You want me for something, Comrade?"

"That's right." Wilder took a couple of steps to one side and gestured for Charlie to precede him. "Come on in." On in Charlie came. The warehouse manager followed, closing the door behind him. "Sit down if you care to."

"Okay." Charlie did. The politeness felt like a roast-beef dinner just before the blindfold and the bullet.

Wilder sat, too, in the nicer chair on the other side of the desk. "I regret to have to say, Comrade Simpkins, that you have been insubordinate and politically unreliable for some time."

"I deny that, Comrade Wilder. I want it on my permanent record that I deny it," Charlie said.

"So noted." The manager actually did scribble on one form or another. "So noted, but it doesn't matter. Because you have fallen into the habit of unpunctuality in addition to your other failings, my own superiors and I have agreed that the only way to ensure proper discipline here is to dismiss you from this facility, effective immediately. Give me your work card."

Numbly, Charlie took it from his wallet and put it on the desk. The manager wrote the date and stamped it in damning red ink, then shoved it back across to him. Those scarlet letters—SACKED—would make it next to impossible for him to find another job. Of course, so would a blank space at the end of his work record.

"This isn't fair. I protest," he mumbled.

"So noted," Horton Wilder said once more. He wrote something else on the form. Then he looked up at Charlie. "But we both know that protest will never go anywhere. You're fired. Get the hell out of here."

Charlie stood up. Just for a second, he leaned forward. If he whaled the living snot out of Wilder, no one in the warehouse would come to the manager's rescue. Hell, he knew his fellow workers would buy him all the bad bourbon he could drink. And something in the manager's eyes admitted he knew that, too.

But afterwards .... Charlie knew he'd catch it afterwards. So would Lucille. So would the kids, even more than they were already. He turned around and walked out. He didn't even slam the door behind him.

Naturally, the buses that took him back up to his flat in the northwest end of the Valley came right on time. If they'd worked like that in the morning .... *Wilder would've found some other way to screw me*, Charlie thought. He was as sure of that as he was of his own name.

The light seemed strange when he walked from the bus stop to his apartment building. He wasn't used to coming home at this time of day. Nikita and Sally would have just got back from school.

"Fired!" he said, and kicked a pebble from the sidewalk into the street. He'd known Wilder had it in for him, but he hadn't expected this.

There it was, the building he and Lucille had called home since they got married. It had been shabby and rundown when they'd moved into the flat. It was fifteen years shabbier and more rundown now. Well, so was he.

Cooking odors came from the kitchen when he let himself in. Sally looked up in surprise from the book she was reading. "Mom, Dad's home early!" she called.

Lucille hurried out, alarm on her face. "Are you all right, Charlie?"

"I'm fine, I'm ... fine. We'll talk about it later, okay?"

That was code. Lucille deciphered it without much trouble. She rounded on their daughter. "Go back into the bedroom for a while."

"Aw, Mom! Nikita told me to come out here and quit bothering him."

"Go back into the bedroom," Lucille repeated, steel in her voice. "Don't bother your brother, that's all." Sally went, her back arched like an affronted cat's. Lucille turned back to Charlie. "What happened?"

Before answering, Charlie walked into the kitchen. "Smells good," he remarked. He meant it as real praise. Getting tasty food out of what their ration book let them buy and what the stores carried wasn't easy. He also meant it as a stall.

His wife wasn't having any. "What happened?" she said again, as implacably as she'd spoken to Sally.

Charlie'd hoped to talk around it, to sugarcoat it as much as he could. Realizing that would wouldn't work, he spread his hands and gave her the bald truth: "Wilder canned me."

She flinched as if he'd slapped her. "My God! Why?" Whatever she'd looked for, it wasn't anything nearly that bad.

"Buses ran late again, so I got there late again. You know he has it in for me. He was just looking for any excuse to shaft me he could find, and the Rancid Trapid District gave him one." People had been making sour jokes about Los Angeles's buses for longer than Charlie'd been alive. It wasn't so funny when the incompetent reality kicked you in the teeth.

"Can you appeal it?" Lucille sounded like a drowning sailor thrashing around in the forlorn hope of grabbing a spar.

"I already told him I was protesting. We both know how much good that'll do me, though."

"But … ." His wife took a deep breath, then asked the question that had to be asked: "What happens now?"

He'd been asking himself the same thing. None of the answers he'd come up with was any good. "I guess I gotta go out and look for some other kind of work," he said, giving her the least horrible one he'd found.

She looked at him the way wives do when their menfolk tell them something particularly idiotic. "Good luck with that!" she exclaimed. "He put the scarlet letters on your work card, right?"

"Yeah. He did." The name for that fatal stamp reminded Charlie of something he'd read a long time ago, but he couldn't remember what and didn't have the energy to dig very hard. Trying to sound hopeful, he went on, "Maybe I'll land something. Not everybody cares about a work card."

"Everybody who matters does," Lucille said, which was, unfortunately, bound to be true. She added another truth a moment later: "Besides, the kind of things you can do with a red-lettered work card won't keep them from tagging you with an Article 203 whenever they get around to it."

Not only was that true, it was, if anything, an understatement. A lot of the things you could do with that kind of card, or with no card at all, would win you a nice, long stretch of corrective labor if they caught you at it. The most you could get for Article 203 was three years. You could earn yourself ten for some of that other stuff—twenty-five if you were lucky.

Charlie'd never thought of himself as a serious criminal before. Everybody bent the rules; you couldn't live if you didn't. He hadn't really broken them—not till he wadded up the WORKERS OF THE WORLD, UNITE! poster and chucked it in the trash. But even that was only ideological crime (not that the authorities thought ideological crime was an *only*). It wasn't stealing or robbing or chiseling or whatever the hell so many people without work cards did.

"One way or another, I'll make out. We'll make out," he said, conscious of the silence that had stretched too long.

She sent him that look again, though it didn't seem quite so deadly this time. Then her eyes narrowed. Charlie noticed the tiny wrinkles at their outer corners. Those hadn't been there when they first got together. Chances were he'd put a lot of them there himself. But she wasn't thinking about that, luckily. She said, "Can you ask Comrade Eichenlode to check into it?"

His jaw dropped. He hadn't thought of that. He might have eventually—he hoped he would have, but he sure hadn't yet. "I can!" he said, and then tempered his flash of excitement by adding, "I don't know how much good it'll do, though."

"What's the worst thing that happens? He ignores you or tells you he can't do anything. How are you worse off?"

"The worst thing that happens is, the NBI knows I'm writing to him, he gets purged, and they send everybody who ever liked him to a labor camp. Doesn't seem all that unlikely, either," Charlie said. Tony Newman had run the West Coast People's Democratic Republic long enough to have got his hands on all the levers of power here. Plainly, Eichenlode wanted to grab some of those levers himself, which made him no friend of Newman's.

His wife only shrugged. "You're already on the shit list. You think a letter will shove you that much further up it?"

"Maybe not," Charlie allowed. "What I think is, I want a drink. Have we got any bourbon left?"

"It says it is on the bottle, anyway. You ask me, it's paint thinner." Lucille took it out just the same. She poured him a good slug, and a smaller one for herself. "Here's to new and better!" she said. They clinked glasses. The stuff burned its way down Charlie's throat like a trash-can fire. Lucille made a face as she swallowed, too.

"New and better," Charlie repeated after his voice box unfroze. "I like that. Comrade Eichenlode likes it, too. Everything's been the same here for too darn long. I think I will write him. See what happens, y'know?" He took another knock of the so-called bourbon. This one didn't sting so much, maybe because the first swig had stunned his insides.

"What do we tell the kids?" Lucille asked.

He wished she hadn't; that reminded him how much of his hope was blue-sky fantasy. Even so, he answered, "We tell 'em the truth. They're old enough to take it, and I'm sick to death of lies."

"That's what got you into trouble to begin with," Lucille said.

"Sure is!" But no matter how proud Charlie sounded, he knew how much out of his weight he was trying to punch.

He threw his letter to Alex Eichenlode in the mail the next morning. Maybe it would do something for him, maybe something to him. He hardly cared either way. He told himself he hardly cared, anyhow.

Then he walked to the bus stop at the corner of Gresham and De Soto and sat on the beat-up bench to wait for the next bus. He had the bench to himself; most people had already headed off to their socially productive labor. He'd finished one Progress and was thinking about lighting another when a bus squealed to a halt in front of him.

Parting with a quarter gave him a small pang—he had no idea when more money would come in. But he had to go to where the jobs were, and he didn't feel like walking that far.

He got off at Sherman Way, probably because he'd worked there for so long. He headed east along the street, though, not west. He didn't want to see the produce store he'd run for so long. He didn't want to see Manuel Gomez, either. And Gomez wouldn't want to see him. Hanging around with somebody who had a red stamp on his work card might make the snoops wonder how reliable you were yourself.

A florist's shop stood only a few doors down from the corner of De Soto and Sherman Way. *Flowers, they're plants. Taking care of 'em's gotta be a lot like handling carrots and pea pods*, Charlie thought. He walked in.

The woman behind the counter was taking care of a customer. Charlie eyed mums and sniffed red and yellow roses—the red smelled sweeter—till the fellow left with his newspaper-wrapped bouquet. The woman asked, "Help you, Comrade?"

"I hope I can help you." Charlie put on his best smile and most ingratiating manner. "If you're looking for somebody to give you a hand here, I mean. I'm ... . Well, I'm hoping to get into something new."

"What have you been doing up till now, Comrade ... ?" she asked cautiously.

"Simpkins. Charlie Simpkins. I've been in produce the past few years." It wasn't even a lie. With what he hoped was a charming grin, Charlie went on, "But I'll tell you, when you've seen one turnip, you've seem 'em all. Flowers, now"—he waved at the colorful, fragrant expanse—"there's always something new with flowers."

"Well, Comrade Simpkins, I'm Ella Freeman. I didn't think I was looking to take anybody on, but you never can tell. Let's see what you know." She threw a string of rapid-fire questions at him, questions aimed at finding out whether he really did have a notion of how to take care of plants.

He answered as best he could. He thought that was pretty well. People would complain about you, for instance, if you didn't put the bottoms of your cut asparagus spears in water so they wouldn't dry out. (Some people would complain, anyway. More would figure it wouldn't do any good. And some produce managers wouldn't trouble to take care of their wares. They figured they'd move them any which way, so why put in extra work? But Charlie'd mostly tried to do his job right.)

Ella Freeman rubbed her chin. She was about Charlie's age, skinny, with green eyes and dark brown hair just starting to show gray. "You weren't just spinning me a line," she said. "That's something."

"No, Comrade. I sure wasn't." Charlie shook his head.

"Okay. All by itself, that makes you interesting. I use a lot of fertilizer. I hear a lot of fertilizer, too. You'd better believe I do. So when somebody can back up what he tells me … . Let's see your work card."

And there it was. Charlie didn't sigh—not outside where it showed, anyway. He took the card from his wallet and set it on the counter between them. "Here y'are."

Of course the red stamp on the otherwise black-and-white card leaped out at the florist. Horton Wilder'd put it there so it would leap out at anyone silly enough to think about hiring Charlie. "Oh, dear," Ella Freeman said. "Do you want to tell me about what happened?"

"Would it make any difference if I do?"

She thought about that. Watching her, Charlie gave her credit for doing even so much. But then, reluctantly, she shook her head. "No, I'm afraid it wouldn't. I'm sorry. Please believe me—I *am* sorry. I think you would have worked out nicely. But I just don't dare take the chance of getting my block chairman or the labor-organization supervisors mad at me. You know how things are."

"You bet I do," Charlie said with more bitterness than he'd expected. "You better not try and give a worker a break in the workers' paradise." He noticed she had a WORKERS OF THE WORLD, UNITE! poster, just like the one he'd thrown out, taped inside her front window. It had hung there long enough, it was starting to sag and crinkle around the edges.

"Comrade Simpkins, I'm going to do you a favor," the florist said. "No matter who asks me, I didn't hear a word you said now."

"Even Comrade Hannegan?" Charlie asked.

Ella Freeman's eyes widened. He'd just told her part of why he had those scarlet letters on his work card, even if he hadn't come right out with it. But she nodded. "Yes, even her. Maybe especially her."

"Okay." As Charlie put the work card back in his wallet, he realized that wasn't enough. "Thanks, Comrade."

"I hope you find something," she told him. "I hope you find somebody who's got more nerve than I do."

"Yeah. Me, too. Well, I won't take up any more of your time." Charlie walked out of the shop. He looked at the poster from the sidewalk. The sun had started to fade it, to make it look older and sleazier than it was.

He looked up and down Sherman Way. This was an old part of town. It also looked older and sleazier than it was, though. Paint didn't get touched up as often as it should have. Cracks in the concrete sidewalk didn't get patched; they got bigger. So did potholes, in spite of the occasional corrective-labor repair gang.

Unless you looked at them almost from the outside, you took such things for granted, the same way you did with not hiring somebody whose work card had a red stamp. A whole lot of things had pushed Charlie to the outside, though. Looking, he wondered, *Does it really have to be like this?* He didn't know of any place where it was better, but couldn't help thinking it should have been.

A Broz chugged past him, heading east. The boxy little car spewed out as much stinking black exhaust as the bus he'd ridden down here. He coughed when the noxious cloud enveloped him. He lit another cigarette so at least he'd be breathing his own smoke. *Does it have to be like this?* he thought again.

Whether it had to be or not, it damn well was. And, as long as he'd come down here, he needed to do some more job hunting. That meant walking past the Log Cabin, a class-four tavern that reminded him of the Valley Relic. He felt virtuous after he put it behind him. Of course, feeling virtuous wouldn't help him find work, either. Odds were, nothing would.

"Gotta try," he said out loud. Anyone who knew him even a little knew he was a stubborn bastard. That was his blessing and his curse, not that he took much stock in either. Right now, it was also the only thing he had going for him.

So he stuck his nose into every place he passed, asking if anybody was looking for a worker. Most people just said no. He thanked them and went on his way. A man who ran a bicycle-repair shop told him, "Before I waste my time talking to you, show me your work card."

"Right." Knowing what was coming, Charlie took it out and handed it to him.

One glance did the trick. The man shoved it back—almost threw it back. "Get the hell out of here! You think I'm nuts or something?"

"I can always hope." Charlie sounded more cheerful than he felt.

"Yeah, sure. Go on, beat it. I wouldn't even look at anybody who's not reliably socially productive." The man sounded scared and mad at the same time. Maybe he thought Charlie was a snoop trying to inveigle him into doing something shady so the government could come down on him like a landslide. In the West Coast People's Democratic Republic, only fools and crooks took chances like that.

Charlie left. He pounded the pavement for the rest of the day. Ella Freeman had at least been unhappy she couldn't take him on. That was as close as he came. As the sun slid west toward the smog-shrouded hills, he trudged back to the corner of Sherman Way and De Soto to wait for the northbound bus to take him home.

Thinking of the Valley Relic made him head down there the next day. It was the kind of place where nobody looked at you sideways because you'd got shitcanned. It was the kind of place where losers hung out, in other words. *Losers like me*, Charlie thought, not without a certain sour pride, as he walked in.

It was still early afternoon. A lot of people who'd come in later were at their jobs, the way he would have been till a couple of days before. The ones who'd started drinking early sent him quick, hooded sidelong glances. A stranger was liable to be a cop in mufti or, worse, an NBI man.

Then they realized he wasn't a stranger, but another sorry son of a gun like themselves. They relaxed. A couple of them let hands drop away from pockets. Charlie walked up to the bar. "What'll it be?" asked the man behind it.

Charlie didn't feel like bourbon so early. "Lemme have an Eastside," he said. It was swill, but better swill than Brew 102, at least to him. Those were the choices here. If you wanted good beer, you didn't drink at a class-four tavern.

The bartender worked the tap. He didn't give Charlie the glass half full of foam, anyhow. *A conscientious worker*, Charlie thought as he paid. He'd tried to be one himself, and a whole hell of a lot of good it had done him.

He looked around. He didn't see anybody he much wanted to unburden himself to, so he sat down at an empty table. This time of day, he had plenty to choose from. Nobody would give him a hard time now if he drank slowly, either. He sighed and sipped, sighed and sipped again.

He wasn't quite halfway down his second beer when Ervin came in. Charlie waved before anyone else could. "Whatever he wants, I'm buying," he told the barkeep.

"This must be my lucky day!" Ervin chuckled harshly. "Gimme a scotch on the rocks, Pat."

"You got it," the bartender said. As Pat built the drink, Charlie came over and put money on the counter. He and Ervin went back to the table together.

"Obliged," Ervin said, and raised his small glass. Charlie touched his larger one to it. They both drank. Ervin went on, "Hear you got the axe the other day."

"Yeah. 'Fraid so. If I'd been a good little boy, I probably wouldn't've, but I ain't no good little boy." He sketched a salute. "And whose fault is that?"

Ervin chuckled again, but shook his head. "You don't get to pin that one on me, guy. You were a troublemaker before I ever set eyes on you, right?"

"I guess I was." Charlie lowered his voice: "Know anybody who'd maybe want to hire a fella with a red stamp on his work card?"

Instead of answering right away, Ervin made a small ritual of lighting a cigarette. He took a drag and coughed. "These goddamn things'll kill me, but not just yet, *alevai*," he said, sucking in more smoke. He tried to blow a smoke ring up at the grimy ceiling, but made a mess of it.

"Do you?" Charlie persisted. He knew he shouldn't push, but couldn't stop himself. Article 203 was enough to make anybody jumpy. They didn't even have to be looking for him in particular. All a cop who was looking to make his day's quota of checks had to do was say, *Hey, Comrade, show me your identity card and your work card*, and he was screwed.

"Not right now," Ervin said, and something small inside Charlie died. Ervin was his best hope—not a good hope, but his best. The older man continued, "Even if I did, I might not tell you. Some kinds of stuff, you don't want to do. You're a political like me, not a proper bad guy."

"I guess." Charlie couldn't deny he wasn't cut out for strongarm work or anything like that. "But what am I gonna do?"

"Roll with it. What else can you do? You don't poke the power structure without figuring they're gonna poke you back—and they can poke harder than you can. So you make it hard for 'em. Unless you're looking for work, stay home so they don't spot you. If you find something, grab it, whatever it is. Shoveling gravel? So what? Right now, you don't care."

"Gotcha." Charlie nodded. What Ervin said made a dismal kind of sense.

"And the other thing you're gonna do is, you're gonna bang on a teakettle," Ervin said, as if he hadn't spoken.

"I'm gonna what?" Charlie wondered if he'd heard straight.

"Make a racket. Make a fuss," Ervin explained. "Appeal what the bastards did to you. Write to everybody you can think of. They want you to lay there and take it. As long as you're quiet, they've got it all their own way. But if you start making a stink about things, then they have to come out and tell why they were treating you like dirt. Most of the time, they don't have any real reason. You got some big shots mad at you, that's all. That ain't a crime, no matter what they say."

"I've already started doing some of that," Charlie said.

"Good. Do more." Ervin looked at his glass and seemed surprised to find it empty. Grunting, he got to his feet. He waved Charlie down. "I'll buy this time. I'm not broke. Not quite. Not yet. Is that horse piss you were pouring down Eastside or 102?"

"Eastside," Charlie said, and then, "Thanks."

"Don't mention it. Part of the service."

As time rolled by, the Valley Relic started filling up. Charlie wasn't the only guy who wanted to bend Ervin's ear. Ervin made the same astringent sense with other people as he did with Charlie. Not all of them took it so well, though.

"You make it sound so easy!" said a man with a long, sad, permanently disappointed face.

"Easy? No. Hell, no!" Ervin answered. "It's hard. It's the hardest thing in the whole damn world. You want to know what's easy, Louie? I'll tell you what's easy. Going along is easy. Doing what they want you to do, doing what they tell you to do, that's easy. The hard part comes when you say no and try and make it stick. Then you find out what trying to hold back the tide is all about."

Somebody'd done that, or was supposed to have done that. An old-time king. They'd told Charlie about him in elementary school. They'd said he'd failed because the old, outmoded ways of doing things couldn't stop or even slow down the tide of history. That had impressed Charlie then, the way any good story will impress a kid. He hadn't even noticed the propaganda. He did now. Like everybody else in the WCPDR, he'd seen enough of it and then some.

A hand fell on his shoulder. He jumped. Had a cop walked in while he was remembering ancient days? But it wasn't a cop. It was Eddie, who laughed and punched his arm. "How you like getting free of Wilder's bullshit, man?" the other produce worker asked.

"Except for Article 203, it's great," Charlie said.

"You gonna piss and moan about every little thing? I'll give you something to piss about—I'll get you another beer. Is that Eastside?"

"Yeah."

"Okay. Be right back." Eddie headed for the bar. He returned with the beer and with something clear in a small glass for himself. Rum or gin or vodka—whatever it was, it would be cheap and bad, because the Valley Relic didn't sell anything that wasn't.

"Thank you," Charlie said.

"Any time, buddy, any time." Eddie clinked glasses with him, then knocked back his shot at a gulp. "Just so you know, everybody thinks you got a crappy deal. We know what the buses are like. So does he. He was lookin' for an excuse to come down on you, that's all."

"Thanks," Charlie said, more warmly this time. But he couldn't help adding, "Fat lot of good it'll do me."

"Are you in the struggle or aren't you?" Ervin said. He'd been talking to somebody else, but that didn't mean he hadn't been listening.

"Oh, I'm in. I'm stuck with being in," Charlie said. "But that doesn't mean I think I'm gonna win."

"You don't do it to win. You do it to do it," Ervin declared. Charlie knew where he was coming from: the state and the Party held all the cards. But wasn't winning every once in a while nice, too? That Party center on Gresham wouldn't go up. And that was bound to be part of the reason he'd lost his job. Some triumph!

chapter

The Labor Exchange was on Vanowen, one big street south of Sherman Way. Charlie'd taken a couple of aspirins before he went to the bus stop. He still had the edge of a headache from the night before. The morning sun burned straight into his brain, seeming to bypass his eyeballs.

He bought a *Daily Worker* and sat down on the bench. He wanted the paper at least as much to shade his face as for reading. He wished he could have stayed home. But the authorities had to see he was looking for work. Passive acceptance of joblessness was one more thing that could buy him an Article 203.

Here came the bus. Either this one was noisier than usual or he had the jimjams worse than he'd thought. The doors hissed open. At least they weren't broken. Charlie climbed aboard. A couple of guys at the back of the bus were passing a bottle back and forth. That was one way to take the edge off a hangover, anyhow.

Down De Soto the bus rolled, stopping every block or two to let people on or off. Charlie did look at *The Daily Worker*, hoping it would tell him Alex Eichenlode had done something no ordinary apparatchik would have dreamt of, much less tried.

It didn't. Instead, it gave the full text of Tony Newman's speech to the Politburo the day before. Newman praised the ties between the

West Coast People's Democratic Republic and the USSR, and the fraternal bonds that linked socialist republics all over the world, especially on the North American continent.

Full and cadet Politburo members interrupted Newman with ovations no fewer than eighteen times. Several of those, *The Worker* said, were stormy and even frightening in the enthusiasm they showed for his remarks. Charlie wouldn't have wanted to be the reporter who counted and then characterized the ovations.

If there was a reporter. If there had been ovations. Charlie was pretty sure Tony Newman had made a speech. That was what politicians did. He imagined Politburo members doodling or dozing in their comfy chairs while the words rolled over them and past them. By the column-inches it took up, it had been a long speech.

Charlie didn't read it all. He kept looking up from the paper to see where the bus was. Sherman Way .... He wouldn't think about the produce shop, or about the poster he didn't put in the window. Somebody else ran it now, somebody who surely did whatever the Communist Party of the WCPDR wanted him to do.

Vanowen. Charlie got off. The aspirins were working better now. That was something, anyhow. He walked west.

Like government buildings all over the world, the Labor Exchange boasted an entrance guarded by columns and was made of marble (well, actually, of marble cladding on concrete; the thin marble slabs had cracked and chipped here and there, showing Charlie the dull gray underneath). The red Spanish tiles on the roof didn't go with the rest of the architecture, but did reflect regional consciousness.

Charlie killed his cigarette in a sand-filled urn outside the door. You weren't allowed to smoke inside. The urn was made to resemble a drum from one of the nearby columns. He couldn't decide whether that was attention to detail or stupidity.

In he went. He'd had steady work for a long time, so he hadn't been here for a while, but he knew the routine. Everybody did. The inside was much less grand than the exterior. Red-and-green linoleum covered the floor; faded, scuffed tracks showed where countless men and women had queued up and slowly—so slowly!—shuffled forward.

He found a place at the end of one of those lines. Getting to the front would take a while. In the meantime, he tried to ignore all the posters praising socialist labor. Ignoring posters was how he'd got into trouble to begin with, but he didn't want to think about that.

Like most people, the Labor Exchange clerks worked no quicker than they had to. They'd shown up, their attitude said, and wasn't that plenty all by itself? So Charlie needed close to half an hour to work his way to the window.

"Let me see your identity card, Comrade," said the Asian man on the other side.

"Here you are." Charlie slid it across to him.

The clerk tilted his head back so he could read it through the bottoms of his bifocals. He made a note in his case register, then handed back the card. "All right, Comrade, ah, Simpkins. What kind of socially productive labor are you looking for?"

"Something in the produce business, if I have my druthers. I've got experience there," Charlie said. "But I'll take anything I can land right now, really."

"I ... see." The Asian man had probably sat behind that window long enough to gather dust and cobwebs. He would have heard every kind of story under the sun, and he'd recognize each one from the first few lines. "Show me your work card, if you would be so kind."

Resignedly, Charlie pulled it out of his wallet. Of course that was next on the agenda. "You got it."

That scarlet stamp made it obvious why Charlie needed to visit the Labor Exchange. "How unfortunate," the clerk murmured. "Things are more difficult because of this, you understand."

"Tell me about it!" Charlie said.

"You would have a better chance to be hired if the red mark could be expunged," the clerk said.

No shit! jumped into Charlie's mind. He stifled it before it jumped out of his mouth, settling for, "Yeah, I know," instead. He went on, "I don't think it was right. I've protested it. I've written to, to everybody I know to write to." Mentioning Alex Eichenlode was liable to do him more harm than good.

"Maybe that will help." The Asian man didn't sound as if he believed it.

Well, fair enough. Charlie didn't believe it, either, not for a minute. He asked, "Have you got any listings for places that'll take a chance on somebody like me? I'll bust my hump for anybody who gives me a shot."

"Wait here." The Labor Exchange clerk disappeared into the back of the building. *Checking up on me*, Charlie thought at the same time as the woman behind him in the queue let out a loud, annoyed sigh. He wanted to apologize to her. Had he been where she was, he would have done the same thing.

Five minutes later, the clerk came back. Instead of looking expressionless, the way he had before, he wore a frown. Charlie beat him to the punch: "Any luck, Comrade?"

"You did not tell me there were ideological concerns involved with that mark on your work card," the man said in accusing tones.

"I didn't do anything illegal. Not a single thing. If I did, I'd be in jail or in a corrective-labor gang right now, not standing here trying to do what I'm supposed to do," Charlie said.

"It still presents … problems. Many are more willing to hire a thief than a political. Thieves are more likely to be socially useful than people who … who cannot recognize how wise and progressive the West Coast People's Democratic Republic is and how it continues to move forward along the path to true and complete Communism."

People like Ervin. People like me. People who don't want Sacramento always looking at us, always telling us what to do, always telling us what to think. People who want more elbow room in their lives. Charlie had no trouble understanding what the clerk meant.

"Comrade, the state says I've got to look for socially productive labor," he said. "If the state also says I can't get socially productive labor, where does that leave me?"

"In an unfortunate predicament," the Asian man said, which was true. He filled out a form and gave it to Charlie. "Report back in two weeks. Detail your efforts to acquire appropriate employment. The west wall lists possible openings. Good day to you."

Good day to you meant *Get the hell out of my hair*. Charlie vacated his place. The woman in back of him made a grateful leap forward to claim it. He mooched over to the job listings. The clerk would have noticed if he didn't. You had to be seen doing the right things.

He couldn't pretend to be a bricklayer or a steel puddler or a physician's assistant. He might have made an office manager, but that job was down in Westwood, too far to go on the sad local bus lines. He made himself pretend to look at other slots he couldn't fill, then gave up, left the Labor Exchange, and headed back to the bus stop to go home.

"You going anywhere today?" Lucille asked, a certain edge in her voice.

"I got the newspapers already." Charlie was reading the *Times* and smoking a Progress. He wished for the finer tobacco in the black-market brands only the nomenklatura could openly buy, but even Progresses took a bite out of your wallet when you had no money coming in.

"That's all you do. The rest of the time, you're here in the apartment." By the way Lucille sounded, so much close contact with her husband failed to fill her with delight.

"Not when I'm out looking for a job," Charlie said. He'd made a couple of forays after his visit to the Labor Exchange, with no more luck than on his earlier venture out.

"But you're just … here. You're in the way. I'm sorry, but I can't think of any other way to put it."

Charlie shrugged, though the newspaper kept his wife from seeing that. "Don't know what to tell you, babe. I get nervous every time I stick my nose out the door. All they have to do is ask to see my papers and I'm in deep, uh, doodoo." He tried not to cuss too much around Lucille. He didn't always succeed—nowhere near—but he tried.

She said, "I gotta tell you, I liked it better when you were heading out to work every day."

That was a different way to say *Get the hell out of my hair* from the one the Labor Exchange clerk had used, but Charlie knew it meant the same thing. He counterpunched: "Maybe I should spend all my time down at the Valley Relic, then."

"You were the one who said you didn't want the NBI or the cops nabbing you," she answered.

He scowled. He had said that. He'd meant it, too. "Something will turn up," he said. "I'm not gonna stay stuck here forever."

"You'd better not!" Lucille said. "Jane Montgomery already asked me if everything is all right."

"What did you tell her?" Charlie asked.

"I said sure. Jane's okay—not like she'd squeak to anybody 'cause she's noticed you're sticking around. But other people will notice, too, sooner or later, and you can't trust everybody. I wish you could, but you can't."

Every block of flats had at least one informer. That was a law of nature in the WCPDR, same as it was all over the world. So did every workplace. The nomenklatura praised the proletariat to the skies, but kept a nervous eye on it down here on earth.

"I'll go out again tomorrow," Charlie said resignedly. "At least I'll look like I'm doing something then."

"Okay. I think you're being smart," his wife said.

"If I'm so smart, how come I got myself canned?" Charlie'd asked himself the same questions again and again. Yes, he could blame the buses. Yes, he did blame them. But he also knew Horton Wilder would have cut him a lot more slack if he hadn't already been giving the people who told other people what to do a hard time.

"Because you're so sweet and everybody likes you so much." No, Lucille hadn't come to town on a load of rutabagas. She understood what his problem was. Her nod, though, said she was willing to change the subject. So did her next words: "What's in the paper?"

"*Something's* going on in Sacramento. I can't work out exactly what—either the clowns who write for the *Times* and *The Worker* don't know themselves or the bosses don't want them talking about it yet. But something."

"Does it have to do with the guy you got the letter from?" Lucille knew somebody might be listening. She didn't even mention Alex Eichenlode's name.

"I wouldn't be surprised," Charlie said. "The papers've been quiet about him lately, though."

"Huh," Lucille said, which was pretty much what Charlie thought. Maybe the papers weren't talking about Eichenlode because they'd heard Tony Newman was going to purge him. Or maybe the word was that the new guy would try to take Newman down. Somebody on the outside could only wait and see how things played out. The newspaper writers might be doing the same thing.

"It would be nice if we knew more," Charlie said, and not another word: he too understood when to stop. Like those of other people's democracies, the WCPDR's Constitution enshrined freedom of speech. As was also true elsewhere, things got enshrined because they'd died.

The next morning, Charlie felt enshrined himself, or maybe embalmed was the better word. He drank an extra cup of coffee before heading for the bus stop on the corner of Gresham and De Soto, but it didn't seem to help. He was still yawning and rubbing his eyes when he crossed the street to catch the northbound bus.

He headed that way instead of going south as he usually did because a *Daily Worker* story had heaped praise on the big apartment blocks going up on the far side of Devonshire Boulevard. *These will be models of egalitarian socialist housing*, the writer claimed.

Charlie doubted that. Nothing ever turned out as egalitarian or as socialist as *The Worker* said it would. But if they were building blocks of flats, they might need guys with strong backs, and they might not ask them too many questions. *If I can lug beans and spuds, I can lug cement, too*, he thought.

De Soto heading north was smoother than it was heading south. Not so many people lived out toward the foothills, though that would be less true once those humongous apartment buildings started filling up.

He could see them as soon as he got off at De Soto and Rinaldi, or rather see their steel skeletons. They were eight or ten stories tall, each one as long as a city block; they dwarfed the older place he lived in. A growling crane swung a prefab concrete panel towards a frame. Workers on a horizontal beam secured it and started moving it into position.

All the buildings were made from the same kinds of panels. When they were finished, their addresses would be the only way to tell one from another. Charlie pitied the poor bastards who'd come home drunk and walk into the wrong block of flats or stagger through the grass and shrubs between the buildings, trying to figure out where the hell they lived.

Now, though, there wasn't much in the way of greenery between the apartment blocks: just dirt and blowing dust and construction machinery and men and women in work boots and plastic helmets. Charlie looked around for a few seconds, then ambled over to a guy carrying a clipboard: a supervisor, obviously.

"Who're you?" the man asked. Charlie, bareheaded and in ordinary shoes, as obviously didn't belong there.

"Name's Charlie Simpkins. Looking for work. Anything you can give me'd be great," Charlie said.

The guy sized him up. "Bet you don't want me asking for your work card."

"I'll show it to you if you want." Charlie felt something new and rare: hope. The guy in the plastic helmet hadn't asked for it right away. That seemed promising.

And sure as hell, the fellow said, "I can give you a couple-three days, anyway. You haul cement, you haul rocks, you haul whatever the hell somebody tells you to haul. I can only pay you fifteen a day. Officially, you aren't even here, but you'll help us stick a little closer to the schedule."

If he had schedule worries, he needed bodies. "Make it twenty," Charlie said.

"Feh." The guy spat in the dirt. "You've played these games before." Charlie just waited. "Awright, twenty. But you better bust your ass like Stakhanov come back to life for that."

"I'll pull my weight," Charlie said. Lucille'd probably guess he'd gone to the Valley Relic and tied one on, but he'd be making money for a change, not spending it.

"You better. I'm Kurt. You need anything, yell for me." Kurt raised his voice: "Hey, Paco! Bring Charlie here a hat. We got us another draft mule."

The plastic helmet fit badly, but Charlie didn't say boo. A big stack of sacks of cement stood next to the street, where the truckers who'd brought them had unloaded them. Charlie joined the men taking them to where they needed to be, alongside the apartment blocks. They were fifty-pound sacks. He'd hauled worse. Pretty soon, his shirt was as cement-grayed and sweaty as anybody else's. When the other guys—most of them as unofficial as he was—saw him doing his share, they started treating him like anybody else.

After a while, he remarked, "We could do this quicker if we had wheelbarrows or dollies or something." He felt as if he were back in the produce warehouse again.

"If I had wings, I could fly to the moon," one of the other draft mules answered. Charlie thought his name was Milton. Everybody who heard him laughed.

At the end of the day, Kurt gave Charlie two ten-dollar bills. Spartacus stared up at him from the banknotes, steely-eyed and jut-jawed. As he stuck the money in his wallet, he remarked, "We could move more in the same time if we had something with wheels."

"I've said the same thing to my bosses," Kurt answered. "From what they tell me, we're goddamn lucky we have as much stuff as we do. So we work the best we can with what's on the ground here."

"Okay," Charlie said. They both understood it wasn't, but what could you do?

"Comin' back tomorrow?" Kurt asked, not quite casually.

"Yeah, if I'm not all crippled up in the morning. What time you want me here?"

"We start at eight."

"If the bus doesn't screw me, I'll be here."

Kurt said something about the Rapid Transit District it wasn't physically equipped to do. He thumped Charlie between the shoulder blades and gave him a little shove toward the bus stop.

A lot of tired, grimy, sweaty men were waiting at the stop. Quarters rattled and clanked into the fare box as they boarded. Charlie got off sooner than most of them. His walk back to the apartment was more like a shamble. Yes, he could feel what he'd been up to.

"Good God in the foothills!" Lucille exclaimed when she got a look at him—and probably a whiff of him, too. "What were you doing all day?"

"Socially productive labor. Twenty bucks' worth." Charlie displayed the two tens. "Up at the big blocks past Devonshire. They need bodies—they need 'em bad enough so the guy who took me on didn't ask about my work card. He wants me back tomorrow, too, and maybe Friday."

"That's good ... I guess," his wife said. "But how much will it help when you go back to the Labor Exchange or—?" She didn't mention a cop picking him up, but he heard it anyway.

"All I can do is all I can do," he replied. "All I can do right now is go soak in the tub for a while. I'm beat. But some cabbage is coming in, and I'll be out of your hair for a while, anyway." The Russian slang for money had long since naturalized itself in English.

"I don't know if I'll ever get that shirt clean," Lucille said sadly.

"I'll wear something grubbier tomorrow," Charlie promised. "Today, I didn't know if I'd get anything or what it would be, so I tried to look halfway neat."

He was stiff and sore when the alarm clock alarmed him the next morning, but not so badly as he'd feared. Even if he was moving different things at the big block of flats, he was using most of the same old muscles to do it. He ate toast smeared with plum jam—the only kind the grocery'd had the past two months—and gulped harsh instant coffee, then headed out the door. If he did show up late at the construction site, he wanted it to be the RTD's fault, not his.

To his pleased surprise, he got there five minutes early. Kurt looked happily surprised to see him, too. "You did come back for more!" he said.

"Shows what I know, huh?" Charlie answered. "What, you figured I'd drink up my dividend and stay home?"

"You never can tell," the supervisor said. "I hoped you'd come back—you didn't stink like rotgut when I took you on, and you did fine yesterday. But I've seen too much to count on anything."

"Fair enough," Charlie said, nodding.

Paco gave him a helmet that fit better today. Was that an accident, or had he earned it with a solid shift? He didn't ask. He just got to work. He was seeing how much you had to do so you didn't look like a shirker, and also when to dial it back so you weren't pushing the other guys.

At the end of the day, Kurt handed him a twenty with Frederick Douglass's face on it. He said, "Take the hat home with you. Bring it back tomorrow."

"Sounds good," Charlie said, and then, pushing his luck, "How about Monday?"

"That ... probably isn't in the cards," Kurt said. "Sorry—I *am* sorry; you pull your weight—but that's how it goes. I've only got so much cash to spread around to people who aren't on the books, if you know what I mean, and some of the others have been here longer'n you."

"Well, shit," Charlie said without heat. It wasn't as if that made no sense.

"Take the hat home tomorrow, too," Kurt told him. "Come back Monday a week and I may be able to give you a few more days. If you haven't landed anything else, I mean. If you have, don't worry about the helmet. I'll find some kind of way to write it off."

"I didn't hear a word you said," Charlie said. They grinned at each other: the grins of two men who understood the system's gears meshed loosely. Kurt used that looseness to take on unofficial labor and write off equipment, confident no one would ask him questions he couldn't answer. Charlie wanted things looser still, though he didn't trust the supervisor enough to tell him so.

Friday, he almost got killed. Somebody on the seventh floor dropped a monkey wrench. It thudded to the ground maybe eighteen inches in front of him. If he'd taken one more step .... The helmet wouldn't have done him much good in that case.

"Jesus!" he said, and set down the sack of cement he'd been carrying. All of a sudden, he felt weak in the knees.

"Oh, man!" one of the other guys said. "You look green around the gills—first time that happened to you?"

"Uh-huh." Charlie managed a nod.

"You gotta sit down for a few, go ahead. Nobody'll give you grief. Most of us know what it's like when the goose walks over your grave."

"I'm okay. Mm, I think I'm okay." Charlie bent to pick up the sack again. He needed two tries, so maybe he was less okay than he wished he were. The man who'd dropped the wrench didn't come down to get it. Charlie might have tried to clean his clock if he had.

At quitting time, Kurt said, "If I see you a week from Monday, I'll be glad. If I don't, I'll figure you got something better."

"Way things are, I bet I'm here." Charlie touched one finger to the brim of the plastic helmet. "Take care."

"You, too." Kurt chuckled. "Oh, and I'm glad that wrench missed you. You don't know how many forms I woulda had to fill out if you got squashed."

"Thanks a bunch. Nice to know you care," Charlie said. The supervisor gave him the finger. He gave it back, then turned and trudged over to the bus stop.

He didn't say a word to Lucille about the thump the wrench made when it landed in front of his feet. After all, nothing bad had happened, had it? No, of course not. All the same, he knew he'd remember that thump for the rest of his life. At least he'd have a rest of his life to remember it in.

On Saturday, he looked for other unofficial work. He didn't find any, and nearly walked into another disaster. On Roscoe Boulevard, the cops had set up a checkpoint where they examined the papers of everybody who came by. That was one of the ways they pulled people in on Article 203. Luckily, Charlie knew what sawhorses painted in broad stripes of black and white meant.

For him, they meant trouble. Instead of going on toward the checkpoint, he paused to stare in fascination at the secondhand clothes in a shop window. Then, casually, as if he'd forgotten something, he went back the way he'd come. He was smooth; he was cool. The police didn't notice him moving away. He turned at the first little street he came to. Once they couldn't see him any more, he breathed easier.

He used side streets and alleys to work his way back to Roscoe beyond the checkpoint. Then he could walk away from it without seeming guilty. He knew better than to look back at the police once he'd slipped their trap. Somebody'd got turned into a pillar of salt for doing something stupid like that.

He did tell Lucille about that escape—but only after the kids went to bed. School taught them that kids who informed on their parents were heroes; they hadn't lived enough to know how much of what school taught them was crap. Better to take no chances. His own folks must have been careful about what they said when he was around, even if he hadn't noticed at the time.

"I'm glad you saw 'em," Lucille said.

"You and me both, babe," Charlie answered. "Nobody in his right mind ever wants to have anything to do with cops. And especially not right now, not when my work card looks like it does."

His wife smacked her lips: a sound of unhappy resignation. "Maybe you'd better stay here till you can go back up to those big blocks again." She didn't sound very happy, either, but she said what she said anyhow. Charlie gave her credit for it.

"I'll try not to get in your hair too much while I'm stuck inside," he said. He thought of it as meeting her halfway.

She didn't. She paused, as if knowing she was taking a chance, but she did go on: "Maybe you could even, y'know, help out some if you're gonna be around all the time."

"What? You mean like cleaning and washing dishes?" *Women's work* was how Charlie thought of such things. He didn't mention cooking. He and Lucille both knew how useless he was at anything more complicated than slapping baloney and cheese on bread to make a sandwich.

"That stuff doesn't do itself, you know," she said. "It would help me out."

"I … guess." Charlie couldn't make himself sound enthusiastic—he wasn't. And he quickly added a caveat: "Not while Sally and Nikita can see me do it."

"Might be good for them if they did." But Lucille left it there. She might not have expected to get so much from him as she had.

Pushing a carpet sweeper felt like any other kind of stupid work to Charlie. Dusting, too. To his surprise, he found he liked washing dishes. It was a job with a beginning, a middle, and an end. You started with dirty and you wound up with clean. And the soothing sound of running water let his mind slip away while he did what needed doing.

After he got over his construction-work weariness, he found his own reasons to be glad he wasn't pounding the pavement every day. "This is like a second honeymoon, almost, being alone with you once the kids go to school," he said. "Haven't been able to do that since I don't know when."

"Almost." Lucille could pour cold water on a notion with just one word. No matter how sarcastic she was, though, she didn't say no all the time. They got along spikily sometimes, but they did get along.

While Charlie wasn't washing or cleaning, he studied the papers harder than he had before he threw that stupid poster in the wastebasket. He still got the *Times*, but more for the sports than anything else. *The Daily Worker* was the rag to go to for politics, and politics mattered more to him now than they ever had before.

The Worker was the rag to go to for official politics, anyhow. It was the organ of the CPWCPDR, which meant it was Tony Newman's organ. It showed the leader and the Party to the world as they wanted to be seen.

One story, for instance, was headlined *Eichenlode Engages in Self-Criticism*. The new man from Spokane had proposed another trifling reform, and the Politburo'd voted it down. He'd apologized for taking up so much of its valuable time. Whether that was self-criticism or a jab depended on who wrote the headlines.

When Charlie grumbled about how the headline was worded, Lucille answered, "Never mind that. Worry about what your fair-haired boy is up to. If he keeps poking the big boss, he'll be sorry."

"Yeah, probably." Charlie didn't want to agree, but didn't see that he had much choice. Mary Ann Hannegan had said the same thing, and she knew more about how the WCPDR's political winds blew than Lucille and Charlie put together.

Friday night, Charlie did the dishes after dinner. Sally and Nikita both stared at him as if he were a capitalist in a top hat and tuxedo twirling a walking stick. "Why are *you* doing *that*?" his son demanded.

"It's not so bad," Charlie answered. "It's kinda fun, even. You should try it yourself. You might like it."

"I don't *think* so!" Nikita backed out of the cramped little kitchen in a hurry, plainly afraid Charlie would grab him and stick a wet sponge in his hand.

After the kids had retreated—almost fled—back to the bedroom, Lucille said, "I thought you didn't want to wash dishes when they could see you."

"So I changed my mind. So sue me." Charlie winked at her. "They shouldn't be able to take their old man for granted all the time."

"Nobody can do that, not even the apparatchiks."

"Yeah." His good humor popped like a soap bubble. "I know we'd have an easier time if they could, but…. Sometimes you just get fed up. I get fed up, anyway."

"Do you? I never would've guessed," Lucille said.

He laughed, mostly because she sounded fond, not furious. "I don't know how come you put up with me, but I'm darn glad you do."

He hoped she'd answer with something like *It must be love*. What she did say was, "Half the time, I don't know, either." That might have meant the same thing; then again, it might not.

When she brought in the mail Saturday, she dropped an envelope into his lap. It was another of those official envelopes that warned of a $300 fine for unauthorized personal use. He looked at it only a little less joyfully than if she'd tossed him a live rattlesnake. "Uh-oh," he said.

"Yeah." Lucille nodded. After a few seconds, she asked, "Aren't you going to open it?"

"I don't know. Am I?" After a few seconds of his own, Charlie did open the envelope and take out the folded sheet of official stationery that lurked inside. He unfolded it with the wary care of a man defusing an unexploded bomb.

"Well?" Lucille said after another wait.

He handed her the sheet. "Here," he said. "Tell me if you think it says the same thing I think it says."

She started to read it out loud: "Effective Monday the twenty-third—"

"That's day after tomorrow," Charlie broke in.

"Yeah. But how am I supposed to read if you keep interrupting?" Lucille started from the beginning again: "Effective Monday the twenty-third, you are reassigned to your former position as manager/proprietor of Produce Store V27 at 21132 Sherman Way. If any errors were made in the prior handling of your case, be assured they were unintentional." She stared down at the letter. "I can't believe it says that, either."

"They never make mistakes. They never say they make mistakes, anyhow. I looked at that and I thought I was dreaming. But I read it the same way you did." Still dazed, Charlie took back the sheet of official stationery. It was very neatly typed, and bore a regional subcommissar's illegible signature. But its message was not the kind of thing that happened in the West Coast People's Democratic Republic ... or anywhere else Charlie knew of.

Unless it did.

"Who would've thunk it?" Lucille said, wonder in her voice. "He really *did* come through for you."

She'd got a beat ahead of him. He was still in awe of the miracle, not trying to work out how it had come to pass. As soon as he heard her, though, he knew she had to be right. "He really did," he breathed. He didn't say Alex Eichenlode's name, not only because the flat might be bugged but also because he didn't want to jinx anything.

"You've got a job again. A real job. The Labor Exchange can't give you a hard time any more," Lucille said.

"Not just *a* job. My old job." Charlie couldn't help adding, "Now if only they'd make up all the pay I lost after I got transferred and then fired—"

"Don't push it!" Lucille said quickly.

"Don't worry. I won't. I guess I won't. But if people pushed more, what do you want to bet they'd get more and have more?"

"What do you want to bet the cops would call in soldiers and they'd start machine-gunning everybody in sight?"

He grunted. She had a point. He read the letter again. Damned if it didn't still say the same thing. The paper was fine and white and smooth, too. Nothing but the best for the Party. And if they threw an ordinary proletarian dog a bone, wouldn't he grab it and run? *If people pushed more* .... But Charlie had the unexpected bone. For now, it would do.

chapter

Getting off at the corner of De Soto and Sherman Way felt familiar and strange at the same time. He hadn't gone west from there since they yanked him out of the produce store and sent him to work at the warehouse. Seeing his old place again would have hurt too much.

But here he was, back again, not because he'd done anything special but because he'd made somebody important notice him. The WCPDR said things weren't supposed to work that way. As he'd found out, the WCPDR said lots of things that weren't true.

He walked past Manuel Gomez's junk shop. Manuel was already in there, fiddling with something or other. He didn't look up from whatever it was when Charlie walked by.

Here was the produce store. Tears stung Charlie's eyes, as if it were his and not the state's. It was his to run again, anyhow. That counted for ... well, something. The front window had a poster now. TOGETHER, WORKERS AND PEASANTS ARE INVINCIBLE! it shouted in big red letters.

He tried the door. It was locked. He looked in the three likeliest places to stash a key. He didn't find it in any of them. Triumph threatened to turn to low farce. Produce Store V27 was his to run again ... if he could get in.

He crouched to check under a chunk of loose concrete near the corner of the building. Nothing there, either. Chances were whoever'd been in charge of the place after him hadn't even noticed the chunk was loose.

"You lookin' for the key, man?" somebody asked from no more than three feet away. Startled, Charlie jumped to his feet, which made his knees creak. There stood Gomez, looking as surprised as he felt himself. "Charlie! What the hell you doin' here?"

"Taking charge of this place again. Or I will be if I ever make it inside. Good to see you, Manuel. You know where the key's at?"

"I better." Manuel Gomez reached into his pocket, took out the key, and ceremoniously handed it to Charlie. "Guy who was here before—Leonid, that was his handle—he gave it to me Saturday afternoon, told me to pass it on to his replacement. He didn't say nothin' about that bein' you."

"I bet he didn't even know. Thanks." Charlie slid the key into the lock. It turned smoothly. He thumbed the latch and opened the door.

"But what're you even *doin'* here?" Manuel asked. Sure enough, that was *the* question. The heavyset man went on, "When you got in trouble with … well, with the people you got in trouble with, I didn't figure I'd ever see you again."

"'If any errors were made, be assured they were unintentional.'" Charlie had no trouble quoting the letter; he'd practically memorized it.

"Oh, sure. Right, man. Those people, they don't never make no mistakes. Listen to 'em, you don't believe me."

"I just work here. I really *do* work here." Charlie sounded surprised again, in a different way this time. He couldn't help it. He still was.

"I didn't think you had that kinda clout. You gotta know somebody with some serious juice." Manuel Gomez spoke with genuine respect—and also with a thorough understanding of how things worked.

Embarrassed, Charlie shrugged. "Sometimes you get lucky, is all."

Gomez leaned forward and ran a hand up and down his arm. "I hope it rubs off," he said, then headed back to his own shop.

Charlie went into the produce store. He didn't turn the sign on the inside of the glass door from CLOSED to OPEN yet. He didn't even flip on the lights. He did go to the front window and take down the TOGETHER, WORKERS AND PEASANTS ARE INVINCIBLE! poster. Into the trash it went. Standing behind the counter, where no one could see him from the street, he aimed both middle fingers at

Party headquarters on Topanga Canyon Boulevard. It felt good—no, better than good. It felt great.

Ervin would have laughed at him. Ervin would have called it a meaningless gesture. He would have said only something that changed the system really counted. As far as Charlie was concerned, Ervin was a good guy, but he missed out on a lot of the juice in life.

Having made his two-fingered gesture of defiance, Charlie did flick the light switch and take a look at what he had. He compared that with what the paperwork Leonid had left him said he should have. Here and there, he was a little light. Here and there, he was more than a little light. Chilies, asparagus, avocados, artichokes …

He smiled to himself. If either Manuel or Vissarion Gomez hadn't paid the place a nighttime visit, key in hand, he would have been amazed. Reporting them might put him back in the authorities' good graces. He didn't even think about it. Theft was another way to work the system.

And fudging the records was, too. Up at the construction site, Kurt wrote off unofficial workers and at least one plastic helmet. Charlie knew he could get the missing veggies off the books, too.

As he did turn the door sign to OPEN, he wondered how long people would need to notice the produce store was once more without its Sacramento-sponsored propaganda poster. Longer than he'd thought after he threw out WORKERS OF THE WORLD, UNITE!—he was sure of that.

His first customer bought ten- pounds of potatoes. Ordinary people could either put them in stringbags or get ten- or twenty-five-pound sacks, not the ninety-pound monsters he'd wrestled with in the warehouse. This fellow wasn't anybody he'd seen before, and didn't ask him anything about Leonid. Whoever he was, he'd stocked up on spuds.

Pretty soon, though, a woman he'd known before came in. She did a double take when she saw him behind the counter. "What are you doing here again?" she asked.

"I got reassigned for a while, but I'm back. You know how these things go." Charlie was bold enough to throw out a second poster, but not bold enough to badmouth the people who ran things to somebody he wasn't familiar enough with to trust completely.

"Well, good," said the woman—he thought her name was Bernice, but wasn't sure he remembered straight. She went on, "That fella who took over from you, he didn't keep things as nice as you did."

"I'll keep doing my best. You know how it goes, though—it depends on what they give me to put out, and I don't have any say over that. Now, what do you need today?" Charlie stayed businesslike. He didn't want to show Bernice—if she was Bernice—how much her words pleased him.

He took care of her, and of the other people who came in. Several of them said they were glad to have him back. He thanked them all, trying not to grin each time. No one seemed to notice he'd taken down the propaganda poster. That only went to show how much attention they'd given it before. In the back of his mind, he could hear old Ervin laughing.

But, as he was locking up and getting ready to walk over to the bus stop, Manuel Gomez came out of his shop and asked, "How'd it go?"

"Pretty good, I think. I still remember what to do, anyway," Charlie said.

"Yeah, I noticed that." Gomez's eyes went to the spot in the front window where that poster had been but wasn't. "Are you asking for it, or what? You'll get it. You gotta know that, *vato*. So how come?"

Charlie didn't pretend not to understand him. "I dunno. Same reason as last time, I guess. Just because."

"Some people, they gotta eat fire even if that means lighting it themselves. I always thought you had more sense," Gomez said. When Charlie didn't answer, the man who ran the junk shop sadly shook his head.

"Take care of yourself, Manuel," Charlie said, and started east toward De Soto. He lit a Progress before he got to the bus stop. As he tossed the match onto the grimy sidewalk, he wondered whether smoking counted as eating fire.

Wednesday morning, the first person who walked into the produce store after Charlie opened up was Mary Ann Hannegan. As Manuel Gomez's eyes had before, hers went to the spot where the TOGETHER, WORKERS AND PEASANTS ARE INVINCIBLE! poster had been taped. Like Gomez, she shook her head. But she looked disgusted, not sad. "I might have known," she said.

"Morning, Comrade Hannegan. Nice day today, isn't it?" Charlie said, as if she'd dropped in for a friendly visit or to buy some tangerines.

She fired up a Marlboro, making a point of letting him see the red and white pack. When you were part of the nomenklatura, you could get cigarettes that didn't taste like horseshit whenever you wanted. You didn't have to pay black-market prices for them, either. "You think you can get away with anything, don't you?" she said, her voice flat and deadly.

"No, Comrade. Believe me, I know better than that," Charlie answered honestly.

"Ha!" She stared at him—stared through him, really. She had to be trying to make him afraid, but what he noticed was how beautiful her eyes were. Yes, she would have been to die for when she was half her age. Come to that, she wasn't bad at all now ... and the nomenklatura could probably buy makeup ordinary proletarians couldn't, too.

She might not have known why she wasn't scaring him, but she realized she wasn't. That made her look more fierce, not less. "What do you want from me, Comrade?" Charlie asked. "I'm just trying to do my job."

Her head swung toward the front window, toward the tape marks that showed where the poster'd been displayed. "You're trying to subvert the West Coast People's Democratic Republic."

"Do you think I'm nuts, Comrade Hannegan? Nobody can do that." Once more, Charlie told the truth as he saw it. He thought Ervin had bigger hopes, but he wasn't Ervin.

"Nobody can do it from the outside, but there's such a thing as subversion from within," Mary Ann Hannegan said. "Don't play innocent with me, Comrade. You know what I'm talking about. You wouldn't be back in this store if you didn't. You'd be getting what you deserve—some of it, anyhow."

He thought of places like Manzanar. He thought of rooms where NBI goons took people apart an inch at a time. He thought of all the things that happened to the family of someone who went to a camp like that or to rooms like those. The cold wind he felt on the back of his neck had to be his imagination ... didn't it?

If the WCPDR had to do things like that, didn't it deserve subverting? Charlie wondered what Comrade Hannegan would say if he asked her that, but not enough to want to find out.

She ground out the Marlboro under the sole of her shoe, as if she were a man, or as if the cigarette were one Charlie Simpkins.

Then she said, "If you think you have an angel, I'm here to tell you you're wrong."

"Comrade, I don't think anything. I got a letter Saturday that told me I was supposed to report here Monday morning. So I did that. I got the keys from Comrade Gomez next door, and—"

"Yes, I know. He told me," Mary Ann Hannegan broke in.

"Okay," Charlie said. Only it wasn't. Nowhere close. Now he'd never be able to gab with Gomez again, not so openly as he had before. He could ask the junk-shop man if he'd talked with Comrade Hannegan, but what good would that do? Either Gomez would say yes and prove he was an informer, or he'd say no and Charlie wouldn't be sure whether to believe him or not. Half a dozen words, and Mary Ann Hannegan had ruined something he valued.

As if she cared. "You wouldn't have got that letter if Comrade Eichenlode"—she freighted the title with scorn—"hadn't pulled levers for you. You know it, too. Sooner or later, though—sooner, I think—Comrade Eichenlode will pull one more lever. I've told you this before. You know which lever it is, too, don't you?"

"I'm sorry, Comrade, but you've lost me," Charlie said.

She considered him, realized he meant it, and visibly decided he was dumber than she'd thought. "The lever on the gallows that drops the trap from under his feet. *That* lever, Comrade Simpkins. Tony Newman's given him about enough rope to hang himself." She sounded as if she was looking forward to it.

Charlie tried to hide how alarmed he was. "I don't know anything about politics. I don't care, either. I just want to do my job."

"You keep saying that. You keep lying." Mary Anne Hannegan half turned and pointed to the spot where Leonid had taped up the poster. "If you don't care about politics, why did you throw that away?"

He shrugged. "Leaving it up would've been political, too, huh?"

She considered him once more. He imagined slot-machine wheels spinning behind those lovely eyes. *Recalculating me again*, he thought, and guessed he might have risen in her estimation this time. Was that good or bad? Too late to worry about it now.

Slowly, she said, "Every action, every inaction, is political, true. But leaving the poster where it was would have been political in a socially constructive way."

Would have been doing what the West Coast People's Democratic Republic wanted me to do. Charlie had heard the jargon his whole life. He understood what it meant in plain English. "I don't know what to tell you," he answered, no more than half a beat more slowly than he might have.

"You associate with undesirable elements," she said, like a judge passing sentence. *Yeah, just like that,* Charlie thought. He understood what she meant there, too. *You drink with Ervin down at the Valley Relic.* Of course they were watching him. And Ervin. And everybody else they wondered about even a little bit. How many people in the WCPDR made part of their living spying on other people? *Lots,* was what occurred to him. Manuel Gomez, for instance.

He wanted to say, *Well, I'm standing here talking with you right now.* He didn't have the balls. He did say, "The kind of changes I'd like to see, they wouldn't do anything to hurt the way things are."

"Any change threatens the system. Any unauthorized change, all the more." Mary Ann Hannegan sounded very sure of herself—and when didn't she? "Deviationism will not be tolerated, will not be permitted. Unlike Comrade Eichenlode, Tony Newman understands that. He has his finger on the pulse back in Moscow. He knows what General Secretary Zhuravlev requires."

As General Secretary of the Communist Party of the USSR, Yuri Zhuravlev was of course the most powerful man in the world. *The Daily Worker* and the *Times* never failed to sing his praises. Charlie didn't think he'd ever heard Zhuravlev's name in the produce store till now. He said, "The General Secretary? No matter how far I crane my neck back, I can't look up that high."

"That's the first—mm, possibly the second—sensible thing you've said today," Comrade Hannegan replied. "Maybe you should remember it more often." Without another word, she walked out of the produce store. The door clicked shut behind her.

Charlie's knees didn't want to hold him up. He had to stiffen them with a conscious effort of will. He'd had the same feeling when that falling wrench almost punched his ticket for good. There was one big difference, though. If the wrench had got him, everything would have been over in a hurry. People like Mary Ann Hannegan and her friends knew how to make pain last.

"Fuck," he muttered under his breath. A lot of people stashed a pint, or sometimes a fifth, in a drawer or on a shelf behind the counter. It took the edge off the joys of socially productive labor. Charlie'd never done that. Right this minute, he wondered why the hell not.

He'd figured out a while before that Comrade Hannegan had a line to Sacramento. She knew what was going on there long before people less well connected—people like, say, Charlie Simpkins—had a prayer of finding out.

As casually as it could, a story below the fold on the front page of Friday's *Daily Worker* announced that a no-confidence vote against Tony Newman had been scheduled for that afternoon. *This is purely a procedural matter, and no structural changes are anticipated*, the paper said.

He looked at that. Someone was proposing to throw Tony Newman out of the slot he'd held for the past twelve years? No, it wasn't Alex Eichenlode—that was the first thing Charlie checked. It was a more senior Politburo man, Colin McCarrick, from Fresno. Charlie'd seen photos of him every now and then. Gray hair, nice suit, face full of pasted-on sincerity. An apparatchik.

An ambitious apparatchik, if he figured he could bring down the WCPDR's longtime leader. Had he thought what might happen if the no-confidence motion failed? If he hadn't, why not?

Just for a moment, Charlie wondered what Mary Ann Hannegan thought of McCarrick. Probably not much, since she seemed a staunch Newmanist. But even if McCarrick plopped his backside into the leather seat at the center of the Politburo dais, Charlie expected Comrade Hannegan would do all right for herself. People like her always did.

Purely a procedural matter. That phrase jumped out at him again. *The Daily Worker* was playing it cool. That made sense to Charlie. Nobody wanted to risk falling afoul of the big boss, no matter who the big boss ended up being.

"Hey," Vissarion Gomez said as Charlie walked by on his way to the produce store.

"Hey," Charlie answered.

"Good to have you back, man," Manuel Gomez's son went on.

"Thanks. Good to be back." Charlie wondered whether Vissarion was an informer, too. Even if the younger Gomez wasn't, Charlie knew he couldn't trust him or his old man any more. Life sucked sometimes.

"That Leonid guy, he was kinda boring. Did everything by the book, know what I mean?" Vissarion looked at Charlie, and at the window that once more displayed no propaganda poster. "Not like you."

"Probably just says he had more sense than I do." No, Charlie didn't want to do anything stupid around Vissarion or Manuel. *Anything stupid except pitching a poster. Twice*, he corrected himself. Too late to worry about that now, though. Way too late.

He opened up the store. He was supposed to get a shipment of peas and green beans today. So they'd told him, anyhow. Maybe it would show up, maybe not. As with so many other things, just because they told you didn't make it so. Charlie didn't believe the shipment would show up. He might have his old job again, but to the people who ran things he remained an unreliable. They'd find ways to make him pay.

In the meantime, he wiped dirt off the carrots and scallions and spritzed the lettuces with a little water so they'd look their best. He chucked a few potatoes and onions that had seen better days into the trash bin in the alley behind the store. He wanted everything he sold to be as good as it could.

Some of the potatoes and onions he threw out weren't very far gone. Charlie knew they'd disappear long before the garbage truck came for what was in the bin. The West Coast People's Democratic Republic was a paradise for workers and peasants—it said so, loudly and often—but they didn't all have enough to eat.

As he went back inside and closed and locked the door behind him, he wondered what was going on in Sacramento. Wonder was all he could do. You had to be a Party insider to know which way the wind blew.

He also wondered how Eichenlode would vote, and what would happen to him if he voted the wrong way. He wouldn't get a pat on the head—Charlie was sure of that. Caring what happened to a politician felt strange, unnatural, wrong. But Eichenlode gave a damn about people like him. That felt strange and unnatural, too.

A little old woman came into the store and looked at Charlie through thick glasses that magnified her eyes enormously. "I heard you was back," she said. "So how did that happen?"

"They reassigned me here, Comrade Nussboym, so here I am." Charlie was pretty sure Abbie Nussboym was okay, but he'd been pretty sure Manuel Gomez was, too. Finding out he'd probably been wrong about that left him not wanting to stick out his neck.

She bought some of the scallions he'd spruced up and some potatoes that had passed inspection. He took her money and her ration coupons. She went off to see what else she could find in the little shops that lined both sides of Sherman Way.

There was an enormous department store—GUM, they called it, after the one in Moscow—in downtown Los Angeles that sold food and clothes, appliances and furniture, tools and stationery, all under one roof. It sold them when it had them, anyway, which wasn't very often. People here joked about all the things GUM didn't sell. Somebody'd told Charlie people in Moscow joked the same way, only in Russian.

A truck rumbled down the alley. Its brakes squeaked as it stopped ... behind the produce store? "I'll be damned!" Charlie said, and hurried out back. Sure as hell, the shipment was here after all.

The guy driving the truck gave him a funny look. "Haven't I seen you somewhere before?" he said.

"You sure have, Jack," Charlie answered. "I worked in the warehouse on Ventura Boulevard for a while. That where you got this stuff?"

"Yeah," Jack said. "What are you doing here, then?"

"It's a long story," Charlie said: not the smallest understatement he'd ever come out with. Saying that also meant he didn't have to tell the story, and he didn't want to. He knew Jack well enough to recognize him and say hello, no more. His story had political overtones, so he'd be a fool to spill it to anybody he didn't trust. That calculation saddened him, but people had to make them all the time all over the world.

Jack didn't seem put out. If he had any brains at all, he made those calculations, too. He reached into the truck and pulled out a clipboard with forms clamped in its steel jaws. "Here. You gotta sign all these."

While Charlie signed (and checked the forms, to make sure nobody'd planted one that would land him in trouble), the truck driver loaded crates onto a dolly and wheeled the green beans and peas into the store's back room. Charlie counted them and made sure they matched the numbers the forms said he was supposed to get. Only after he was satisfied did he give the clipboard back to Jack.

"Thanks." The driver touched a forefinger to the bill of his cap in an almost-salute. "That Wilder item, I bet he's gonna shit rivets when he sees who this stuff's gone to."

"That'd break my heart," Charlie said dryly. Jack guffawed. Then he climbed into the truck, fired it up, and drove off.

Charlie went back inside. He opened a crate of peas and one of green beans with a pry bar. The fresh smell rising from the vegetables made him smile. So did their bright green goodness. He didn't usually see such fine produce; most of it went into the special shops for the nomenklatura. As long as he had it, though, he'd put it in the bins out front.

He didn't know how the locals knew when he got a shipment, but they always did. For the next couple of hours, he was very busy. People made a beeline for those bins. He had to break into a second crate of beans and one of peas, then a third. His customers knew he didn't get vegetables like these every day, too.

Vissarion Gomez bought a couple of pounds of peas and a couple more of green beans. "You're gonna be my mama's favorite fella tonight," he told Charlie. "I dunno what she'll do with these, but it'll be good, whatever it is." He smacked his lips.

"Make sure she knows I'm taken," Charlie said, and got a laugh from Vissarion. Some peas and beans already sat under the counter, in paper bags tied with coarse twine. Charlie intended to be Lucille's favorite fella tonight, too. He'd never brought unofficial produce home very often. He didn't want to be a pig, or to get caught being a pig. With produce this special, he made an exception.

He stayed so busy, he hardly thought about the no-confidence vote in Sacramento or about Alex Eichenlode till he closed down and headed for the bus stop. There were vending machines near the benches. Peering through the thick, dirty glass, he saw that neither *The Worker* nor the *Times* had headlines screaming about Tony Newman's ouster. Either the vote had failed or the papers had gone into the stands before it happened.

When he got home, he set the sacks on the kitchen counter. "What have you got there?" Lucille asked.

"See for yourself," Charlie said.

She opened first one, then the other. "Oh, these are pretty," she crooned. "I don't remember the last time I saw such nice veggies."

"Me, neither. I figured they'd give me old moldy stuff that wasn't worth putting out, or else maybe nothing at all. But they surprised me," Charlie said.

"You know why? You scare the crap outa them, that's why," his wife said.

"Don't be silly. That's—" Charlie stopped. It might not be ridiculous after all. People might not be scared of him as Charlie Simpkins, but some would be scared because he'd got his old job back. They'd be scared of Alex Eichenlode, scared of change. Change scared even Mary Ann Hannegan.

He looked at his watch. It was just about six straight up. He clicked on the radio. "What's so important, you've got to hear it right now?" Lucille said.

"The no-confidence vote!" he answered. Then he had to explain. She hadn't seen a newspaper, and she'd only listened to music on the radio. He couldn't blame her for that. Most of the time, the news wasn't worth paying attention to.

Once she understood what was going on, she said, "I don't really think they'll throw him out. Do you?" She pointed to a cabinet, then to the wall the refrigerator covered: both good places to hide bugs.

Charlie got the message. "No, of course not," he answered. "I'm surprised it came to a vote at all. Tony Newman's doing a terrific job." He imagined an earphone-wearing NBI snoop cursing in disgust when he heard that.

The news came on. The broadcaster reading it didn't even mention the no-confidence vote, or say it had been postponed. She talked about the overfulfillment of the latest Four Year Agricultural Plan, and about General Secretary Zhuravlev's upcoming visit to the North American fraternal socialist republics. She gave the latest on a fire at a galoshes factory in Compton, and about a little boy who'd been killed by a police car.

"This foolish child unexpectedly darted into the street," she said. "The dedicated officer at the wheel could not have anticipated anything of the sort."

Charlie and Lucille looked at each other for a moment. Neither said anything, because you never could tell. But Charlie knew his wife had to be thinking the same thing he was. Newsreaders never suggested the police could be wrong, the driver wasn't paying attention, maybe he'd had a few, or maybe he just didn't give a damn. No, it was always the ordinary person's fault.

The newscast ended without a word about the no-confidence vote. Charlie scratched his head and turned off the radio. He didn't care about the upcoming show. It was a paean to socialist forestry in northern California, Oregon, and Washington. That made it more interesting than thinking about killing himself, but not a whole lot.

Instead of suicide, he contemplated the story the news hadn't covered. Why the devil not? Was the Politburo trying to figure out how to tell the world it had ousted Tony Newman? Was Newman, having won the vote, trying to decide how to punish the people who'd moved against him? Were secret policemen and soldiers shooting at one another in the streets of Sacramento? That wasn't likely, but it had happened down in Bogota about the time Nikita was born, so you never knew.

That's the trouble, Charlie thought. *You never know.* If the radio and the newspapers told more of the truth and less of what the Party wanted people to hear .... He laughed at himself. *I'll be goddamned if I'm not turning into Ervin.*

He kept worrying at it all through supper, though he did remember to tell Lucille how good the steamed peas were. She smiled. "I wasn't going to mess those up, not after you brought 'em home."

"Is that where those came from? I didn't think we had 'em before," Sally said.

"That's where they came from, and you can thank your father for 'em," Lucille said.

"Thank you, Daddy," Charlie's daughter told him.

"It's okay." He only half heard her. He'd gone back to puzzling over politics. He knew that was silly; like anybody who wasn't a Party member, he didn't know enough about what was going on inside the halls of power. But he couldn't help himself.

Mary Ann Hannegan would know. He'd had that thought before. One corner of his mouth twisted. Nothing would have made him happier than never seeing her again. Seeing Comrade Hannegan would mean he'd landed in more trouble. And he figured the odds were good he would.

He bought *The Worker* and the *Times* Saturday morning, and sat down on the bus bench to read them. The produce store stayed open only till one on Saturday; he'd come home in the afternoon. A half holiday, the WCPDR called it. Charlie still had to get up early to go over to De Soto, so he thought of it in less generous terms.

He was scratching his head when he hopped off the bus. Neither paper said a word about what had happened in the capital. For all he knew, they'd called off the vote and nothing had happened. If they had, though, wouldn't the newspapers have mentioned that?

Manuel Gomez was opening up as Charlie came by. "You don't even have to be here today," Charlie said.

Shrugging, Gomez answered, "I like to come in on Saturdays sometimes. I see people who can't get here the rest of the week."

"You're a sucker for sob stories, is what you are," Charlie said as he pulled the store key out of his pocket. Only after he'd gone inside did he realize he'd jawed with Gomez as if Mary Ann Hannegan hadn't told him the junk-shop man had talked with her. It wasn't even protective coloration, the way so much of life in the WCPDR was. For a couple of minutes, he'd just forgotten.

He put out more peas and green beans. Sure enough, his customers snapped them up. Like Manuel Gomez, he did a lot of business on Saturday. He would have got more excited if he'd got paid more for selling more. But he didn't. As long as he hit—or could pretend to hit—his sales norms, his salary stayed the same.

When he got back to the flat, he turned on the radio and waited for the news. The lead story was that the French Democratic Commune had overproduced the planned steel output in the third year of its current Six-Year Plan by thirteen per cent. "General Secretary Zhuravlev telephoned his congratulations to Premier Henriot," the broadcaster said, and went on to the next item.

Not a word about the no-confidence vote. Charlie began to wonder whether he'd imagined the whole thing. He knew he was crazy, but didn't think he was crazy that way.

He brought the Sunday *Times* and *Daily Worker* back from the corner of De Soto and Gresham the next morning. The kids grabbed the color comics in the *Times*. Charlie wanted *The Worker* first anyway. He went through it methodically, front to back. All the same, he almost missed the story. It was buried on page eleven, next to one about improved millet production in the People's Democratic Republic of Ethiopia and Eritrea.

"No-Confidence Motion Resoundingly Defeated," the small headline said. The story said the Politburo had voted 16-5 to retain Tony Newman at the helm of the West Coast People's Democratic Republic. It mentioned by name the five members who'd presumed to vote against him. One was Colin McCarrick, who'd made the motion. Three of the others were only names to Charlie. The fifth was Alex Eichenlode.

I told you messing with Tony Newman was stupid. Charlie could hear Mary Ann Hannegan's low, tobacco-roughened voice inside his own head. He wanted to stick his fingers in his ears to block it out, but that wouldn't do any good.

"Did you say something, sweetie?" Lucille asked, so he must have made a noise, even if he couldn't remember doing it.

"I didn't, but I will," he said. "The no-confidence vote failed. It wasn't close."

"Well, that just goes to show what a popular fellow Premier Newman is." Lucille sounded bright and cheery, the way anyone sensible would when praising the ruler in a flat that might be bugged.

"I was thinking the same thing," Charlie answered in the same upbeat tone. If some bored NBI tech was monitoring a microphone, he'd be sure Charlie was lying through his teeth. Charlie didn't want to make it easy for the state to build a case against him, though.

As he read the short news story again, he wondered whether what he didn't want mattered even a dime's worth. If the WCPDR decided to build a case against him, it could build one out of moonshine and cobwebs if it chose to. He might protest his innocence till he was blue in the face, but no judge would listen to him. Judges were teeth in the system's gears, too.

"How many people were disloyal enough to vote against Comrade Newman?" his wife asked.

"Five. Five out of twenty-one."

"I didn't think there'd be many more. I'm surprised there were even that many," Lucille said. "Nobody wants folks he can't trust around him."

"That's right. That's exactly right." Instead of imagining he heard Mary Ann Hannegan, in his mind's eye Charlie saw that NBI snoop tearing off his earphones, slamming them down on his desk, and cussing a blue streak. The bastard would know he was being played, but what could he do about it?

"Everything's gonna be just fine now," Lucille said.

"Sure it will. Tony Newman'll make sure it will." In spite of everything, Charlie smiled. He really wished he could see the look on that NBI guy's ugly mug.

chapter

The first shoe dropped quickly. Reading the *Times* on his way down De Soto Tuesday morning, Charlie saw that Colin McCarrick had been appointed to head a WCPDR trade delegation to the Socialist Democracy of Manchuria. *His expertise in forestry and paper production will be invaluable*, the story said blandly.

McCarrick was an expert on forestry? Charlie didn't remember ever hearing that before. He might not have paid attention. Or somebody sitting in front of a typewriter in Sacramento might have made up a reasonable-sounding excuse for throwing Colin McCarrick the hell out of the West Coast People's Democratic Republic.

There were still people's republics where trying to overthrow the big cheese and failing would get you a noodle—Russian slang for a bullet—in the back of the neck. A lot of people had got those noodles in the Northeastern Soviet Socialist Republic when Charlie was young. That kind of thing hadn't happened here for a long time. Just because it hadn't, though, didn't mean it couldn't.

Another *Times* story talked about General Secretary Zhuravlev's upcoming visit to North America. The Russians wanted to snuff out trouble in this part of the world before it could get bad.

Manuel Gomez's place was already open when Charlie walked by. Gomez looked up from whatever he was doing. Charlie waved back. Yeah, the junk-shop man had probably informed on him. In spite of that, he was still a pretty good guy. What were you supposed to do?

What were you supposed to do? You were supposed to put up the propaganda posters they gave you. His life had got more interesting since he hadn't done that—no doubt about it. Had it got better? He wasn't so sure there.

Today, Charlie did do what he was supposed to do. He opened up the produce store and got ready for customers. He more than half expected Comrade Hannegan to come in to gloat about the no-confidence vote. She didn't. If she'd decided he wasn't important enough for gloating, he didn't mind a bit.

Nobody who came in said word one about the Politburo vote or about Comrade McCarrick's sudden departure for the Socialist Democracy of Manchuria. Did people not know? Did they not care? Or did they just have better sense than to talk politics with anybody they didn't know well?

A shipment of nice avocados and artichokes came in. The driver happened to be Jack again. "You're getting all kinds of good stuff," he remarked as he moved boxes into the back room.

"I'm as surprised as you are, believe me," Charlie said.

"I know what it is." The truck driver winked. "I bet you got photos of that Wilder hemorrhoid with a sheep."

Charlie laughed so hard, he had to lean against the back wall for a few seconds. "I wish!" he said.

"I tell you, Wilder'd have to pay even if it was a goddamn sheep. Nobody'd do him for free, bet your ass," Jack said.

"Probably," Charlie agreed, laughing still, and left it there. He couldn't be sure Jack wasn't taking his words back to Wilder, or to Mary Ann Hannegan, or to the police or the NBI. Hell of a thing, when you had to watch every word that came out of your mouth. This was exactly what Ervin meant when he wished the system had some looseness in it. It sure as hell needed some.

On Tuesday morning, *The Daily Worker* reported that Madeleine Jeter had been chosen as the new WCPDR ambassador to the People's Democratic Republic of Yemen. Comrade Jeter had voted to remove Tony Newman Friday afternoon. *Another one down*, Charlie thought mournfully.

Wednesday passed without the axe's falling again. On Thursday, a story in the *Times* announced that Roger Villasboas, another anti-Newman Politburo member, was heading a commission charged with studying Bulgarian Black Sea harbor installations. Yes, the purge was on.

The Friday *Times* and *Worker* both let people know Feofan Trowbridge, who had also voted against the Premier, was bound for the Sinkiang People's Republic on some unspecified mission. *He will assist our fraternal socialist partner in advancing the world proletarian revolution*, *The Worker* added. It didn't say how.

"Crap," Charlie muttered, and slammed the paper down on the empty bus seat beside him. The woman across the aisle looked at him out of the corner of her eye. When he didn't do anything else, she relaxed ... a little.

What went through his mind like the tolling of a sad bell was *And then there was one*. He would have expected Newman to drop on Alex Eichenlode before any of the others except perhaps Comrade McCarrick. Eichenlode was a comer, not just an apparatchik. But nothing had happened to him yet.

Which meant—what? Charlie couldn't believe the Premier would put up with anybody who threatened his power. Would he stage a show trial, with Eichenlode confessing he'd spied for the Canadian Federated Socialist Republic before they executed him? Or would he simply vanish from the Politburo without a word of explanation?

Late at night, in bed, with the kids snoring in the other bed and with the covers pulled up over his head, Charlie whispered his worries to Lucille. He felt her shrug. "If he does go away like that, they'll take him out of the photos, too," she whispered back. "It'll be like he never happened!"

"Just like that!" Charlie exclaimed—louder than he should have, though not loud enough to wake Sally or Nikita. Everybody knew about those photos, though no one talked about them. Most were old. There'd be a gap in a Politburo group picture, a gap that often didn't quite match the background. Whoever'd filled that gap while the photographer snapped away had got airbrushed out of history since.

It still happened, too. Charlie remembered a Marxist-Leninist-Stalinist ideologist named Clem Gottwald, who'd been erased after the downfall of the NESSR. People said—said quietly, if they knew what was good for them—he'd wanted to bring those radical policies here to the West Coast. He'd disappeared, from the Politburo and from the official record.

"Eichenlode's a good guy, though," Charlie said, once more in tones mindful of his safety.

"He is to you." Lucille always had better sense than to raise her voice when they talked like this. "What looks good to you won't to Newman and people like him. The big shots, they don't like it when anybody rocks the boat."

"Yeah," Charlie whispered sadly. Mary Ann Hannegan had said pretty much the same thing. Like every other country in the world, the West Coast People's Democratic Republic promised total proletarian revolution, the coming of true Communism, and the withering away of the state. In the meantime … In the meantime, the nomenklatura liked the way things were just fine.

"Why don't you go down to the Valley Relic tomorrow after you close up and blow off some steam?" his wife said.

He stared at where her voice was coming from—there in the blackness under the bedclothes, he couldn't see anything, but he stared anyway. "You never tell me anything like that!" he blurted.

"Well, now I did," Lucille replied. "Can we go to sleep, already?"

"Okay," Charlie said. Thirty seconds later, she started snoring. He lay awake a lot longer than that.

The Saturday papers still said not a word about Alex Eichenlode. Charlie got another shipment of top-quality vegetables for the shop, though. He had no idea whether that meant anything, but rode the hope. It cost nothing, and it was what he had.

After he locked up, he took Lucille's advice and rode the bus south on De Soto, not north. Another bus carried him east on Ventura. After he got off, he walked to the tavern near the warehouse. As soon as he came through the door, somebody at a table in the back let out a whoop: "Look what the cat drug in!"

"Hey, Dornel!" Charlie waved.

"C'mon back here and let me buy you a drink," the big black man said. "I figured you done run out on us for good."

"I'm not that smart," Charlie said, and won a laugh.

Dornel got him what passed for bourbon in a class-four joint. They clinked glasses and sipped. Charlie tried not to make a face. He saw Dornel trying not to make one, too. The warehouse worker said, "Jack, the way he tells it, you got your old job at the produce store back. Is that the straight goods? Don't know if I wanna believe a raggedy-ass truck driver, know what I'm sayin'?"

"Hate to break it to you, but he's telling the truth," Charlie answered.

"Damn! How'd you pull that?" Dornel asked with what sounded like genuine respect.

"Luck. Luck like eight or ten sevens in a row." Charlie had no idea whether Dornel had ever heard of Alex Eichenlode, or what he thought of him if he had. He'd never seen any signs that the black man informed, but he'd never seen those signs with Manuel Gomez, either. He didn't show his cards.

"More'n that, by the sound of it." Dornel knocked back his whiskey. Charlie finished his, too, and went to the bar to get another round. "Obliged," Dornel said when he set his glass down, and then, "No wonder Wilder makes like he wants to bite somethin' whenever he hears somebody say your name, then."

Charlie smiled. He couldn't help it. "Does he?"

"Bet your sweet ass he does. That man never did take a shine to you, did he? Neither did the fella what was there before him. Muldberg, that was his name. How come you don't get along with the folks who tell other folks what to do?"

"They're jealous of how handsome I am," Charlie said, deadpan.

Dornel snorted and coughed. "Goddammit, that almost went up my nose," he said without rancor. He cocked his head to one side as he examined Charlie, then slowly shook it. "Nope. Gotta be some kind of explanation that makes sense instead."

"Thanks a bunch," Charlie said. Dornel tipped the hat he wasn't wearing, a gesture oddly bourgeois even in play.

Ervin came in a few minutes later. Charlie had no idea what the old-timer did when he wasn't at the Valley Relic. Here, Ervin was a big wheel, or as big a wheel as you could be in a class-four tavern. He talked with people at several tables, and shook hands with people at several more. He already had a beer by the time he made it back to where Dornel and Charlie were sitting.

"Waddaya know for sure?" Charlie asked him.

"If I knew anything for sure, I'd know enough to stay away from this crummy place." Ervin snagged a chair from a nearby table with his foot and sat down. "How's it going, Dornel?"

"It's going. Might go better if some o' this brown"—Dornel touched the first two fingers of his right hand to the back of his left wrist—"washed off, but it's going."

Ervin nodded. "Uh-huh. The workers' and peasants' paradise likes black people even better than it likes rootless cosmopolites like me." That was political jargon, too. It stretched *kike* out into six syllables.

Dornel clicked his tongue between his teeth. "Man, one o' these days they gonna shoot you for real, you keep talkin' like that."

"Why? It's the truth," Ervin said.

"That's why," Dornel answered. Ervin chuckled in appreciation and lit a cigarette.

He spent the next fifteen minutes talking with Dornel and paying no attention to Charlie. Charlie felt miffed. He'd thought he was in Ervin's good graces; that was one big reason he'd come down here. He wondered what he'd done to put Ervin's nose out of joint. He couldn't think of anything.

Dornel stood up. "Gotta see a man about the pipes," he said, and headed off to the Valley Relic's sour-smelling men's room.

Ervin started to rise, too. It was so obvious he didn't want to stick around that Charlie exclaimed, "What, am I cancer?"

"I was wondering the same thing," Ervin answered, but he sat back down.

"How come?" Charlie asked, bewildered.

The older man looked at him as if he were an idiot. "You got your old job back, that's how come." He spoke as if to an idiot, too, in words of one syllable.

"Oh, fuck me!" The light that went off inside Charlie's head was brighter than a hundred flashbulbs. Ervin thought he managed to go back to running the produce store because he'd done something the state or the Party wanted him to do. "It isn't like that!"

"No? How is it, then?" Shrouded in tobacco smoke, Ervin seemed a million miles away from believing him.

Charlie explained about Alex Eichenlode. Dornel came back when he was halfway through. Charlie was upset enough, he didn't even care. "That's how," he said when he got done. "You don't like it, say the word, and you'll never see me again, 'cause I won't come back."

"I'm not worried about you on account of me. They want me, they always know where to find me. I don't keep secrets. I don't sneak around," Ervin said. "I'm worried about you on account of other people."

"Fine." Now it was Charlie's turn to get up. Grief almost choked him. "So long."

"Hold on." That was Dornel, not Ervin. He looked at the longtime dissident. "I don't think Charlie's a good enough liar to blow smoke up our asses. I don't think he would, neither. He drives those people nuts." He didn't explain who *those people* were, or need to.

"You never know. I mean, never," Ervin said harshly. "Fastest way to win a ticket to Manzanar or Hanford is to trust somebody you shouldn't have." He grudged Charlie a nod. "So long. Luck—I guess."

"Luck," Charlie echoed, his voice empty. He sketched Dornel a salute. "Take care of yourself." Out of the Valley Relic he walked. The door closed behind him. Tears stung his eyes, but he didn't look back once, all the way to the bus stop.

Tony Newman nominated four new people to fill the Politburo slots he'd emptied. The surviving members of the WCPDR's senior governing body confirmed his picks. *The Daily Worker* duly recorded the roll-call votes. Alex Eichenlode voted for two of them, abstained once, and voted against one.

Every time Charlie saw Eichenlode's name in print, he had to work to keep from grinning. In another time and place, he might have sent up prayers of thanksgiving and relief to God. Being who he was, living where and when he did, he never once thought of that. But the feeling was there even if the gesture wasn't.

In another of those under-the-bedclothes talks with Lucille, Charlie whispered, "They haven't purged him. I don't know why they haven't, but they haven't."

"Could he kick up that much trouble if they tried?" she asked.

"By himself? Nah, not a chance." Charlie shook his head. "The people who like what he's trying to do—"

"People like you."

"People like me," Charlie agreed. After a few seconds' thought, he shook his head again. "I don't see it. I wish I did, but I don't. Newman's got the Nibbies. He's got the ordinary police—oh, maybe not in Spokane and up there, but most places. He's got the soldiers. Anybody starts trouble, he finishes it."

"That's how it looks to me, too. I wondered if I was missing something. Why haven't they got rid of him, then?"

"Beats me." Charlie moved a little. Not quite by accident, his hand came down on Lucille's thigh.

Not at all by accident, she knocked it away. "Tomorrow. Not tonight, okay? I'm really tired tonight."

"Okay," he said. It wasn't, not quite, but he was tired, too. And if you wanted to stay married, you had to give to get. His own troubles and the way Lucille stuck by him had reminded him how much he wanted to stay married.

So he got home the next evening in an optimistic mood. That optimism blew out like a candle in a tornado when Lucille thrust three official envelopes at him as soon as he walked in the door. "These came today," she said, as if he couldn't work that out himself.

"Oh, for Chrissake! What now?" he said.

"I dunno. Open 'em up and find out."

"I don't want to." The envelopes were from Sacramento. How often did good news ever come from there? What went through Charlie's mind was *Shit flows downhill*. He knew too well how far downhill from the capital he was.

"Open 'em anyway. We'd better find out what they think we did now." As usual, Lucille was relentlessly practical.

"Yeah, yeah." Charlie murdered one of the envelopes and unfolded the letter inside. Then he did the same thing with the other two. Without a word, his face somber, he passed her all three letters.

She took them with the look of dread most people wear just before the dentist goes to work. She read the one on top. She stared at Charlie. "They … they put us back in our old place in the queue for a TV set?" She didn't sound as if she believed what she was saying.

Charlie had trouble believing it, too, but he'd already read them both. "And for the car," he said. "That's the second one. The last one says I've got my full tobacco ration back."

"It is regretted that administrative sanctions were inappropriately applied in your case. Corrective adjustment is hereby made," she quoted. Then she said, "They *never* do things like that!"

"Only they did." After a moment, Charlie made a connection. "They did when I went back to the produce store, too."

"That's right. They did. Is it because … ?" Lucille leaned toward him and spoke softly in his ear: "Is it because Eichenlode's still pulling for you?"

"I was thinking the same thing. I sure hope so," Charlie murmured, also leaning close. He nibbled her earlobe. She squeaked and hopped back.

"It's good that important people, people in the Politburo, pay attention to what's going on with regular workers," she said, for Charlie's benefit and for that of anyone else who might be listening.

"It's very good," Charlie said, also pitching his voice to the unseen audience. Alex Eichenlode had had that kind of reputation up in Spokane. Having that kind of reputation was what propelled him to the Politburo. But when somebody ordinary found out the reputation was deserved … . Charlie might have been more surprised to see a unicorn trotting along Sherman Way past the produce store. Then again, he might not have.

"You know what else is good?" Lucille said.

"Tell me," Charlie urged.

"I think the kids are tired. They may hit the hay earlier than usual."

"Oh, yeah?" He eyed her. Not to put too fine a point on it, he leered at her. "How about that?"

A week later, General Secretary Zhuravlev landed in Sacramento to discuss the state of the West Coast People's Democratic Republic with Tony Newman. Both the *Times* and *The Daily Worker* splashed the Soviet leader's visit all over their front pages. The *Times* even splurged on printing a big color photo of Zhuravlev coming down the wheeled stairway from the Red Star, the enormous Ilyushin airliner that was his personal steed. *The Worker* used the same photo, only in black and white.

A *Worker* editorial said, *Anyone can see that relations between the USSR and our own nation have never been stronger, that their alliance has never been firmer or more unshakable. The General Secretary's visit only underscores and emphasizes this incontrovertible fact.*

Charlie felt one eyebrow rise. Somebody'd written something about someone protesting too much. Shakespeare? Dickens? One of those old guys. Every so often, he wished he'd paid more attention in school. Some of the stuff he'd almost learned might have come in handy if only he remembered more of it. *Maybe if the teachers weren't so goddamn boring*, he thought.

And he wondered whether Comrade Zhuravlev and Comrade Newman would talk about Alex Eichenlode. He didn't see how they could avoid it, though he would have bet Tony Newman wanted to. Or maybe Newman hoped to talk. Maybe he was waiting to get the Soviet General Secretary's okay before he purged Eichenlode along with the rest of the apparatchiks who'd had the gall to vote against him.

Charlie still didn't have a propaganda poster in his front window. After that visit from Mary Ann Hannegan, nobody'd given him any more trouble about the big blank space. None of his customers seemed to have noticed. Of course, he knew that didn't prove anything.

Pretty soon, a work crew with a tall ladder came along Sherman Way. They set up the ladder in front of a light pole. A worker wearing a plastic helmet like the one gathering dust in Charlie's closet went up the ladder. In one hand, she carried a red flag with a gold hammer and sickle in the top left corner: the flag of the USSR.

When she came down, she wasn't holding the flag any more. Sly as Sherlock Holmes, Charlie deduced that she'd fixed it to the horizontal holding the actual streetlight away from the pole. Two men closed the ladder and lugged it off to the next pole. The helmeted woman followed, puffing on a cigarette. So did another man, who was carrying a big box of Soviet flags.

That afternoon, they went along the other side of Sherman Way, moving in the opposite direction. The whole street would be decorated to celebrate Yuri Zhuravlev's state visit, though Charlie didn't think Zhuravlev would get within three hundred miles of Los Angeles.

When that occurred to him, he first thought it wasted time and effort, because the Soviet boss would never know one way or the other. But Zhuravlev might know. Chances were he had informers, spies, whatever you wanted to call them, telling him just how thoroughly this North American satellite was honoring him.

On the way home, Charlie saw hammer-and-sickle flags hanging from light poles up and down De Soto, too. He nodded to himself; De

Soto was also an important street. Walking back to his block of flats, he noticed Gresham wasn't flag-bedizened. He laughed. *His* street didn't count enough to ornament.

He turned on the radio after dinner, hoping to unwind with a game or some music. Instead, all the stations carried Tony Newman's speech of welcome and solidarity. Newman laid it on with a trowel; no one had ever denied that he had a strong sense of self-preservation.

"You commanded us to be free, Comrade General Secretary, and free we have become!" the leader of the WCPDR declared. The functionaries he was speaking to blistered their palms as they clapped. Charlie wondered whether tomorrow's *Worker* would call the applause stormy or thunderous. Some people bet on things like that.

It was a good line, anyhow. Or it was till you thought about it—not that you were supposed to think much about political speeches. How free were you if you were free because somebody ordered you to be free?

Charlie glanced up at the light fixture that held two bulbs and was a good place to hide a bug if someone needed a hidden bug here. His head bobbed up and down, once, twice. Yeah. About that free.

"Penny for 'em," Lucille said. "You look like you're thinking about something."

"How great this speech is, that's all." Charlie lied without hesitation.

"Well, sure." So did Lucille.

More applause greeted the end of Tony Newman's speech. It wasn't as loud as some of the bursts during the address, but lasted longer and struck Charlie's ear as more sincere. *The applause of relief*, he thought. *He's finally done.*

But the ordeal wasn't over. After Newman sat down, General Secretary Zhuravlev spoke. He used Russian, pausing every sentence or two to let the interpreter do her job. The interpreter had a faint accent, so she would have come to North America with Zhuravlev. Most people in the WCPDR had studied Russian—Charlie'd taken two years' worth—but few knew it well. He'd started giving it back as soon as he didn't need to remember it for the sake of a grade.

"Thank you for your warm and fraternal welcome, Comrade Newman," Zhuravlev said through the translator. "Friendship and cooperation between the USSR on the one hand and the North American socialist republics on the other is an essential component of our long-continuing world peace and of our progress on the road to true Communism."

Again, loud applause came out of the radio speaker. No one who got invited to a gathering that featured the WCPDR Premier and the General Secretary of the Communist Party of the USSR would fail to clap at a line like that. Even more to the point, no one who came to such a gathering would want to be seen not clapping.

After spouting more platitudes and getting more cheers, Yuri Zhuravlev said, "I am glad to see the West Coast People's Democratic Republic so prosperous, so serene, and so stable. The Party here governs so well, no disruptive elements are able to raise their voices."

The apparatchiks applauded once more. *Says who?* Charlie mouthed to Lucille. She stuck out her tongue at him.

"We in the USSR want no adventurism in ideology. No such trends appear to be growing here, as was unfortunately the case farther east in days still well within living memory," the General Secretary continued—a not-so-veiled dig at what had happened in the NESSR when Charlie was escaping from school.

He got another hand, this one more scattered and less confident than those before it. The important people in Sacramento had to be wondering where he was going. Well, Charlie wondered the same thing.

Zhuravlev spelled it out: "As zeal in the pursuit of perfect Marxism-Leninism-Stalinism must not exceed certain reasonable limits, though, so must the quest for stability stop short of trapping internal affairs in an inescapable straitjacket that paralyzes all evolution and development and leads only to stagnation."

The General Secretary paused. One or two people clapped, no more. Before the near-silence could get too revealing, Zhuravlev added, "Of course, the Premier and Politburo here, along with the required security organs, have long merited praise for the way they comport themselves. It lies squarely within the tradition whose acceptance unifies all the world's socialist states."

If the applause when Tony Newman shut up had been relieved, what came now put Charlie in mind of a bunch of people suddenly reprieved from a tenner in a labor camp or from a bullet in the back of the neck. He would have bet Premier Newman was clapping louder than anybody else.

"Our special friendship with the North American socialist republics has long endured. I confidently hope and expect it to continue far into the future. Thank you; I bid you good evening," Yuri Zhuravlev finished. He got one more relief-filled ovation. He wasn't going to send all the people who'd been listening to him to Manzanar ... or to a Soviet camp like frozen Vorkuta.

Thoughtfully, Lucille said, "I wonder if you know who is there."

"Yeah, that's an interesting question, isn't it?" Charlie would have bet Tony Newman hadn't wanted to invite Alex Eichenlode. If the General Secretary told him to, though, what choice did he have?

Neither the *Times* nor *The Worker* said anything about Eichenlode the next day. The day after that, Zhuravlev took off for Denver, the capital of the Rocky Mountain People's Republic. *The Daily Worker* went right on saying nothing about Eichenlode. The *Times* didn't name him, but one sentence buried in its story caught Charlie's eye: *Before departing, Comrade Zhuravlev held brief private meetings with three Politburo members.* Charlie had no way to be sure what that meant, but it left plenty of room to jump to conclusions.

The next day, he found he wasn't the only one playing that always-exciting game. Mary Ann Hannegan strode into the produce store, imperious as ever. "Good morning, Comrade," Charlie said. "I'm lucky enough to have some oranges from the People's Democracy of Chile. I may not be patriotic for saying so, but they're as good as the ones we raise here."

Her expression said she hadn't come in for oranges. She looked as if she wanted to spit on the worn linoleum floor—or in Charlie's face. "Don't laugh at me," she said. "Don't you ever laugh at me."

"I wasn't. Really," Charlie said, which held some truth, anyhow.

Going on with her own train of thought as if he hadn't spoken, Comrade Hannegan said, "You know as well as I do, the General Secretary doesn't get how things work here in the WCPDR."

"I'm sorry, but I don't know anything," Charlie said. "If you don't believe me, ask my wife. Or my kids. *They'll* tell you."

"Don't play games with me, either," she said. "Comrade Zhuravlev has no idea how much he's emboldened the Eichenlodist Menshevik clique."

Charlie knew what a Menshevik was: anybody not Communist enough to suit the person throwing the name around. Hearing it thrown at Alex Eichenlode annoyed him enough to make him ask, "How did he make it to the Politburo, then?"

He didn't like the way Mary Ann Hannegan looked at him. He'd already had the thought that some questions marked you as too smart for your own good, smart enough to be dangerous to people who mattered. After a short, tense pause, she answered, "Didn't I ask you before if you'd ever heard of giving someone enough rope to hang himself?"

"Yeah, you did," he said, and not another word. Comrade Hannegan seemed to be doing that with him right now.

When she saw he wasn't going to stick his neck out far enough for the noose to go around it, she continued, "That's what Tony Newman was doing. It would have worked, too, if the General Secretary understood how things are here in the WCPDR. But he doesn't, dammit." She swore as casually and unselfconsciously as a man.

"Oh?" Charlie doled out another word.

"That's right." She nodded. The shift in light made him notice how much gray her hair had mixed with the golden, but she was so fair, he still couldn't judge exactly where one started and the other stopped. "He thinks Premier Newman needs a rival to keep him nervous and to keep him from making more trouble with his neighbors, but it's more complicated than that."

"Is it?" He chanced two words this time.

"Of course it is." Mary Ann Hannegan spoke as if she had not a doubt in the world. "It starts with things like you and that stupid poster. It starts with things like that, but it never ends with them. Give the reactionaries an inch and they take a mile."

"Reactionaries?" That one word came out before Charlie could stop it. He'd never thought of himself so.

Comrade Hannegan had, and did. "What else are you?" she asked; her tone flayed him with scorn.

"Me? I'm just a guy who wants to live his life and not be bothered as long as I don't bother anybody else." Charlie wanted to scratch his head, but didn't. Wasn't that obvious?

As she had when he declined to get a new poster for the front window, she shook her head as if he'd failed a test. "You can't do that. The state has an interest in your being a socially productive as well as an economically productive citizen."

"I am. I've stayed married. Lucille and me, we've got two good kids. I even do my bit at block meetings."

"You make trouble for the Party there, too," she said.

"The Party wanted to make trouble for a bunch of my neighbors," Charlie answered, figuring he was in too deep for telling the truth to hurt him any more. "If it cared more about ordinary people, ordinary people might care more about it. Then they wouldn't need to make trouble. I kinda think Alex Eichenlode feels the same way."

"You aren't an ordinary person. You wouldn't be so difficult if you were. And the only thing Alex Eichenlode cares about is making himself stronger. Premier Newman would have nipped that in the bud, but the General Secretary wanted him to hold off. So of course he held off. He's not Eichenlode—he's loyal to the Soviet Union."

"Oh, yeah?" Charlie said. Mary Ann Hannegan nodded as she lit a fresh Marlboro. He believed her. He felt as if he were in the Stars' dugout at Gilmore Field, listening to the manager explain why he'd pulled a pitcher. He'd never expected an inside-baseball lesson on Communist Party politics, but he'd just got one.

"If we're lucky, we can cut out this right-deviationist cancer before it hurts us too much," she said. "As for you, if you're really as clever as you seem to be, maybe you'll be lucky enough not to get caught when we do. An outward show of proper behavior would still probably do it."

They didn't always kill everybody who gave them grief, or send those people to labor camps. They scared a lot of folks into silence and going along for fear of what would happen if they didn't. Comrade Hannegan scared Charlie. But Ervin already thought he was going along for the sake of getting his job back. He'd wanted to hate the old man for that. He didn't want to hate himself because it was true.

When his silence stretched, Mary Ann Hannegan said, "Never tell anyone you weren't warned, Comrade Simpkins. I hoped for better from you." Out she went. She didn't look back.

At lunch, Charlie crossed De Soto and walked into the Log Cabin. He gulped two slugs of almost-bourbon. They helped, but not nearly enough.

chapter

"Dad, I need four dollars and ninety-five cents," Nikita said after dinner one night a few weeks later.

"How come?" Charlie asked.

"For a new Falcons sweater," his son answered. "I threw the other one away after they wouldn't let me wear it any more."

"For your—? They said you could come back in? Really?" Charlie couldn't believe it. When it came to holding grudges, kids were even worse than the Party.

But Nikita nodded. "They sure did. Votsy Leeb told me they'd heard something that wasn't so when they blackballed me before. He didn't exactly say he was sorry, but that's what he meant."

Charlie didn't know who Votsy Leeb was. Some teenage apparatchik, he supposed. He pulled his wallet out of his pocket and gave Nikita a five-dollar bill. Nikita stuck it in his own pocket and went into the bedroom. He came back with a nickel, which he handed to Charlie. Charlie took it. He'd meant it when he told Mary Ann Hannegan he'd raised two good kids. Of course, Lucille might also have had a little something to do with that.

"I'm glad they're letting you in again. I'm sorry they threw you out the way they did. I know that was on account of me," he told Nikita.

"I was mad at you for a while. Now . . . . With everything that's going on now, I don't know what to think. Nobody seems to."

Maybe the kids paid more attention to what went on in Sacramento than a lot of grownups did. Charlie wouldn't have been surprised. What went through his mind was, *Why can't people think whatever they want to think?* Even he recognized that as something he shouldn't say to anybody except maybe Lucille, and then late at night and under the covers. If Comrade Hannegan heard it, for instance, he'd find out how fast the NBI could show up.

He did say, "We all have to do the best we can. What else is there?"

"They tell us that in school, too." Nikita looked at Charlie. "I don't think you mean it the same way they do."

"You're a smart kid. You must get it from your mom," Charlie answered. Nikita looked at him again, this time uncertainly. That suited Charlie well enough. If you couldn't convince 'em, confusing 'em was the next best thing.

Saturday night, they went to the movies at the Holiday over on Topanga Canyon Boulevard. The feature was a comedy called *Means of Production*. Charlie didn't care much about it, but he was willing to sit through it to see the newsreel beforehand. He knew Lucille and the kids would yawn through the newsreel waiting for the feature, so things worked out.

Everybody got popcorn and soda. A sign at the snack counter said WE EXPECT MORE CHOCOLATE SOON. By the way it looked, the sign had been there a while. Since the kids didn't seem upset, Charlie didn't worry about it. He and his clan went into the theater itself and found seats.

The lights dimmed. The usual little propaganda pieces played on the screen. Work like a Stakhanovite! Build the path to true Communism! Don't be a deviationist! They'd been playing the same ones since Charlie was Sally's age, maybe longer.

Then the newsreel came on. Sure enough, it featured Yuri Zhuravlev's visit to the WCPDR. There he was, shaking hands with Tony Newman. There he was, accepting salutes from an honor guard outside the Capitol. There he was, eating a hot dog at a Solons game and looking, well, bored—nobody played baseball in the Soviet Union.

And there he was, listening to Newman's speech and giving his own at that banquet. Several times, the camera showed the important people applauding. That fellow with the slicked-back hair and the pointed nose ... Charlie recognized him from newspaper photos. He leaned toward Lucille. "That's Alex Eichenlode," he whispered.

"Is that what he looks like? Okay," she whispered back—less of a response than he'd hoped to get.

She paid more attention when *Means of Production* started. The pretty girl (she *was* pretty, so Charlie didn't doze off in his seat) had to choose between the handsome young worker and the older, dumber, but richer capitalist boss. In the nick of time, the worker developed a process that made the boss's factory obsolete and left him on the street and hungry. And, of course, that also meant the pretty girl picked the handsome young guy.

It was as much propaganda as the WORKERS OF THE WORLD, UNITE! poster Charlie hadn't taped up. It had a sugar coating, though. Some of the jokes were stupid, but some, especially the ones aimed at the capitalist, were pretty funny. The movie didn't come right out and call him a Jew, but he looked like one. Charlie wondered whether he would have noticed that if he hadn't heard Ervin grousing at the Valley Relic.

On the way home, Charlie asked Lucille, "What did you think?"

"It was cute. It was kind of silly, though," she said. He nodded; that was a milder version of his own reaction. He thought more about propaganda now than he had before he threw out that poster.

The newsreel was propaganda, too, of course, and hardly pretended to be anything else. And it had shown Alex Eichenlode—more than once, in fact. Which meant ... what? Probably that Comrade Hannegan had it right. Whatever Tony Newman might have wanted to do with Eichenlode, General Secretary Zhuravlev must have told him not to. When the General Secretary of the Communist Party of the USSR told you not to do something, you didn't.

Charlie wondered whether Comrade Hannegan had seen that newsreel. A slow smile spread across his face. He hoped so.

Two weeks went by. Alex Eichenlode proposed another of his little reforms, this one to require showing an internal passport only when crossing a state line, not a county line. The motion passed the Politburo by a 12-9 vote. Three of the four new members Premier Newman had appointed voted for it.

Not a word about the reform made it into the *Times*. *The Daily Worker* gave it three paragraphs, noting, *Regulations implementing the change will be formulated in due course.* Charlie stared at the story, bug-eyed. Though short, it was vast; it contained multitudes. When he got off the bus at Sherman Way, he left *The Worker* folded so the little piece was uppermost. Anyone with eyes to see could read it and understand.

How many people had eyes to see? That was an interesting question, wasn't it?

Manuel Gomez greeted Charlie as he came west on Sherman Way toward the produce store: "Waddaya know for sure?"

"Not very damn much," Charlie answered. He wasn't going to say anything to give Gomez the chance to screw him over. *Especially not now*, he thought. He didn't know what would happen soon—he didn't *know* anything would happen soon—but he had hopes. He wasn't used to having hopes, not when it came to politics.

Gomez took the reply in stride. Charlie might have come out with the same thing even before he found out the junk-shop man was (probably was) ratting him out. "I hear you, buddy," Gomez said. "Life sucks, then you die."

"About the size of it," Charlie said. Cynicism made a useful shield in the WCPDR, the same as it did everywhere else. As long as you kept the shield up, you didn't have to show what lay behind it.

"Have a good one," Gomez said, and went into his place. Had he seen *The Daily Worker* story about the vote on internal passports? The only way to find out would be to ask him. Charlie didn't want to know that badly.

He opened up his shop. As he walked past the wastebasket where he'd thrown the WORKERS OF THE WORLD, UNITE! poster, he noticed it wasn't empty, the way it should have been. Somebody'd eaten an apple and tossed the core in the wastebasket.

Somebody who'd come in after he went home. Charlie went through the storage room and checked the back door. It seemed fine, same as the front door had. Whoever'd visited the store had had a key or a great set of picks.

A cop. A Nibbie. Someone who could get into any place he wanted to. Why would he want to? To plant bugs. That was the only answer that made any sense to Charlie. And it didn't make much sense. The only person to whom he'd ever said anything subversive here was Mary

Ann Hannegan. If he'd made her angry enough to talk to the police or the NBI, he knew he'd be under interrogation or in a camp by now.

The other question was, why would a Nibbie or a cop who was bugging the produce store leave a calling card for Charlie to find? Did the security organs hire idiots? In a way, that wouldn't have surprised Charlie at all. In another way .... He shook his head. No.

They wanted him to know they'd been here. They were sending him a message. He read it that way, anyhow. And the message was something like *You aren't such hot shit. We can do whatever we want to do to you, whenever we want to do it.*

That was what they'd thought last night. Last night, he would have thought the same thing. Now .... Now he wondered how many police captains and NBI colonels had read that short *Daily Worker* story with eyes to see.

He whistled as he started doing the early-morning paperwork. He knew he whistled badly. Lucille and the kids had told him so often enough to make him believe it. If one of the security organs *had* hidden a microphone here, he hoped he was annoying whoever'd got stuck with monitoring him.

A woman he hadn't seen before came in and made a beeline for his tomatoes and carrots. As she paid for them, she said, "My neighbor was right!"

"Right about what, Comrade?" Charlie asked, careful as anyone talking with a stranger had to be.

"I usually go to the store on Canoga—it's closer to where I live," his new customer answered. "But all they ever have is the same old kolkhoz trash. My neighbor said your vegetables were as good as anybody could get in a nomenklatura store. She wasn't kidding, either! You'll see me again, for sure. From now on, I'm a regular." She left happily, her produce in a stringbag.

Charlie started whistling again. Sure as hell, people were noticing he'd started getting better stuff than usual. His shoulders shook with silent laughter. The collective farms in California's Central Valley raised most of the vegetables people in the WCPDR ate. And the kolkhozniks there took no better care of them than they had to. Why should they? They were raising them for the state, not for themselves.

A lot of Four-Year Plans had tried to solve that. None had worked. The peasants cared more about their tiny private plots than they did about the broad state fields. Apparatchiks and intelligentsia ate the pampered produce from those plots. So did people who bought on the left.

After a moment, Charlie laughed out loud. Now he hoped some NBI man was listening to what went on here. The bastard's ears would be burning if he was.

He idly wondered what would happen if he got a piece of cardboard and wrote ALEX EICHENLODE WOULD MAKE A GREAT PREMIER! on it in big letters, then taped it up in the front window. The only answer that occurred to him was *Nothing good*. Like most people's, his courage had limits. No homemade sign went up.

When he headed home that evening, he bought the afternoon edition of *The Daily Worker*. To his disappointment, it held nothing new or interesting about goings-on in Sacramento. He did leave this copy with the little story face-up, too.

"How'd it go?" Lucille asked.

"You know what? It wasn't too bad," Charlie answered. He didn't say anything about the vote Eichenlode had won. When he talked about that, if he talked about that, he'd do it in a whisper late at night in the bedroom. Even if he didn't talk about it now, though, it still kept making him smile when he didn't expect to.

He waited for the other shoe to drop. If you were watching a movie or reading a story, you not only knew that shoe would drop, you had a pretty good idea when it would. A movie or a story was going to have a happy ending, and could only be so long. It had to finish.

Real life was sloppier. Things took as long as they took. Sometimes they never happened at all. Sometimes they didn't work out the way you hoped they would. Tony Newman might yet manage to send Alex Eichenlode on a trade mission to the Algerian Democratic People's Republic. If he did, Mary Ann Hannegan would stroll into the produce store and blow Marlboro smoke in Charlie's face.

If he was still there. If he didn't get more scarlet letters on his work card. If Newman won the power struggle, his people would go after everybody who'd favored Eichenlode, and especially after everybody whom Eichenlode had favored. That was how the game worked. You paid for picking the wrong side.

Charlie studied *The Daily Worker*. He studied the *Times*, which was a tiny bit less likely to spout the pure Newman line. He listened to the radio news more carefully than he ever had before, and tried to squeeze meaning not just out of every word but from every incidental cough and mumble the announcers made.

None of that got him very much. On the outside, things in Sacramento seemed to run smoothly. Routine measures passed the Politburo on unanimous votes. Alex Eichenlode didn't waste his time fighting against things like highway repairs and improvements in the Bay Area, a big irrigation canal for the Central Valley, or flood-control projects along the Columbia River.

"You'll drive yourself crazy if you keep worrying about every single thing," Lucille told him. That was not only general enough but sensible enough for her to say it without worrying about secret listeners.

"I'm already crazy," Charlie replied. So was that—and anyone monitoring a bug in their flat was bound to agree with it.

"Fine. You'll drive yourself crazier," Lucille said. He maintained a dignified silence, which meant she'd won that round.

A couple of days later, a *Times* story said, *Soviet Ambassador Yanukovich consulted with Premier Newman yesterday on discussions he'd had with Yuri Zhuravlev during the General Secretary's recent North American visit. Neither the embassy nor the Premier's office released a statement about the meeting.*

The only thing that made Charlie notice the page-seven squib was that he'd already gone through *The Daily Worker* and hadn't seen anything like it there. He flipped through *The Worker* again. No, it wasn't in there.

And that might mean something, or it might not. He didn't have any sure way to judge—and he did have to get off when the bus stopped at De Soto and Sherman Way. As he walked to the produce store, he worried at it like a man trying to work a chunk of gristle out from between his teeth with his tongue.

At least a man with something stuck like that knew if he got it out. Try as Charlie would, he could only guess. After he opened the produce store and closed the door behind him (and after he checked the wastebasket for fresh apple cores—none), he started to laugh.

He'd thought about Mary Ann Hannegan coming in here with her fancy cigarettes. What if he went up to her apartment-rental office, asked what he most wanted to know, and blew nasty Progress smoke all over? What would she do? Did he want to find out?

Again, he needed no more than a couple of seconds to decide he didn't. Opposing the state and its apparatus wasn't a lark or a game. You did it when you couldn't not do it. Otherwise, you just gave the security organs another excuse to kick you in the kidneys till you pissed blood.

Charlie laughed again, on a different note this time. "Like they need one!" he said. A snoop wouldn't make anything out of that.

Vissarion Gomez ambled in a few minutes later. He bought a pear and ate it right there. "That's really tasty, man," he said, tossing the remains into the wastebasket. Charlie suddenly wondered if *he'd* come in after hours. His dad had had the key, and was bound to know how to make a duplicate.

Maybe I don't need to worry about NBI monitors, Charlie thought. *Or maybe I still do. If Manuel talks to Comrade Hannegan, Vissarion could plant a bug.* He hated making such calculations. Everybody did. And everybody made them, because what else could you do?

Almost as quickly as he should have, he said, "Glad you like it."

"Oh, yeah." Vissarion nodded. "You been gettin' the good stuff lately, huh?"

"I guess. I just put out what they send me. What else can I do?" Charlie said.

Vissarion sent him a sidelong glance. "You know where the bodies are buried. I bet that's what it is. Shit, man, gotta be! I didn't expect to see you around here no more, but here you are, and you still ain't got no poster in your window."

"I just want 'em to leave me alone. I don't bother anybody. I don't want anybody bothering me, either." Charlie didn't think that was too much to say. It sure as hell wasn't anything the authorities didn't already know.

"Good luck with the world," Vissarion said. Charlie had no comeback ready; the junk-man's son was much too likely to be right about that.

But he's not bound to be right. I don't think he's bound to be right, anyhow, Charlie told himself. Hope was a hothouse plant. You had to keep it warm and moist and protect it from …. *From what?* he wondered. *From reality*, was what occurred to him first. Not too long before, he would have been sure about that. Now, hope might get to flower. It just might. And how beautiful would that bloom be?

Do the Dialectic was almost over. Charlie was willing to put up with the last couple of minutes of the stupid quiz show so he could hear the nine o'clock news. But he didn't have to listen to the emcee's closing comments. A bell chimed three times—once for each state in the WCPDR—and an announcer said, "We interrupt this program for a special bulletin!"

Charlie and Lucille looked at each other. "What went wrong now?" she said, beating him to the punch.

"Earthquake up north? Train wreck? Airplane crash?" He came out with the first three things that crossed his mind.

He had no time for more. The radio announcer went on, "This afternoon, in Sacramento, the Politburo approved a motion of no confidence in Premier Newman by a vote of sixteen to five. Accepting the result of the Politburo's ballot, Newman resigned, effective immediately. The Politburo named Alex Eichenlode of Spokane, Washington, to replace him. Here is Premier Eichenlode."

"Holy crap!" Charlie exclaimed.

Again, he got no time for more. "Comrades! Fellow citizens of the West Coast People's Democratic Republic! I'm Alex Eichenlode, the man the Politburo has chosen to guide the country forward. The honor humbles me. I promise I'll do the best I can for everybody in the WCPDR," Eichenlode said.

It was, Charlie realized, the first time he'd heard the new Premier talk. Eichenlode had an ordinary voice, on the border between tenor and baritone, and a twangy, slightly old-fashioned way of speaking. Well, it wasn't as if anything happened in a hurry in a place like Spokane.

Eichenlode went on, "The government expects the people to do what it needs them to do. That's to be socially responsible and patriotic. But the government needs to remember that the people expect it to do what they need it to do. That's to let them get ahead as much as it can and to get in their way as little as it can. I aim to see that we try and do that."

He's saying what I said to Vissarion Gomez, Charlie thought. *I meant it. Does he? Christ! What if he does?*

"I was lucky enough to meet General Secretary Zhuravlev when he visited Sacramento not long ago. The first thing I did when the Politburo chose me as Premier was to send him a cable. I promised that the WCPDR's support for our alliance with the Soviet Union would continue unchanged, and told him our support for Marxism-Leninism-Stalinism and the march toward true Communism was strong and unwavering," Eichenlode said. "I just now got an answer back. The General Secretary writes, 'I congratulate you on your promotion and look forward to the successful unfolding of the historical dialectic in your land.'"

Charlie understood what that meant. Eichenlode was telling Tony Newman's followers—people like Horton Wilder and Mary Ann Hannegan—that the USSR was on his side. You could think about intriguing against a new Premier whose policies worried you. If you intrigued against the Soviet Union, you'd regret it.

"We have a lot of work ahead of us. I'll try to hold up my end," Eichenlode said. "I told the General Secretary we're all for Marxism-Leninism-Stalinism. I meant every word of it, too. What I aim to do here, with your help, is to give the West Coast People's Democratic Republic Marxism-Leninism-Stalinism with a smiling face. We can do it. We will do it. Thanks. Good night."

"That was an address by Premier Alex Eichenlode. We now resume our regularly scheduled programming," the announcer said, as if Eichenlode had been running the WCPDR for the past twenty years.

"Marxism-Leninism-Stalinism with a smiling face? I like it," Lucille said.

"Same here. Who wouldn't?" Charlie said. He wondered how many different pictures of Karl Marx, Vladimir Lenin, and Joseph Stalin he'd seen. They were on coins. They were on posters. They were on billboards. They were on postage stamps. They were on embossed seals that made documents official. They were on wrapping paper, and on wallpaper, too.

Had he ever seen a picture of any of the three men smiling? He couldn't remember one.

"Who woulda thought you knew the Premier?" Lucille said.

"I don't *know* him. He gave me some help. It ain't the same thing," Charlie said.

"Close enough for me," she said.

He thought about it for a few seconds and decided not to argue. When you got right down to it, that was close enough for him, too.

Naturally, the *Times* and *The Worker* both sported banner headlines the next morning. NEWMAN OUT, EICHENLODE IN!, the *Times* shouted. *The Daily Worker* seemed more restrained. NEW WCPDR PREMIER, it said, without spending an exclamation point and without naming Alex Eichenlode. Charlie would have bet the people who ran the paper were as Newmanist as Mary Ann Hannegan. He wondered whether Eichenlode would make them pay for that.

They had connections, though. Unlike the one in the *Times*, their story said Tony Newman had accepted an appointment as the WCPDR's new ambassador to the People's Socialist Republic of Albania. Newman had sent people who opposed him into exile. Now he was going himself.

Manuel Gomez greeted Charlie with, "You watching TV last night?"

"Watching what?" Charlie asked wryly. Even back in his old, proper place in the queue, he was still years away from getting one. He wondered whether Gomez had sweated out his wait or just made his own from pieces of sets that didn't work. The junk-shop man knew how to fix almost anything. Charlie went on, "I did listen to the radio, though."

"Okay. Okay." Gomez waved that aside. "You think the changeover's gonna make a big difference?"

"Who knows?" Charlie shrugged. "Have to wait and see, that's all." Whatever else he thought, he was sure he'd better not show what was on his mind.

"Yeah, I guess. One big shot or another one, it's all the same to people like us, huh?" Gomez said.

"That's how it usually works, sure as hell." Charlie kept playing it safe.

Gomez needled him: "You figure now they'll stop giving you grief on account of you don't got no poster in your front window?"

"You know what? That never even crossed my mind," Charlie answered. It was even true, though he knew he would have thought of it pretty soon. He studied the poster in Gomez's window. "Yours has been up there a while now. Getting kinda ratty."

"Yeah. Maybe I'll get another one. Or maybe they'll start a fresh campaign and send everybody different ones. What'll you do then?"

"I got enough troubles without borrowing more," Charlie said. Manuel Gomez chuckled. Charlie knew what he'd do if the authorities did mail him a new poster. He also understood the difference between knowing and admitting.

He wasn't even surprised when the first person who walked into the produce store was Mary Ann Hannegan. Without preamble, she said, "I suppose you're happy now."

Bet your ass I am. Charlie didn't say it. He tried not to let it show on his face. He did say, "All I am, Comrade, is surprised."

"'Marxism-Leninism-Stalinism with a smiling face.'" Once more, she didn't quite spit on the linoleum, but she came close. "Building the road to true Communism is serious business, dammit. Not a game or whatever that, that clown thinks it is."

"What's wrong with being happy while you're building Communism?" Charlie asked.

"Alex Eichenlode is a deviationist, a right deviationist, Comrade Simpkins. You know it as well as I do, too. The difference is, you like it. I don't. And when you see what Eichenlode does to this country, you'll understand why I don't."

"If you want to spice up dinner tonight, Comrade, I have some jalapeños and even some habaneros, up from the Mexican SSR." Charlie waved to the bins where the peppers sat.

Could looks have killed, Mary Ann Hannegan's would have incinerated them. "So you do." She made it sound like an accusation. "I've heard you're getting all kinds of interesting things. How are you managing that, Comrade? The produce store a block from my house doesn't do nearly so well."

You mean you don't shop at the fancy nomenklatura place all the time? Charlie didn't say that, either. "I have nothing to do with what they send me, Comrade. You know how these things work. I just put it out and try to make it stay fresh and look nice."

She aimed that blowtorch gaze his way. "I've heard stories about your connections, Comrade. The more I see, the more I believe them. But let me tell you one thing. I don't care what kind of connections you have. In the long run, you'll wish you didn't, and they won't do you one goddamn bit of good."

"You don't get it, Comrade Hannegan. I'm just a guy trying to get along and keep my nose clean. That's all I ever wanted to do."

She looked out toward Sherman Way. So did Charlie. Nothing was going on, not so far as he could tell. Then he realized Mary Ann Hannegan wasn't looking out at the street. She was looking where the propaganda poster wasn't, the way she had the last time she dropped in.

"Right," she said tightly, and left without a backward glance.

"Jesus Christ!" Charlie wished he could change his shirt. It was all wet at the armpits and down his back. He could smell his own fear. He wondered whether Mary Ann Hannegan had a part-time gig with the NBI. She hadn't even threatened him, not really. She'd scared the living piss out of him even so. How many interrogators had that kind of talent?

Maybe if you're lucky, you'll find out, he thought.

"Lemme have a bourbon," Charlie told the bartender at the Valley Relic.

"Here ya go." The man in the boiled shirt and the black bow tie remembered him well enough to clink a couple of rocks into the glass along with the rotgut. He also remembered him well enough to say, "You ain't come in for a while."

"Nope." Charlie slid a quarter and a dime across the bar. Everybody said tipping wasn't socialist: it paid workers to act servile. Everybody did it anyway: workers who didn't get tipped acted worse than servile. The barman put the quarter in the cash box and the unofficial but necessary dime in his pocket.

Charlie sipped the bourbon, then turned around to eye the tavern so the bartender wouldn't see the look on his face. You'd always be disappointed if you expected good stuff in a joint like this. What he had, though, was miserable even for a class-four tavern.

Despite the lousy booze, the Valley Relic was crowded. Saturday afternoon: men who didn't feel like going home after the half day ended came here and drank instead. Cigarette smoke fogged and fugged the air. He lit a Progress of his own. It wasn't great tobacco, nowhere near, but it got some of the taste of the bourbon out of his mouth.

There sat Ervin, talking with a couple of people at a table near the guys shooting pool. If he hadn't been here, Charlie would have finished his drink and left. But he made his way over to the table, stopping a couple of times to say hello to people he knew. He hadn't been—he didn't think he'd been—a regular, exactly, but he'd shown up enough so the fellows who were knew who he was.

He got into Ervin's line of sight and waited to be noticed … or not noticed, which would also tell him what he needed to find out. Ervin finished the story he was telling and got a laugh. Then he did a pretty good job of acting surprised at seeing Charlie. "I know you, don't I? You're Steve Delgado, right?"

The younger guys sitting with him laughed again. So did Charlie. "That's me—I wish," he said. Of all the people he wasn't, the Stars' slugging first baseman stood high on the list.

Ervin went on, "Long as you're here, you may as well drag up a rock."

"Okay." Charlie grabbed a chair from another table. He didn't say anything more. He just waited.

After a little while, Ervin said, "Eichenlode, huh?" He picked up their conversation as if it had broken off minutes before, not weeks.

"Yeah, Eichenlode. How about that. Pretty crazy, isn't it?" Charlie said.

"I hope it works out. We're cruising for a bruising if it doesn't," the old man said.

"Funny—funny-peculiar, I mean, not funny-ha-ha—but somebody I know who's as Newmanist as you can get said almost the same thing," Charlie replied.

"You don't have to be a genius to figure that out. Hell, even I did it." Ervin's chuckle turned into a cough. He soothed his throat with some beer. "I've been on the Nibbies' shit list for a long time now on account of I keep saying we need to loosen up some."

"Marxism-Leninism-Stalinism with a smiling face," Charlie quoted.

Ervin's mouth twisted. "That's Eichenlode. That ain't me. The difference is, the NBI knows I mean it. Him? We'll find out." He coughed again. "'Course, the other difference is, I can talk from now till everything turns blue and it won't matter half a buck's worth. He can do things. Damfino if he will, but he can. Like I told ya, we'll see."

"I hope he does. We could sure use something new. Something better than *this*," said one of the younger men sitting with Ervin. Charlie didn't know him. The wave he used to accompany *this* took in not only the Valley Relic but all of Los Angeles or all of the West Coast People's Democratic Republic.

"Everybody knows we need a kick in the pants. Jesus, Zhuravlev knows it—that's gotta be why he wouldn't let Newman finish his purge," Ervin said. "Zhuravlev's an SOB, but he's not a dumb SOB. If

Eichenlode can make it work here, it may spread. If he can't—" Ervin shook his head.

"Huh!" Charlie said. He felt glad he'd come back to the tavern. The idea of the WCPDR as a guinea pig hadn't crossed his mind. He pointed at Ervin. "Was what went on in the Northeastern Soviet Socialist Republic the same kind of deal?"

"It coulda been, I guess. Or the bastards who were running things there might've decided they were gonna take care of all the people who didn't like them—take care of 'em but good, I mean. And the more people they took care of, the more there were who didn't like 'em. If the Russians hadn't come in when they did, that would've been an uprising like nobody's seen for a long time."

Reactionaries who rose against the progressive governments guiding the nations of the world toward true Communism got what was coming to them. Anybody who knew anything knew that. It was why uprisings were so rare.

"Eichenlode won't get into that kind of trouble," Charlie said.

"He better not. If he gets into it, we all get into it," Ervin replied.

"He wants to make things better. Like I told you before, I wouldn't have my old job if he didn't," Charlie said.

"Yeah, you told me." Ervin left it there: a less than ringing endorsement. After a moment, though, he resumed, "It could be so. I hope it's so. That's better'n any of the other things I can think of. You don't seem like that bad a guy."

"Thanks. Neither do you." Charlie tried to match him dry for dry.

"I know my limits. The Nibbies do, too. Eichenlode? Nobody knows for sure about him. That's the good news and the bad news, both."

"Way it looks to me, things have to get better. The way they are now…. How can they turn worse?" Charlie said.

Ervin looked at him over the tops of his glasses. "They talked the same way in Pittsburgh and Syracuse and Boston twenty-odd years ago. 'How can things get worse?'" The old man put a mocking whine into his voice. "By God, the NESSR found how they could get worse. You're old enough to remember that, right?"

"Oh, sure. It's been on my mind, too. I think it's been on everybody's mind here—everybody who is old enough to remember, I mean," Charlie said. "But c'mon. Say what you want about Eichenlode, you know he isn't gonna go off the deep end the way they did there."

"No, not the way they did there," Ervin—agreed? He ran his hands through the hair he had left above his ears, so it puffed out on either side of his head. "All kindsa different ways to go off the path the people who count like, though. Only way to stay on it is to keep them happy."

He didn't name the Russians. He might be a gadfly or a pissant, but he knew how easily small annoying bugs could get squashed. Even a gadfly had to be careful about how it buzzed. "I understand that," Charlie said. "But we can't be just like them. We *aren't* just like them."

"That's true. They're bigger than we are." Ervin held up a hand. Charlie saw the yellowish nicotine stains on his first and second fingers. He had those stains himself. Ervin went on, "Oh, sure, like I told you, we've got some different laws in the old books."

"You did tell me. And I used 'em. My block leader hated it, but he had to go along," Charlie said proudly.

"Uh-huh. He didn't want to find his tires slashed or dog shit in his mailbox," Ervin answered. "I've done it, too, lotsa times. You gotta watch it, though. Not everybody gives a rat's ass about that stuff." He fired up another smoke.

chapter

When Charlie walked back into his apartment, he wanted to tell Lucille all about how he'd squared things with Ervin. How big a load off his mind that was amazed him. But before he could say a word, his wife beat him to the punch: "Well, I've got some news for you."

"Oh, yeah? What?" Charlie asked, because he didn't see any way not to.

"Vince Gionfriddo's gone," Lucille said.

"Waddaya mean, gone? He's not block chairman any more? He quit?" Charlie had to admit, that was news. Gionfriddo'd always enjoyed being important—or at least seeming important, which was about as much as a block chairman could really do.

"He quit, yeah, but that's not all. He's *gone*," Lucille said. "His family moved out of their flat night before last. Nobody knows where they moved to, either. Svetlana Tompkins, who I heard it from, she told me they didn't even leave a forwarding address. They just took off, like … like I don't know what."

Like people scared of the NBI went through Charlie's head. So did *Like people scared of their neighbors*. He put that into safer words: "They didn't have a lot of friends, did they?"

"No, but to just disappear like that?" Lucille shook her head. "You can't get away with it. You have to fill out a million forms before you move. You have to get official permission."

"You do. I do. Gionfriddo and his wife belong to the Party. What do you want to bet somebody's taking care of 'em right now, wherever they are?" Charlie thought about the bugs that might be picking up his words, but he didn't care. Everybody—even cops, even Nibbies—knew Party members got away with things ordinary people didn't.

"You know what Svetlana told me?" Lucille said. Of course Charlie didn't, so she continued, "Somebody told her the Gionfriddos were worried about what was liable to happen to them on account of—you know. On account of that."

For a second, Charlie didn't follow. Lucille stayed wary, almost too wary. Then the light dawned. He started to laugh. "They're scared because ... because ... ?"

"That's right." She saw that he got it.

He laughed some more. The Gionfriddos might have feared flat tires on the car they, as CPWCPDR members, hadn't had to wait nearly so long to buy. Or they might have thought somebody would put a stinking surprise in their mailbox instead of a Party newsletter. Did they think Alex Eichenlode would encourage people to do things like that?

They might. They just might. *The wicked flee where no man pursueth.* Charlie didn't know what that was from, but the funny, old-fashioned verb ending had made him remember it. And it seemed to fit here.

Lucille said, "I wonder who's gonna be the new block chairman."

Charlie thought about the likely replacements for Vince Gionfriddo: Communist Party members who would enjoy being a big frog in a block-long puddle. More of the same, in other words. Some of what he'd drunk down at the Valley Relic must still have been buzzing through his veins, because he answered, "How about I try and grab it myself?"

"Are you nuts?" Lucille said, which seemed a perfectly reasonable question.

"Probably," Charlie answered. "But you know what? Everybody cries and moans about how miserable things are. If you don't try and do something about it, what's the point? If Gionfriddo hadn't tried to put that Party center next door, he wouldn't've had to bail out the way he did."

"He tried to put it there because the people above him told him to," his wife said, and that was also bound to be true. "What will you do when they give *you* an order like that? They will. You know they will. They'll probably do it fast, too, if you're the block chairman.

They'll make you look like a crock of crap to the people you say you're trying to help."

"That depends," Charlie said.

"On what? It's how things work." Lucille set her hands on her hips, wondering why he couldn't see the obvious.

"It depends on how clean the new broom sweeps, that's what," he said. "With a guy like Eichenlode in charge, we have a chance to clean out some of the people who've gummed up the works since before Marx was born."

He made Lucille smile, anyhow. But she replied, "How much can any one man do, though? How much will they let one man do?"

He wasn't sure whom she meant by *they*. The apparatchiks who'd been entrenched in Sacramento and all of the West Coast People's Democratic Republic for far longer than Tony Newman'd been Premier? Or the apparatchiks who'd been entrenched in Moscow and Leningrad even longer than that?

How big a difference did it make, one way or the other? Not much, not so far as Charlie could see. He said, "You can either try or you can give up. Somebody's gotta try, I think. I'm here. Block chairman isn't a big thing. They may not even pick me, for Chrissake. But I oughta give it a shot."

She stood on tiptoe to kiss him on the forehead. It wasn't a gesture of affection; it was what she did when Sally or Nikita didn't feel well and she was checking whether they had a fever. She sighed. "Well, the next meeting isn't for a couple of weeks," she said. "If we're lucky, you'll have come to your senses by then."

"Thanks a bunch, babe." Charlie made as if to swat her on the behind for sassing him. She made as if to skip out of the way. Neither of them went through with it. They both grinned.

He never did tell her about making up with Ervin. That seemed less important now. If he aimed at taking over Vince Gionfriddo's slot, wouldn't he be doing what the old man wanted? Or would Ervin ask if he was nuts, too? He didn't worry about it, not then. Lucille was right—he still had time to change his mind.

Alex Eichenlode proposed his measure to give zeks back their citizens' rights after five years of post-release good behavior to the Politburo once more. He wasn't a junior member now, not somebody the old-timers undoubtedly suspected of grandstanding. He was the Premier, their boss. He had the whip hand—they'd given it to him. The proposal passed unanimously.

Nobody on the radio said a word about it. Charlie caught the story in *The Worker* a couple of days after the vote. It quoted Eichenlode: "Either corrective labor and reeducation do their job or they don't. If they do, we need to recognize that and stop lifelong punitive sanctions against reformed offenders. If not, we should try some other way to cope with political and social crimes."

Charlie nodded, there on the southbound bus. That made sense to him. Had he been the one to tell the country what to do, he might even have gone further. But he still wasn't used to nodding at things he found in *The Worker*.

A few days later, Eichenlode made a speech. Because he was the Premier, it blanketed the airwaves. The people who controlled the news might have tried to minimize one reform. They couldn't very well block him from the microphone if he wanted to use it.

"Thank you for listening to me, my fellow citizens," he said. "I want you to hear that I plan to reintroduce my measure to eliminate the yearly radio tax—and also the tax on televisions, for those who have them. Radio is as much a public utility as water or electricity or housing or medical care. It shouldn't come with a fee attached. If the Politburo agrees, from now on it won't.

"Radio entertains the people. It also informs them. Making access to programs that are so important in their daily lives depend on whether they can afford the tax is a capitalist survival in a state that seeks true Communism. That's how it seems to me, anyhow. The Politburo will have the last word.

"But I did want you to know what I have in mind here. Not everything gets into the papers as soon as it should—which shows again why radio is so important, and why nobody should have to do without it. Thank you, and good night."

"Any time they get rid of a tax, I'm for it," Lucille said. "Only thing I wish is, they'd do it more often."

"Yeah." Charlie nodded. But he thought more was going on than that. The new Premier had gone on the radio tonight so nobody could get between him and the audience he wanted to reach … which meant he recognized that people had been trying to do that. And what would happen to those people now?

If anything did happen to them, neither the *Times* nor *The Daily Worker* reported it. The radio didn't say anything about it, either. Charlie carefully read both papers and listened to even more news than he'd been in the habit of doing. It was possible that some bloodletting went on behind the scenes. That kind of thing had happened often enough in the WCPDR, as it had in every other socialist state in the world.

Or was it possible that Eichenlode was letting the people who'd tried to silence him get away with it? Charlie wondered why he'd do something like that. He might not have all the backing he needed to go after them full bore. He might be giving them more rope so they could hang themselves with it, the way Mary Ann Hannegan had said ex-Premier Newman was doing with him.

After a few days, one other thing occurred to Charlie. Alex Eichenlode might have brought the newspaper commissars over to his side, or he might simply have forgiven them. Charlie was a grown man. Most of the time, he didn't believe in fairy tales. Eichenlode tempted him, though.

He said as much to Lucille, in one of those late-night conversations under the covers. "He'd better not be that nice," she answered.

"What do you mean?" Charlie asked.

"What do you think I mean? He pushed Tony Newman out of the top spot. Do you think he can get rid of all the people who want Newman, or somebody like Newman, calling the shots? Do you think he can make those people like him by being nice to them? If he thinks so, he's too dumb to last real long."

"Oh," Charlie said, and, after a moment, "Here all the time I thought I was the hard-boiled one."

"You are, mostly, but not about this. I haven't seen you go head over heels like this since … . I don't remember when."

Charlie remembered when. "The last time I went head over heels like this, it was on account of you. That worked out okay, huh?" He reached for her. They had to be quiet so they wouldn't wake the kids, but they had plenty of practice at that.

Lucille fell asleep right away. That was what everybody said men did, but Charlie lay awake on his back, staring up at the blackness between him and the ceiling. His wife made more sense than he wished she did. She had a way of doing that.

Mary Ann Hannegan didn't sit in her office hoping Premier Eichenlode could change the way things worked. Neither did Horton Wilder. Neither did Vince Gionfriddo and his family, wherever the hell they'd run to. Neither did tens of thousands of other small-time apparatchiks from Seattle to San Diego. They liked the way the WCPDR ran now just fine. So did a lot of people who gave the small-timers their marching orders.

So how could Eichenlode get those people to go along with his reforms? Lucille was bound to be right: making nice wouldn't do it. The new Premier could purge everybody he worried about, with show trials and executions and everything else that went with settling into power. That might scare the rest into behaving. But if he did it, how was he any different from the apparatchiks he was getting rid of? Why would people hope he could make life better?

Was Marxism-Leninism-Stalinism with a smiling face only … Marxism-Leninism-Stalinism? "It can't be!" Charlie exclaimed, loud enough to make Lucille stir beside him but not loud enough to wake her or the kids.

He had to be right. He thought he did, anyhow. The idea of Eichenlode as Premier wouldn't have scared people like Comrade Hannegan so much if they figured he was just slapping a fresh coat of paint over what was already there. If they reckoned something about his policies was fishy, didn't ordinary folks, folks doing their best to get along, have to believe he was trying to help them?

"Damn right," Charlie said, more quietly this time. Lucille didn't move. Almost whispering, he added, "I hope." Even hopeful, he tried to keep in mind what was real. Ervin might show gruff approval. He might.

Charlie dozed off trying to decide whether the old man would.

As usual, Charlie and Lucille were enthusiastic about the walk to the mandatory monthly block meeting. She praised it with faint damn: "More fun than going to the dentist, anyway."

"Is it?" Charlie said. "At least the dentist gives you painkiller before she starts drilling on you." Lucille laughed, for all the world as if he were kidding.

He stumbled over a crack in the sidewalk concrete and had to take two quick hopping steps to keep from falling on his face. "You okay?" Lucille asked.

"Yeah. That one's been there a long time. Got me just the same. Somebody needs to come down the street and fix it, along with all the others," Charlie said. "If Vince'd been doing his job, somebody would have three years ago."

His wife sighed. "If they put you in there, do you really think you can make things like that happen?"

"I can try. Somebody's gotta try," Charlie answered. "If we don't try, the clowns who let all this stuff slide and pocket the cabbage they get to take care of things, they go on doing it forever while everything runs down more."

"They'll do it anyhow," Lucille said.

"Not if they can't get away with it," Charlie said. Lucille went on toward the recreation center without another word. No, she wasn't convinced.

When they walked into the center, a man from down the street whom Charlie didn't really know came up and asked him, "You going to do it? No kidding?"

"You bet I am." Charlie'd been spreading the word, and asking people he told to do the same. He hadn't had any hints till now about whether that was doing any good. If a near-stranger buttonholed him, it might be.

The near-stranger said, "Good luck. I hope you get it."

"Thanks," Charlie said, but he was talking to the fellow's back.

With Lucille, he went into the big meeting room. They sat down in the third row: not right up front and obvious, but close enough to the tables up on the raised platform so Charlie could make himself heard when he needed to.

One of the comfortable chairs behind those tables was empty. Elsa Payne and a couple of other Party members sat in the rest. Charlie'd heard the recording secretary wanted to become block chairman. He didn't know if that was true, but he'd find out pretty soon. Stalin had used being a secretary as a springboard to power. Maybe Elsa dreamt of doing the same thing.

He looked around. The room seemed fuller than usual. The meetings were mandatory, but people still found excuses to stay away from a lot of them. Today, everybody knew Vince Gionfriddo had taken it on the lam, and everybody had a pretty good notion of why. The whole block wanted to see what happened next.

Bang! A man in a nice suit, a suit from a nomenklatura store, used the gavel. "Meeting will come to order," he said. "A lot of you know me. For those who don't, I'm Chris Donlin. I work out of the State Prosecutors' Office over in Van Nuys. I'll be running things tonight, since Comrade Gionfriddo, ah, can't be here."

"Bailed out, you mean," a guy behind Charlie said, loud enough for the whole room to hear. Giggles and coughs ran through the crowd. Charlie'd thought the same thing. He'd kept quiet, though. He was glad someone else hadn't.

"No one quite knows what's going on there," Comrade Donlin answered smoothly, as a state prosecutor would. When he smiled, though, his eyes didn't say *good joke.* They said *labor camp.* He went on, "We'll start off the usual way, with Comrade Payne reading the minutes of last month's meeting and the agenda for tonight's."

Her voice as flat as a tire that had hit one of the big potholes on De Soto, Elsa Payne went through the minutes … or maybe they were pages from a Four Year Plan from seventy-five years ago. Charlie tried not to yawn and fidget. He knew he wasn't the only one. One of the best ways to calm people down was to bore them to tears.

Nobody voted against approving the minutes as written. Charlie thought they were accurate enough. Even if they weren't, approving them wouldn't matter a dime's worth in the grand scheme of things.

"Thank you, Comrade Recording Secretary," Donlin said. "Now we proceed to this evening's business."

Most of it was as unexciting as the minutes had been. The block passed a resolution congratulating Alex Eichenlode on becoming Premier and wishing him success. Charlie didn't know what the people up there thought of Eichenlode. If it was what he suspected, they weren't dumb enough to admit it out loud.

A motion to consult with civic authorities on park improvements also passed. They'd passed a motion like that a couple of years before. Charlie wondered how many besides him remembered. The park still needed improving. He voted for the motion anyhow. Something *might* happen this time.

Then Elsa Payne said, "As the block chairmanship has unexpectedly fallen vacant, nominations are now in order for that position."

Still slick—and still with those labor-camp eyes—Prosecutor Donlin said, "I'm going to take the moderator's privilege and place your name in consideration, Comrade Payne." He chuckled to show what a man of the people he was at heart. He asked, "Do I hear a second?"

"Second!" three voices—a man and two women—chorused.

Charlie stood up. "I'm Charlie Simpkins. A lot of people know who I am and what I've done. I nominate, uh, me for block chairman."

The gavel banged. Chris Donlin shook his head. "I'm sorry, Comrade, but self-nomination is out of order."

Lucille got up. "*I* nominate Charlie Simpkins. Do I hear a second?" A lot more than three people answered her.

"Spousal nomination is also invalid," Donlin said, still doing his damnedest to head things off.

It didn't work. Too many people shouted for Charlie's name to be entered in nomination for Donlin to ignore them or pretend not to hear. He might have had a riot on his hands if he'd tried.

He saw as much. No longer smiling or pretending to be an ordinary guy, he ground out, "Very well. Let Comrade Simpkins's name also be considered. Perhaps the candidates will briefly speak to their qualifications and let the meeting know how they will serve the working people on the block. Comrade Payne, if you'd like to go first ... ?"

"Thank you, Comrade Donlin," the recording secretary said. "If the people of the block choose me as their new chairman, I promise continuity with the progress we've made in the past. I am familiar with the things that need to be done to ensure that citizens' needs are met on an ongoing basis and in a timely fashion. I have the honor to be a member of the Communist Party of the West Coast People's Democratic Republic, and will use my position of membership to assist my fellow block residents in any way practicable. You know me. You can count on me. I trust I will have your support."

"Very well put, Comrade." Chris Donlin fixed that nasty gaze on Charlie. "Your turn, Comrade Simpkins."

"Thanks." Charlie didn't go up onto the stage. He turned around and faced his neighbors. "Comrade Payne says she'll do things the way they've always been done. I believe her. That's what I'm afraid of. If we'd had business as usual a little while ago, the Party would have a new center here on the block and a whole bunch of you would need new places to live without any help getting 'em. I don't know about you folks, but I'm sick and tired of that nonsense. I think the new Premier is, too. And if you are, you'll back me. I mean, this *is* the West Coast People's Democratic Republic, and we *are* the people." He sat down.

A woman in the crowd yelled, "That's right! We *are* the people!" Others took up the cry. Charlie realized that, if he'd been smart, he would have slipped somebody a couple of bucks to stand up and say that. He hadn't been, but it had worked out anyway.

Prosecutor Donlin's face said he figured Charlie'd arranged the call. He gaveled for quiet. He gaveled and gaveled, and finally said, "Comrades, if you please! We can't go on to the vote till we have order!" Charlie stood up and turned around with his arms raised and his hands open. Little by little, the tumult ebbed.

Charlie won by better than two to one. Had it been closer, he guessed the apparatchiks on the stage would have tried to cheat in the count. They couldn't, though, not when it would have been so obvious.

"Congratulations, Comrade Block Chairman," Donlin said through clenched teeth. "We will do everything we can to ease the transition and acquaint you with the way things are required to be done."

"Thanks very much." Charlie knew Donlin was lying as hard as he ever did in court. He and Elsa Payne would do everything they could to screw him over—he'd just screwed them. He shrugged mentally, if not physically. He hadn't expected anything different.

After the meeting adjourned, people came up and pumped his hand and thumped him on the back. A man asked, "You really think Eichenlode will make a difference?"

"Early days yet, Bert. I hope so." Charlie glanced toward the stage. Nobody was left up there. They'd sneaked out while he wasn't paying attention. Yes, he had a pretty good notion what they thought of Alex Eichenlode.

"You did it!" Lucille said while they were walking home. Two steps later, she added, "You damn fool."

"If that's how you feel, you could've stopped me just by keeping quiet. Now you're on one of their lists, too," he said.

"I'm married to you, so I already must be," she answered, which had to be true. She continued, "Maybe you *can* do some good. It'd be great if somebody could, that's for sure."

"Don't worry about me. Worry about Eichenlode. We'll swim with him, or else we'll sink," Charlie said.

Charlie saved money at a WCPDR Bank branch on De Soto: a big, sturdy building that had been there longer than anybody could remember. It stayed open Saturday afternoons, to give the many people who worked five and a half days a week the chance to use it.

The Saturday after he got elected block chairman, he hopped off the northbound bus at Saticoy and walked the half-block to the bank. Three police cars were in the parking lot, their lights flashing. A cop held up a hand when Charlie walked past them toward the entrance. "You can't go in," he growled.

"How come?" Charlie asked.

"On account of three stupid goddamn yeggs knocked it over an hour ago. They got away with a whole buncha cabbage. Bank's closed now. Detectives are in there getting evidence and stuff. So beat it, before I ask to see your ID."

Beat it Charlie did. His shoulders shook with laughter as he went back to the stop to wait for the next bus. He could see robbing a jewelry store or a watch-repair shop or something like that. But a bank? Food and rent were cheap. Other things cost a lot more, but you mostly had to queue up to get them. You couldn't do that much with a whole buncha cabbage. No wonder the cop called the yeggs stupid.

When Charlie told Lucille about it, she thought it was funny, too. "What'll they do, corner the market on radishes or Brussels sprouts?" she said. "Good luck with that!"

"You're reading my mind, babe," he answered. "Maybe they think they can make a killing on the black market, but even so... ." He shook his head. He didn't believe it for a minute.

"Doesn't seem likely, does it?" she said. "But every time you think you know how stupid people can get, they go and surprise you."

"You got that right." Charlie wasn't thinking so much of the yeggs as he was of the bureaucrats who kept on doing the same old thing even though they didn't have the same old leader any more. He guessed Alex Eichenlode had to be thinking about them, too. How were you ever going to change anything if the weight of inertia kept the WCPDR moving in the same direction it always had?

Two nights later, Eichenlode gave the beginnings of an answer to that in a speech broadcast up and down the country. When Tony Newman spoke, Charlie made a point of doing something else. Newman would give either no news at all or bad news. Who wanted to hear that? With a new Premier in Sacramento, though, Charlie'd changed his ways. He wondered how many other people also had.

Eichenlode's voice came from the radio speaker: "Good evening, my fellow citizens. Tonight, I'm going to talk about something that's been an open secret in the West Coast People's Democratic Republic for much too long. The news you see on television or hear on the radio or read in the newspapers isn't always the whole truth. Much too often, it's what the state wants you to see or hear or read instead."

"Did he really say that?" Lucille exclaimed.

"Yeah," Charlie answered, as startled as she was. Ordinary people knew the government lied all the time, of course. They joked about it when they thought they could get away with that. He hadn't been so sure the apparatchiks understood it, though.

Lucille started to say something else. Charlie waved for her to wait. He wanted to see where the Premier was going.

"Propaganda is necessary, to a degree. It builds social solidarity," Eichenlode said. "But lying straight-faced to the people is unacceptable. You don't have to be as clever as a fox to know fair and balanced reporting of the facts is more valuable in the long run than any number of clever falsehoods.

"Too often, we've lied to keep the government from looking bad and to protect it from embarrassment. If people don't know something is wrong, nobody will try to fix it. The truth needs to be public, not a closely held, closely guarded secret.

"Because we need the truth to be out there, I am ordering a suspension of all news censorship, effective immediately. If press organs find stories worth reporting, they are free to do so, even if those stories point a finger of blame at local, state, or national authorities.

"Laws against slander and libel will continue to apply. Private parties may not lie in public, any more than the state may. But officials won't get away with using those laws to muzzle people who report events. I hope this policy will give us a new openness as we begin to restructure our institutions.

"One more thing—be patient. Change won't happen overnight. Our problems have grown over many years. We won't solve them before the sun comes up tomorrow. But we won't solve them at all if we don't start working on them now. Thank you, and good night."

"That was Comrade Alex Eichenlode, Premier of the West Coast People's Democratic Republic," the announcer said. Then she started to explain what Eichenlode had just talked about.

Charlie turned off the radio. He knew what the Premier had talked about; he'd heard him. Wasn't explaining too much a kind of propaganda, too?

"Do you think he means it?" Lucille asked. A moment later, she found the other question that counted: "Do you think he can do it?"

"With anybody else, I'd say it was hot air," Charlie answered. "With Eichenlode? Yeah, I think he does. I hope he can do it, too." He remembered once more all the functionaries who'd been sitting at their desks doing the same kinds of things over and over for years. How would they like it if they suddenly got told to stop doing those things? Not very much, Charlie feared.

"You were right about him," his wife said. "He *is* trying to shake things up. I didn't think so before, but I do now."

"Good. If it all goes wrong, we'll get in trouble together," Charlie said.

"We would anyway," she said. He nodded. She understood how things worked, all right.

The next morning, the *Times* ran an editorial headlined *We'll Work to Do Better*. It admitted it had been censored in the past, which was a lot like admitting Los Angeles air wasn't fit to breathe. Walking barefoot through the obvious, somebody'd called admissions like that. *The Daily Worker* reported Eichenlode's speech without commenting on it, which was ... interesting.

Manuel Gomez greeted Charlie with, "Okay, man, when do they put you on the County Board of Commissars?"

"You're funny. Funny like a truss," Charlie answered.

"And your mama, too," Gomez said without anger, aiming his middle finger in Charlie's general direction.

Charlie returned the gesture. They both grinned. Charlie had to remind himself that Gomez probably told tales to Mary Ann Hannegan. But even if he did, he wasn't the worst guy in the world. You just had to watch yourself around him.

The junk-shop man said, "You liked that guy before anybody else ever heard of him. How'd you do that? You don't look so smart."

"You know why? 'Cause I'm not," Charlie said. Gomez laughed. Inside, Charlie didn't think it was so funny. Manuel Gomez had slipped up. Charlie knew he hadn't talked about Alex Eichenlode with him. Gomez must have heard that from Comrade Hannegan or someone else he reported to. Which meant she hadn't been lying when she said he'd talked with her. Too bad, but knowing was better than not knowing.

"You think he can change stuff for true?" Gomez asked.

"I hope like hell he can." Charlie wasn't telling him anything the people he passed things on to didn't already know. If Eichenlode crashed in flames, they'd make Charlie pay. But they would have anyhow. Charlie understood that only too well. Telling the truth was a relief, the same way taking a big dump would be.

He wondered how long the papers, the radio, and the TV would need to discover that truth-telling relief and satisfaction. He wondered whether they would at all. They'd been plugged up for years and years and years. In spite of the editorial in the *Times*, could they ever look at the world as it seemed to them, not as someone told them to?

Gomez looked back at his POWER SPRINGS FROM THE BARREL OF A GUN poster. It had stayed in his window a long time now. "Sometimes I wish I woulda had the *cojones* not to put that thing up," he said with a rueful shake of his head.

If Charlie reported that, he'd catch it. But he had to know Charlie wasn't about to report anybody. Charlie, in fact, was feeling more subversive than ever. "Why don't you take it down, then?" he said. "If they ask you how come you did it, you can blame me."

"It's tempting, y'know? But honest to Pete, I still ain't got the balls."

That struck Charlie as honest. *As honest as an informer is likely to be*, he thought. He gave a mental shrug. Most people didn't have the nerve to chuck a poster the Party sent them. He still had no idea how he'd done it himself. He had, though, and now he'd got help from the guy who'd become Premier of the WCPDR.

Life sure turned crazy sometimes.

As if embarrassed to have admitted so much, Gomez turned toward his shop. "I'd better make like I'm working, man."

"Okay. I'm expecting a fresh shipment of cabbages this morning. I'll open up so the swarms of housewives who want 'em won't break down the door," Charlie said.

"Save a couple for me under the counter, like," Gomez said.

"You got it," Charlie said. "Those heads'll have more brains in 'em than mine does, for sure."

"Go on, beat it." Gomez waved him toward the produce store, then went inside his own place.

When the cabbages showed up, they disappointed Charlie. All the fancy produce they'd sent him lately had spoiled him and left him expecting he wouldn't get anything less. These were ordinary at best; some of them should have gone into a bin a week before they did.

He wasn't the only one who noticed, either. "I was hoping you'd have something nicer," an old lady sniffed.

"So was I," Charlie answered. "This is what the truck brought, though."

"You've had such good vegetables … and now these." She sighed. "I was going to make sweet-and-sour cabbage rolls if I could get some ground meat, but with these raggedy leaves it's more trouble than it's worth."

"I'm sorry. I can't do anything about it. I wish I could."

"Maybe Comrade Eichenlode will make it so regular people get good produce all the time, not once in a while when we're lucky," she said.

"You never know." Charlie left it there. She'd been coming in for a long time, but it wasn't as if he knew her even the way he knew Manuel Gomez. Would she take whatever he said to Mary Ann Hannegan or to some Newmanist NBI officer counting the days till he got a chance for revenge on the deviationists?

You never know, he thought again. Life in the WCPDR worked like that. Till Alex Eichenlode came along, he'd taken it for granted. Now? Now he wondered.

chapter

A week later, the *Times* ran a story about somebody who really was on the County Board of Commissars, and about how she'd landed her nephew a staff job he wasn't remotely qualified for. The piece had an odd feel to it. Reading between the lines, Charlie got the idea the reporter was thinking *Am I going to get away with this?* as she wrote.

County Commissar Rivers denied everything. Normally, that would have been plenty to quash the story (normally, of course, the *Times* never would have dared print it in the first place).

Things weren't normal any more. The *Times* had got its hands on a note she'd written to the guy who'd hired her nephew. The gist was *I know he's not too smart. Give him the slot anyhow, and I'll pay you back when I get the chance.* Important people made deals like that all the time. They never dreamt they'd get called on them.

The Board expelled the commissar. The apparatchik who'd taken on her nephew suddenly found himself managing a trout fishery outside Crowley, Oregon. Even the kid lost his soft job.

When Charlie recounted the story for Lucille, she said, "Wow! You always figure they'll believe the commissar." Her mouth twisted. "What else are you gonna figure? That's how things work."

"Uh-huh," Charlie said. "What I want to see now is, what happens to the reporter? What'll they do to her for landing a big shot in trouble?"

"If she just disappears, how will you ever know?" his wife asked.

"Oh, I'll know. I'll know *because* she disappears. If I don't see any more stories with her name on them, it'll mean she's getting what troublemakers usually get." *What they started giving me*, he thought. He wasn't even bitter about it, or not very. Lucille had it right: that *was* how things worked. When you went against the people who ran things, of course they hit back.

She looked at him with more admiration than he saw on her face most of the time. "You *do* know how this stuff happens."

Charlie snorted in surprise and pleasure; no, he wasn't used to praise from Lucille. "Yeah, well, it's not like I haven't had to take things apart and put 'em back together lately. Kinda like Gomez next door does with his clocks and can openers and gadgets like that, only inside my head."

"You've got a lot more serious since … everything started." Lucille shook her head. "Not serious, exactly. But you're thinking more before you do things. Like you said, you're taking them apart and putting them back together."

He almost laughed at that. All he'd thought when he threw out the WORKERS OF THE WORLD, UNITE! poster was, *This stupid old line—again?* Since then, though … . "Yeah, I guess so. I have to, don't I, the way things are?"

"Maybe you're finally growing up," Lucille said.

Charlie did laugh then. "If you're gonna come up with an explanation, come up with one that makes sense, why don't you?" His wife snorted.

For a week or so after that, he didn't notice any new stories by Olga Rizzuto—and, with a byline like that, he wasn't likely to miss them. He started to fear the worst. Was she covering chicken farms in Hawthorne now? Did she have the scarlet letters on her work card? Or had the cops or the NBI grabbed her?

But then she was back again, with a piece detailing how the police had beaten a bunch of people breaking up a party at a park. The park was south and a little west of downtown L.A.: the black part of town. The story didn't say much about that, not in so many words. Just because the story didn't say it, though, didn't mean it wasn't there.

Nobody in the WCPDR was supposed to treat people differently because of what color they were. It happened anyway. It wasn't as horrible or as open as it was in the Southeastern Confederated People's Republic, but it was there. Everybody knew that. Dornel sure did. Things a cop would laugh off from a white man got a black man a bloody head … if he wasn't "shot while resisting arrest."

Someone in the police department must not have realized Tony Newman wasn't Premier any more. Their statement read, "We will maintain social order and cohesion by whatever means prove necessary. Resistance to state authority, especially by disruptive elements, will not be tolerated even for a moment."

One of the men at the park had been a fellow named Du Bois Burghardt. Olga Rizzuto's story described him as an activist. To Charlie, he sounded like Ervin's black cousin. He got statements detailing the way the cops had waded into the crowd of partiers from just about everybody who'd stayed out of jail. He took them to the City Administrative Board and made a fuss.

The *Times* reported the fuss. So did *The Daily Worker*. It had come late to the dance, but now it was starting to kick up its heels, too. And even a radio news show let people who'd got kicked or billy-clubbed tell their stories on the air.

Charlie figured it would all blow over. Nobody ever did anything to cops. Only this time somebody did. Two of them got canned; two more were suspended without pay. The *Times* quoted Du Bois Burghardt as saying, "I am amazed. I am delighted, but mostly I'm amazed. The West Coast People's Democratic Republic has always talked about justice for everyone. Now we're finally starting to see it."

Not long before, that by itself would have been plenty to land him in a cell, or else in a labor camp. Nothing happened to him, though. Charlie didn't think so, anyhow. He was starting to believe the cops and Nibbies couldn't up and grab somebody like Burghardt and keep it quiet.

That Saturday, he went down to the Valley Relic. Sure enough, Ervin was there. "You know the fella down in South Central?" Charlie asked him.

"Du Bois? Oh, hell, yes," Ervin said. "For years—he ain't much younger'n I am. First time we ran into each other, believe it or not, we were both looking for the same book at the big library downtown. He's got stones, Du Bois does."

"I guess so!" Charlie said, and then, "The library, huh?"

Ervin laughed his raspy laugh. "Bet your ass. Where ya think all the damn nuisances hang out? The stuff is there. The bastards just make it hard as hell to find."

"I've seen that myself," Charlie said. "Why don't they get rid of it, make like it never happened?"

"They think it's so old, it's embalmed, and nobody but them knows anything about it." Ervin laughed some more. "You should see the looks on their faces when some regular guy gives it back to 'em."

"I found that out, too. I kept 'em from knocking down that block of flats for the Party center, remember?"

"That's right, you did." Ervin lit a Progress. He offered the pack to Charlie, who also took one. After a long drag, the old man went on, "There's another reason they don't trash all those ancient laws, too. They're bastards—you better believe they are—but some of 'em are smart bastards. They remember what happened with the Northeastern Soviet Socialist Republic. The older laws, the freer laws, give them a chance to stop that from happening again without going in with soldiers."

"Okay. That's what they do if somebody goes around the bend that way," Charlie said, and Ervin nodded. But Charlie hadn't finished: "What happens if somebody tries getting too free, though?"

Ervin coughed. He coughed several times, in fact, and had trouble stopping. He stared reproachfully at the cigarette between his fingers. After a moment, he answered, "I'll tell ya one thing—it ain't a problem they've had to worry about a whole hell of a lot."

"I know, but I bet they are now."

"It's like I said to you before. Zhuravlev wants to see what happens when Eichenlode pulls the cork halfway out of the bottle."

"I think you're right. But does Zhuravlev understand how many bubbles are in the beer?"

"Good question." Ervin nodded in something closer to real approval than Charlie'd seen from him for a long time. "We'll all find out, won't we? And the other good question is, does Eichenlode understand that?"

Charlie grunted. It *was* a good question, and one he hadn't thought of himself. He'd pretty much assumed the new Premier knew exactly what he was doing. But what if Alex Eichenlode was making it up as he went along, too? And what if he had feet of clay like everybody else?

We'll all find out, won't we? Ervin's words echoed inside Charlie's head.

"I'll do what I can for you, Comrade Vanderpool. I don't know how much that'll be, but I'll try." Charlie glanced down at his watch. It was five past eleven. Dmitri Vanderpool showed no signs of wanting to leave. In fact, he started telling his tale of bureaucratic woe for the fourth time. Charlie decided to be more blunt. "Listen, Comrade, it's getting late. I've got to go to work in the morning. So do you."

"Oh." Vanderpool looked startled. "Maybe I should go, then?" He didn't sound as if he meant it.

Whether he meant it or not, Charlie steered him out of the flat, slammed the door in his face, and noisily locked all the locks and deadbolts. Then he turned to Lucille and clapped a hand to his forehead like a bankrupted capitalist in a movie. "Tell me again why anybody ever wants to be a block chairman."

"I don't know why anyone else wants to. You wanted to because you're an idiot," his wife answered.

"Boy, you got that right!" Charlie didn't try to argue with her. How could he? He agreed with her.

"Can you do anything for him?" Lucille asked.

"If I'm real lucky. I mean, *real* lucky. If I find a licensing clerk or somebody else with the right connections who's in a good mood, or maybe one who wants a couple of crates of vine-ripened tomatoes. If I feel like wasting a day and a half on it. If I don't have to try and fix four other people's problems."

"You should've let Elsa Payne have it," Lucille said.

"I'd like to let Elsa have it, right in the snoot." Charlie balled up his fist. "And that Donlin item, too. They still haven't let me get a good look at the records."

"What do you think they're hiding?"

"How much Gionfriddo feathered his nest while he ran the block. And how much stuck to their fingers, I bet. They wouldn't be making so many excuses if their hands were clean."

"Can you do anything about it?"

"If I want to talk to the cops, maybe. Or if I want to talk to the Party area leader. But I don't wanna talk to him unless I have to, and

I bet he doesn't wanna talk to me, either. He probably thinks I'm not supposed to poke my nose into private Party business, no matter how crooked it is."

Slowly, Lucille said, "I've heard Party members aren't supposed to talk much about what they're doing with people who don't belong."

"Yeah, I've heard the same thing. Like we're not pure enough or something." Charlie yawned. "I'll worry about all of it later. Vanderpool's stolen enough sleep from me."

"Well, you still have some sense left, anyway," his wife said.

"Not much," Charlie answered. "Maybe some."

Whether he wanted it to or not, his quest to do something for Dmitri Vanderpool—actually, his quest to get Vanderpool to shut up and quit bothering him—did lead him to the area leader's door three evenings later. An Asian man with graying hair opened the door when he knocked. "Yes? What can I do for you?" the fellow asked, in tones that suggested he figured Charlie wanted him to do something.

"You're Comrade Yang, aren't you?"

"That's me. Nelson Yang, at your service. I don't think we've met … ?"

"I'm Charlie Simpkins, the new block chairman up on Gresham. One of the people there is having some fun and games with a licensing board. I was hoping you could help me help him."

"Charlie Simpkins? Pleased to meet you, Comrade!" Yang stuck out his hand. Cautiously, Charlie shook it. But the area leader seemed to mean what he said. Standing aside, he went in, "Come in, come in! I've heard a lot about you."

"Oh, yeah?" Charlie went in. The flat was larger, nicer, and newer than his. Nelson Yang had a television. It was on: his kids were watching. He chased them out of the front room. As he did, Charlie said, "Whatever Comrade Payne and Comrade Donlin told you, I hope you'll listen to my side of the story, too."

Yang laughed. "You bet I will. But I knew about you before they said boo. I'm on the West Valley Central Committee. Comrade Hannegan's been cussing about what a stubborn right deviationist you are for months."

"Has she?" Charlie didn't like the sound of that, even if Comrade Yang seemed amused, not annoyed.

"She sure has, but what would you expect from a Newmanist? Why don't you sit down? Can I get you a beer or a drink?"

"Bourbon on the rocks, thanks." When Charlie sat on the sofa, it didn't groan under his weight like the one in his own apartment.

"Coming up." Nelson Yang went into the kitchen. He continued, "If everybody in the country wanted to keep it in the deep freeze, Comrade, Alex Eichenlode never would have made it out of Spokane. Jim Beam suit you?"

"Uh, sure," Charlie said dizzily. It wasn't just that the area chairman turned out to favor Eichenlode. Jim Beam was one of those fancy brands you only found at nomenklatura stores. When you drank the hooch you could buy yourself, at a package store or in a class-four tavern …

When you drank that kind of nasty hooch, your first taste of Jim Beam showed you you'd no idea what bourbon could be. Charlie wanted to jump up and yell *Hurray!*, as if a Star had just hit a grand slam. He contented himself with remarking, "That's mighty good."

"Glad you like it," Yang said with a smile. "Now, what's going on with this person on your block?" As best he could, Charlie explained Comrade Vanderpool's troubles. The area leader nodded. "This kind of strangulating bureaucracy is a problem all the socialist states have these days. Alex Eichenlode is going to try to loosen it up. You know that, don't you?"

"Oh, yeah. That's how he made his name up in the north." Remembering *The Daily Worker* article he'd read served Charlie well.

Comrade Yang beamed. Charlie might have, but he was drinking more of that lovely bourbon. "There you go!" Yang said. "So sure, I'll do what I can for your fellow—Vanderpool, you said his name was? How do you spell that?" When Charlie told him, Yang wrote the name on a sheet of scratch paper.

Finding out that the area leader was an Eichenlode man made Charlie bolder. "There's one other thing you may be able to help me with," he said, and explained how Elsa Payne and Chris Donlin didn't want to show him all the old block records.

"Ah," Nelson Yang said, and then nothing more for a few seconds. After that pause for thought, he went on, "That may be more complicated, I'm sorry to say. Sharing internal Party business with non-members is something we don't normally do. You're not a CPWCPDR member, are you?"

"No, I'm not. But I'm a legally chosen block leader even so. Which counts for more?" Charlie replied.

"As long as Tony Newman was Premier, that question had only one answer, and you know what it was as well as I do," Yang said. "Now? It's still complicated now. As time goes on, as Comrade Eichenlode's reforms go forward, it may get easier. Or it may not. You have to understand, I don't *know* what Eichenlode is aiming at. I've never met him. I'm doing the same thing you are—I'm seeing what he does and guessing what he may decide to do next."

"Gotcha." Charlie drained his glass and got to his feet. "If you can do something, great. If you can't, well, I gave it a shot. I won't hang around bending your ear. If I didn't already know better, Vanderpool would've taught me a few nights ago."

"There are certain joys in taking one of these posts, aren't there?" the area leader said, deadpan. "It's good you can learn lessons like that. People who can't—"

"Don't get much sleep," Charlie finished for him.

Yang grinned. "True, but that isn't what I was going to say. People who can't learn those lessons shouldn't become block leaders to begin with. I wondered about you, but I think you'll do fine. Thanks for coming by. If you need anything else, I'm here."

"Thanks." Charlie hadn't expected to like Nelson Yang or to think he might have found an ally. But he did, and that was how it looked to him.

People needed a while to decide Premier Eichenlode meant what he said about removing censorship. After they did, stories about corruption and nepotism filled the papers for weeks. Lots of people who had been prominent found themselves either without a position or doing unimportant work in unimportant places.

"You can't say they don't have it coming to them," Lucille told Charlie. "You can't say watching the so-and-so's going down in flames isn't funny, either."

"You sure can't," he agreed. "I've laughed a time or three, you bet."

"We've needed a good cleanout," she said. "Sort of like the whole country's had a big slug of milk of magnesia, and now we're sitting on the pot."

"Sort of, yeah. Now let's see if they do a proper job," he said.

"What do you mean?" Lucille asked.

They were in the kitchen; she was fixing dinner. He made a gesture he might have borrowed from an orchestra conductor. She started rattling and clanging pots and lids and big metal spoons. With luck, that would foul up whatever microphones might be hidden there. With even more luck, the cops and the NBI might not be spying so much these days. Charlie hoped that was true, but didn't count on it. What he could do to make life hard for them, he would.

Quietly, he spoke through the din: "When will they start getting around to letting zeks out of camps, and to admitting most of them never should've got sent to those places to begin with? Will they ever get around to that?"

"Oh." His wife's eyes widened. She rattled and clanged harder than ever. Under cover of the racket, she said, "You don't think small, do you?"

"Not any more. If they give me a little, I want a lot. And zeks are only part of it. Will they ever have the nerve to say the show trials were a bunch of crap, too, and the people they shot didn't deserve it?"

Lucille banged another aluminum lid down on the counter. She stirred the stew in the pot with a spoon that scraped the sides and bottom. While she did all that, she said, "How can they, without telling us they've been lying to us all along?"

"They darn well have. The more you look, the more you see it," Charlie said savagely. "The more I look, the more I just want to get the truth, to find out what they've done to us for so long. Before Eichenlode came along, I didn't dream that could ever happen. Now I think it might—and I don't think I'm the only one, either."

Rattle! Crash! Bang! Lucille might have had a solo for drums and cymbals. Through it, she said, "No, I don't think you are, either. Some of the things you hear when the stores don't have what people are looking for …"

"No kidding!" Charlie said. "I'm on the receiving end there myself, remember. Everybody grumbles. They've always done that. Now it's more 'The apparatchiks will have apricots in their stores. Why don't we?'"

She nodded. "Like that, yeah."

"Everybody wants a lot. How do you let people be a little bit free and then say they can't go any further?" Charlie scratched his head. "I wonder how much Eichenlode thought about that before he started loosening things."

"You could write him another letter and ask him." Lucille's voice was sly.

"Oh, yeah, I'm really gonna do that!" Charlie rolled his eyes. "Last thing he wants is another letter from that crazy guy in Los Angeles."

"He helped you before."

"All the more reason not to push it now. He'll figure I'm just another clown trying to get more out of him. He's gotta get a hundred letters like that every day, or a thousand."

She kissed him, which caught him by surprise. "You know what you are? You're a stubborn fool who wants to go his own way no matter what anybody else does. You'll end up paying for it, too. The only reason you wrote Eichenlode before was, you didn't think it'd do you any good."

"Huh!" He scuffed his foot on the linoleum. "Y'know what's wrong with you? You know me too well."

"I'd better by now, don't you think?" She stirred the stew again, tasted, and nodded. "Go call the kids, will you? We're about ready."

"Okay." By then, Charlie felt relieved to escape.

A few days later, *The Daily Worker* ran a story headlined *Politburo Mulls Reevaluation of Certain Political Convictions*. It wasn't a big story, and was buried on page nine. If you weren't looking for it, you wouldn't find it or understand it. That had to be why it was there at all. As things were, it didn't say the Politburo or the courts actually would reevaluate those convictions. It only said the WCPDR's bosses were thinking about it. All the same, Charlie made sure he left it face-up when he got off the bus.

When he got home that evening, Lucille said, "Guess what?"

"I dunno. What?" Charlie didn't feel like guessing.

"The Donlins aren't in their apartment any more. Elsa Payne isn't in hers, either," she said. "They're gone like the Gionfriddos."

"Jesus!" Charlie said. That was news, all right—block news, anyhow. "Did they take all the old papers with them?"

"Beats me. I bet you're the only one who cares, though."

"I may be, but there's no guarantee. The cops may have some questions for them, too. Five gets you ten they were grabbing everything they could get. A lot of people join the Party for the chance to do that."

Lucille sniffed. "A lot of people join the Party for the chance to do that without worrying about the cops, you mean."

"Things have worked like that for a long time. I'm not so sure Eichenlode wants them to keep working that way," Charlie said.

"He may be the greatest thing since sliced bread, but I don't care what he wants. Getting that to change will take more than one person. Tell me I'm wrong. Make me believe it." Lucille looked a challenge at her husband. Charlie spread his hands, silently admitting he couldn't, regardless of how much he wanted to.

The headline on the morning *Times* made Charlie open his eyes as wide as another cup of coffee would have. "GENERAL FLEES TO MEXICAN SSR!" the paper screamed. He would have bought it anyway, to have something to read waiting for the bus and riding it. As things were, he shoved a quarter into the coin slot and pulled the lever so hard, he almost jammed the vending machine's works. After yanking at the top a couple of times and swearing, he finally managed to extract a copy.

Sure as hell, Major General John Sejna had crossed from Calexico to Mexicali, by all the signs one short jump ahead of the NBI. Major General Sejna was suspected of selling wheat across the border instead of turning it into bread or hardtack and feeding it to his soldiers.

By itself, that would have been a scandal. The more Charlie read, the juicier things looked. Sejna was only thirty-nine, which was mighty young to wear stars on his shoulder boards. One possible explanation for his rise was that he happened to be married to Tony Newman's daughter.

Before Charlie could get to the *Continued on page 5*, the bus rumbled up in a cloud of diesel fumes. Reluctantly, he folded the *Times* under his arm, dug another quarter out of his pocket, and stuck it in the fare box. As soon as he found a seat, he started reading again.

"That this happened at all is most unfortunate," Premier Eichenlode was quoted as saying. "That it seems to have happened for several years without being detected is even worse. We will investigate our security and accounting failures. We will also seek to extradite General Sejna from Mexico."

Charlie didn't think the WCPDR needed to do a hell of a lot of investigating. Who would check to see what the Premier's son-in-law was doing in his spare time (or would it be on his official time?)?

Nobody who wanted to stay in one piece. And even if someone did notice, what could he do about it? Tell Tony Newman? Tell a senior general who reported to Newman? Neither seemed a cunning plan.

The story ended, *The Mexican government states that General Sejna has requested political asylum, and that its extradition treaty with the WCPDR does not apply because of this.* That seemed a lot like *We've profited from him, so we'll keep him,* which struck Charlie as a very capitalist thing for a fraternal socialist republic to say.

He took the *Times* with him when he got off the bus. Instead of throwing it in the trash in the produce store, he set it on the counter. In his own small way, he wanted to make as much trouble as he could for the regime that had fallen.

A woman who bought potatoes and carrots and onions must have already read the story. As she was paying and handing over coupons, she said, "I bet when I go into the bakery they'll charge me more for bread on account of everything that son of a bitch stole."

"I don't know anything about that, Comrade Kirchner." Charlie spoke from a lifetime's automatic caution. You never could be sure who was a provocateur. He didn't care to think Alex Eichenlode would use people like that, but he knew damn well the Nibbies would. How much control did the new Premier have over them?

"We all know. We've known all along. Up till now, though, we were too scared to talk about it. Some of us still are." Out Comrade Kirchner went, her nose in the air. Charlie knew he'd fallen in her opinion.

Was she genuine, and not a security-service plant? She'd been shopping here for a while now, and she'd never come out with anything like that before. He remembered what Ervin had said. Could Eichenlode keep the cork halfway in the bottle? Or would people here try to grab more freedom than he wanted to give them?

He lit a Progress and blew a stream of smoke at the ceiling. "I sure hope so," he said, though nobody was there to hear him. Nobody was there unless the NBI had bugged the store, anyway. And they wouldn't know what he was talking about.

He'd just ground out the cigarette when Mary Ann Hannegan walked into the store. Of course she saw the *Times*. He'd stuck it there so people would see it, and she noticed things. She looked disgusted, as if he'd displayed a filthy picture, not a newspaper. "Throw that out!" she said.

"But it's news, Comrade," he answered. "What can I do for you? I'm expecting some radishes—red ones and the big white ones that'll curl your hair—but the truck hasn't come yet."

She told him where he could stick a big white radish. "Sideways," she added. Yes, she swore like a man, all right.

After a moment, he managed, "If you feel that way, I don't know why you came in at all."

"Because I'm disgusted," she said. "With Alex Eichenlode, who's a fool; with Nelson Yang, who's laughing at me; and with you. You started all this, you and the rightist bourgeois nationalists like you."

Charlie looked at her. "Why is Comrade Yang laughing at you? On account of me? Why would he do that? I've only met him once."

"Why do you think?" Mary Ann Hannegan growled. "Because you're a block chairman now." She rolled her eyes in disgust at the very idea. "And because three Party members with sound political understanding had to leave their positions as if they were so many undesirables."

"Had to run out, you mean," Charlie said. "Nobody made them do it. They just took off in the middle of the night. Who knows what they'd been doing before they decided they had to beat it? Who knows how long they'd been doing it, too?"

"Were you always this stupid, or have you been practicing? They tried to find somewhere safe before Eichenlode and his thugs threw them into a corrective-labor camp. People, good people, are doing that all over the country. They see it's the only sensible thing they *can* do."

"Wait. They think the new Premier will jug them because they like the old one? That's the kind of things Eichenlode's trying to get away from!" Charlie said.

"You really *are* that stupid." Mary Ann Hannegan shook her head. "Don't you recognize propaganda when you hear it?"

"Comrade, recognizing propaganda was what got me into trouble to begin with," Charlie answered. "But don't you have it backwards? Eichenlode took censorship off the papers and the radio and things. He didn't stick it on."

"It's a reactionary regime. Of course it will have a reactionary press," she said. Charlie couldn't remember much of his geometry. Since he escaped from school, he'd never had to see whether two triangles were congruent with each other. He remembered the mad certainty with which the teacher'd rammed proofs home, though. In all the years since, he'd never heard anything like it. Till now.

He said, "If they'd kept the lid on, we never would've found out Tony Newman's son-in-law was stealing from the state."

"Do you believe that?" she said scornfully. "If they make you hate the people in a government, you'll hate the things the government was doing, too, no matter how important and how necessary they were. It's the oldest trick in the world."

"He ran off to Mexico because he was innocent, right?" Charlie jabbed.

"Comrade, I told you—people *are* running off. I know some of them. There are refugees from the West Coast PDR in the Mexican SSR, in the Rocky Mountains, and up in the Canadian FSR. There are even refugees in the Southeastern Confederated People's Republic."

Charlie thought about that. He didn't know if it was true; he wondered whether Ervin would have a better idea. He was sure Mary Ann Hannegan believed it. Which meant ... what?

He thought a little more. Then he said, "You know, if Sacramento hadn't been lying to us for as long as I can remember and probably a lot longer'n that, I might take you seriously. The way things are, if what I see in the paper and hear on the news doesn't smell like bullshit all the time for a change, I'll pay attention to it and try and forget the crap from before." He found himself swearing back at her.

"You would," she replied. "You and all the other would-be bourgeois here. But the men and women who're escaping from this tyranny have their own stories to tell. The Premiers and First Secretaries who are in charge of our neighbors will listen to them. You can count on that, Comrade. And General Secretary Zhuravlev will listen. You can count on that, too."

Charlie bit down on that idea as if it were an unexpected cherry pit. It jolted him just as much as a cherry pit would have. "The Russians won't do anything to us!" he gabbled. "Comrade Zhuravlev backed Eichenlode against Newman. That's why Eichenlode didn't get purged!"

"Eichenlode wants to abandon Marxism-Leninism-Stalinism. He wants to throw away the Communist Party's leading role in the government and in the state and to foist a bourgeois democracy on us." Again, terrible certainty filled Comrade Hannegan's voice.

"None of that's true, you know," Charlie said, as if to someone who was plainly nuts and might be dangerous. "It's what people like you always come out with when things might loosen up a little and let ordinary folks catch a break."

"Think whatever you want. Say whatever you want, since one of the things you think is that censorship is gone. Think about how much what you think and what you say matter. Then think about how much what Comrade Zhuravlev thinks matters." She walked out without waiting for a reply.

The door clicked shut. She strode up Sherman Way. "Fuck!" Charlie said. He sagged against the counter. His legs didn't want to hold him up.

For the rest of the day, he tried to shake off the visit. He had less luck than he wished he would have.

By the next morning, though, he'd managed to convince himself that Mary Ann Hannegan was full of sour grapes because Tony Newman had lost and Alex Eichenlode'd won. In political fights, somebody always lost. Comrade Hannegan just wasn't used to seeing the man she'd backed defeated. The West Coast People's Democracy would go on the way it always had—maybe even better than before. She'd get used to the new boss.

Then he read a story on page three of the *Times*. The headline, *Rocky Mountain First Secretary Expresses Concern*, wasn't too alarming. But the piece told how Jan Nagy, who ran the WCPDR's eastern neighbor, had sent Premier Eichenlode a note saying he was worried about the direction in which the new reform program seemed to be going.

The Premier has replied that his program is suited to the country's needs, is purely an internal matter, and does not affect the WCPDR's foreign policy or its unwavering commitment to Marxism-Leninism-Stalinism in any way, the story ended. Charlie muttered to himself on the bus. Mary Ann Hannegan might have nasty politics, but she was nobody's dope.

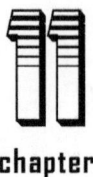
chapter

I could get used to this, Charlie thought as he sat down in one of the comfortable chairs on the stage in the rec center meeting room. He had a new recording secretary up there with him. Vicki Hayashi had volunteered for the job. She was home from her work as a stenographer because she'd had a baby a couple of months before, and wanted to keep her shorthand sharp while she was away.

Dmitri Vanderpool came up in front of the first row of seats and stared at Charlie as if he were the reincarnation of Friedrich Engels. "You did it, Comrade Simpkins! You really did it! You cut through that red tape like it was never there to begin with!"

He'd already come to Charlie's apartment to thank him. He was so grateful, Charlie worried about him. Hadn't anybody ever done him a favor before? With his hangdog air, maybe not. "Happy to help, Comrade," Charlie said now. "Why don't you sit down, so we can get on with the meeting?"

"Oh! Okay." Vanderpool seemed to need reminding anyone but Charlie and him was there. Reluctantly, he sank into one of the hard seats out there on the floor.

Charlie banged the table with the gavel Vince Gionfriddo'd left behind. Lucille had cracked walnuts with it in the flat, but he wasn't going to say so. "Let's come to order, okay?" he said. When people didn't, he used the gavel again and repeated himself, louder this time. After something like quiet descended, he went on, "Comrade Hayashi will talk about the minutes from the last meeting."

"There aren't any minutes from the last meeting. Or if there are, Comrade Payne took them with her when she lit out for the tall timber," Vicki Hayashi said bluntly. "But everybody who was here knows what happened. Comrade Simpkins got elected block chairman, which is why he's up here now." She turned and half waved to Charlie, as if the crowd might not have noticed him sitting beside her.

"That's why I'm here, all right," Charlie agreed. "This isn't going to be all neat and formal, the way it was when the Party people were running the show. Sorry about that, but it won't. Some of you have asked me to do little things for them or help them do those little things themselves. I've managed once or twice—"

"With me!" Dmitri Vanderpool said loudly.

Bang! Charlie discovered he liked plying the gavel. "You're out of order, Comrade," he said. "A couple of times, I struck out, too. You always try, but you don't always win."

"I think Comrade Eichenlode looks at things the same way," Vicki Hayashi said.

"Huh!" Charlie laughed uneasily. "He's got a few more things to worry about than I do. Yeah, just a few." The understatement drew a few chuckles. He'd been kidding on the square, though. The First Secretary of the Canadian Federated Socialist Republic had also sent Sacramento a note complaining about the WCPDR's policies ... and the Canadians were famous for never complaining about anything.

He looked out at his neighbors. Some of them were looking back at him the same way. Others eyed him as if they hoped he'd be on a train to Manzanar soon. *She's a Party member*, Charlie thought. *So is he. Her, too.* Chances were they were Newmanists, too.

I can sic Nelson Yang on them ran through his head. Yang would probably enjoy taking them down a peg. But once you started using the Party against the Party, where did you stop? Anywhere?

Aloud, Charlie said, "I don't have much of an agenda. Let's take questions from the floor for a while and then go home. How's that sound?" Nobody said no. He pointed at a woman. "What can we do for you, Comrade? Uh, tell us your name first."

"I'm Olga Sullivan, Comrade Simpkins. What do you people up there think about lifting censorship?"

"I'm for it," Charlie said at once. If the unsmiling faces in the meeting room reported to the NBI, the Nibbies wouldn't hear anything they didn't already know. He went on, "Matter of fact, I was tired of getting treated like a mushroom."

"A mushroom?" Vicki Hayashi sounded puzzled. Some people in the hard seats looked that way.

Charlie nodded. "Sure. You know. They keep you in the dark and feed you ... well, what they feed mushrooms." He didn't quite say *bullshit* in his first meeting, but he came close.

"Oh!" The recording secretary giggled. Then she nodded, too. "I wouldn't have put it like that, but I feel the same way."

No one out there stood up and spoke in favor of censorship, though the looks on some people's faces said they wanted to. Charlie had a good idea why they kept quiet. For one thing, the change in how things worked was government policy, and not many people even imagined going against that. For another, they had to fear they'd go on one list or another if they spoke up.

Charlie wanted a country where the authorities didn't make lists like that. He thought Alex Eichenlode did, too. That seemed to be where the new Premier was heading. Charlie hoped so.

Then one of the men with those hard, set faces did raise a hand after all. Charlie pointed at him. "Yes, Comrade? Who are you, please, and what's on your mind?"

"My name's Walter Lefebvre, Comrade Simpkins. My question is, when does freedom turn into license?"

He'd managed to speak up for censorship without mentioning it by name. In a way, Charlie admired his ingenuity. "I've thought about that some myself, Comrade Lefebvre," he answered. "The way things are these days, you have to, don't you? It looks to me like freedom turns to license when you start using it to tell lies and hurt people with them. As long as you're saying what's true, where's the problem?"

"Suppose you claim what you say is true and I say it's a lie. Then what?" Lefebvre asked.

"If it's important enough, the courts can figure it out, can't they?" Vicki Hayashi said before Charlie could respond. He nodded; he liked that. Comrade Lefebvre still didn't look happy, but he sat down.

"Okay, who's next?" Charlie asked. He pointed to a middle-aged man with a bushy Stalin-style mustache who lived in his building. "You're Pete Villareal, right?"

"That's me." Villareal nodded. "Now, this getting rid of censorship is fine, but how much does it mean if we only have one candidate every time we vote? When do we start fixing *that*, Comrade Simpkins?"

A buzz ran through the meeting. Men and women leaned forward in their seats, as if they'd been waiting for a question like that. And if they had … . If they had, then Charlie wasn't as far ahead of most folks in his opinions as he'd thought.

Still, he had to watch his words here. "I don't think Comrade Eichenlode is questioning the Communist Party's leadership in the West Coast People's Democratic Republic," he said. "We aren't a great big country. We're just trying to get along a little better. We aren't doing anything that ought to make our neighbors and our allies nervous or upset."

Take the hint. For God's sake, man, take the hint. Charlie didn't know what all might make Yuri Zhuravlev get angry at the WCPDR's new Premier. Loosening the Party's grip on the government sure seemed likely to do it, though. Talking about that—even thinking about it—had to be dangerous.

He hoped he didn't look as alarmed as he felt. If he did, he looked scared to death. He must have looked scared enough to get through to Comrade Villareal. The man with the mustache said, "Well, you're bound to be right about that," and sat down.

Part of the crowd seemed relieved. Part seemed mad. Mad that Villareal had asked the question? Or mad that Charlie hadn't answered it the way they'd hoped he would? He couldn't tell.

He didn't much care. "Any more questions?" he asked. *There'd better not be, not after that*, his tone suggested. There weren't, either. *If there are no more questions, class is dismissed.* Charlie turned that into meeting talk: "Do I hear a motion to adjourn?"

He did. He heard seconds, too. The motion passed without opposition. He used the gavel one more time.

"That was interesting, wasn't it?" Vicki Hayashi said as they both stood up.

"Interesting. Yeah." Charlie was just glad to get away in one piece.

Rehabilitation notices started showing up in the *Times* and, more often, in *The Daily Worker*. *The Worker* ran a little statement from Alex Eichenlode with the first bunch. *Not everything our country has done over the years was perfect*, the Premier wrote. *We've made mistakes. Some of the men and women we recognize in those notices are gone, but admitting they were wrongly condemned may make their families happier. No further condemnation will apply to family members, either, and those who still live will enjoy full civic rights like any other citizens.*

How did you give ten years in a labor camp, or twenty-five, back to someone? You couldn't. Charlie'd known people who went into camps. Not many came back—not to Los Angeles, anyway. When they did turn zeks loose, they'd keep them in internal exile, in the desert or the Sierras or someplace else where they couldn't stir up trouble.

That might change now. If censorship was gone, ordinary people might hear what life in the camps was truly like, not the rumors that floated here, there, and everywhere. What would happen when they did? Would they be terrified or furious?

He left *The Worker* behind on the bus when he walked west down Sherman Way to the produce store. Manuel Gomez came out of the junk shop. "How's it goin'?" he asked, and then, before Charlie could answer, "How's it feel, bein' a block leader?"

"How'd you know I was one?" Charlie returned. He knew damn well he hadn't said anything about it himself.

"Oh, hell, you hear shit like that," Gomez said. "You're on the block where all the people who used to matter up and split. That's how they wound up stuck with you, huh?" He winked.

"Damn right," Charlie said, not without pride.

"Crazy times we live in, man. Not just you drivin' people nuts, neither," Gomez said. "You see how they're startin' to give people who got in trouble in the old days their good names back?"

Charlie nodded. "Sure did. In *The Worker*, no less." Even with censorship turned off, *The Daily Worker* came as close to being an official organ as the West Coast People's Democratic Republic had.

"Saw that myself before I got over here today. One of the guys in there is Pedro Perez, cat who was on the County Board of Commissars way the hell back when. And do you know who Pedro Perez was?"

"No, but you're gonna tell me, aren't you?"

"Bet your ass I am." Gomez's head bobbed up and down. Maybe he'd read *The Worker* instead of shaving this morning; graying stubble showed on his cheeks and both chins. "Pedro Perez, he was my mama's grandpa. We were hotshots once upon a time—that side of the family, anyway."

"Not the Gomezes?" Charlie asked.

"Nah. Hell, no." As Charlie had a minute before, now the junk-shop man sounded proud of being disreputable. "My father's people, we've all been a bunch of chicken thieves as far back as anybody can remember."

"My old man would've got along with you. He could make anything, fix anything. But he liked the coffin nails even more'n I do. By the time he was coughin' enough to go see the docs, they had to take out a lung. He didn't last long after that." To take the edge off his feelings, Charlie lit yet another Progress.

"They say you oughta quit. They don't tell you how." Gomez fired up a cigarette of his own. "But it's kinda nice to get the blot off the family, know what I mean? They don't hold it against you this long, but my mom's people, they got plenty of the shit end of the stick. Better believe they did. So I gotta give Eichenlode credit for that."

"Rehabilitation may even do people who landed in that kind of trouble not so long ago some real good," Charlie said.

Manuel Gomez looked startled. "Yeah, you're right. It just may. I never even thought o' that. Tell you somethin' funny?" When Charlie didn't say no, Gomez went on, "I got no idea what old Pedro Perez looked like. After the Nibbies sent him to whichever camp they sent him to—I don't know which one, either—his wife and his kids, they got rid of all the pictures of him they had. They didn't want anybody thinking they still liked him or anything, y'know?"

"Oh, sure." Charlie'd heard stories like that before. When the authorities cracked down on your family, things only got worse if you didn't grin and bear it. He was lucky, in a way. As far as he knew, he was the first one in his clan to get fed up with the way things worked.

"I better quit bendin' your ear." Gomez looked up the street. Two women with stringbags were heading toward the produce store. Gomez finished, "They'll get you in dutch if you don't open up for 'em."

"Yeah. That scares me," Charlie said. Gomez laughed and went inside his own shop. As Charlie walked over to unlock the front door, he wondered how much truth he'd heard. Maybe all, maybe none, maybe something in between. Chances were he couldn't even find out. If they'd purged Pedro Perez, they were liable to have written him out of the record, too. Charlie'd also heard stories like that.

He was still fiddling with the lock when one of the women said, "The lady who lives in the flat next to mine says you've got summer squash in, *and* zucchini."

"That's right, Comrade." Charlie's thumb came down on the latch. He pulled the door open. "Sold most of them yesterday, but there are still some left."

He found himself talking to the woman's back. She and her friend hadn't even waited for him to turn on the light. They'd made a beeline for the squashes. If a store had something you wanted, that was what you did. Lucille operated the same way. So did everybody who couldn't shop at a nomenklatura store.

Does it always have to work like this, though? he wondered. The door clicked shut behind him.

Red Fleet landing craft rolled up onto a beach north of San Diego. Fierce-looking soldiers—or would they be Russian marines?—stormed out of some of them, rifles at the ready. Others disgorged tanks. Helicopters filled the sky above them.

Red Army and Fleet Exercise at Encinitas, the *Times* headline announced. A couple of divisions' worth of Soviet troops would be maneuvering on the beach and in the desert farther east. So would some units from the WCPDR. "Maintaining cooperation between allies is vital for worldwide security," said General Mikhail Ogarkov, who headed the contingent from the USSR.

Charlie wanted to see Russian soldiers in California—or anywhere else in the WCPDR—the way he wanted a hole in the head. A spokeswoman from Alex Eichenlode's Foreign Commissariat, though, was quoted as saying, "These maneuvers were agreed upon before the change of administration in Sacramento. We are pleased to train alongside Soviet forces, however, as they are the strongest military power the world has ever known, and we can always learn from their example. We remain completely confident that they will withdraw as soon as this exercise ends."

In the ordinary world, any time you said you were completely confident about something, you weren't confident about it at all. Did that work the same way in the rarefied air of international diplomacy? Since nobody'd ever accused Charlie of being a diplomat, he didn't know for sure, but he had a good idea how he'd bet.

The Russian landings on the beach also figured in the newsreel when he and Lucille and the kids went to see a new movie a couple of weeks later. On the big screen, in color, with the roar of the helicopters' motors blaring from the theater sound system, the soldiers storming the beaches seemed even more intimidating than they had in smudgy newspaper photos.

As for the movie, *Sorry—Wrong Telephone* was the same kind of two-guys-after-one-pretty-girl comedy as *Means of Production* had been. It was, and then again, it wasn't. *Means of Production* laid on propaganda with a trowel. Try as he would, Charlie couldn't find any ideological message in *Sorry—Wrong Telephone*. It was just, well, funny. Party bureaucrats didn't save the day. The only one who had any role in the movie was a fussy bumbler who made things more complicated, not less.

"What did you think?" he asked his family as they waited for the bus that would take them home.

"I liked it," Lucille said.

"Me, too," Sally agreed. "It was silly." She paused. "It was made to be silly, I mean. It wasn't silly by accident, the way a lot of dumb movies are."

"It was just a story. It wasn't a story trying to teach a lesson or anything. There aren't a whole lot of movies like that," Nikita said, echoing Charlie's own thoughts. *Anybody'd think we were related or something*, he thought as the bus grumbled up to the corner.

The Soviet corps maneuvering in the WCPDR was supposed to leave the Tuesday after the family saw *Sorry—Wrong Telephone*. In fact, it didn't start heading out till the next Saturday. General Ogarkov blamed "technical difficulties." The *Times* claimed Ogarkov had conferred with the Soviet ambassador in Sacramento before the force did withdraw.

On Sunday, Premier Eichenlode went on the radio to say, "I'm glad our nation had this chance to work with the peace-loving forces of our much larger socialist brother state, the USSR. The recent maneuvers were a valuable experience, and we learned a great deal from them."

Nikita glanced up from his geometry homework. "What did we learn? That they don't go home when they say they will."

Charlie coughed. "Be careful who's around when you say that kind of stuff."

"It's okay, Dad. Censorship's gone. You can say whatever you want," Nikita answered. He didn't tack on, *You dumb old drip*, but he might as well have. He was a kid, and got used to changes and to taking them for granted faster than older people did.

"Be careful even so," Charlie told him. "If they can turn censorship off like a light bulb, they can turn it on again the same way. And if they do, they'll remember everything you said while it was off."

"They wouldn't do—" Nikita stopped before he finished. He looked thoughtful, then sheepish. "Oh. I guess they might."

"Yeah, they sure might. If they don't, fine. But they can always hang a charge on you if they want to. No point making it any easier for 'em."

"Can they get away with tightening the screws after they've loosened up? Would anybody go along?" Lucille said.

"I don't know whether Sacramento can do that," Charlie said. "But the Russians darn well can, if they decide to. If Eichenlode wants to loosen up, he's gotta make them decide not to, 'cause otherwise—"

"Otherwise we're cooked," Lucille said.

Charlie nodded. That was what he'd meant, all right. He didn't think General Secretary Zhuravlev had decided to hold those maneuvers where and when he did by tossing darts at a map of the world and a calendar, either. Zhuravlev was sending a message. Being a Russian, he wasn't especially subtle about it, either.

"What can we do if the Soviet Union decides we've gone over the line?" Nikita asked. "I mean, if we like how things are going now?"

He'd been horrified when his old man turned into a right deviationist before his eyes. Now that the whole country was swinging that way, though, he was delighted to swing with it. So was Charlie. "What can we do? Not much but … hunker down and hang on tight, son, 'cause the ride's gonna get bumpy."

"Comrades, I have an important question for you." Alex Eichenlode's voice came out of the radio and into Charlie's living room. Charlie figured the Premier was bound to be on TV, too, but, even though he and

Lucille had got back their old place in the queue, that wouldn't matter to them for years to come. Eichenlode continued, "That question is, What is to be done now?"

"What?" Charlie's head jerked up as if someone had given him an electric shock. Lucille jumped, too. Anybody who heard that particular question would, in the WCPDR or anywhere else in the world.

Eichenlode knew it, too. With a dry chuckle, he said, "Have I got your attention now? Good. Yes, I know I'm asking the same question Vladimir Ilyich Lenin did in 1902, when he wrote *What Is to Be Done Now?*, the work that began to push the Bolsheviks into the revolutionary vanguard of the socialist movement."

Eichenlode coughed twice "He was looking at the movement in Russia and in the world as a whole. Russia was a great power even before it became the Soviet Union, and Vladimir Ilyich was a great man. Our own West Coast People's Democratic Republic is much smaller and much less significant. And, as anybody who knows me will tell you, I'm a very ordinary fellow myself."

"He's downplaying," Charlie exclaimed.

"He sure is." Sweetly, Lucille added, "Why don't you shut up so we can listen to him do it?"

That was such good advice, Charlie took it. The Premier continued, "Many years have passed since Vladimir Ilyich wrote his inflammatory pamphlet. Marxist-Leninist-Stalinist thought has developed significantly since those days. That's why I'm asking *What is to be done now?* in terms of the current economic and social reality prevailing in the WCPDR."

Charlie used Marixst-Leninist-Stalinist talking points against ordinary Communist bureaucrats in small ways. Alex Eichenlode thought bigger, much bigger. You had to admire his nerve, anyway.

"I am going to ask the Politburo and the People's Assembly to consider how we can govern our own small country in more perfect accordance with Marxist-Leninist-Stalinist principles, and in accordance with the needs of our populace," Eichenlode said. "I will offer some suggestions, and I'm sure the distinguished members will also have their own ideas." What he suggested would sail through, of course. Things worked that way. Who could guess what his cronies might come up with?

"We've already started this program, of course. Relaxing censorship and rehabilitating people wrongly convicted of political crimes are essential foundations for the action plan. But, once more, what is to be done now?

"We need to look at how we manage our enterprises. Having people at the top tell those below them what to do without worrying about actual conditions strikes me as inefficient. In the same way, having California in a position to dictate to Oregon and Washington because it's the biggest part of the country has always struck me as unfair."

Eichenlode chuckled again. "Some of you will say I only notice this because I come from Washington, and from Washington on the far side of the mountains at that. And you know what? You're probably right. Your foot notices it itches before the rest of you does.

"Maybe the Politburo and People's Assembly members from the sunny south will persuade us northerners we're being foolish by complaining. I don't think so, but it could happen. That's why we'll discuss these things and others—to find out."

Charlie heard him take a deep breath. "I need to be very clear about two things we *won't* discuss. As our recent joint maneuvers with Soviet troops show, our loyalty to our allies has not wavered, is not wavering, and never will waver. In the same way, the leading role of the Communist Party of the West Coast People's Democratic Republic remains the rock to which we moor the state. As it was in Lenin's day, it is still the vanguard of world revolutionary thought and deed. That we recognize this simple truth goes without saying.

"Together, all the progressive nations march toward true Communism. We ask *What is to be done now?* only to guide our steps in that direction. Thank you, and good night."

"That was Alex Eichenlode, Premier of the—"

Charlie clicked the radio off. He didn't think he'd been listening to the King of Sweden, not that Sweden had had a king for a good many years. "Well," he said brightly, "*that* was interesting."

"Oh, maybe a little." Lucille's voice was as dry as his own ever got, which didn't happen very often.

She went into the kitchen and came back after a minute or so with half a sheet from a scratch pad. She'd written, *Can he get away with it?*

That was the question, all right. It was also a question you didn't want to say out loud if you worried the flat was bugged, not even when censorship was said to have been lifted. Lucille held out a pencil so Charlie could answer, but he didn't need it. A shrug said everything he knew.

He crumpled the little piece of paper, put it in one of the ashtrays on the coffee table, and lit a match. A minute later, the evidence was gone. Lucille silently clapped her hands. "That's the way to do it," she said.

"Yeah." Charlie didn't say anything about which was the way to do what. Lucille hadn't, either.

He wondered what he could do to help change the way things worked in the WCPDR. *What is to be done now?* he thought, and laughed.

"What's funny?" Lucille asked.

"Nothing. It's just stupid," Charlie answered.

His wife didn't push him. If she was used to anything from him, it was stupidity. She put up with him anyway. That said he'd done *something* right in his life, or he could hope it did.

As for his question to himself, he saw no real answer except *Keep going the way you're going*. If people all over the WCPDR suddenly started telling apparatchiks to go fly a kite, change had to follow … didn't it?

No, as a matter of fact, it didn't, or the world would have seen a lot more change. Even so, they couldn't fling *everybody* into a labor camp. Or could they? The maniac who'd run the Northeastern Soviet Socialist Republic when Charlie was young sure had given it his best shot.

But Yuri Zhuravlev had stopped him and thrown him out. Zhuravlev didn't want everybody in labor camps, only troublemakers. What if everybody in a country *was* a troublemaker, though? What would the most powerful man in the world do then?

Charlie went into the kitchen and poured some bourbon over ice cubes. That didn't solve the problem, of course. It did keep him from worrying about it for a while, which was almost as good.

Before Alex Eichenlode replaced Tony Newman as Premier, Charlie'd bought newspapers to kill time and to see what the Party and the government wanted him to think. Most people, he felt sure, threw quarters into vending machines for the same reasons. It wasn't as if newspapers held much news.

Or it hadn't been. These days, the newspapers were much more interesting. The *Times* was, anyhow. *The Daily Worker* stayed stodgier. It was the Party paper, after all. It still seemed to have trouble believing that the Party and the government were changing, or at least trying to change.

But a *Worker* headline grabbed Charlie's eyeballs a few days after Eichenlode asked what was to be done now and tried to answer his own question. *North American Party Leaders to Confer with Zhuravlev,* the headline said.

Meetings like that were usually scripted and planned long in advance. Yuri Zhuravlev's last visit to North America had been. This one seemed different. Charlie supposed the General Secretary of the CPUSSR had needed a little while to decide what to do about Eichenlode. By the signs, he had now.

And, by the signs, he wasn't happy. When Charlie saw the meeting would be on Long Island, he felt as if the bus he was riding down De Soto had bounced over a really big, really deep pothole. It hadn't. That was only his stomach lurching all on its own.

He'd been thinking about the NESSR after Eichenlode finished speaking. He hadn't particularly thought about the Long Island gulags, but he remembered them. Anybody old enough to did. After Red Army soldiers liberated the Northeastern Soviet Socialist Republic, the papers and newsreels had been full of pictures of starving zeks and the horrible barracks they lived in. The Russians wanted to be seen as the good guys, and on the whole they got what they wanted.

Now . . . . Charlie muttered to himself. Yuri Zhuravlev didn't do things by accident. If he wanted to meet on Long Island, he was sending a message, to Alex Eichenlode and to any other North American Party boss who might want to do what Eichenlode was doing. You had to be an idiot to get the message wrong, too.

Don't. It was that simple.

He opened the shop. A woman came in and bought parsnips and turnips. "Stew tonight," she said as she gave him ration coupons and money, and then, "If I were the Premier, I wouldn't go anywhere near Long Island! The nerve of that Russian bastard!"

Charlie couldn't very well pretend he didn't know what she was talking about. "Sometimes saying no is worse than saying yes," he answered.

She tossed her head. "Nothing's worse than Long Island. You've gotta be uncultured to think about that place, let alone want to meet there!"

If some Nibbie was listening to a bug in the store, he had to be spitting out his teeth about now. *Uncultured* was one more thing that had passed from Russian to English. It was a muscular insult; words like *shitkicker* didn't come close. If you were a San Francisco city slicker, a very bold San Francisco slicker, you might call somebody from outside Spokane, somebody like Alex Eichenlode, uncultured—as long as you were talking to people you trusted.

To tell a shopkeeper Yuri Zhuravlev was uncultured .... The woman was either stupid or brave or ...

Or the world is changing. Is trying to change, Charlie thought. He dared hope it was number three.

She went on, "All we're doing is trying to live our own lives. The Russian have no business messing with us as long as we don't bother them."

She was halfway through that when Mary Ann Hannegan walked into the produce store. "Propagandizing, Comrade?" the Party official asked Charlie.

"As a matter of fact, no," he answered.

"I don't need any propagandizing," the woman snapped, rounding on Mary Ann Hannegan. "I know what I see with my own two eyes. I see a Party hack right now, for instance. Well, Premier Eichenlode'll help us settle the likes of you!"

Comrade Hannegan stared at the woman as if she'd never seen anything like her before. And she might not have, or not for many years. An ordinary person who presumed to tell a Party member where to head in? Such strange, abnormal beasts weren't supposed to exist.

She quickly gathered herself. She had a way of doing that. "Suppose you tell me your name," she said crisply.

"Suppose I don't," Charlie's customer replied. "You'll know cops who'll come around to give me grief. People like that'll get stuffed pretty soon, too. Wait and see. Suppose you get the hell out of my way, *Comrade*." She started for the door as if she'd go through Mary Ann Hannegan if the other woman didn't step aside.

Mary Ann Hannegan did, though she seemed astonished that she moved. The woman stomped out of the produce store, then headed east on Sherman Way toward De Soto. Comrade Hannegan glared at Charlie as if everything were his fault. "You see what happens?" she said. "As soon as control weakens even a little, everything starts falling to pieces."

"Yeah, how about that?" Charlie said cheerfully.

"Not you, too!" Mary Ann Hannegan exclaimed.

"Oh, you bet, me, too. And you already know my name, so you don't need to ask what it is. I've been a troublemaker since the last big propaganda campaign started, remember?"

"I remember." By the way she said it, nothing about him would ever be forgotten. "But you've shown you have a political consciousness, even if you are a right deviationist. When someone from the … from the lumpenproletariat starts spouting this nonsense, the country's in more trouble than you can imagine."

"Is it? Well, then, what is to be done now?" Charlie asked with malice aforethought.

Comrade Hannegan's expression warned she was making another note in his file. "Funny, Comrade Simpkins. Funny like cancer. Your marvelous Eichenlode made the same stupid joke, and now he gets to explain it to Yuri Zhuravlev. I don't think the General Secretary will laugh."

"Long Island isn't a great place for jokes, no." Charlie paused, then said, "Some folks'd be happier if the Russians hadn't stepped in when the NESSR went nuts. Some folks'd be happier if all the North American socialist democracies threw half their people into labor camps and worked 'em to death. I'm not naming any names, you understand."

"I understand. I understand very well," she answered in the flat voice of formal hostility. "And in case you're wondering, I'm not one of those 'folks.'" Her lip curled.

"You say that. You may even believe it. I kinda think you do. I told you I wasn't naming names. But from where I sit … ." He broke off with a disgusted gesture. "What's the use? You aren't gonna listen to me."

"How right you are." Mary Ann Hannegan walked out. She went west on Sherman Way, not east as the other woman had. Her office lay in that direction, but it fit only too well.

chapter

Three days later, Alex Eichenlode flew back across the continent. When he landed, Charlie sighed in relief. He hadn't been sure General Secretary Zhuravlev would let the Premier of the WCPDR come home. He would have bet his last dime that Eichenlode hadn't been sure, either.

After a couple of days resting up, the Premier spoke on the radio. "Along with the other North American Party leaders, I had a frank and comradely discussion on Long Island with the General Secretary of the Communist Party of the Soviet Union. An exchange of views on important issues is always welcome. I emphasized once more to Comrade Zhuravlev and to my North American colleagues that the West Coast People's Democratic Republic remains committed to our alliances and to our ideology, and that all changes underway here are purely an internal matter, of no importance to any foreign government. I believe we reached an understanding on that point."

"Let's hope he's right!" Lucille said.

"That would be good," Charlie agreed. If the NBI came down on him for wishing the Premier well . . . . He shook his head. If the Nibbies wanted to come down on him, all they had to do was talk with Mary Ann Hannegan.

Yuri Zhuravlev didn't fly off to the USSR right after he let Premier Eichenlode leave. He stayed in the Northeastern Soviet Socialist Republic for what the *Times* called "sightseeing" and *The Daily Worker* termed "further consultations with North American leaders."

Charlie hoped *The Worker* had it right. What would Zhuravlev look at in the NESSR? The weathering remains of the camps carved out in the middle of the great north woods in Maine? The mass graves alongside those camps? Was anyone caring for those graves these days? Or were the second-growth pines, fertilized by zeks' moldering flesh and bones, getting tall above them?

Then the General Secretary and all the North American Party heads except Alex Eichenlode issued what they called the Long Island Declaration. It sounded as if Tony Newman had written it. When you read phrases like *Marxist-Leninist-Stalinist thought is the font of world revolutionary progress* and *the necessary leading role of the Communist Party in the state and in social advancement* one more time, your eyes wanted to glaze over.

As Charlie walked from the bus stop to the produce store, Gomez greeted him with, "What do we do when the Russians invade and they're not holding maneuvers?"

"You read the paper too this morning, huh?" Answering a question with another question let Charlie pretend that what the junk-shop man'd asked had an answer besides *Give up—what else can we do?*

Gomez shook his head. "Nah. Heard it on the radio while I was drinking coffee. It's kinda big news, you know."

"Think so, do you?" Charlie said. Manuel Gomez snorted. Charlie went on, "Eichenlode's right. We aren't doing anything that's got anything to do with people who aren't here in the WCPDR. We're still a waddayacallit, a fraternal socialist state. Nobody's nuts enough to try and change that. I don't even think Eichenlode wants to."

"Nobody gives a shit what you think, Charlie," Gomez said. Charlie couldn't tell whether the other man was calling him by his name or would have said the same thing if he were Vasili Simpkins. Gomez added, "Only thing anybody gives a shit about is what Zhuravlev thinks. The rest? Big fucking deal."

"You know what's a big fucking deal, Manuel? I'll tell you what. If everybody can get a phone. Or a typewriter. If you don't have to wait years for a car or a TV or a trip to the Rockies. If they don't chuck you into Manzanar for saying a Politburo member's a dumb asshole when everybody knows he is. *That's* a big fucking deal."

Gomez looked at him with wise, sad eyes. "When the Russians come, man, you're gonna hope they only chuck you in Manzanar."

Charlie sighed. "Yeah, probably."

"Yeah for sure. You don't even try and keep your mouth shut any more, do ya?" Gomez sounded more admiring than otherwise.

"No, not very much. Know what else? I'm not the only one, either. Not even close." Charlie told the junk-shop man about the customer who'd reamed out Mary Ann Hannegan. He finished with, "A whole bunch of people are sick to death of the way things've been for Christ only knows how long. Not just here, either. All over North America. All over the world, I bet. Who knows? Maybe even in the workers' and peasants' paradise, the model for socialist states everywhere."

"Guy, I like you, swear I do. Listen to your Uncle Manuel, hey? You go on like that, you won't need to wait for the Russians. I don't give a shit what a sweetheart Eichenlode is. The Nibbies'll pitch you into a goddamn labor camp any which way."

"I wish I could tell you you were wrong." Charlie sighed. "But you aren't. Wanna know what else? I hardly even care any more."

"You say that now, on account of you never been in. You been a *good* boy till now, Charlie. Talk to a zek who's done ten or twenty-five. He'll tell you what a dumb piece of shit you are. Bet your balls he will."

"You keep being right, dammit," Charlie said. Manuel Gomez smiled a smile so thin, it was almost emaciated. In spite of knowing the junk-shop man was talking sense, Charlie didn't think he'd change his wicked ways. Something inside him had snapped when he pulled the WORKERS OF THE WORLD, UNITE! poster out of that mailing tube. He had no idea how to fix it. He didn't want to fix it.

"I sure do. How come you don't care?" Gomez held up a hand. "Never mind. I don't wanna know. What I don't know, they can't rip outa me. And you better believe they'll ask me questions about you. They'll ask everybody who's ever laid eyes on you."

"Nah. I'm not a big enough deal for them to get excited about. They'll save that for the politicians and the bureaucrats."

"Unh-unh," Gomez said. "You're the kind who scares 'em, 'cause you don't give a shit no more. Those are the dangerous ones."

He'd nailed how Charlie felt, sure as hell. Whether that meant what he thought it did … Charlie could hope it didn't. He said, "I give a shit about opening up for my counterrevolutionary customers." Comrade Hannegan would agree he had at least one.

Several people talked about the Long Island Declaration as they bought potatoes and cabbages and apples. Nobody said that the Soviet Union needed to intervene to keep Alex Eichenlode from traveling down the road he'd chosen. One woman suggested that Yuri Zhuravlev could use the fat cucumber she laid on the counter for things that had nothing to do with salads, or even pickling.

"Sideways," she added sweetly. She was young and pretty, which only made Charlie's ears heat more than they would have otherwise.

Because she was pretty, he added, "With a twist."

She smiled. "You bet, with a twist! I thought you were like that, but I wasn't sure till now."

"How come you thought so?"

"You haven't had one of those dumb posters in your window for I don't know how long now." She looked at him as if he was dumb for having to ask.

"Oh." Charlie wondered how many other people had noticed but never mentioned it. More than he'd guessed, it seemed.

Most of the mail went straight into the trash, as usual. He almost chucked a letter from the collective farm connected with the agricultural college farther south, but decided to open it instead. *I can throw it out once I've read it*, he reasoned.

He read it and didn't throw it out. Instead, he thoughtfully stuck it in the drawer under the cash box. The letter talked about how the collective's members, following the suggestions in Premier Eichenlode's *What Is to Be Done Now?* manifesto, had decided to try to sell some of their produce directly to local stores.

We naturally have to charge more than state suppliers do, but we think our fine quality will make our prices seem like a bargain, the collective farmers wrote. *If this interests you, let us know.*

Normally, Charlie would have had to get his supervisor's approval before he did anything that far out of the ordinary. The functionary responsible for the West Valley's produce stores would probably have to get four or five levels of bureaucrats senior to her to sign off on it before she could tell Charlie to go ahead.

Normally …. But things weren't normal any more, were they? No, not even close. Charlie tapped the drawer with a fingernail. "Y'know, I just may take you up on that," he said.

Charlie'd gone by the agricultural college and its attached kolkhoz any number of times when he worked at the warehouse down on Ventura Boulevard … and, later, when he headed to the Valley Relic. He hadn't paid any special attention to it. Chain-link fencing covered with green tarps kept people going along De Soto from peering at the crops and at the workers tending them.

He told Lucille he'd visit the place on his Saturday afternoon half-holiday. "Down that way, huh?" she said. "You sure you aren't just going to that crummy joint you drink at?"

"Maybe afterwards, but not instead of."

She made a face at him. "That's what you say." They both laughed.

He got off the bus at De Soto and Victory and walked south till he came to an entrance. A large young man in a little shack asked, "Need something, Comrade?" He gave the clear impression that, if he didn't like the answer he heard, Charlie wouldn't get in.

"I think I do," Charlie said. "I manage the produce store up on Sherman Way, and I got this letter." He took it out and showed it to the large man. "I want to talk about it with your people."

The fellow's attitude changed. "Oh, you're one of those! Okay. Go to Building Four and ask for Friedrich. Tell 'em Mike passed you through." He stepped out of the shack, unlocked the swinging gate, and held it wide for Charlie.

"Thanks," Charlie said as Mike closed and locked the gate behind him. He wondered how he'd find Building 4, but not for long. There were paths through the growing crops, and neat signs directing people to whatever they might be looking for.

Men and women were working in the small fields, and tending to chickens and pigs. Movies and magazines showed tractors and harvesters rolling across the vast expanses of collective farms in central California and eastern Washington, the expanses where the wheat and barley and corn that went into the WCPDR's daily bread, beer, and breakfast cereal came from.

These fields were nothing like that. They put Charlie more in mind of collective farmers' private plots, the ones where they worked when they weren't laboring for the kolkhoz's common good. The care the people here lavished on them gave him the same impression.

When he walked into Building 4, a woman looked up from a typewriter and said, "Yes?" Again, he got the feeling he might land in trouble if he answered wrong.

He showed off the letter once more. "Mike at the gate on De Soto told me I should talk to Friedrich here."

"Oh, sure." She relaxed and pointed to a stairway. "Top floor—room twenty-seven. Go on up. I don't think he's with anybody now."

"Okay." Up he went. It was only a two-story building. He walked along the hall till he found room 27. The door was open. A gray-haired man behind a desk looked up at him. "Are you, uh, Friedrich?" Charlie asked.

"That's me, Comrade. Friedrich Papadakis. Come on in. What's on your mind?"

Charlie set the letter on the desk. "I run a produce store. I want to find out what kind of deal you've got in mind."

"Sit down, sit down." The collective-farm man waved Charlie to a chair. Unlike the ones for visitors in Horton Wilder's office, it had padding. The air smelled of pipe smoke. Sure enough, a pipe sat in a bronze ashtray. Papadakis said, "Smoke if you want to. I'm glad to see the response we're getting."

"You've come up with a ... different way of doing things." Charlie lit a Progress. "This is a different kind of kolkhoz, too, isn't it?"

"Just a little." Papadakis smiled. "We're the college's research arm, you might say. We don't work for profit—or we haven't, till policies started changing. We investigate the most efficient ways to grow the best crops. What we learn, we pass on to collective-farm managers all over the country."

"Is that what the deal is?" Charlie said. "No wonder your plots get so much tender loving care, then."

"No wonder at all," the kolkhoznik agreed. "Some of what we do is too labor-intensive for big farms, but some isn't."

"Well, I'm interested. What are you trying to unload? What are your prices like? Can you deliver to my place?"

"We can deliver. We have a beat-up pickup truck we use. As for what we've got, let me show you. Come along to the next building. You've seen a lot of produce, so you can tell me what you think of ours."

Friedrich Papadakis led Charlie to a building with thick adobe walls and a roof that had plenty of overhang on all sides. Charlie nodded to himself; rain didn't come to Los Angeles all that often, but you had to protect unbaked clay all the same. Fluorescent lights came on when Papadakis opened the door. He waved Charlie in ahead of him.

It was ten or fifteen degrees cooler in there than outside. That was what adobe was for. Charlie grinned, saying, "Smells like my store, only more so."

"I expect it would. See for yourself what we have," the kolkhoz man said.

The radishes were crimson golf balls with leaves and roots. Charlie rubbed one against his trousers, then bit into it. He gave Papadakis a thumbs-up. You couldn't ask for more crunch or flavor. Green beans, a couple of varieties of peas .... He'd thought the state warehouse had sent him fine produce after he got his manager's job back. So had other people. Now he discovered there was a step up from what he'd had then.

"I've seen worse," he said, trying not to show how impressed he was. "You didn't answer when I asked about prices before. Now I really want to know." Papadakis told him. He winced. "That's twice as much as I shell out to the warehouse, three times as much for the snow peas."

"When was the last time you got snow peas from the warehouse?" Papadakis asked.

"Been a while," Charlie admitted. "But it's like you said in your letter—I'd have to charge more, too, and I don't know how many people will go for it."

"Some will," the kolkhoz man said. "Some will pay extra for a good meal, some just want to shove any old thing into their faces. Room for both kinds. Room for both kinds of food, too."

"What I'm trying to figure out is whether there's room in my budget. I'm gonna have to start small. If I make enough on my first order, I'll get more when I come back."

"You sound like somebody who knows what he's doing," Papadakis remarked.

Charlie snorted. "Only goes to show, you never met my wife." The kolkhoznik laughed. Charlie bought thirty pounds of radishes, thirty pounds of green beans, and fifty pounds of snow peas. "Like you say, I don't have those very often. I figure they'll move," he told Papadakis. "You can get 'em to me Monday morning?"

"Tell me when you want 'em, and they'll be there then."

"Half past eight. I'm supposed to open at eight straight up, and I try to, but the buses are the way they are, so I can't always."

"We all know that song, don't we? I hope things will get better now. I don't know they will, but I hope so. Even hoping feels funny, if you know what I mean. Sometimes you thought it would all go on forever, the same as it always has."

A few months ago, Charlie reflected, he wouldn't have said that to anyone he hadn't known for years and years. Even now, it seemed bold. Automatic habits of self-preservation were hard to shed. Charlie had to make himself nod. "Yeah, you sure as hell did. And if Zhuravlev is serious about the Long Island stuff, it still may."

"I don't see how he can be," Papadakis said. "We aren't trying to change anything anywhere else. We're only cleaning up our own house."

"I said the same thing not long ago to a Party kinda big shot I know—Newmanist. She didn't want to hear it."

"If you're on top, the way it always was looks good. Why don't you come back to my offices? You can fill out a pile of forms for me." Friedrich Papadakis smiled crookedly. "The way it always was, one more time."

"Oh, yeah." Charlie knew he'd have to fill out forms at the produce store, too. Extraordinary expenditures forms. New-vendor forms. Others, too. He had drawers full of them.

If nobody wanted the fancy vegetables and fancy prices, he figured he could get away with making the experiment. He probably couldn't have before Alex Eichenlode became Premier. But then, the little collective farm here never would have tried selling to stores before Eichenlode took power.

If things did work out, his customers could buy something good that they couldn't get otherwise. He cared enough about what he was doing for that to matter to him.

Monday morning, the kolkhoz's truck showed up at eight thirty on the dot. The guy who lugged in the produce was Mike from the guard shack. He nodded to Charlie. "Here y'go, man. Glad you decided to do business with us."

"Me, too," Charlie said. *Do business* sounded almost as old-fashioned as something from Shakespeare. What else would you call this unregulated, unplanned commerce, though? Charlie couldn't think of a better term.

He put up cardboard signs above the bins where the snow peas and radishes and beans went. EXTRA FANCY! FROM THE AGRICULTURAL COLLEGE COLLECTIVE FARM! He put up the prices, too, in big red numbers. People needed to know. Then he posted one more sign. LIMITED SUPPLY! it said.

That might or might not make shoppers want to spend money. In the West Coast People's Democratic Republic, as in most socialist republics and people's democracies around the world, lots of things were in limited supply most of the time. Charlie took the chance, hoping his customers would want to grab while they could.

The first woman who came in after the vegetables went on display took a couple of steps toward them before she saw what they cost. Then she stopped and sent Charlie a reproachful stare. "Those look nice, but I can't afford them," she said.

"Comrade Wilson, I wish I could charge less, but I paid more to get them myself," he answered. "If you don't want them, nobody's gonna make you buy 'em. The regular stuff is still here."

She got some turnips and carrots, but her eyes kept going back to the snow peas. Charlie didn't smile as she yielded to temptation, scooping a pound of them into the hanging scale. "Just this once," she said, as she brought her produce to the counter. "Eugene will enjoy them."

"Hope so. Hope you do, too," Charlie said as he took her money.

Some people did steer clear of the pricey produce. Others grabbed it as if fearing they wouldn't see the like again if they held back. They weren't far wrong, either. By the time the day ended, Charlie had only a few green beans left from what he'd got at the agricultural college.

That worked at least as well as I hoped it would, he thought as he took down the signs where the radishes and snow peas had been. He knew the green beans would sell out first thing in the morning. He also knew he'd visit Friedrich Papadakis again.

He was about to close up shop and go home when Mary Ann Hannegan walked in. She saw the remaining sign over the beans and nodded as if it confirmed something she'd heard. It probably did. She nodded again, this time to Charlie. "Well, well," she said. "Congratulations on bringing capitalism back so soon."

He nodded, too. It wasn't as if he hadn't wondered whether somebody'd say something like that. "Don't be silly, Comrade," he answered. "How can it be capitalism when I got my vegetables from a representative of the collective managing the kolkhoz at the state agricultural college?" Yes, he could sling Marxist-Leninist-Stalinist phrases around as well as anyone.

Mary Ann Hannegan's lip curled. "The people at that experimental collective farm have been right deviationists for years. Some of them have taken what they know to places like Manzanar and Folsom and Hanford. Of course they'll try to take advantage of Comrade Eichenlode's foolish policies. I hoped for better from you. I didn't expect it, but I hoped."

"If I was doing anything against the law, you wouldn't come here to talk about it. Maybe once upon a time, but not any more. The police or the Nibbies'd show up and haul me away."

Her look said he had that right. She answered, "Some people aren't worth bothering with. You at least have a political consciousness—I told you so before. I keep wanting to wean you away from deviationism. You could even be an asset to the Party if you cared to."

Was that an invitation to apply for membership? There'd been a time when Charlie would have been over the moon to get one. He'd always thought of himself as a very plain guy, somebody the CPWCP-DR wouldn't look twice at. And the Party never had … till this moment, when he no longer wanted anything to do with it.

"Comrade, I've finished my quota of socialist labor for the day," he said. "All I care to do now is go home, eat dinner, take my shoes off, and get the answers wrong when I try and help my kids with their homework."

"You won't get away with it, you know," she said, as if dinner and homework were criminal offenses. Charlie knew she wasn't talking about them, though. In case he didn't, she spelled it out: "The Long Island Declaration put us on notice that we won't be permitted to veer off the track."

"We aren't veering off the track. Doesn't every country have the right to find its own way to true Communism? Isn't that what the alliances that bind fraternal socialist states are all about?"

He thought she wouldn't answer. To a Communist of her stripe, only one road ran forward. But she did. "No," she said before she walked out the door.

Charlie left, too. He turned the sign on the front door from OPEN to CLOSED. He locked up. The faint snick of the key coming out of the deadbolt lock seemed dreadfully final. Shaking his head, he walked down Sherman Way toward the bus stop.

After shutting the produce store on Saturday afternoon, Charlie went south to the agricultural college. A different man, though also one tall and well made, sat in the guard shack. "I need to talk with Friedrich," Charlie said. "I'm a customer." He had to work not to laugh. Damned if he didn't sound like a capitalist!

Capitalist or not, he seemed to know the magic words. "You got it," the guard said, and opened the gate for him.

When Charlie went into Building Four, he nodded to the woman at the typewriter and asked, "Is Friedrich here?"

"He sure is. Go on up," she said without even looking away from her copy.

The gray-haired kolkhoz manager greeted Charlie with, "Hello, Comrade! How did the experiment go?"

"I'm here to plow my profits into new stock," Charlie answered. "An apparatchik who keeps an eye on the block where my store is accused me of being a capitalist. I told her she was wrong—what I was doing was square in line with Comrade Eichenlode's *What Is to Be Done Now?* manifesto."

Friedrich Papadakis beamed. "That's the way! The best part is, you aren't even wrong."

"I didn't think I was when I said it, either," Charlie answered. "Now? I'm not so sure."

Papadakis held his right index finger to his lips. "Shh! You're supposed to keep quiet about that. But if our politics are going to loosen up, don't you think our economic policies have to, too?"

"I've only just started worrying about that. I'm nothing but a guy who runs a produce store. I want things looser, yeah. That's why I like Eichenlode so much. How we get there? That's for smart people to figure out. I'll roll with it."

Papadakis studied him. Charlie wondered whether the other man had used whatever connections he had to check him out. Unless Papadakis was a naive fool—which he sure didn't seem to be—he'd want to make sure he wasn't dealing with a Newmanist out to sabotage the collective farm's tiptoeing into commerce.

"Something tells me you aren't so dumb yourself," he said, and, after a moment, went on, "Why don't we see what you'll want for Monday delivery?"

Charlie nodded. "That's what I'm here for."

He followed Papadakis to the adobe-walled storehouse close by. The smell in there was different from what had greeted Charlie's nose a week earlier: spicier, sweeter, more perfumed. "We've been picking the citrus trees," the kolkhoznik said as the overhead lights came on.

"Haven't you just!" Charlie exclaimed. The front of the storehouse was piled high with crates of lemons yellow as the noonday sun and tangerines the color of the same sun when it rose or set. There were also boxes of avocados that hadn't been there on his first visit. Their bumpy, green-black skins reminded him why some people called them alligator pears.

"How much can you spend this time, and what do you want for your money?" Papadakis asked.

"I'll get some lemons and avocados, not too many. They look great—don't get me wrong—but not everybody lives in a flat, and people with houses're liable to have lemon trees or sometimes avocado trees in their yards. They give 'em to friends or sell 'em in the park or back alleys, so not as many folks buy 'em at the store. Tangerines, though, I'll get lots of those. Who grows them at home?"

"And you said you weren't so smart?" Papadakis rolled his eyes. "Sandbagger!"

"My ass," Charlie said, to hide how pleased he was. "I've been doing this a while, that's all. I'll get more avocados than lemons. And I'll buy more of the green beans and snow peas. The peas went like—" He snapped his fingers, then looked around. "No more radishes?"

"'Fraid not. We hadn't planted that many, and we went through them in a hurry. How much have you got to spend, and how do you want to divvy it up?"

"You gotta tell me the prices on the stuff I haven't bought yet," Charlie pointed out.

Friedrich Papadakis thumped his forehead with the heel of his hand. "You may be a smart fellow, but I'm an idiot." He gave Charlie what he needed to know.

Charlie thought for a few seconds, then grinned wryly. "Let's go back to your office, okay? The forms are there anyhow, and I'm gonna want to do a little figuring on paper so I know how I ought to split up my money."

He made his choices. He filled out all the papers he needed to place his order. There would be more paperwork Monday when the kolkhoz driver delivered the produce to the store. Charlie wished all that were simpler. When buying from little outfits that weren't part of the massive state apparatus grew more routine, maybe it would be.

Instead of going straight home after finishing his business with Papadakis, he took the next southbound bus south to Ventura Boulevard, then another one east till he could walk to the Valley Relic. As usual, the place smelled like the class-four tavern it was: smoke, beer, sweat, and, faintly from the bathrooms, puke.

Bourbon in hand, Charlie looked around for a place to sit down. Somebody waved to him: Dornel. He waved back and came over to the black man's table. "How's it going?" he asked.

Dornel made a face. "Going? Man, it has went."

"That good, huh?" Charlie raised his glass in sympathetic salute.

"Even better. I shit you not." Dornel drank some of whatever kind of whiskey he had. Charlie got the idea it was nowhere near his first. "Wilder .... Hell, you know what he was like. He keeps getting worse."

"They said it couldn't be done!"

"They was wrong. Was they ever." Dornel sadly shook his head. "He's like he reckons the Nibbies're gonna come in and haul him away any second now, an' he takes it out on us."

"I know why he thinks that way," Charlie said. Dornel raised a questioning eyebrow. Charlie explained: "It's what he'd do himself if he could. It's what his pals would do—*will* do if they get the chance. He doesn't get that Eichenlode aims to use the NBI less, not more."

"Mm .... Reckon you got somethin' there," Dornel said after a moment's thought. "But I'll tell you, Eichenlode may not be so smart. He don't clamp down on some o' them bastards, they make him sorry."

"I know," Charlie said; that gloomy thought had crossed his mind, too. "If you have to fight dirty, though, how do you clean things up afterwards?"

Before Dornel could answer, Ervin walked into the Valley Relic. Being a celebrity at a class-four tavern was as small a stardom as there was, but the old man enjoyed it. People waved and grinned and offered to buy him drinks and asked him to sit with them. This afternoon, he let Charlie get him a beer and parked his carcass with him and Dornel.

"I was hoping I'd run into you today," he told Charlie. "I finally got it all figured out."

"Oh, yeah?" Charlie said.

"This I gotta hear," Dornel added.

"It's simple," Ervin rasped. He wet his whistle with a Brew 102, then lit a Progress. "Honest to God, it is. You know how all the socialist states go on and on about how they're heading toward true Communism?"

"Never heard that before," Charlie said.

Ervin and Dornel both looked disgusted. Ervin said, "Yeah, yeah, mess things up."

"I try," Charlie said modestly.

"Feh," Ervin said, and then, "Yeah, I finally figured out what they remind me of. They chase true Communism like dogs chase cars. And it's the same way with dogs and with them. If they ever catch what they're chasing, they won't know what the hell to do with it."

He waited for Charlie's admiration. Charlie gave it to him. So did Dornel, who went to the bar to buy him another beer. Charlie said, "That may be the saddest thing I've ever heard in my life."

"Oh, good! I was thinking you'd be one of the people who could see past the joke," Ervin said. "I mean, the joke is funny, sure, but it's on us. All these years, all these gulags, running after something that probably isn't there and that'll put you out of business if you get hold of it."

"Eichenlode's got a better way," Charlie said as Dornel came back with the stein.

"Thank you, Comrade," Ervin said to the black man. His eyes swung back to Charlie. "You may be right. I hope so. I think so. I bet even Zhuravlev thinks so. The difference between me and him is, though, Zhuravlev doesn't fucking care." He swigged the new brew.

chapter

Two days after the *Times* printed a story about a rash of lynchings in and around Atlanta, the Southeastern Confederated People's Republic sent Sacramento a formal diplomatic protest. *The scurrilous farrago of lies appearing in a publication that has lost its moral compass and its socialist obligation to fraternity can only be destructive of good order and of warm relations between our two states*, the note said. To underscore how upset the SECPR was, it recalled its ambassador to Richmond "for consultation."

A *Times* editorial replied, *That the Southeastern Confederated People's Republic doesn't want the world to know how it treats its black citizens doesn't mean that it doesn't treat them horribly. Hushing things up doesn't mean they aren't there. We have too much experience with that here at home.*

"The *Los Angeles Times'* reporting seems credible," a radio newsman said a night later. "The WCPDR stands by the right of newspapers to look for the truth and to print it when they find it. Letting people know what's wrong is often the first step toward setting it right."

"Hanging people because they're the wrong color isn't something a good socialist state should do," Nikita said. "All my friends are talking about it. Everybody's mad at Richmond."

"This didn't just start up now, when the paper ran the story," Charlie said. "It's been going on for … well, forever. Black people catch it here"—he remembered Dornel's sour cracks and the way the police behaved in South Los Angeles—"but it's a lot worse over there."

"That guy on the news is right," Nikita said. "They should fix those things, not hide them. A government is supposed to fix things, isn't it?"

Everything seemed simple when you were a kid. "When a government tries to tell people to do things they don't want to, that's when it has trouble," Charlie said.

His son's expression said he had feet of clay up to his neck. "I suppose the black people in the Southeastern Confederated People's Republic want to get lynched?" Nikita suggested.

"Ouch!" Lucille made as if to chalk up an imaginary point in the air. "I wonder where he gets that from."

"No idea." Charlie felt more proud than annoyed.

"We started something different," his wife said. "Other places aren't used to stuff leaking out."

"If they'd tell the truth themselves, they wouldn't be so surprised when somebody else does." No, Nikita had no compromise in him.

"I won't even try and tell you you're wrong," Charlie said. "But they *don't* tell the truth, they *won't* tell the truth, and we have to deal with that. We were the same way ourselves till just a little while ago, remember."

"I do remember. We were stupid. I thought you were crazy because you didn't go along with that campaign, but now I see you knew what you were doing after all," Nikita said.

Charlie gaped. How many fathers ever hear such things from their teenage sons? Before he could find a way to answer, Lucille brought him down to earth with a thud: "Don't give your dad too much credit. He happened to feel ornery, that's all."

"Everybody ought to feel ornery, then. We'd be better off if more people did, that's for sure." Yes, Nikita was ready to start world revolution now. No doubt about it, kids his age were born Trotskyists.

Three days later, a small story ran in *The Daily Worker*. It said that the Southeastern Confederated People's Republic had referred its quarrel with the WCPDR to the Soviet Union for evaluation. "This is a purely internal matter," said Vyacheslav Martillo, the WCPDR Foreign Commissar. "We do not seek to make the SECPR change what happens within its borders, and it has no call to take offense if we note things that do in fact happen there."

Did Comrade Martillo know what he was talking about? Charlie hoped like anything he did. All fraternal socialist republics were theoretically equal. In real life, some were more equal than others, and the USSR the most equal of all. If Yuri Zhuravlev decided to arbitrate between the two North American countries, what could they do but go along with his decision? Nothing Charlie could see.

If Zhuravlev did decide to put his hand in, neither of the papers said anything about it. In Tony Newman's time, that would have proved nothing. Now …. It might, anyhow. Or it might not. Charlie had no way to judge.

Because he was still worried, he went to see Nelson Yang the next Saturday afternoon. He'd got on with the area leader much better than he'd expected when they first met. If you had connections, you were a fool not to use them.

He had to wait a bit before the important man could talk with him. Well, since becoming block leader he'd had people waiting to talk to *him* a few times, too. It came with the territory. "What can I do for you, Comrade Simpkins?" Yang asked when Charlie's turn came.

"Maybe you can tell me how nervous I oughta be," Charlie said.

"Nervous about what?" Yang asked. Charlie explained. The Party man nodded when he finished. "That's an interesting question. You do find them, don't you? I think—" Before Yang could say what he thought, the telephone rang. He made a sheepish face. "Excuse me."

"Sure." Charlie listened to half a conversation about Party business. You had to be in good odor with the authorities to have a phone, the same way you did to own a typewriter. Governments naturally distrusted gadgets that made it easier for ordinary people to exchange ideas with one another. In the Mexican Soviet Socialist Republic, a typewriter license was much harder to get than one for driving a car, and the authorities took type samples from every machine before releasing it to the licensee.

Would Alex Eichenlode change such restrictions? If you didn't censor papers or books or the radio, why should you keep censoring your own citizens? *A telephone? That'd be nice*, Charlie thought.

Nelson Yang said his good-byes, hung up, and turned back to Charlie. "Sorry about that."

"What were you gonna say?"

"This—I *think* the Soviet Union will leave us alone a while longer. If Comrade Zhuravlev had wanted to back the Newmanists, he could have done it, and Eichenlode wouldn't be Premier now. It wasn't as if Eichenlode hadn't shown what kinds of policies he meant to follow."

"People like what he's doing, too. Most people, I mean," Charlie said.

"That's right. And it's important. The Russians went into the NESSR because they were afraid things there were bad enough to spark a rebellion—and that it might overthrow the government. They want things to stay quiet and orderly."

"Yeah." Charlie nodded. "Thanks. You've taken a load off my mind—some of a load, anyway."

"I've been worrying and wondering about it, too. I believe we can make it work. You said it yourself—Eichenlode's policies are popular here. Only a few holdovers from the old regime are squawking to Moscow."

"And our neighbors," Charlie pointed out.

"Zhuravlev shouldn't listen to them. I don't see any signs that he is. He would have responded to the SECPR differently if he wanted to intervene," Yang said.

"Here's hoping you're right."

"Yes, indeed." Yang changed the subject to show the talk was almost over: "I've heard nothing but good things about the way you're handling your block. You should know that."

"Thanks again. Glad to hear it. It's more work than I expected, and doing it without the old records doesn't make it any easier."

Yang frowned. "I haven't managed to do anything about that. The people who ran off still have friends protecting them. When things straighten out, I'll take care of it."

"Okay." Charlie understood that *When things straighten out* meant *When our side gets stronger*. Even under Eichenlode, Party infighting hadn't gone away. He wondered what could make that happen. The only thing he thought of was *a miracle*.

After leaving Nelson Yang's place, Charlie went down to Ventura Boulevard. He got home an hour after the family's usual dinnertime. Lucille was not pleased. "Why didn't you sleep under a table at the Valley Relic and come home tomorrow morning?" she said.

"Sorry, babe. I went to the Relic, yeah, but that's not why I'm late." Charlie set a paper bag on the kitchen counter and reached into it like a magician reaching into a top hat. Instead of a rabbit, he pulled out two cartons of Lucky Strikes and a fifth of Jim Beam. "Don't say I never did anything for ya."

Her eyes, which had been narrow with annoyance, widened. "Where did you get those?"

"On the left, where else? That alley where you think somebody'll hit you over the head with a wrench every time you stick your nose in."

"How much did it cost? I can guess for the Luckies, but I can't even imagine what bourbon like that goes for," she said. When Charlie told her, she flinched. "So it'll be potatoes and cabbage for the next two weeks?"

"Nope. We're fine."

"How can we be fine when you just spent that much?"

"Because it comes out of what I'm making off the produce from the agricultural college's collective farm. Till now, I've plowed every dime of profit back into buying more goodies from them. The more I buy, the more I can sell, and the more I sell, the more cabbage I make. But I figured, what's the good of making money if you can't enjoy it a little?"

"Will we get in trouble on account of that?"

"I don't see why we should. The money wouldn't be there if I hadn't earned it. I only wish I had more to spend it on."

"Walk in somewhere and come home with a Zil?" Lucille made a joke of it.

"Us driving around in a fancy Russian car? That'd be fun!" Charlie grinned, because it *was* a joke. Only Party bigwigs could buy whatever they wanted whenever they wanted it. It was queue up and wait for ordinary people. Day by day, year by year, you inched forward. Eventually, your name rose to the top and you got to take home whatever you'd waited for.

Charlie wondered whether Alex Eichenlode had thought that that old, well-worn system might change, too. Then he wondered whether Yuri Zhuravlev had. If the General Secretary had …. How much could a big country let a small country get away with?

Lucille took half a step toward the Jim Beam. "Want to have a drink to celebrate getting rich and everything?"

"Sure." But Charlie laughed, because that was a better joke than the one before. "If I was rich, we'd get the good stuff all the time, like people who can go to nomenklatura stores. Progresses? Or the rotgut they scrape out of the barrels? Forget about that crap!"

She busied herself for a moment with glasses and ice cubes and opening the bottle. After she handed Charlie a drink, she said, "It'd be nice if everybody could get the good stuff all the time."

"It would, yeah." He raised his glass. "Here's to the good stuff!" Lucille clinked with him. They drank. He nodded. No matter how much he'd paid for the fancy bourbon, it was worth every penny.

"Oh, that's nice," Lucille said.

"You better believe it." Charlie eyed his wife. "Me, I found the good stuff a long time ago."

She rolled her eyes. "*How* much did you drink at the Valley Relic?"

"I had a couple with Eddie from the warehouse, that's all. From everything he says, and Dornel, too, Wilder did me a favor when he fired me. These days, he's making like a Nibbie colonel in charge of a camp."

"You'd love that, wouldn't you?" Lucille knew him, all right. "But you people down there got rid of one horrible boss."

"We sure did, and we got the other jerk in exchange. At least when I'm at the produce store, I'm the only one running me ragged."

"I wish the one down the street here had somebody running it who cared half as much as you do," Lucille said. "She's not buying from your kolkhoz, let me tell you. Half the shelves are empty half the time. If you didn't bring things home with you every once in a while, I don't know how we'd manage."

"The state's in charge of her store, same as it is with mine. If she does as close to nothing as she can get away with, she gets the same salary I do. So that's what she does. A lot of jobs work the same way. I could act like that, too, but I'd rather do things right if I can. I found a way to make extra with the collective farm. I bet she tossed their letter without opening it."

"Besides, you'd be bored to death if you sat around inside your store all day long," Lucille said shrewdly.

"Who, me?" Charlie tried to sound innocent. He didn't bring it off well. "Anybody'd think we'd been married for a while or something."

"Or something," Lucille agreed. Then she changed the subject—a little, anyhow: "Listen, Comrade Capitalist, next time you spend some of your ill-gotten gains, bring something nice home for the kids. They felt it even more than we did when things weren't so good because of the trouble they got in school. However we can make it up to 'em, we ought to."

"I'll do that," Charlie said. "Good idea."

He opened a carton of Luckies and took out a pack. Under the red circle with the brand name inside, smaller type declared, *Product of the Southeastern Confederated People's Republic*. He peeled back the silver paper and extracted two cigarettes. Handing one to Lucille, he tapped the other on the counter to keep the tobacco from coming out, then struck it in his mouth. He lit his wife's smoke before his own.

"That's what tobacco should taste like," she said after her first drag.

"Sure is. Makes Progresses seem like they're made out of horse manure, doesn't it?" Charlie sighed out smoke. "The SECPR is full of nasty sons of guns, but they turn out good cigarettes and whiskey."

Lucille picked up the package and read the same legend he had. "Why isn't anything ever simple?"

"I can't tell you. Probably because we aren't kids any more." Charlie lowered his voice. "Nikita'd keep smoking our own nasty tobacco to spite the lynch mobs there. And who knows if he's not right?"

"Who knows anything these days?" Lucille said. If that wasn't the best question Charlie'd heard in quite a while, he had no idea what was.

"My fellow citizens, I'm pleased to tell you that day after tomorrow I'll be conferring with General Secretary Zhuravlev." Alex Eichenlode's voice came from the tinny radio in Charlie's front room. "I'm honored that he will travel all the way from Moscow to the West Coast People's Democratic Republic to talk with me. The meeting will take place in Blythe, just on our side of the Colorado River."

Blythe was a sun-blasted, dusty border town where nothing ever happened. Where nothing ever had happened, anyhow. Now it would go into the history books. How it would go into them …

"I want to assure everyone that this will simply be another frank and comradely discussion about issues of concern to the WCPDR and the Soviet Union." Eichenlode sounded as if he meant that. Of course, being a politico, he'd sound that way whether he meant it or not. He went on, "Comrade Zhuravlev has generously offered to help improve our strained relations with the Southeastern Confederated People's Republic, and I'm delighted to accept. I hope and expect Chairman Thurmond will feel the same way."

Charlie was glad he had his latest pack of Luckies in his pocket, where Nikita and Sally couldn't see them. No, the kids had no use at all for the SECPR these days. Sally'd said some of her friends wanted the WCPDR to go to war against a fellow fraternal socialist republic, even if they didn't border each other.

Premier Eichenlode continued, "General Secretary Zhuravlev has given me his most sincere guarantee that his latest visit to North America is completely separate from the joint maneuvers Soviet forces are holding with soldiers from the Rocky Mountain People's Republic. The desert terrain in Arizona and Nevada is different from anything the USSR has in its own territory."

"He'd better mean it," Nikita muttered. He wasn't wrong, either. But if Yuri Zhuravlev didn't mean it, Charlie still couldn't imagine how the WCPDR would fight back. The USSR could send men and ships and planes anywhere in the world. No matter what Sally's friends wanted, Charlie doubted his own country could fight any of its next-door neighbors.

"I'll tell you what the General Secretary and I discuss in Blythe after our meeting ends," Eichenlode said. "As I did on Long Island, I'll do my best to make him understand that our reforms are purely internal, and pose no threat to any other state. I believe he will continue to support our endeavors. Thank you, and good night."

Charlie wondered what Chairman Orval Thurmond thought about that. His country felt threatened because papers here told people what it did. Silence muffled all kinds of things in all kinds of countries. When you couldn't rely on it, you started to get scared.

"I wish we had a TV," Sally said. "Then we'd be able to watch what's going on for ourselves."

"We're moving up the list," Lucille told her, echoing Charlie's thoughts of not so long ago.

"I'll be old by the time we finally get one," Sally said.

"I hope it'll be not long after you start high school," her mother replied.

"That's *years*!"

Years stretched huge when you didn't have many of them. Charlie remembered that. He wished it were still true. Every time he looked around now, he had more of them under his belt, and they piled up faster and faster.

He bought another radio and took it to the store so he could listen to the news while he had to stay at work. You never had to queue up and wait years for a radio. You could get one anywhere, for next to nothing. The WCPDR wanted its people to have them. As long as it had been around, the radio and the newspapers were its main tools for getting the public to think the way the state wanted.

Customers didn't mind listening along with him. He hadn't thought they would. A woman buying beets and avocados said, "The Premier better not sell us down the river!" By the way she sounded, she was ready to take on the USSR regardless of how bad the odds looked. She wasn't the only one, either.

That was brave. Charlie also thought it was less than smart. Almost everybody who came in backed Alex Eichenlode. The only thing the housewives and repairmen and secretaries complained about was that he wasn't going far enough fast enough. Not for the first time, Charlie wondered whether even Eichenlode had understood how much discontent simmered under the surface here.

"On this side of the Colorado is Blythe, in the West Coast People's Democratic Republic," said the radio reporter who'd accompanied Eichenlode to the border. "On the other side of the river sits Ehrenberg, in Arizona in the Rocky Mountain People's Republic. A single bridge links the two countries, a bridge with the usual customs stations and passport-control points at either end. Any minute now, Yuri Zhuravlev will cross the bridge to confer with Premier Eichenlode."

A man set a watermelon on the counter and said, "He should go back to Russia, is what he should do. None of his damn business, what's going on here!" He handed Charlie a silver dollar. That was what people still called the coins, anyhow. They hadn't been silver for a very long time. They were steel plated with nickel to look shinier.

As Charlie made change, he remarked, "Not so real long ago, Comrade Weigel, you never would have had the nerve to say that out loud."

"Yeah, I know. Crazy, isn't it?" Weigel said. "But I'll tell you somethin', buddy. I like it better this way, y'know?" He stuck the change in his pocket and the melon under his arm. Then he walked out.

A moment later, the announcer said, "Several cars are coming west across the river. Some will hold General Secretary Zhuravlev's guards, from the People's Commissariat for Internal Affairs. And one will be his armored limousine, which will have accompanied him on the Red Star."

The Premier of the WCPDR also had a plane he used at need. Charlie would have bet it was nowhere near so big or so grand as the one Zhuravlev traveled on.

"I'm watching from a distance, you understand. Even with binoculars, things aren't as clear as I wish they were, so please excuse me if I make mistakes," the radio man said. "Yes, this is the Soviet delegation. They aren't stopping at the frontier posts, of course, but are proceeding into the WCPDR. The bridge has been closed to ordinary traffic since midnight, naturally, and will stay closed until the General Secretary crosses back into the Rocky Mountain People's Republic."

How many truck drivers on both sides of the border were sitting in the hot sun and fuming—or sitting in a tavern and drinking—because the General Secretary was visiting the Premier? Charlie was sure Yuri Zhuravlev didn't care. He had a nasty suspicion Alex Eichenlode didn't worry about it, either.

"A white pavilion has been set up in which the two leaders can talk. The flags of the WCPDR and the Soviet Union fly side by side in front of it," the announcer said. "A generator powers portable cooling units to keep the General Secretary and the Premier comfortable." Charlie felt a stab of jealousy. The Valley wasn't quite so hot as somewhere like Blythe, but it was hot enough for all ordinary use. Fans ran day and night in his flat and here in the store.

"The Russian cars are pulling up outside the pavilion. As General Secretary Zhuravlev's NKVD men get out, NBI guards come forward to meet them," the newsman said. "Two of the General Secretary's men are walking into the pavilion, I suppose to make certain everything is safe and secure."

"Heh," Charlie muttered. His own acquaintance with the NBI didn't make him love it. The Nibbies were too used to being top dogs. When they dealt with the People's Commissariat, though, they had to roll over and show their bellies. As far as he was concerned, it served them right.

Nothing happened for the next little while. The Soviets would be very careful before they let Zhuravlev go in. Then the announcer said, "They're coming out again. One of them is waving. That's the signal for the General Secretary and his interpreter to get out of his Zil. And here is Premier Eichenlode, walking out of the pavilion to greet his distinguished guest. They're shaking hands for the photographers."

Walking out of the pavilion wishing his distinguished guest would drop dead, Charlie thought. Or maybe not. Zhuravlev had paved the way for Tony Newman's downfall. If not for him, Alex Eichenlode would be a trade official in the Socialist Democracy of Inner Mongolia or a zek in Folsom.

"They're going back to the pavilion," the radio man said. "The Premier's holding the flap wide for the General Secretary and the translator. They duck their heads a little as they enter. The Premier follows. The flap closes behind him. What they'll talk about, they'll talk about in privacy."

A woman had walked into the store while the announcer was talking. "I sure hope everything turns out okay," she said.

"So do I, Comrade Flores," Charlie answered—she was a regular. "Looking for anything in particular today?"

She headed for the bins that held peppers ... when he had peppers for them to hold. She looked at him in reproach. "I was hoping you'd got some more of those jalapeños I bought a couple of weeks ago. My husband really enjoyed them. He smokes a lot, you know, so he wants a kick in what I make him. Otherwise, he thinks it all tastes the same."

"I know what you mean." Charlie'd noticed he was putting ever more salt and hot sauce on things these days. He remembered his father doing the same thing before him. "I asked the truck driver why he didn't bring jalapeños the last time he came, though—they were on the inventory sheet for what I was supposed to get. He said they never made it to the warehouse. They come up from the Mexican SSR, and there's been some kind of trouble on the other side of the border."

She made a face. "Mexico's always been in Russia's pocket. When Comrade Zhuravlev spits, Mexico goes swimming. I bet they're making us pay on account of Alex Eichenlode isn't like that."

"He didn't say anything about why," Charlie replied. "But I don't think he knew exactly what's going on down there."

"Nobody knows what's going on down there. It's one *chingado* country, is what it is." She turned the conversation: "I'm glad Comrade Eichenlode didn't cross the Colorado. They wouldn't have let him come back again, if you want to know what I think."

"I'd be lying if I said the same thing didn't cross my mind, too," Charlie said. "I felt that way when he went to Long Island. Nobody can count on coming home from Long Island."

"You got that right!" Comrade Flores nodded vigorously. She was a few years older than Charlie: plenty old enough to remember the horror that had overtaken the Northeastern Soviet Socialist Republic a generation earlier. "Long Island, that was bad enough to make Manzanar seem like a dacha by a lake."

"Yeah." Charlie wouldn't have spoken so freely himself. When you'd always looked over your shoulder, you had trouble stopping. He did, anyhow. Some people seemed to take the new arrangement for granted. He envied them.

"If you don't have my peppers, I'll see you some other time," she said. "I got other stops I need to make. Take care of yourself, Comrade. You're on the right side." She turned and walked out before he could ask her how she knew.

She might have noticed that front window without the propaganda poster. Others had. Charlie shook his head. And he'd been sure nobody cared whether a stupid poster was there or not. "Shows what I know," he muttered. "Not one hell of a lot."

Yuri Zhuravlev and his entourage drove back into the Rocky Mountain People's Republic only a few minutes before Charlie closed up and went home. He would have stayed in the store longer had Zhuravlev still been talking with Alex Eichenlode. He wanted to know what was going on.

"No immediate statement is expected from either side," the radio announcer said. "Both leaders will want to evaluate what they heard today. As long as the two countries continue to talk, the situation can't be too dire, a thought I'll leave you with till further developments arise."

He sounded like a man whistling past a graveyard at midnight. *Or I might be listening more to myself than to him*, Charlie thought as he locked up. He hoped he was. He couldn't be sure. The older he got, the more it looked as if he couldn't be sure of one single goddamn thing.

Alex Eichenlode talked to the West Coast People's Democratic Republic at nine that night. "I think my discussion with the Soviet General Secretary went well," he said. "I think he understands that our internal processes of change and reform will remain just that: internal processes. We are not trying to tell anyone else how to live or how to govern their state. We trust our neighbors and allies will extend us the same privilege."

He sounded like somebody whistling past a graveyard, too. As for trust .... Charlie's old man had played a lot of poker. One of the things he often said was *Trust, yeah, but cut the cards.* How were you going to do that if the guy you were playing against wouldn't let you?

"What do you think?" Lucille asked after the kids went back to the bedroom.

Charlie noticed she hadn't asked while they were still there. That had to say something about what *she* thought. With a sigh, he answered, "If everything was great, Zhuravlev wouldn't have flown out from Moscow to begin with."

"Yeah." She nodded. "Well, we'll do whatever we can."

"We'll do whatever we have to," he amended.

"Whatever we have to." Lucille nodded again. "It would be nice if we had a choice, though."

"It would. That's what Eichenlode's been trying to do—give us choices, I mean. I like it. Even here, though, some people—quite a few people—don't. Bastards."

"The kind of people who want to get even with us for wanting things to be different," she said.

"With everybody who ever said there are more ways than the one old one to do anything," Charlie agreed. "Last time I saw her, just last month, Mary Ann Hannegan still had her drawers in a twist because Newman got thrown out."

"Something should have happened to people like that," Lucille said.

"Part of me thinks so, too. Part of me thinks that, if you play the same game they do, what's the difference between you and them? You're just another so-and-so who throws people he doesn't like into labor camps."

"You have to take care of yourself. They'll get you for sure if you don't," Lucille said.

"Yeah. I know." Charlie went into the kitchen. He came back with two glasses of Jim Beam on the rocks. He handed Lucille one. "These won't change one damn thing that's going on, but they'll numb us up for a little while."

"Right this minute, I'll take that," his wife said. She drained her drink almost as fast as he killed his.

When he rode down to work the next day, a *Times* story caught his eye. One of their reporters had been arrested in the Mexican SSR, in a town called Michoacán de Ocampo. Charlie'd never heard of it. The story helpfully told him it lay south of Mexicali, which was on the far side of the border from Calexico in the WCPDR.

Brett Avila was calling in a story he said was important when the line connecting him to Los Angeles suddenly went dead, the Times said. We have learned he is being held in the town jail. What the charges are or when he may be freed, we do not know at this time. We are grateful to the government of the West Coast People's Democratic Republic for making inquiries on our behalf.

That didn't sound good. People in the WCPDR made nervous jokes about Mexican jails. Even by the standards of prisons in any other fraternal socialist republic, they were supposed to be places you didn't want to visit for yourself. And everybody said the Seguridad del Estado made the Nibbies seem warm and cuddly by comparison.

As Charlie got off at Sherman Way, he wondered whether Manuel Gomez knew about this. Gomez's family had been in Los Angeles for a long time, but he might have relatives on the other side of the frontier. Even if he didn't, his last name *was* Gomez.

Such murky thoughts filling his head, he walked west. Gomez's junk shop, though, still had the CLOSED sign on the front door. Charlie frowned. Gomez almost always opened up before he did. He stood right in front of the window and peered in. Somebody was moving around in there—Vissarion. Charlie tapped on the plate glass.

Gomez's son looked up, startled. When he saw it was Charlie, he came up to the door and opened it a couple of inches. "Hey, man," he said through the gap, as if ready to slam the door any second.

"What's going on? Is your dad okay?" Charlie came out with the first fear that crossed his mind.

"Pop? Yeah, he's fine." Vissarion sounded surprised he needed to ask. Then the young man realized what he meant. "Oh. You mean 'cause I'm here and he ain't?"

"That's right," Charlie said, less patiently than he might have.

"We're closing down, man. Closing down for good. I'm just getting some stuff that'll come in handy over in Lompoc. We got cousins up there. We'll stay with them a while till we get the place up there going. It's the sticks, but what can you do?"

"You're … leaving? Like that? For good?" Charlie didn't want to believe his ears. Gomez and this shabby store had always seemed as much a Valley fixture as Stoney Point over on Topanga Canyon Boulevard.

But Vissarion nodded. "That's right. My old man, he don't like the way the wind's blowing. He says he don't wanna stay in L.A. no more. Says he'd sooner head for a dumbshit little nowhere town nobody never notices. Matter of fact, he says he knows somebody who can put you up for a while if you come, too. Pop, he thinks you're a pretty good guy."

And if that didn't answer Charlie's questions before he asked them, nothing ever would. "Tell him thanks for me," he said, his voice suddenly husky. "That means a lot. But tell him I don't figure it's as bad as he does. And even if I did, I think I'd stay anyway."

Vissarion nodded again. "He figured you'd say that. You're one crazy stubborn *vato*, is what he says. Far as I'm concerned, he's right, too. Anybody who'd stick his balls on the block for a stupid fuckin' poster …"

"Yeah, well—" Charlie spread his hands. "I did it. I'll wear it."

"Luck, man. You're gonna need it, bet your ass. Listen, I gotta finish up this shit so we can get the hell outa here. Take care." Vissarion shut the door in Charlie's face. In case Charlie missed the point, he locked it again, too.

"Fuck me," Charlie said, alone again on the sidewalk. He went on to the produce store. As he mechanically set about opening up, he kept thinking it couldn't be so bad as Manuel Gomez thought. Then he realized it might not be that bad. It might be even worse.

chapter 14

The West Coast People's Democratic Republic formally asked the Mexican Soviet Socialist Republic to release Brett Avila. The Mexican SSR refused, saying the *Times* reporter was being held on charges of conspiracy and espionage. The WCPDR denied the charges. The Mexican SSR ignored the denials.

Charlie watched all this the same way he watched a Pacific Coast League pitchers' duel: anxiously, with his heart in his mouth. He didn't know what would happen next, but he did know it could be bad for his side.

Even *The Daily Worker* weighed in. *The Worker* had been slower to get behind Alex Eichenlode than other outlets. But it was on board now. An editorial said, *A writer seeking to find and print the truth should not be considered threatening to anyone. If he is, those who feel threatened need to ask themselves why.*

"There you go!" Charlie said when he read that. He was on the bus at the time. A woman across the aisle gave him an odd look, but he never noticed.

A burglar broke into Gomez's shop and stole some of the junk he'd left behind. The police came around to investigate. Charlie wondered who'd called them. He never would have, not in a million years.

"We'd nod to each other, say hello in the morning. That was about it," he told a sergeant with a notebook. "I didn't know him real well or anything."

After scribbling, the cop asked, "Any idea why he closed down or where he went? That place has been there a long time. His house is empty, too."

"I kinda wondered about it. Did he skip town, then?" Giving the police anything went against Charlie's grain, same as it did with most people.

By the sergeant's jaundiced eye, he'd heard a lot of lies in his time and knew he was hearing more now. "That's what we're trying to find out. He's not in any trouble or anything, but you don't just bail out on your life if everything is going great."

"No, you don't." There, Charlie could agree without giving anything away. He added, "I hope he's okay."

"So do we." The policeman pulled a card from his wallet. "You hear anything, use a drugstore phone and call me, will you?"

"Sure. Thanks." Charlie lied again. The sergeant stumped out of the produce store. Torn in half, his card went into the wastebasket that had once held the WORKERS OF THE WORLD, UNITE! poster.

The next morning, a *Times* story said that a *Seattle Post-Intelligencer* reporter had fallen afoul of authorities in Chilliwack, not far north of the border between the WCPDR and the Canadian Federated Socialist Republic. Charlie couldn't tell from the piece just when the Canadians had arrested the woman. Whenever it was, he didn't like it.

Neither did Friedrich Papadakis, when Charlie visited the collective farm. After he'd picked out his next order of fruits and vegetables, the kolkhoz manager said, "I'll send it over to you Monday … if things haven't hit the fan by then, I mean."

"You're cheerful today," Charlie said.

"Sometimes you've got to be," Papadakis replied. Charlie set a hand on his shoulder. They stood there for a moment. Then they went back to Papadakis's office for the paperwork. Charlie almost trotted as he left the farm. He wondered whether he'd ever come back again.

Instead of heading home, he went south down De Soto, and then over to the Valley Relic. He wanted to find out what Ervin thought of the way things were going. But Ervin wasn't there. Neither was anybody he knew from the produce warehouse.

He sat down at the bar and ordered a bourbon. One sip told him that was a mistake. "This sure ain't Jim Beam!" he blurted.

"In a class-four joint? Don't make me laugh!" The bartender rolled his eyes.

Charlie stretched the drink as long as he could, both because it was bad and because he kept hoping Ervin would walk in. But Ervin didn't. Maybe he'd packed up everything and split for Lompoc, too. *Maybe you should*, Charlie said to himself. Instead, he finished the booze and went out to the bus stop.

"I didn't expect you back so soon," Lucille said when he came in.

"You complained when I was late. Now you're complaining when I'm early?" Charlie asked.

"I'm not complaining. I'm surprised. Can I be surprised?"

"I don't know. Have you filled out all the forms you need for that?"

"You're funny today ... . What are you doing?"

"Fixing myself a drink. I need to get the taste of the kolkhoz and the Valley Relic out of my mouth. If you ask me real nice, maybe I'll make you one, too."

"Oh, *please*," she said, her voice as saccharine as the heroine's in one of the sappiest old proletarian movies. He barked laughter and poured another bourbon.

They touched glasses. Charlie sipped. "The only trouble with the good stuff is, it spoils me for everything else," he said, and then, "Kinda like you."

Lucille might have come back with something sharp, but that stopped her. "How many did you have down there before you came back?"

"Just one. Everything's going to hell, I think."

"What can we do about it? Anything?"

"Move to Lompoc, the way Gomez did. And Ervin, for all I can prove. He sure wasn't at the Valley Relic today."

"Lompoc?" Lucille thought about that, but not for long. "I'd rather stay here."

"Yeah, so would I," Charlie said. "But if we're gonna stick around, the best thing we can do is go outside after it gets dark and wish on the first star we see that everything turns out okay."

"How much will that help?" Lucille sounded intrigued.

"As much as anything else," he explained. "Except maybe getting drunk and staying drunk for I don't know how long. That'd make the Russians think we're on their side, anyhow."

"Wishing on a star hurts less."

"You're no fun."

When Charlie rode the bus back to work on Monday, he wondered whether Mary Ann Hannegan would drop in to throw the way things looked in his face. Soviet troops on maneuvers in the Rocky Mountain People's Republic, inquisitive reporters from the WCPDR seized both south and north of its frontiers .... If you were the worrying sort, you didn't have to guess very hard about why the Mexicans and Canadians had grabbed them.

Charlie was the worrying sort, but not about his liver—getting drunk and staying drunk looked better and better to him.

Comrade Hannegan didn't come by. The produce delivery from the collective farm showed up, for all the world as if everything were fine. "Good to see you. I wasn't sure I would," Charlie told the driver.

"Good to be seen," the fellow answered seriously. "I wasn't sure I'd make it, either. Ain't life grand these days?"

"Just peachy. At least," Charlie said. The kolkhoz driver gave him a crooked grin. After setting the last crate from Charlie's order in the storeroom, he drove off to deliver to some other produce-store manager who cared about what he sold. His pickup belched less smoke than most, but still left a trail behind it as it rolled away.

"I'm making all kinds of cabbage on this deal with the farm," Charlie said when he got home. "I really could buy enough Jim Beam to stay fried for a long time."

"Oh, boy," Lucille said, and then, "It's a shame they don't have little plots full of steak and lamb-chop bushes. I don't remember the last time I had a lamb chop."

"That'd be nice. I don't, either," Charlie said. "If you aren't an apparatchik, forget it."

Dinner was stuffed cabbage rolls. More of the stuffing was rice than ground pork. That was how things worked when you didn't have connections. The sweet-and-sour tomato sauce made them taste good even so. And they did fill you up.

Charlie enjoyed an after-supper Lucky. That and after-sex were the best cigarettes around. And the first one after you got up. And when you hadn't had one for too long. And ...

"Good morning, Comrades." Alex Eichenlode's voice came out of the radio in Charlie's living room, as it came out of radios and televisions from Seattle down to San Diego. "The Soviet ambassador called on me today. Comrade Yanukovich delivered Secretary General Zhuravlev's assurances that the USSR has no hostile feelings toward the West Coast People's Democratic Republic. Comrade Zhuravlev himself told me the same thing at our recent meeting in Blythe."

"Talk is worth its weight in gold." That wasn't Charlie or Lucille. It was Nikita. The kid was starting to catch on to the way the world worked.

"Still, I was glad to have the ambassador's assurances, which I'm sure are completely reliable," Eichenlode went on. And if that wasn't another way to say *Talk is worth its weight in gold*, Charlie'd never heard one. After a pause that might have been for a sip of water, the Premier resumed: "I asked Comrade Yanukovich if the Soviet Union would be kind enough to use its good offices to help secure the release of our reporters who are being held in the Mexican SSR and the Canadian FSR.

"There, I'm sorry to say, things didn't go so well. The ambassador expressed a certain reluctance to interfere in the internal-security considerations of fraternal socialist states. He did seem confident things would work out for the best sooner or later. I asked him if he knew how long that would be, so I could pass the news on to the reporters' families. Unfortunately, he seemed unsure."

"I bet he did," Charlie said. By the way his son looked at him, he'd beaten the kid to the punch. Yeah, Nikita was learning.

"Still, hope dies last," Eichenlode said. "Day by day, our reforms take firmer root in fertile soil. Day by day, our society becomes more open and more free. Day by day, we move toward the perfect freedom of true Communism. And these positive developments will surely go forward whatever else may happen. Thank you, and good night."

"None of that sounds good," Lucille said.

"Boy, I wish I could tell you you were wrong," Charlie answered. "When they say something'll surely go on, you know it's in trouble. And the Russians don't tell you they don't feel hostile about you—"

"Tell you twice they don't feel hostile about you," Nikita broke in.

"Tell you twice, uh-huh. They don't do that to tell you they don't really feel hostile about you."

"The USSR is a long way away. How many soldiers can the Russians bring here?" Nikita said. "If they try anything, we should fight them."

"We don't have a big army ourselves," Charlie reminded him. "Nobody in North America has a big army. The Russians don't want anybody else to be dangerous to them, and they know how to get what they don't want." He had the feeling he was drowning in complicated negatives. Was that his own cast of mind or a hangover from listening to Eichenlode's somber speech? He couldn't tell.

Nikita said, "You know, if you fill a bottle with gasoline and put in a cloth wick, you can light it and throw it at a tank and it'll burn the tank up."

Fear filled Charlie. His son was so young, young enough to be brave and stupid at the same time. As calmly as he could, he said, "How close have you got to be to get to hit a tank with a firebomb like that?"

"I don't know. From the mound to the plate? Something like that. A tank's a lot bigger than home plate," Nikita answered.

"Okay. Say sixty feet," Charlie said. "How close does a tank have to be to hit you with its machine gun? Or with its cannon?"

"Uh—" Plainly, getting shot at himself hadn't occurred to his son.

"A bullet can hit you out to a quarter of a mile. Half a mile? I don't know. Somewhere in there, anyway. A cannon can shoot miles. Don't ask me how many—I don't know that, either. But I do know it can knock a house down on top of you, too. So don't go talking about gasoline in a bottle, huh?"

"Don't you *want* to fight for your country?" Nikita looked at him as if he were a black, rotten spot found too late deep inside an orange.

Charlie did want to fight for it. It was starting to turn into something worth fighting for. He'd fought against it in small ways before Eichenlode became Premier. But he said, "This isn't about getting sent to a rotten job, or even to a camp. This is about getting *killed*. Nobody starts over after that. Nobody gets a second chance."

"Your dad's right, Nikita." By the urgency in Lucille's voice, she realized what she was hearing, too. It scared her as much as Charlie.

"That wouldn't happen to me," Nikita said. *That couldn't happen to me*, he meant. He sounded so sure.

"Anything that can happen can happen to you. Don't give it a chance, okay? Not so real long ago, remember, you called me a right deviationist because I didn't tape up a silly poster. Now you want to take on the whole Red Army all by yourself?" Charlie said.

His son turned red. "I was dumb then. I hadn't seen how things ought to work."

Why do you think you have now? Charlie almost asked it out loud. At the last moment, he swallowed it. Not that it wasn't true—much more that Nikita wouldn't see it was true. Such a big part of being young was making mistake after mistake and bit by bit learning from them.

Your first mistake against a tank would be your last one. Ever. You wouldn't learn much after that.

"Let's keep hoping we're fussing about nothing," Lucille said. "Everything's fine now. It can keep right on being fine. Okay?"

"Yeah." Charlie nodded. He remembered not talking about, not even thinking about, the death he saw on his old man's face.

"Sure, Mom," Nikita said in the same tone of voice Charlie'd used a moment before him. He got up and hurried out of the living room.

Lucille stared at the radio as if she hated it. "Oh, *shit!*" she said, softly but with venom a rattlesnake would have envied.

"Uh-huh." Charlie felt very tired, tireder than he ever had coming home from that illicit construction job.

"What do we do now? What can we do now?" she asked.

"A day at a time, hon. An hour at a time. A minute at a time, for all I know. That's about it. That's what we've got right now." Charlie held up his right index finger. "Oh. One more thing."

"What's that?"

"Make darn sure Nikita isn't stashing bottles and cut-up old washrags under his bed or anything."

"You're pretty smart." Lucille paused. "What if he is?"

"Either we lock him up and don't let him out again or we … we pray he's as lucky as he thinks he is." Charlie didn't think he'd ever talked about praying before. It was nothing he took seriously. But when everything you did take seriously seemed useless, what could you lose?

People who lived in Los Angeles boasted that it could be in the eighties any month of the year. They were right, too. When it got up over 105 every day for a week in a row, though, it was summer and you were in the Valley. Charlie's flat had fans, but no air-conditioning. He soaked the sheets with sweat every night, as though he were breaking a fever.

The produce in his store suffered, too. He used fans and misters there, but he spent a lot of time each morning getting rid of fruits and vegetables that gave up the ghost.

While he worked, he listened to the radio. He had it on whenever he was awake these days, except when he rode the bus. As far as the radio was concerned, everything seemed fine. Before Alex Eichenlode, that wouldn't have meant a thing … and he wouldn't have cared what the announcers said. With Eichenlode running things, he didn't think they were lying to hear themselves lie.

He was chatting with a customer about how hot it was when the music coming out of the speaker stopped. A woman said, "We interrupt this program for the following special news bulletin."

Charlie and the customer looked at each other. "Oh, shit!" she exclaimed. "I bet they've gone and done it!"

That told Charlie everything he needed to know about where she stood. "I bet they have," he said sorrowfully.

"Large transport planes have unexpectedly landed at Glory to the Revolution International Airport outside Sacramento," the radio announcer said. "By their markings, they belong to the Red Air Force. Soldiers and tanks are coming off them and making for the center of town, where the Capitol and the Premier's residence are located. Some firing is reported. I will pass on more information as I have it."

She fell silent, but the music didn't come back: only the hiss of the carrier wave. Charlie put the cantaloupes the customer wanted into her stringbag and shoved it back across the counter at her. "Take 'em," he told her. "Money and ration coupons are the last things we've got to worry about now."

"Thank you, Comrade!" she said, and for once the dusty old word sounded as if it meant something. "I'd better head for home."

No sooner was she out the door than the announcer came back on. Soldiers and armor had landed at Portland, Spokane, and Los Angeles, too. More soldiers had crossed the WCPDR's borders from the south and from the north, and there were reports of naval landings outside Seattle, San Francisco, and San Diego. Charlie remembered the military exercises not long before. Here they were again, only this time it wasn't an exercise. The USSR meant it.

"Troops from the so-called fraternal socialist republics of North America are reported to be part of the Soviet-led invasion force," the woman broadcaster said. Charlie savored that *so-called*, as he did her next remark: "Some of them, unlike the Russians, may possibly speak English."

"You tell 'em!" he said. It wouldn't make any difference, but it did make him feel better.

"I can hear tanks outside this building," she said. "I don't know how long you'll be able to keep listening to me. I'll stay on the air as long as I'm able to. There is word that fierce fighting is going on in and around Spokane. I'll tell you more as news comes in."

Spokane, Charlie remembered, was Alex Eichenlode's home town. That it stood up for him made Charlie feel better, and also probably wouldn't matter a nickel's worth in the grand scheme of things.

"Comrades, your attention, please!" the woman said a couple of minutes later. "I've just been handed a statement from Premier Eichenlode. Here it is: 'To the People's Democratic Self-Defense Forces and to the citizens of the West Coast People's Democratic Republic, this is Alex Eichenlode, your commander and Premier. I call on all of you not to fight back against the soldiers now forcing their way into our country. They have entered in overwhelming force. Any resistance is hopeless, and will only bring death and destruction. As long as I'm still free, I will do everything in my power to persuade Yuri Zhuravlev that he's made a mistake and should withdraw his troops immediately. Don't expose yourselves to danger. I'll do whatever I can to set things right.'"

Somewhere in Los Angeles, Russian soldiers—and maybe men from the Rocky Mountain People's Republic and the Southeastern Confederated People's Republic with them—were telling local leaders what to do. No sign of them on Sherman Way. The Valley always seemed a bit removed from the rest of the city. The invasion hadn't happened yet, not here.

As if to prove as much, a woman walked in and asked Charlie, "You have any more of those nice oranges and snow peas?"

He waved toward the bins. "Take whatever you want, Comrade Phillips. Help yourself. On the house."

She gaped at him. "You're joking, right?"

"Not even a little bit. Who cares about money right now, when the Russians have invaded?"

"When the Russians have what?"

"Invaded. You know, marched in. They've got soldiers from our neighbors with 'em, too—on leashes, I bet, like any other sons of bitches."

"Comrade, you've gone out of your mind." The woman turned around and made for the door without either snow peas or oranges.

"I wish I had," he answered, but he was talking to her back. She hurried away, as if afraid whatever madness he had were contagious.

You know what? It is, he thought. *Freedom was spreading all over the country. People liked catching it, too.* He knew that wasn't all true. People like Mary Ann Hannegan and Horton Wilder had hated what was going on. Freedom scared them to death. "It should have, too," Charlie said out loud. "They didn't know what to do with it."

General Secretary Zhuravlev did, though. He knew he had to stamp it out before it spread any more. And the bastard was strong enough to do just that.

Charlie wondered whether Comrade Hannegan would show up to rub his nose in it. In a way, he was surprised and a little miffed she hadn't done that as soon as she heard the news. But then he realized he was only a little fish to her. She'd have bigger ones to fry first. Nelson Yang, for instance. Charlie hoped the area leader would be all right.

After an hour or so, the radio newswoman said, "I've just heard that Premier Eichenlode is in the custody of the invading forces. He did not try to escape. He said, 'If they want me so much, they can have me.' There are also Soviet soldiers, and a few from North America, inside this building. They haven't been ordered to shut us down—yet. As I told you before, we'll go on as long as we can."

Customers came in every so often. Almost all the ones who'd heard about the invasion were hopping mad. The ones who hadn't got angry as soon as they found out. "They can't do that!" a woman said. "What happens in our country is nobody's business but ours!"

"What happens in our country is nobody's business but ours. They can do that anyway, though. That's why they've got all those ships and planes and tanks and guns—so they can do that anyway," Charlie said.

"Well, to hell with 'em," she said.

"Yeah." Charlie didn't charge her or anybody else for what they wanted. He didn't worry about ration coupons, either. If they emptied the store, he figured he'd close up and go home. He didn't want to work for the Russians or whoever they plugged into the Premier's slot in Sacramento.

The woman on the radio said, "Unofficial sources are urging a nationwide general strike against the invaders. The sooner they see how unwelcome they are in the West Coast People's Democratic Republic, the sooner they'll go away."

A moment later, a loud thuttering rumble overhead announced a helicopter. They weren't common in the WCPDR; Charlie would have bet this one wore red stars on its flanks. The Russians might not have entered the Valley yet, but they were looking it over—and warning it, too.

That call for a general strike must have been too much for the invaders in Sacramento. "I am being taken out of the studio," the broadcaster said. "Good-bye and good luck!" The station stayed on the air, but only static showed it was there.

A few minutes later, a new voice, a man's, came from the speaker: "Good day, my peace-loving comrades in the West Coast People's Democratic Republic! My name is Lavrenti Bragg. I'm from the Southeastern Confederated People's Republic, and I'm proud to be a part of the force liberating your country from the grasp of the right deviationist faction that's illegally grabbed power here. Obey orders from the army of liberation and everything'll go just fine for y'all. We'll get the place running the way a proper socialist state ought to again, and then we'll go home. I know you're as sick of the capitalist corruption here as we are, and that you'll be proud to help us stamp it out."

"I don't know what he's drinking, but I sure wish I had some. Gotta be strong stuff," Charlie said.

A woman who was filling her stringbag with broccoli and Brussels sprouts nodded. "He's out of his gourd if he thinks we want this," she said, and circled her finger by her ear to show how far out of his gourd he was.

"He probably does. People from outside don't understand what's going on here, or they'd let us keep doing it. I bet a whole bunch of soldiers are wondering how come everybody's cussing at them," Charlie said.

"When they show up here, I sure will," the customer said.

"You won't be the only one," Charlie replied. But he couldn't help looking at the light fixtures and the corners where the walls met the ceiling: good places for planting bugs. Lately, he'd got used to saying whatever he wanted. He hated watching himself again, but knew he'd have to. *Gotta remind Lucille and the kids, too*, he thought. Nikita, especially, came out with inflammatory talk—literally, sometimes.

The woman headed for the door. Before she left, she said, "Well, it was fun while it lasted."

"It sure was," Charlie agreed. Mary Ann Hannegan had seen this coming. He hated her for being right.

On the radio, Lavrenti Bragg was saying, "Word is coming in that terrorist elements in the West Coast People's Democratic Republic are attacking liberating forces with rocks and bricks and bottles, and that some have even tried to destroy our vehicles with firebombs and explosives. This has to stop *right now*. Even your own deviationist Premier understands that resistance is futile. Terrorists and bandits will be met with all the force at our disposal. If necessary, hostages will be taken. A word to the wise had better be plenty."

He repeated that warning several times over the next couple of hours. As Charlie'd learned from raising two kids, a warning you had to keep repeating was a warning nobody was listening to. He wondered whether the people who were trying to fight back were hurting the invaders or just pissing them off. What he wished and what he thought were two very different things.

He was getting ready to close up—and the store was almost bare—when a woman came in and said, "I heard they burned up a couple tanks in the Sepulveda Pass and blocked the road up from the airport."

"Good!" Charlie said savagely.

He didn't see any invaders on the bus ride north. Whether that was because of a corked road through the pass or not, he couldn't have said. He did see more cops on the street than usual. The cops were meaner than usual, too. From his window, he watched one use a billy club on a man who might have said something but sure hadn't done anything. The man staggered away, blood running down his face. Other people screamed at the cop. He pointed his pistol at them. They scattered and ran.

Jesus, that didn't take long, Charlie thought. Cops became cops not least because they enjoyed telling ordinary people what to do and pushing them around. Now the ones here had an excuse for doing just that. They had it, and they were using it.

As soon as Charlie walked into the apartment, Lucille said, "I knew it was too good to be true."

"A lot of things are." As Charlie spoke, he pointed to the spots where microphones might be hidden. Lucille needed only a moment to catch on. She nodded and held a finger in front of her mouth. Charlie wrote a note: *Tell the kids*. His wife nodded again. While she went in to talk with Sally and Nikita, he burned the note. He hadn't had to play that game for a bit, but the rules were graven on his soul.

During dinner, Nikita looked as if he wanted to explode. He didn't talk about anything that mattered, though. Charlie sent him a thumbs-up and a nod as Sally carried dirty dishes to the sink. Nikita's answering nod was as sober as the ones Lenin must have exchanged with other Bolsheviks in Petrograd (it wasn't Leningrad yet, of course): a conspirator's nod, or a revolutionary's.

"I'm going to take a walk," Charlie said once he'd stubbed out his after-dinner cigarette.

"Where to?" Sally asked.

"Around the block," he answered. Once more, the less he said, the safer he was.

He had no idea whether Nelson Yang would be home, or whether the Party functionary would have time for him if he was. But someone else was just leaving Yang's flat when Charlie walked up to it. He didn't even have to tap on the door; he just stuck his head in.

"Ah, Comrade Simpkins!" Yang said with a strained smile. "I wondered if I'd see you tonight."

"Yeah, well—" Charlie shrugged. "Have you got a minute?"

"Maybe even two. Shall we step outside? It'll be a little cooler."

Even he didn't have an air-conditioner in his apartment. Charlie would have bet Mary Ann Hannegan did. He let Yang lead him downstairs again and out onto the sidewalk. "Can we talk here?" Charlie asked.

"If we can talk anywhere," Nelson Yang answered. "I didn't want to think it would come to this. I didn't want to think Moscow would be so stupid—and so brutal."

"What can you do about it? What can *we* do about it?"

"Not much," Yang said bleakly. "Gum up the works wherever we're able to. Cooperate as little as possible. Make things hard for the bastards without being too obvious about it. I don't know what else we can do unless we want to get a bunch of people killed. Zhuravlev isn't playing."

"Yeah, I know." Charlie told him about the cop who'd beaten the man on De Soto.

Yang made a horrible face. "I've already heard too many stories like that, dammit. The police and the NBI are celebrating like it's May Day."

A police car rolled along the street. A cop aimed a bullhorn at Charlie and Nelson Yang. "Go back inside!" he roared. "Don't you dumb assholes know there's a dawn-to-dusk curfew? Go inside or you'll be sorry!"

They almost stumbled over each other hurrying into the lobby of Yang's building. The police car went on. Half a block farther along, the cop shouted at somebody else.

"I'm sorry about that," Yang said with admirable sangfroid, and then, a moment later, "How will you get home?"

"I'll sneak—how else? If they stop me, I'll tell 'em I'm a block leader who was getting the Party line from my area leader. That'll make 'em leave me alone." Charlie also paused briefly before adding, "Unless our names're already on their shit list, I mean."

"They probably are." Nelson Yang sighed and looked ten years older. "*So* stupid," he muttered.

"Yeah." Charlie peered out. The cop car had turned a corner and disappeared. "See ya." Charlie shook Yang's hand, then headed back to his own block of flats. He clung to darkness as much as he could. Since quite a few street lights were out, that was easier than it might have been. Once he found his hand going to his breast pocket for a cigarette, but he made it fall. Lighting a match when you were trying not to be noticed wasn't the smartest thing you could do.

When he came in, Lucille said, "I'm glad you're back! They've declared a curfew."

"I found that out. But I'm here," he said.

"Did you see anybody while you were, um, out walking?" she asked.

"Yeah. A friend," Charlie answered.

His wife had no trouble working out who that was. "What did he have to say?"

Charlie sighed. "He figures the best we can do is make things tough for the Russians—we don't have a chance of making 'em go away. And he's gotta have worries of his own. He's a Party man, and he picked the wrong side. They're bound to make him pay for that."

"You picked the wrong side, too," Lucille pointed out.

"I sure did," Charlie said, more proudly than not. "But I don't belong to the CPWCPDR the way he does. I'm just an ordinary jerk."

"You're my ordinary jerk," Lucille told him.

He hugged her. "Thanks, babe. Thanks especially now. It's been a godawful day, or whatever's worse than that."

"Whatever's worse than that, is right." She hesitated, then asked, "Are you going down to the store tomorrow, with the general strike called and everything?"

"Not me. I'll stay out a while—don't know how long. I'll have to see, is all. We can't let 'em just think they can get away with this crap." Charlie knew they thought exactly that. He also knew they were much too likely to be right, no matter how the West Coast People's Democratic Republic twisted in the USSR's grasp.

He did walk down to the corner of Gresham and De Soto the next morning, not to catch the bus but to buy the papers. The *Times* and *The Daily Worker* might have been written on different planets. *The Worker's* headline was COUNTRY FREED FROM DEVIATIONISTS! The story underneath toed the Soviet Party line. By contrast, the *Times* said RUSSIAN INVASION! and showed a photo of a tank on fire in the Sepulveda Pass. Yuri Zhuravlev's censors hadn't shown up there yet. Charlie knew they would.

When he turned to go home, he noticed that somebody'd spun the street sign ninety degrees, so *Gresham* pointed down De Soto and *De Soto* along Gresham. Peering across the street, he saw the sign on the other side was wrong, too. A slow smile stretched across his face. That would confuse the hell out of anybody who didn't know the neighborhood—a driver from the Northeastern Soviet Socialist Republic, say.

He found himself whistling as he ambled along what the screwed-up street sign called De Soto. The people here who still liked Alex Eichenlode couldn't win, but they might have some fun while they were losing.

chapter

Officials—some with Southeastern drawls, others with Russian accents—kept telling people to go back to work because the liberators were making sure everything was back to normal. They kept seeming surprised when nobody listened to them. When they told their people to do something, something got done. It wasn't working that way in the WCPDR.

Saturday, Charlie did get on the bus, not to open the produce store but because he wanted to check a couple of places. Walls and fences had sprouted a bumper crop of graffiti since the invasion. RUSSIANS GO HOME! and RUSSIANS OUT! were everywhere, a little more common than obscene embellishments on the same theme.

Also everywhere were smiles that were sometimes little more than quick paint splashes. Others showed dots for eyes and a nose above the smiling mouth. And still others sported MLS in place of the dots. The first one of those Charlie spotted puzzled him. When he saw the second one, he laughed out loud. There it was, Marxism-Leninism-Stalinism with a smiling face, thrown in the Soviet Union's face.

He got off at Victory (he knew that, even if the street signs at that corner had all disappeared) and walked south to the entrance into the agricultural college's collective farm. The tarps covering the chain-link fence bore their share of RUSSIANS GO HOME! and MLS–smile scrawls and then some.

"Hey, Mike," he said, recognizing the fellow sitting in the guard shack. "How's it going?"

"It's fucked, man. How d'you think it's going?" the bruiser answered sourly.

"Can I talk with Friedrich?"

Mike shook his head. "We aren't letting anybody in. We aren't selling produce to outsiders any more, either. We got orders about that. Worth our asses if we buck 'em."

"I didn't want to talk with him about that," Charlie said.

"Even so." The guard seemed as bendable as a boulder. Charlie gave up and went back to the corner.

He caught the next southbound bus (which had a big smile painted on its side) and rode it down to Ventura Boulevard. Someone had splashed white paint all over the street signs at the corner of Ventura and De Soto. Charlie smiled again crossing the street to get the eastbound bus that would take him to the Valley Relic. The placard above the bus's front window didn't say which route it was. Even the drivers, though driving, were making trouble.

The bus rattled along for a couple of blocks, then pulled to the curb at a spot that wasn't a regular stop. "I think you better get out here, Comrades," the driver said. "Something's going on up ahead, and I don't wanna get stuck in it." The front door hissed open. Charlie was sitting near the back. The rear door should have opened, too, but hadn't. It had a handle screwed to the inside. Charlie yanked on it and made his escape.

He walked toward the trouble, not away from it, the way he would have before he threw out the propaganda poster. *Damned if I haven't changed*, he thought with wonder. *I even started before the country did.* He kicked at the grimy concrete under his feet. *Fat lot of good it did me, too.*

People filled not just the sidewalk but the street ahead. They were blocking six or eight tanks from coming any farther west—Charlie could see turret tops and cannons above their heads. And they were shaking their fists and shouting at the soldiers inside the tanks.

All but the lead tank had red stars on their turrets. They belonged to the Red Army, so their crews weren't likely to know English. But the machine in front sported as its emblem a red flag with a blue St. Andrew's cross, a black crossed sledgehammer and sickle in the center. It came from the Southeastern Confederated People's Republic, then. That made some sense: the tankmen could talk with the locals and understand the answers they got.

They might understand them, but Charlie didn't think they liked them. The lead tank's commander rode head and shoulders out of the cupola on the turret, so he could see where the tank was going and so he could talk with the crowd keeping it from going anywhere. "We've come to liberate your country," he called. "Y'all clear the way and let us get on with it, hey?"

"Who invited you?" people shouted back, and, "Go home" and, "Go to hell!" and, "You shitheads suck Russia's dick!"

The tank commander tried again: "Your boss man, he ain't no proper Marxist-Leninist-Stalinist. He's a right deviationist, is what he is."

"Fuck Marx! And Lenin! And Stalin—twice!" a woman screeched at him. He looked shocked. Not being religious himself, Charlie didn't know what an orthodox believer hearing heresy shouted in his face looked like. But that was the expression the tank commander wore.

"You— You can't talk that way!" he stammered.

"Like hell we can't! No censorship here!" the woman said. "We don't have to watch our mouths the way you do in the shitty place you come from. We don't hang black folks for the fun of it, neither." She was black herself, or at least dark brown. Charlie doubted whether the tank commander cared for that.

"Marx and Lenin and Stalin were great geniuses," he said.

"They stuck it up little boys' assholes," the woman retorted.

Before the man from the SECPR could get properly offended at that, somebody threw a rotten orange at him. It hit him in the shoulder and splashed his face. Cursing, he wiped his eyes with the butternut sleeve of his coverall.

Since the people who'd got there ahead of Charlie were keeping that tank busy, he pushed on to the next one. The Russian in charge of it was also looking out of his cupola. He had a broad Slavic face and pale eyes almost as cold as Mary Ann Hannegan's.

A few bits of Russian Charlie hadn't learned in class still lingered in his memory. "*Yob tvoyu mat', blyad!*" he yelled gleefully. "*Pizda! Khuy!*"

Only a moment later did he notice that the Russian was holding a submachine gun with a fat drum magazine. The fellow could fill him full of more holes than a colander had in less time than it took to tell. Had he seen it before, he might not have shouted *Fuck your mother, whore!* He might not have called the tank commander a cunt or a dick, either.

This isn't a game. This is real. He'd told that to Nikita. Maybe he should have told himself, too.

The tank commander's hands twitched, but he didn't quite point the machine pistol at Charlie. He might have had orders to be nice to the locals. He also might have needed a moment to remember them.

Charlie went on his way. He looked back at the Russian two or three times. Each time, his gaze met that icy one. He kept going, glad he could keep going.

He'd just reached the end of the tank column when somebody ran up and smashed a wine or whiskey bottle with a blazing wick on the rearmost machine's engine decking. Flames dripped down through the screening over the fans and into the engine compartment. The young man—older than Charlie's son, but not much—whooped and ran like hell.

That seemed like such a good idea, Charlie ducked off Ventura Boulevard and made his way east down an alley behind the businesses on the street. A minute or two later, machine guns chattered and people shrieked. A bullet slammed through a shop and spanged off the brickwork on the other side of the alley no more than ten feet in front of Charlie. He shivered. If he'd smoked less, if his wind were better, if he'd gone a little faster, if he'd gone a little farther …

No, it wasn't a game. And, when somebody tried to wreck one of their tanks, the Russians started playing for keeps. He didn't suppose he could blame them for that. For invading his country to begin with? A different story.

He walked into the Valley Relic all sweaty and panting. The tavern was open, general strike or no general strike. He'd been sure it would be. When did people not need to drink?

"Let me have an Eastside," he told the bartender—he wanted something long and cold.

"Here you go." The man in the black bow tie drew it. As Charlie paid, the barman added, "You know what was going on fifteen, twenty minutes ago when all hell broke loose?"

"Yeah." Charlie told him.

"Jesus!" the man said, and then, "They aren't just farting around, are they?"

"Not hardly. You don't run tanks down the main drag to give somebody a big kiss with 'em." Charlie wished he'd thought of that before he trotted out his bits of remembered Russian obscenity.

Then he spotted Ervin at a corner table. He waved. The old man waved back and lifted his own beer in invitation. Charlie made his way over. As he sat down, Ervin said, "Looks like we scared 'em even worse'n I thought we did, huh?"

"Why in the world would you say that?" Charlie asked.

Ervin laughed and coughed and laughed some more. "I was hoping for two steps forward, one step back. Now we've got one step forward, ten steps back."

"A hundred. A thousand," Charlie said.

"Feels that way, don't it?" Ervin shook his head. "Yeah, we scared the piss out of 'em, all right. Zhuravlev must not've believed Eichenlode'd go through with all the stuff he said he was gonna do."

"What could be worse than keeping your promises?" Charlie didn't try to hide his bitterness.

"Nobody's tried goin' this way not just in a month o' Sundays but in a year o' Sundays," Ervin said. "Really giving workers' councils the power to decide what their outfits're gonna do? Listening to what the ordinary sons of bitches want, what they need, not just the nomenklatura? Anybody'd think this was turning into a people's democratic republic or something."

"Or something, is right," Charlie said. "Now they sit on us for the next fifty years."

"I bet they don't," Ervin said. Charlie looked at him in surprise. The old man explained: "We cost the Russians money, probably a ton o' money. Invasions don't come cheap, you know, and this is a big one, and halfway around the world for them. Soldiers, planes, ships, who can say what all? So they'll find a stooge and put him in Sacramento so he can sit on us for 'em, do the dirty work so they don't got to."

That made a certain kind of horrible sense to Charlie. People like Mary Ann Hannegan, Emmett Muldberg, and Horton Wilder sprang to mind. So did ... . "You think they'll bring Tony Newman back?"

"They may, but I figure Zhuravlev thinks he's damaged goods. Zhuravlev damn well ought to—he did the damaging," Ervin answered.

"Plenty of other clowns around who can do whatever the Soviet ambassador tells 'em to and enjoy it while they're doing it."

"You make good sense. You really understand how all that shit works," Charlie said.

"Don't remind me. If that was all it took, I mighta been a big wheel in Sacramento myself." Ervin shuddered at the idea. "I never could stand the idea of crapping on other people to get ahead, though. So here I am—a shlemiel with a big mouth, showin' off how smart he is in a fucking class-four tavern. See? I'm a success!" He laughed, for all the world as if it were funny.

"Me, I came at it from the other way," Charlie said slowly. "I got sick of Sacramento—and Moscow, even if I didn't think much about Moscow then—crapping on *me*."

"You're more dangerous to 'em than I am. All I do is talk. Guys like you, they find ways to hit back," Ervin said.

"So did that fellow who firebombed the Russian tank. Then the others cut loose and chewed up who knows how many people," Charlie said. "The WCPDR is so big, it took all this time before anybody tried to change anything. And the Russians are so big, they stepped on that like me stepping on a Progress."

"You try, is all. You tried. I tried. Eichenlode tried. It didn't work. Sooner or later, somebody somewhere else'll give it another shot. With luck, that one'll go better." The hope seemed to console Ervin. Charlie … still felt crapped on.

Lavrenti Bragg did a lot of talking on the radio. Like anybody else with two brain cells to rub together, Charlie knew the man from the Southeastern Confederated People's Republic did a lot of lying. He listened to him anyway. Every so often, bits of truth sneaked in.

"Comrade Eichenlode is going to fly to Moscow to talk with General Secretary Zhuravlev," Bragg said one evening about ten days after the invasion. "Gus Goslin, the WCPDR Commissar for Economic Advancement, will come along with him to discuss outstanding financial arrangements."

Nikita had no trouble seeing what that meant. "They're gonna make us pay for the invasion!"

"About the size of it," Charlie agreed. He noticed something else about how Bragg told the story. Yuri Zhuravlev had his proper title. So did this Goslin fellow, whoever he was. But Lavrenti Bragg just called Eichenlode *Comrade*, not *Premier*. *Comrade* was the handle for a secretary or a plumber, not somebody who ran a country. Or who had run a country, anyhow.

"The Russians'll tell him what he has to do, and they'll stick a gun to his head to make sure he does it," Lucille said. That was also about the size of it.

"I still don't have a poster in my window," Charlie said. The produce store was open again; the general strike had fizzled out as people got hungry and as the invaders warned them about Article 203. He told himself not pandering to propaganda meant he was still fighting. No matter how often he told himself, he didn't really believe it.

His son said, "You stood up against the way the government oppressed us even before Alex Eichenlode was Premier."

Nikita sounded proud of his old man. That was nice. He was probably doing his best to forget how mad at Charlie he'd been back then. Charlie didn't call him on it. He didn't see the point. Instead, he changed the subject: "Did you hear about the ballgame last night?"

"I sure did!" Nikita's face lit up.

To show there were no hard feelings, the Pittsburgh Proletarians had come out to San Francisco for an exhibition game against the Seals. Only there were hard feelings. It turned into a beanball war, with two benches-clearing brawls. The Seals won, 7-3.

"I just wish the Russians played baseball. If they came themselves instead of sending their puppets ... ." Charlie said.

"Ooh!" By Nikita's grin, he liked that idea.

Three days later, Premier Eichenlode came home from Moscow. The Soviet government put out a statement about the meeting. Eichenlode and Gus Goslin had signed for the WCPDR, along with the Foreign Commissars of the other fraternal socialist republics of North America and the USSR. "This is not the agreement I would have wanted," Eichenlode said on the radio, "but my talks with the Soviet General Secretary made it more reasonable than the first draft I saw."

The Daily Worker printed the whole text, because that was the kind of thing *The Worker* did, especially now. Charlie waded through the

Marxist-Leninist-Stalinist phraseology on the bus. The document talked a lot about suppressing counterrevolutionary tendencies, consolidating and defending socialism, normalizing the situation, and gradually sending the invaders home once the threat to socialism in the WCPDR had passed.

It also pledged that the invasion force wouldn't interfere in the WCPDR's internal affairs. Charlie thought that was pretty funny, all the more so as he read it half a minute before the bus stopped at an identity-control checkpoint near the bank. It was sandbagged, and sprouted machine guns like dandelions.

He showed a Soviet captain his ID card, wondering if his name was on a list. The Russian officer only looked it over and gave it back. He and his bully boys did haul a woman off the bus, though. "I didn't do nothin'!" she said. The Soviet soldiers or security men had submachine guns. They looked ready to use them. Nobody on the bus tried to rescue the woman. Charlie never found out what happened to her.

He opened up the produce store, wondering why he bothered. These days, he was back to getting the usual junk from the warehouse. It was as if the authorities had decided to remind ordinary people they didn't deserve anything better. For all he knew, they'd done exactly that. The potatoes with lots of big eyes and limp carrots sure argued for it.

"You haven't got anything decent?" a woman asked, shaking her head at the sad display.

"If I did, don't you think I'd put it out?" Charlie said.

"You? Yeah, you would. Some of these shitheads, they don't give a damn one way or the other," she said. At least she'd noticed he did.

Half an hour later, Mary Ann Hannegan walked in. Charlie eyed her without warmth. "I knew trouble always came in threes. First the garbage they made Eichenlode sign, then the garbage they gave me"—he waved at his sorry shelves and bins—"and now you."

"This is what you bought, Comrade, you and your precious Premier," she answered. "You don't like it now that the whole price has come due? I told you this would happen, remember."

Charlie did remember. He didn't want to, but he did. "So much for fraternal socialist states."

"The West Coast People's Democratic Republic wasn't one any more. That was the problem, and the Soviet Union had to fix it. They did," she said.

"Oh, cut the nonsense, will you please? We weren't going to pull out of our alliances. Eichenlode isn't nuts," Charlie said. "He was just trying to get out from under all the stupid nonsense that weighs everything down."

"He was moving against the Communist Party's continued leadership role in the state." Mary Ann Hannegan couldn't have sounded more disgusted if she'd said Eichenlode ate babies for breakfast—and raw babies at that.

"So what?" Charlie said. "If the Party's so wonderful and perfect, how come you don't think it could win an honest election?"

Her eyes widened—not in horror this time, Charlie judged, but in surprise. Hadn't she ever asked herself anything like that before? Charlie was damned if he thought she had. "Because of the lies and mystifications reactionary forces spew when given the license to say whatever they want," she answered after a moment's thought.

"Oh, you mean like the ones they tell in the Southeastern Confederated People's Republic that make it okay for white folks to lynch black folks?" Charlie took sour pleasure in throwing the SECPR's full name in her face.

She glared at him. "I never said we were perfect. But we are moving toward true Communism, and that's as close to perfection as we'll ever see."

"Not moving towards it very fast. Anybody'd think the people who run things like telling everybody else what to do or something. Anybody'd think they like it more than moving toward true Communism."

"People have gone to corrective-labor camps for saying things like that. People have got a bullet in the back of the neck for saying them." Mary Ann Hannegan spoke in a soft, deadly voice. She didn't even call the bullet a noodle, the way almost everybody did.

"Are camps on the road to true Communism? Once it does get here, will there still be camps?" Charlie jeered.

Still grimly serious, she answered, "Comrade, there will always be camps. Keep talking and you'll learn all about them."

Not so long ago, the thought of getting ten or twenty-five would have kept him in line. To his surprise, he hardly cared now. When something seemed inevitable, what point to letting it scare you? "I'm just tired," he said. "If you wanna buy some vegetables, buy 'em. If you don't, get the hell out of here."

"You're on the list," she said.

No, I'm not. Not yet, anyhow, he thought. He didn't say it. He knew better; if he wasn't on the list now, she could land him there. But if he had been, the identity check would have nabbed him. He just stood there and waited.

She shook her head in what he thought was bewilderment. She wasn't used to people who wouldn't show fear. Still shaking it, she turned her back and walked out of the produce store.

Charlie lit a Progress and let it do what it could to calm him. He might not show fear, but he sure as hell felt it. He never smoked his expensive black-market cigarettes in the store. They smelled so much better, anyone who came in was bound to notice. He wasn't Mary Ann Hannegan, who used her Marlboros to show off the privilege she enjoyed in a society that called itself classless.

He wondered what the Russians would end up doing with, doing to, Alex Eichenlode. They couldn't keep him as Premier very long. Charlie was sure Ervin had that right. They wouldn't trust him to stay a reliable puppet.

Would they appoint him ambassador to the Lao People's Democratic Republic or some other insignificant fraternal socialist republic far, far away? Or would he end up something like a second assistant salmon-fisheries supervisor in Eureka, internally exiled and always watched? Charlie had trouble deciding which was worse.

Then something new and different happened: three Russian soldiers came in. One of them was smoking a cigarette that smelled even worse than a Progress. He and one of his friends had slung their rifles on their backs. The third man carried his, in case of trouble.

That kind of trouble, Charlie didn't want. He dredged up a phrase from his long-ago language class: "*Dobry den, Tovarishchi.*"

"*Dobry den!*" said the guy who was smoking. He and his pals grinned; Charlie'd hit the right note. In Russian, the soldier went on, "You speak Russian?" Charlie held his thumb and forefinger a quarter-inch apart to show he didn't speak much. The Red Army men laughed.

They all went over to the oranges. Those were nothing much, not to Charlie, but they seemed to entrance the Russians. Each chose two. They set them on the counter. "How much?" asked the fellow who did the talking for them. He was a corporal, so he outranked his buddies.

"One dollar." Charlie tried to keep it as simple as he could.

They didn't have any WCPDR money, though. He was about to say they could have the oranges for nothing when the corporal dug a crumpled five-ruble note from a pocket and solemnly handed it to Charlie. He unfolded it. A bust of Lenin stared up at him. He wanted to tell the Russian he couldn't make change, but had no idea how.

The Red Army man didn't care, either. "*Bolshoye spasibo*," he said, and motioned to his friends. They all headed for the door.

"*Pozhalusta*," Charlie said faintly. The corporal waved without turning back. Out onto Sherman Way he and the other two soldiers went.

Charlie felt he should have thanked them, not the other way around. Five Soviet rubles were something like seventy-five WCPDR dollars, which might have made those the most expensive oranges ever. But it had to work the same way in the USSR as it did here. When you saw something you wanted, you grabbed it and didn't worry about the cost, because ten minutes later it wouldn't be there.

He laughed a shaky laugh. The Russians might have banned the few faint buds of capitalism Alex Eichenlode had allowed, but they'd just given him a mighty fat profit.

One problem with a Soviet banknote: unless you belonged to the Red Army, you couldn't casually stroll into a hardware store and buy something with it. You had to turn it into local loot. On Saturday afternoon, then, Charlie got off the bus at Saticoy and headed for the WCPDR Bank.

Two armored personnel carriers squatted in the parking lot not far from the entrance, but he didn't worry about that till a soldier stepped out of the building and asked, "Watcha want, buddy?"

He spoke English, not Russian. Charlie noticed then that the two APCs had the flag of the Southeastern Confederated People's Republic on their flanks rather than the USSR's red stars. He took the five-ruble note out of his wallet and showed it to the sentry or whatever he was. "I got this from some Red Army men who came into my store. I want to change it into dollars."

That Cyrillic writing seemed to impress the trooper from the SECPR. "All right," he said, and stood aside. "I reckon you can go on in."

"Thanks." Charlie did.

He figured it would be business as usual in there. It wasn't. The bank was full of SECPR soldiers—mostly officers, by their uniforms.

The handful of tellers and managers inside wore expressions either worried, frightened, or both. Maybe what was going on was supposed to be an investigation, but to Charlie it looked as much like a bank robbery as the one the yeggs had pulled off here not that long before. The vault stood open, for instance, and men with those butternut SECPR uniforms kept going in and out.

Charlie stood a few feet inside the entrance, waiting to be noticed. It took a while; the soldiers from the Southeastern Confederated People's Republic seemed intent on whatever they were doing. After a couple of minutes, a skinny young man with hair as red as a new penny walked up to him and growled, "Who the hell are you, and why the hell did Caleb let you in here?"

He'd given Charlie long enough to get over his jitters and to figure out how to play this. As he had with the sentry—Caleb?—he displayed the five-ruble Soviet note. "I came here because I need to get this changed," he said, as if he dealt in money from the USSR every day.

"Oh." The young SECPR officer came down a peg right away. The fancy Cyrillic printing and Lenin's grim, chin-bearded profile worked on him the same way as they had on the ordinary soldier. He didn't know how important Charlie was or what he could get away with. Since he didn't, he did what any sensible fellow would do. He passed the buck, or rather, the rubles. "You'd better talk to Major Douthit or Lieutenant Colonel Watkins." He pointed back toward the vault to show Charlie where to find them.

"Thanks, sonny." Charlie headed that way as the junior officer stiffened. The redhead only stiffened, though. He had to figure nobody who didn't have the right to talk to him that way would have the nerve to try it. Since Charlie'd started being a deviationist, he'd found himself surprised again and again at how far gall would take him.

Two older SECPR officers sat at a card table they'd set up inside the vault. One was bald and jowly, with two stars on each collar tab. The other, a few years younger, had straw-colored hair and a wispy mustache, and only one star on each tab.

They were both laughing like loons when Charlie stepped in. A nearly empty bottle of bourbon on the card table helped explain that. So did the stack of open safe-deposit boxes with it. The officers had two big rings of keys they must have taken from the bank officials. More open boxes and papers from them lay all over the floor.

It wasn't any kind of investigation—it *was* a robbery. They cared nothing for papers of any kind. Each of them, though, had an untidy pile of gold coins, fancy pocket watches, jewelry, and other valuables in front of him. Charlie doubted stealing the loot was in their orders. He also doubted whether any SECPR or Soviet higher-ups would care, except possibly to redistribute the wealth so they got some.

After tossing aside an empty safe-deposit box with a clang, the bald man noticed Charlie. "What d'*you* want?" he said. His tone added, *You'd better make it good.*

Charlie set the banknote from the Soviet Union on the table. "I need to turn this into WCPDR dollars," he answered. "The kid with the carrot top sent me back here—he said you'd take care of it." He did his best to seem altogether matter-of-fact, as if he dealt with invaders inside a bank vault all the time.

He didn't think his acting would win him a Bulganin Prize. But he didn't have a critical audience, and that five-ruble note made Watkins and Douthit sit up and take as much notice as their sozzled state allowed. "What's it worth in your money?" the blond major asked.

"About seventy-five bucks," Charlie answered truthfully. He would have lied had he thought he could get away with it, but he didn't care to take the chance here.

Major Douthit nodded. "About a hundred in ours," he said, which made Watkins nod, too. To his superior, Douthit went on, "What do you want to do, sir?"

"Let's give him something to remember us by," the bald lieutenant colonel said. That alarmed Charlie. But then Watkins reached into his pile. He tossed Charlie a goldpiece about the size of a half-dollar. Automatically, Charlie caught it out of the air. Watkins gestured to Douthit's takings. "Give him one o' those fat fifties, Taylor. We'll make it up next juicy box we open."

"I'll do it." Douthit tossed another gold coin to Charlie, who caught this one, too. It was even bigger and heavier than the first, and eight-sided rather than round. He stuck them both in his pocket.

"Since you're getting it in gold, you won't fuss about still being five dollars short, right?" By the way Lieutenant Colonel Watkins said it, bad things would happen if Charlie fussed.

But he didn't intend to. "I guess it'll be okay," he said, his voice as casual as he could make it.

"You're a smart boy, Comrade," Watkins said. "Now get outa here, smart boy. We gotta finish liberating this place." He and Douthit laughed some more. Douthit reached for the whiskey bottle. He was drinking from it as Charlie left.

The redheaded officer scowled as he walked to the door. If the light colonel and the major had let him go, though, what could a lowly lieutenant or whatever he was do about it? Caleb the sentry even held the door open for Charlie as he came up to it. "Thanks," he said grandly.

Out in the almost empty parking lot, with nobody close by to see what he was doing, he took out the coins for a longer look. The round one was a twenty-dollar goldpiece from the Confederate States of America, the name the southeastern part of North America had carried before the Revolutions. The date under Jefferson Davis's head was 1871, which was ... a hell of a long time ago now.

The heavy octagonal coin came from the Pacific Confederation, which had split off from the rump of the United States after the CSA won its independence. Under the eagle on the back were an SF mintmark and the date 1880. The San Francisco mint still struck coins for the West Coast People's Democratic Republic, though these days none of them was made of gold or even silver and none was worth anything like fifty dollars.

Charlie realized both coins had to be worth a lot more than their face value to a collector. He also realized he was bound to get stiffed if he tried unloading them to somebody like that. He knew as much about coin collecting as he did about the sea life at the bottom of the Indian Ocean. Zero equaled zero. Half of being smart was knowing what you were dumb at.

As he stuck the goldpieces back in his pocket, he wished Manuel Gomez hadn't run off to Lompoc. Gomez had Party connections but, running that junk shop, he was also bound to have shady ones. Charlie didn't think Gomez would have cheated him ... too badly.

No point to worrying about it now. The way the WCPDR was locked down these days, Lompoc might as well have been on the far side of the moon. Shaking his head, Charlie walked over to the bus stop.

A man smoking a nasty cheroot looked up at him as he neared the bench. "Were you inside the bank just now?" he asked.

"Yeah," Charlie said warily. Had the guy noticed him checking out the gold coins? That might spell trouble.

But the man only asked, "What the hell's going on in there? Those damn carriers with the machine guns on top … ." He made as if to spit.

"I was lucky. They let me do what I needed to do and then leave. They're cleaning the joint out, is what they're doing," Charlie said.

This time, the guy with the stinking stogie did spit on the sidewalk. "Fucking Russians!" he said in disgust.

"They aren't even Russians. They're from the SECPR." Charlie waved back at the APCs to show how he knew.

The man clapped a hand to his forehead. "*Those* shitheads! That's even worse. The Russians, at least they're strong enough so we can't tell 'em no. But the Southeastern bastards—the other ones from around here, too—they're just along for the ride."

"That's about the size of it," Charlie said. The other man hadn't worried about him being a Nibbie. He wouldn't worry, either. *I won't worry yet*, he corrected himself. The way things were going, the old apparatus for keeping an eye on everybody all the time would be back in place before long.

Up rattled the bus. Charlie made damn sure he put a quarter in the fare box, not the Confederate goldpiece. He found a seat and perched on it. The fellow with the cheroot sat nowhere near him.

He got off at Gresham and headed west to the apartment block. When he walked into his flat, Lucille called, "That you, honey?" from the kitchen.

"Nah. It's Father Frost," Charlie answered.

"You're funny, Charlie, funny like a wooden leg. "There's no Father Frost, not in this weather there isn't. Did you manage to change that note at the bank?"

"I did, yeah." He went into the kitchen and kissed her.

"How much did you get?" she asked as soon as he let her go.

"They gave me seventy dollars."

She brightened. "That's good! That's almost what it's really worth, right?"

"Pretty much, uh-huh." Charlie fished out the Confederate gold coin and the bigger one from the Pacific Confederation and set them on the counter. They both rang sweetly; they didn't clank the way steel and aluminum did.

Lucille blinked—blinked twice, in fact. "Good Lord! Where did you get these?" she said in a near-whisper.

"At the bank." He quietly told her the story, finishing, "It's a good thing they were smashed out of their skulls. Otherwise, I bet they would've shot me. Good thing I had Russian money, too—the Russians make everybody think twice."

"How much are they really worth?" she asked.

"No idea. I don't want to try and find out, either, not now." He explained why, and she nodded. He went on, "We'll stash 'em somewhere as safe as we can. If we have to, we'll use 'em. If we don't, we've got 'em to fall back on, that's all." Lucille nodded again.

chapter

A few weeks went by. As fall came on, the weather in the Valley eased from unbearably hot to hot. The papers kept saying the Red Army troops and other invaders would start going home to their motherlands soon. The soldiers kept staying. "We will depart as soon as normalization is complete," the Soviet commanding general declared through an interpreter.

People in the West Coast People's Democratic Republic gradually stopped resisting the army they didn't want. They mostly ignored the foreign soldiers in their midst and did their best to pretend the invaders didn't exist. That annoyed the unwelcome guests, too, which was the point.

No more Russians came into Charlie's store. Two soldiers from the Socialist Republic of Quebec did, though. They had no English, and he no French. They could read numbers, though, and unlike the Red Army men, they had money from the WCPDR. Oranges entranced them, too, so much so that he didn't have the heart to make as if the men in grayish green weren't there. They bought four apiece and left all smiles.

A few days later, the *Los Angeles Times* ran a front-page editorial. *Times change, and our coverage has to change with them*, the piece said. *Newspapers, ours included, are part of the new normalization process.*

The authorities have told us we can only continue publishing if we fully conform. This being so, we must resume submitting our copy to the People's Board of Editorial Supervision. We hope and trust that we will still be able to bring you interesting and entertaining news in a timely fashion.

The unnamed people who wrote the editorial might have meant, *We hope we'll be able to keep sneaking the truth past the censors when it counts.* They might have, but Charlie couldn't make himself believe it. More likely, they meant, *We've got to parrot the Party line, the way* The Worker *does.*

He'd enjoyed reading real news, news that cared more about what actually happened than ideology. Knowing he wouldn't be able to any more left him gloomy and grouchy all day. He felt as if someone he cared about had died. And that wasn't so very far wrong, was it?

When he got home that evening, Lucille wordlessly handed him an envelope. "What's this?" he asked, a sinking feeling in his stomach—the return address showed it came from the West Valley Central Committee.

"I don't know. It's got your name on it," she said.

"Yeah, yeah." He opened it and unfolded the letter inside. When he'd read it, he folded it again, saying, "Well, it could be worse, I guess."

"What does it say?" Lucille asked.

He unfolded it and read it out loud: "Dear Comrade Simpkins: This is to inform you that your services as block chairman of Gresham Block 21200 will no longer be required. A replacement will be chosen at the upcoming meeting. Your efforts are appreciated." He smiled a lopsided smile. "Only one good thing about it I can see."

"That's one more than I can. What is it?"

"Mary Ann Hannegan didn't sign the stinking thing. I mean, I'm sure she voted for it, but she didn't get to laugh in my face on paper, anyway."

"Oh, boy," Lucille said in hollow tones. A moment later, she brightened. "Do you want to go to the meeting and run against whoever the apparatchiks put up?"

"I don't know. Do I?" That hadn't occurred to Charlie. He thought about it for a few seconds before shaking his head. He'd never felt beaten before, but now he did. He hated it, which made it no less real. "I'm tempted, but I better not. It's not on account of me—sooner or later, they'll get around to doing whatever they're gonna do to me. But you think they'd let me win even if I won? You think they wouldn't note down the name of everybody who votes for me and then make them pay for it?"

She did some thinking of her own. Like him, she didn't need long. "That sounds about right. I wish it didn't, but it does .... It would be nice to rub their noses in what we think of them, though, wouldn't it?"

"It would, yeah. But they already know that. You better believe they do. The thing is, they don't care." Charlie crumpled up the letter and threw it at the wastebasket. As he walked over to drop it in, he asked, "What's for dinner?"

"Noodles and cottage cheese, cauliflower on the side." Lucille held up a hand before he could say anything. "I know. But all the shops are as empty as I ever remember them. It's almost like they want us too hungry to try and make trouble."

"Ha! Waddaya mean, almost?" Charlie said. They both laughed. It was laugh or scream.

After he ate, he went over to Nelson Yang's apartment. To his surprise, he didn't have to wait at all to see the area leader. "Ah, Comrade Simpkins!" Yang said, and pumped his hand. "I might have known it would be somebody like you."

Charlie's surprise lasted only a moment. He could see what lay in front of his nose, see it and understand it. "Somebody with nothing left to lose, you mean? They just told me I wasn't block chairman any more."

Yang's grin was perfect gallows. "Let me fix you a drink, then!" he said with joviality he plainly didn't feel. "I'm not area leader any more, either."

"No wonder your place isn't crowded like usual, then," Charlie said.

"No wonder at all," Nelson Yang agreed. "You like bourbon, don't you?"

"That's right." Charlie wondered how many people's favorite drinks the other man remembered. Quite a few, he was sure.

Yang built the bourbon on the rocks as smoothly as one of the barkeepers at the Valley Relic. He poured himself a slug, too. "What shall we drink to?" he asked.

"Success—what else?" Charlie said. They touched glasses. Charlie sipped and sighed. "You've spoiled me, man. I shelled out for a bottle of good stuff myself."

"Proud to be a corrupting influence, my friend."

"You're a lot more on the inside than I am. How bad are things?" Charlie asked.

"As bad as you figure they are, they're worse," Nelson Yang said. "I don't *think* we'll go the way the Northeastern Soviet Socialist Republic did, but I could be wrong. That scares me. It should scare you, too. And I'm not on the inside any more. They haven't expelled me from the Party yet, but I can see it's coming."

Charlie sucked in a slow breath, as if he were the wounded man himself. "That … won't be easy for you," he said. Getting thrown out of the CPWCPDR was the political equivalent of the scarlet SACKED on your work card. It meant you weren't to be trusted. It meant you were fair game.

"Nothing's easy for anyone these days, except for people like Mary Ann Hannegan and Gus Goslin. Comrade Hannegan was honest, at least. She never made any bones about being a hard-liner. But Goslin?" Yang wrinkled his nose, as if smelling skunk.

"I know he went to Moscow with Eichenlode. Past that, he's only a name to me."

"That's all he's ever been to anybody. He's from Oregon on the wrong side of the mountains—same kind of backwoods fellow as Eichenlode. He came up with Eichenlode, too, made sure he did whatever Eichenlode needed. And how he's doing whatever Yuri Zhuravlev needs, damn him."

"Oh. One of those guys who always knows which side his bread is buttered on," Charlie said.

"Congratulations! You understand everything you have to about Comrade Goslin," Nelson Yang said.

"Happy day! Happy goddamn day!" Charlie said. "So the Politburo will plug him in like a toaster and he'll toast us for the Russians?"

"Ha! That's funny even if it isn't funny."

"Funny, is right. I'm a card, and they've dealt with me. But what's gonna happen to Alex Eichenlode? What will they do to him?"

"I don't think they'll kill him. Except in the NESSR twenty-odd years ago, murdering your political rivals has gone out of style in North America. They'll figure out whatever will humiliate him most, and then they'll do that."

As Charlie sipped fancy bourbon, his eyes slid around the big, luxurious flat. Would somebody who'd been expelled from the Party be able to keep a place like this? Would he and his family be able to go on shopping at nomenklatura stores? None of that seemed likely.

"I'm sorry, man," Charlie said. "For everything. I'm sorry as hell."

Nelson Yang understood him. He'd figured the area leader—no, the ex-area leader now—would. Yang replied, "Like they said when the Russians rolled in, it was fun while it lasted, wasn't it?"

A month later, the other shoe finally dropped. There'd been hints in *The Worker* and the *Times*, but only hints. Everything that went on in Sacramento was wrapped in a thick wadding of secrecy. Part of that, no doubt, was because the actors in Sacramento were just actors; they took their cues from the director in Moscow. And part of it was because they didn't usually want their people to know what they were up to. Alex Eichenlode had been an exception there, as he had been so many other ways.

He spoke on the radio one evening, with no announcement beforehand. If you happened to be listening, you heard him; if not, not. The regular newsreader said, "Here is the Premier of the West Coast People's Democratic Republic," and then Eichenlode was on the air.

"Comrades, fellow citizens of the West Coast People's Democratic Republic, this is Alex Eichenlode," he said. "This is the last time I'll be talking to you as your Premier. I expect it will be the last time I'll talk to you in any official capacity. Tomorrow, the Politburo of the WCPDR will meet to confirm the selection of Gus Goslin as my successor."

"Oh, shit," Nikita said loudly.

"Couldn't have put it better myself," Charlie said.

Lucille shushed them both. Eichenlode was still talking: "Our fraternal socialist allies have determined, and the Politburo has agreed, that in these difficult times Comrade Goslin is the best choice to lead the WCPDR toward normalization. As he takes control of the country, our autonomy will increase and the occupying troops from our fraternal allies will gradually begin leaving our soil.

"Having them leave can only be good for the country. If my also leaving is part of the price for that, I pay it willingly. I've always tried to put the country's good ahead of my own.

"I still think our allies misunderstood what we tried to do here, but my opinion is not the one that counts. Believe me, I wish Comrade Goslin success. If he does well, the WCPDR will do well. Compared to that, what happens to me isn't important. I won't worry about it. Neither should you. We'll all do the best we can. Good night, and thank you."

Charlie wiped his eyes with his sleeve. Lucille was dabbing at hers, too. Nikita and Sally lay on the floor, both sobbing. Getting your hopes smashed to bits came harder the first few times, before the thick, calloused hide of experience gave much protection.

Lucille lit a Progress. "Toss me the pack, will you?" Charlie said. She did. He fired up a cigarette, too.

Nikita looked from his mother to his father. His eyes were wet and red, his face blotchy. "Let me have one of those, okay?" he said.

"That's a bad idea," Charlie said. "You aren't used to 'em. It'll make you sick."

"I don't care," his son answered. "The whole stinking world is sick."

"It sure is. You can wait a while longer anyway," Charlie said. Lucille nodded. In the face of a united front from his parents, Nikita threw his hands in the air and stormed into the bedroom. Sally followed.

"I'll tell you, I feel like throwing rocks at the first Party people I see, and we both know I'm not the only one," Lucille said.

"People from San Diego to Seattle are saying the same thing right now. Some of them are doing it. Throwing rocks at cops, too, unless I'm nuts," Charlie said. "But it won't help. And not all the Party people are bastards, either. Even Eichenlode is Party to his fingertips. Nelson Yang, too."

"You said he thought they'd throw him out."

"He did, uh-huh. Normalization, you know. Gotta clean out the rubbish before you can turn the clock all the way back."

"It *does* stink, Charlie. Sacramento. The country. The whole goddamn world. Nikita's right."

"You think I don't know it? We tried to make things a little better in a little country. That was all Eichenlode ever aimed for, swear it was. But the Russians couldn't stand the idea of a Communist who really cared about ordinary people. They were scared it would spread, like chicken pox or measles. And so they squashed it before it could."

He didn't sleep much that night. He didn't think anyone else in the family did, either. Gummy-eyed in spite of as much coffee as he could hold, he rode the bus to work. He got through the day. A mild-looking woman who was buying parsnips and beets told him, "They're all fuckers, you know."

He didn't suppose she was talking about the root vegetables. "Really, Comrade Boileau? I never would have noticed," he said. She laughed a laugh that seemed to come from beyond the grave as she peeled off ration coupons and paid him.

Several other people said the same thing, if less pungently. And, just before Charlie closed up, a man filling a stringbag with potatoes said, "It's official. The Politburo crumpled him up like a piece of paper and tossed him in the trash."

Charlie's eyes slid to the wastebasket. The WORKERS OF THE WORLD, UNITE! poster'd gone there. Everything felt connected, and not in a good way. "Sometimes you wonder why anybody ever even tries," he said.

"You do. You sure as hell do. What do I owe you for these?"

"Take 'em. On the house. What difference does it make?"

The man eyed him, suspicion mingling with concern. "You okay, man?"

"Not even close. But nothing else is, either, so I fit right in."

"Uh, yeah. Uh, thanks." Cradling his free potatoes between his left arm and his ribcage, the man left like a robber with his loot.

A few minutes later, Charlie left, too. Only force of habit made him lock the door. The feeling that nothing mattered any more was very strong. If somebody came in at night and stole vegetables ... well, so what?

When he walked into the flat, he kissed Lucille. That still seemed good, anyhow. Then he said, "You heard?"

"I heard." She turned a thumb down like a Roman Emperor saying good-bye to a wounded gladiator. With the gesture, Charlie's hopeless despair came down again, too.

He hardly noticed what he ate for dinner. As he'd locked up from habit, he turned on the radio the same way. He dully wondered why he bothered. The news was all lies and propaganda again.

The announcer said, "Newly selected Premier Gus Goslin will address the West Coast People's Democratic Republic. Here is the Premier."

"Comrades, fellow citizens, I will labor like a Stakhanovite to move the WCPDR forward along the road to true Communism," Goslin said. His voice had some of the same far-side-of-the-mountains twang as Alex Eichenlode's, but none of the excitement at what he was doing. His words were just ... words.

He went on, "I am proud and humbled that the Politburo has chosen me to lead the country in these trying times. With the aid of our fraternal socialist allies, I will do whatever I can to end our social discordances and normalize our economic, political, and foreign relations."

"Same old horseshit." That wasn't Nikita or even Lucille. It was Sally. How she'd got to be a connoisseur of old horseshit Charlie couldn't have said, but he also couldn't have said she was wrong.

Goslin talked for another fifteen minutes, but he'd said everything that mattered in his first few sentences. From now on, whenever Yuri Zhuravlev sneezed, Goslin promised to catch a cold. Anybody who didn't catch a cold when the General Secretary of the Communist Party of the USSR sneezed was a dangerous right deviationist, as far as Comrade Goslin was concerned.

As soon as the new Premier finished at last, Lucille turned off the radio with a decisive click. "Well, that was fun, wasn't it?" she said brightly.

"I don't remember the last time I enjoyed anything so much," Charlie said.

Nikita glared at each of them in turn. "If you guys were half as funny as you think you are, you'd be twice as funny as you really are."

"Don't worry about it. We love you, too," Charlie said. He'd only thought Nikita'd given him a dirty look before. Now he got a real one. The kid definitely showed promise.

Every morning, Charlie bought *The Daily Worker* and the *Times* at the bus stop. He wanted to find out what the West Coast People's Democratic Republic would do to Alex Eichenlode now that the Politburo (and the Soviet Union) had ousted him from the Premiership. He knew his curiosity was morbid, but he couldn't help having some.

For more than a week, neither paper said anything. Charlie began to wonder whether the people who were running things now had thrown Eichenlode into a cell and lost the key, or just quietly given him a noodle in the back of the neck. He didn't think they could hide anything like that, or that the WCPDR would stay quiet once the word leaked out. But those arrogant bastards might calculate differently.

Then a one-paragraph story ran on a back page of *The Worker*. It said that former Politburo member Alex Eichenlode had been appointed an assistant mining superintendent in Mojave, California.

"Fuck!" Charlie said. A couple of people on the southbound bus gave him funny looks. He didn't notice. He wouldn't have cared if he had. Mojave! That was internal exile with a vengeance! Both the exile and the vengeance had to be intentional, too. The little town was out in the middle of the, yes, Mojave Desert. You got sent there, you weren't just forgotten. You were obliterated.

He dropped *The Daily Worker* down between his seat and the one in front of it. Now that he had the answer he'd been looking for, he wished he didn't. Shooting Eichenlode might have been kinder than marooning him in Mojave. Even leaving him in a cell might have been. Chances were, a cell would have been cooler.

Charlie shook his head all the way from the corner where he got off the bus to the produce store. He wished Manuel Gomez still ran the junk shop next door. He would have had someone to talk to then, even if Gomez was an informer. But no one had taken over the building after Gomez left. The big front window showed only darkness within, as if Charlie were looking into a skull through an empty eye socket.

As he was opening the store, a column of Red Army tanks and armored personnel carriers clattered west along Sherman Way. A tank commander standing head and shoulders out of the cupola waved to Charlie. The Russian wore a grin. Maybe he and his comrades were heading home. Charlie wanted them gone, but not enough to wave good-bye back. The tanks' tracks chewed up the asphalt. They turned right on De Soto and disappeared, leaving only stinking diesel smoke behind. Charlie went inside and closed the door. It helped … a little.

Another day to get through. Had all the days before Alex Eichenlode tried his brief experiment with freedom seemed as gray and dull and meaningless as the ones since the invasion? Charlie didn't think so, but couldn't be sure. He hadn't had standards of comparison then.

He almost wished Mary Ann Hannegan would come in to rub his nose in what had happened to Eichenlode. Then at least he'd get honestly pissed off instead of being stuck with this oppressive, leaden hopelessness. But she stayed away. He supposed he didn't matter enough to worry about any more.

Or maybe she was busy making whatever arrangements she had in mind for him. He'd drawn her notice and her anger even before anybody outside of Spokane had heard of Alex Eichenlode. The Communist Party of the West Coast People's Democratic Republic, like every other Communist Party in the world, remembered slights forever.

"Fuck!" he said again. Nobody but him was in the store. He might have sworn even if he'd had customers. But the obscenity couldn't lift him out of his funk. Nothing could.

No. That wasn't true. He knew what could bring him back to life—the same thing that could revive the whole WCPDR. But it wouldn't happen. The Politburo wouldn't pick anybody like Eichenlode again for years and years. For generations, if ever. Even a glimpse of freedom had been plenty to scare the living shit out of the apparatchiks.

Saturday afternoon, he rode down to the Valley Relic after closing up at one. He wanted to talk to Ervin. He understood it wouldn't do any good, but it would let him get some things off his chest that Lucille didn't want to listen to.

The old man wasn't there when he went in. Eddie and Dornel were, though. He sat down with them. Eddie raised a beer in salute. "Ain't life grand these days?" he said.

"Wonderful. Terrific," Charlie answered. He sipped his bourbon and winced. Now that he knew what Jim Beam was like, this stuff had only one use: anesthetic. Well, that was what he needed now. He asked, "How's it going for you guys?"

"Wilder, he thinks they chose him Premier, not Goslin," Eddie said.

"Wilder, he thinks they chose him King. King Shit, that's what he's like these days," Dornel amplified.

"Jesus! I'm sorry," Charlie said.

"Everybody's sorry. Don't do nobody no goddamn good," Dornel said.

"You're lucky you don't have the son of a bitch on your back these days, man," Eddie added. "You don't know how lucky you are."

Charlie had no idea how his troubles compared to Eddie's and Dornel's. Troubles were ... troubles. Everybody had them. These days, everybody had nasty ones. What could you do? You could drink. Charlie did. Lousy bourbon was only a small trouble.

After a bit, he went to the bar and bought a round. He figured he'd do some drinking this afternoon. As long as he didn't get too fried to remember which buses to take to get home and when to get off, what difference did it make? Buses didn't have many advantages over cars, but that sure was one of them.

Eddie bought a round. Dornel bought a round. Charlie bought another one. They munched peanuts and pretzels to give the booze some ballast. After a while, Charlie asked, "You guys think Ervin's coming in today?"

Dornel looked at Eddie. Eddie looked at Dornel. For close to half a minute, neither of them said anything. Then, with startling gentleness, Dornel asked, "You didn't hear, man?"

"Hear what?" Even as Charlie spoke, more than half of him already knew the answer.

Sure as hell, the black man said, "They dropped on him, God damn them. Right here, they dropped on him. Last Monday, it was. I seen it happen. The fuckin' Nibbies, they grabbed him an' hauled him away. He was cussin' a blue streak, Ervin was. I wanted to go fight them bastards, but I got me a wife'n kids like everybody else, y'know?"

"Shit. Oh, shit," Charlie said, his voice numb with ... no, not shock, because it wasn't a surprise. With something more like self-disgust or self-loathing. "No, I didn't know."

Sadly, Eddie said, "He always said they knew where to find him. Wish like hell he was wrong."

"Yeah." Charlie stared down into his glass. He wasn't looking at the ice cubes and the half-inch of tawny liquid he hadn't swallowed yet. He was looking at his own future. If they'd come for Ervin, how long till they came for him? How come they hadn't come for him already?

Where he looked ahead, Dornel looked back. "I shoulda took 'em on," he said, also sounding as if he hated himself. "If one guy woulda done it, bet your ass everybody in the place woulda jumped in. We woulda kicked the Nibbies around so good, they never coulda remembered who all we was. But I didn't have the balls. Nobody did."

Charlie offered what sympathy he could: "You try and fight the NBI, you're in over your head. Way over."

"I know it. I keep tellin' myself the same thing, over'n over." Dornel covered his face with his big hands. "But this was *Ervin*, man."

"When the Russians came in, Eichenlode told everybody not to fight 'em, remember," Charlie said. "Sometimes you can't, that's all, no matter how much you want to."

"What ever happened to Eichenlode, anyways? He didn't seem like too bad a guy for somebody who wore a tie all the time." Eddie wasn't a political man. He was just somebody who hated bosses. And, considering the bosses Charlie'd known at the produce warehouse, who could blame him?

He was also a man unlikely to read *The Daily Worker*, which would mean he really didn't know. Charlie told him.

"Mojave? Jesus! Shooting him would've been a favor next to that," Eddie said.

"I thought the same thing," Charlie said.

"You guys got it straight," Dornel agreed. "They hate on that man *hard*."

"No shit. Anybody ever needs to give the WCPDR an enema, Mojave's where he plugs it in," Eddie said.

In spite of everything, Charlie giggled. But he knew the West Coast People's Democratic Republic held worse places than Mojave. Ervin would be in one of them right now. *How long till you are, too?* Charlie asked himself. Not liking the answer he found, he did his damnedest to blot it out with bad bourbon.

He never quite remembered how he made it home after stumbling out of the Valley Relic. Sunday morning, he woke up with a hangover that made him want to swear off drinking forever.

"They got Ervin. They left him alone for years and years, but they got him this time," he said to Lucille as she fed him a breakfast of black coffee and aspirins.

She nodded. "You told me that last night."

"I did?" Charlie started to shake his head, then quickly gave it up as a bad idea. "I forget all the stuff I oughta remember, and I still remember all the crap I wanna forget." No matter how much rotgut he'd guzzled, no matter how miserable he felt right now, *How long till you are, too?* still burned in letters of fire in his mind's eye.

"You want some toast? That might help." Lucille knew there were things she could fix and things she couldn't. Letters of fire were out of her league. A hangover wasn't.

"Later on. I'm not ready for it yet." Charlie drank more coffee. He usually liked it with condensed milk and sugar, but this was for medicinal purposes.

"Aspirins started working yet?"

"A little. Not enough. Maybe the hair of the dog would help."

"You sure?" she asked. Charlie nodded—cautiously. She poured him half a shot of Jim Beam.

He knocked it back. "Oh, that's good!" he said. "If I'd been drinking that instead of Old Undershorts yesterday, I wouldn't feel so awful right now."

"Yes, you would. Too much of anything'll hurt you, and you had way too much," Lucille said. "I don't blame you, but you did."

"Ain't it the truth?" he said sadly, and then, a moment later, "I think it helps. Give me about the same again, okay? I won't ask for any more after this, honest. Or if I do, tell me no."

"You!" Fondness and exasperation warred in his wife's voice. She did what he wanted, though. With bourbon, aspirins, and coffee in him, he felt almost human. He stayed in the apartment all day, though. When Sally complained about not being able to see the Sunday comics, he gave her forty cents and sent her to the machine by the bus stop. He didn't care enough about the lies in the Sunday *Times* to walk the three blocks and back, not when he'd damaged himself the night before.

He had more toast and coffee for lunch, then ate noodles and meatballs in tomato sauce for dinner with the rest of the family. All that java meant he didn't sleep as well as he wished he would have Sunday night. To wake himself up Monday morning, he drank an extra cup with breakfast.

Off to the bus stop he went. The *Times* and *The Worker* had almost identical editorials singing the praises of normalization. They did that about every other day, whenever they weren't saying what a wonderful leader Gus Goslin was. Charlie wondered how the people who wrote those editorials looked at themselves in the mirror.

He sighed when he opened up the shop. He'd enjoyed selling good produce. He wasn't getting good produce any more, though. He hoped other produce stores in the Valley were getting better than what the warehouse sent him. If they weren't, the WCPDR looked to be on the edge of famine.

A woman who was buying the best of his sad cauliflowers said, "You used to have such nice things. How come you don't any more?"

"I don't like it any better than you do, Comrade," he answered. "This is what gets delivered to me. I have to try and sell it."

"You must have got 'em mighty sore at you," she said. He only shrugged. Telling her she was right wouldn't have helped.

He made it through the day. The bus that took him home pulled up to the stop at De Soto and Sherman Way just five minutes late. By Rapid Transit District standards, that made it early. It didn't get any further behind on the way north. So he was in a pretty decent mood when he walked into the flat.

It lasted about fifteen seconds: till Lucille handed him an official envelope. "What's this?" he asked with something less than delight. Nothing the government had to say to him these days was likely to be good news.

"Why are you asking me? It's got your name on it," she said. "If you want to find out, you can open it and see."

"I don't *want* to find out." Charlie braced himself, as if he were about to get a shot. "I guess I better, though, huh?" He pulled up the flap and took out the letter. He read it. "Oh, *fuck* me," he said, softly but with great sincerity.

"What now? Do I want to know?"

"I've been reassigned," he said. "Assistant manager of Produce Store L2, starting the fifteenth of next month."

"Assistant manager?" Lucille said indignantly—that meant a pay cut. "Where is it? What kind of horrible bus ride will you have to do to get there?"

Charlie realized she didn't know how the produce-store system worked. All the stores in the San Fernando Valley had a V code—his was V27. An L code .... "It's worse than that, babe. This place isn't down here. It's up in Lancaster. We've got to move. They've assigned us a flat up there."

"Lancaster?" she said, and the way she said it made him see he'd only thought he was cussing when he went *Oh, fuck me*. "That's ... ten miles past the end of the world."

"Tell me about it! The end of the world is Palmdale," Charlie said. Both little towns lay up the Sierra Highway from Los Angeles, in what people called the High Desert. Not many places regularly got hotter in summer than the west end of the Valley, but Lancaster and Palmdale were two of them. It was winter now, but, as if to make up for things, the High Desert got colder than the Valley this time of year. It even snowed up there every once in a while.

And, because Lancaster and Palmdale were surrounded on all sides by miles and miles of miles and miles, a lot of the people who lived there were zeks who'd served out their terms in camp. Just because you'd finished your sentence didn't mean the West Coast People's Democratic Republic was through with you. Oh, no. It stamped your internal passport so you couldn't live anywhere but a place like Lancaster. If you tried to move to the big city and they caught you, right back into a gulag you went.

Lucille realized that at the same time as Charlie did. "It's internal exile!" she exclaimed in dismay.

"It sure is," Charlie said. "They did it to Alex Eichenlode, and they did it to us. Didn't I ever tell you I'd take you places if you stuck with me? We got the same thing pinned on us the Premier did."

"Oh, boy." She shook her head. "I knew they were gonna give it to you when they got around to it. I was ready. I thought I was, anyway. But *Lancaster*? I didn't think they'd do that to you."

Charlie said the obvious: "I've got to go. You ... you probably don't."

"You're a damn fool, but you're *my* damn fool," Lucille said. "And we talked about this before, remember. I'm on their list, too. If I don't go now, they'll get me pretty soon. We may as well stick together."

He squeezed her. "I was lucky when I found you. I'm smart enough to know it—you better believe that. What I don't know is whether you were lucky when you found me."

"Kinda late now to worry about that, don't you think?"

"I guess. Thanks, sweetie." Charlie hugged her again.

She hardly noticed. "We've got a million things to do before we can leave. Boxes—you can get boxes from the store, right? Everything we don't throw out has to go in boxes."

"I'll bring 'em home on the bus, break 'em down and pile 'em up," Charlie said.

"We have to see what the closest schools are, too." Lucille kept talking as if he hadn't spoken. "And—schools, kids—we've got to tell Nikita and Sally, too."

"They probably ought to know," Charlie agreed, his voice dry. When he got old and creaky, he suspected he'd sound a lot like Ervin. Poor Ervin! Wherever'd the NBI'd sent him, it was bound to be someplace a hell of a lot worse than Lancaster.

Again, his wife went on as if he weren't there. "God, I wonder what they'll think!"

"Either they'll be sore at us for taking us away from all their friends or they'll be proud the government is scared to let us stay in Los Angeles any more. Nothing in between, unless I'm crazy," Charlie said.

"Of course you're crazy." Lucille noticed that. She raised her voice: "Sally! Nikita! C'mere! I've got something important to tell you."

chapter 17

On the map, it was not quite seventy miles north and east from the west end of the Valley to Lancaster. The distance from one to the other, though, had nothing to do with what was on the map. It felt more like going from the Earth to Mars, or maybe ten miles farther.

When the time to move came, Lucille and the kids rode the bus north. Charlie went along with the moving-van driver and his helper. The big truck was wide enough so they weren't all squashed together.

Once the Sierra Highway got out of the woods, the High Desert was yellow-brown and barren. It had rained a couple of days before, so the plants that grew there were green. But not many did grow there. Dirt. Sand. Rock. Gullies that channeled the rain when there was any rain to channel. When there wasn't, which was most of the time, they baked as dry as everything else.

Charlie practically pressed his nose against the side window. "Looks like you can see forever!" he said.

Pausing in the middle of lighting a Progress, the driver answered, "Yeah, and there ain't one goddamn thing worth seeing all the way out there, either."

He had a point, or at least part of one. Except for the highway, the power and telephone poles that flanked it, the train tracks that ran alongside, and the occasional narrow crossing road, the landscape might never have heard of humanity. It seemed all the more empty to someone like Charlie, who'd lived to the edge of middle age in the WCPDR's biggest city. To the driver, too, evidently.

Palmdale was small and flat, and looked about as uninteresting as a town could. As it disappeared behind the van, Charlie asked, "How far till Lancaster?"

"About another ten miles, maybe not quite," the assistant said. "Man, what the hell'd you do to get sent way out there?"

"Worst thing you can do. I opened my mouth when I shouldn't have," Charlie answered with an odd, sardonic pride.

He seemed to impress the assistant. But the driver said, "Naw, there's gotta be worse shit than that. Sometimes Lancaster's too good for people. They ship their sorry asses all the way out to Rosamond or Mojave or even California City."

"Mojave!" Charlie exclaimed.

"Uh-huh. It's up the road a ways."

"How far?"

"Twenty-five, thirty miles. Something like that. How come? You know somebody there?"

"Yeah. I sorta do," Charlie said. "And you know what? You're right. The bastards who sent him there think he did way worse than I ever dreamt of."

"Told ya," the driver said smugly.

When they got to Lancaster, it looked to be much the same kind of place as Palmdale: low-slung, spread out, and unlovely. The driver got off Sierra Highway at Avenue I. He went west to Tenth Street, turned north again, then west on Avenue H-8. Lucy, Nikita, and Sally stood in front of a block of flats. It seemed newer but shabbier than the one the family'd had to leave.

"They better watch themselves, standing around like that," the driver's assistant said. "People that live around here, you gotta keep an eye on 'em."

"You mean people like me?" Charlie asked.

"You said it, buddy. I didn't," the young man replied.

When the moving van stopped moving, Charlie got out. "What's it like?" he called to Lucille and the kids. They would have seen the new place by now. He hadn't.

"It's … an apartment. It's smaller than the one we had. I think the walls are pretty thin," his wife said.

"Oh, joy," he said.

"The kitchen's decent, though," she said. That mattered more to her than to him.

The driver came over and asked, "What's the apartment number again?"

"They've given us 267," Lucille said.

"Okay." The man turned to his assistant. "It's 267, Mickey. Let's do it."

They did it, hauling boxes and furniture and appliances into the flat till it bulged. Charlie and Nikita helped with the boxes. Nikita wore down, but Charlie kept going. Mickey gave him a nod. "You've had some practice doing this," he said.

"Lugging shit around? Yeah, just a little. This time, it's my own shit." Charlie spoke lightly, but he could feel what the hauling was doing to his shoulders, back, and legs. He'd shamble around like an arthritic chimpanzee in the morning, but that was tomorrow. Today, he kept going.

This new place *was* smaller than the old. "We should have thrown more stuff away," Lucille said sadly, threading her way through the mountain range of boxes in the front room to get to the bedroom.

"If we have to, we'll get rid of it here," Charlie answered. "If we don't, we'll figure out some place to stick it." He paused. "Crap! I didn't tip the movers! Did you?"

"Five bucks apiece," she said.

"Good for you!" He hugged her. Then he sagged as if all his bones had turned to jelly. "Jesus! I want to sleep for a year!"

"You and me both," Lucille said. "The packing, the moving…. Now we get to unpack, and that'll be fun, too."

"Fun. There's one word." Charlie sighed. "Tomorrow I get to check in at the police station, let 'em know we're in town. Gotta do the things citizens do." He chose his words with care. The authorities had assigned the family this flat. They'd sent him up here because they didn't like his politics. If they wanted to bug the place so they could build a case against him, they'd had a perfect chance. He went on, "Gotta see what the new store's like too, see who my new boss is."

Lucille nodded. "All kinds of fun."

"You said it again! But yeah. You probably won't be able to cook tonight, either. Did you see any place not too far from here where we can get something to eat?"

"There's a fried-chicken place on this street, the other side of Tenth Street West. I was already thinking about that."

"Sounds good to me. The van came up Tenth Street, so I didn't see what was on the far side of it." Charlie'd known the west end of the Valley like the back of his hand. Now he had a whole new town to learn. It wasn't a very big town, but he was starting from scratch.

"We've got to get the kids into their new schools, too. I don't know what all else!" Unflappable Lucille sounded rattled.

Charlie felt the same way. "What we do tonight is, we find the sheets and blankets and bedspreads and pillows and something for us to wear tomorrow. Maybe the coffee, too. Then we collapse."

The chicken place was nothing fancy. Charlie didn't care. After the day he'd put in, he thought he would have happily eaten fried feathers. Everybody else in the family was at least as ravenous. They could have built two or three chickens from the bones that piled up on their plates.

As he started to slow down, Charlie glanced around at the other customers. Quite a few of them were skinny, leathery men with worried eyes. He'd seen enough released zeks down in Los Angeles to recognize the type. There seemed to be more here. Sure enough, Lancaster was one of the places where the government stashed them.

He was already starting to stiffen up on the walk back to the new building. "Oh, I should be great tomorrow," he said, wincing as he went up the stairs.

"We're here. We made it. Whatever we have to do, we'll take care of it, that's all." A full stomach had given Lucille some of her usual manner again.

"Yeah." Charlie looked at his watch. "It's not even eight o'clock yet? I don't just wanna sleep, I wanna hibernate like a big old bear, and not wake up till it's spring." He muttered under his breath. "I must be getting old."

"Moving will do that to anybody," Lucille said.

He sent her a grateful grin. "I love you, babe. So you know, and everything."

Charlie woke the next morning convinced that whoever was responsible for maintaining his carcass had fallen down on the job. The fool had forgotten to oil any of his joints during the night. They all creaked. He lurched around the apartment, trying not to knock down any of the piles of boxes. Coffee and aspirins helped a little, the way they did with a hangover. As with a hangover, they didn't do nearly enough.

He went downstairs anyhow, convinced he deserved a Hero of the WCPDR medal for his bravery. He had to ask the building superintendent where the police station was and how to get there.

"You're the fella what moved in yesterday," the man said, scratching a white-stubbled chin he hadn't shaved in two or three days.

"Sure am." Charlie nodded. Even that hurt.

"So you gotta go let 'em know where you're at, uh-huh. Believe me, sonny, that's the only time folks around here wanna know where the cops are." The super gave him the directions he needed. He was another one with the look of an old lag.

The station was not quite a mile away, in what passed for Lancaster's civic center. When Charlie'd asked about buses in town, the building superintendent laughed in his face. He'd never dreamt he would miss the Rapid Transit District, but life was full of surprises. He walked. It wasn't too bad. He didn't suppose he would have enjoyed it so much in August, though.

A cop at the door patted him down before letting him go inside. Like policemen anywhere in the WCPDR—anywhere in the world, when you got down to it—the ones here knew how much the people loved them. Anybody who wanted to walk in of his own accord was automatically suspect.

"Waddaya want?" the desk sergeant asked. His warmth and friendliness reminded Charlie why he hadn't set foot in a police station since they dragged him in after that bar brawl.

He showed the sergeant the letter that had turned his life, and his family's, upside down and inside out. "I'm here," he said. "I need to report to you guys so you officially know I'm here, right?"

"Oh. Yeah. You do." The sergeant nodded. He had to be ten or fifteen years older than Charlie, but Charlie wouldn't have wanted to mess with him. His blunt features, broad shoulders, and thick chest suggested he'd been in a lot of fights and won most of them. But, since Charlie was playing by the rules, the cop pointed down the hall and said, "You gotta talk with Lieutenant Peterson. Room 103—second door on the left. You got your internal passport, too, right?"

"Sure do. My family's, too." Charlie patted his breast pocket and went down the hall, adding, "Thanks," over his shoulder.

He stuck his head into Room 103. A pretty redhead of about thirty sat behind a desk near the door. He almost asked her where Lieutenant Peterson was. Before he opened his mouth, though, he spotted a name plaque on the desk. ROSA PETERSON, it said, and under that, in smaller letters, *Lancaster Police*. He was glad he hadn't shot from the lip. Women hated it when you just assumed they were secretaries or whatever the hell.

Instead of being dumb, he said, "Comrade Lieutenant?"

She rewarded him with a smile that almost made him forget how sore and achy he was. "Yes? What do you need, Comrade?" she asked. It was the same question he'd got from the desk sergeant, but she made it seem a lot friendlier.

He set the letter on her desk. "The guy up front told me you were the one I should check in with."

"That's right, Comrade, uh"—she glanced at the letter—"Comrade Simpkins. Let me check your file. I should have it with the Incomings." She stood up, went to a sheet-steel cabinet, opened it, and extracted a manila folder. After she'd quickly gone through it, she closed it and said, "Well … ." The word hung in the air.

Charlie had a good idea of what that meant. More proudly than not, he answered, "Yeah."

"You haven't been convicted of anything. You haven't even been formally charged with anything. You're a political offender anyway. You understand that, don't you?"

"I didn't figure they made me move to Lancaster on account of they thought I'd done anything *good*," he said.

Rosa Peterson opened the folder again and flipped through pages till she found what she wanted. "The said Simpkins has a sardonic cast of mind and turn of phrase, which makes him resistant to norms of social utility," she read. "What do you have to say about that?"

Straight-faced, he answered, "One of your snoops was listening to my wife?"

She laughed, then looked as if she wished she hadn't. Closing the folder, she said, "You'd better watch yourself, Comrade. During normalization, we have no patience with that kind of foolishness. Some people come to Lancaster from camps. Some move in the other direction. Is that plain enough, or shall I draw you a picture?"

"That's real plain, Comrade Lieutenant," Charlie said. She might be pretty, but she was a cop, all right.

"For your family's sake, I hope it is," she said, as if to stab him with another icicle. Then her manner lightened once more. "For now, it isn't a criminal matter. I hope it won't become one. You've reported, fulfilling that legal requirement." She inked a rubber stamp and thumped it down on his letter. "Here is verification that you've done so."

"Thanks." He stuck the letter in his pocket.

"Only doing my job. Now, you have your internal passport?"

"Yup. And my wife's. And the kids'." Charlie took them out.

"Give them to me, please." Lieutenant Peterson picked up another stamp. She used it on the Amendments and Endorsements page of each passport in turn. It showed that the bearers were in internal exile, and couldn't leave the restricted zone without special permission. As she handed them back, she asked, "Is there anything else?"

"One more thing." He showed her the letter again. "This is the address of the produce store where I'm supposed to start working Monday. Can you tell me how to get there from here? I'd like to meet the manager before I jump in."

"Yes, of course." Lieutenant Peterson gave quick, competent directions. To back them up, she sketched a rough map on a piece of scratch paper.

"Ah, that's great. Appreciate it," Charlie said. Having the map was great, anyhow. What it showed, rather less so. The store was another mile east of the police station. He wasn't thrilled about walking a couple of miles each way every day. *Maybe I can get a bike*, he thought. It would have to be secondhand. He'd need to go into a state queue if he wanted a new one.

He escaped the station with nothing but relief. Walking across a fair part of Lancaster wasn't so bad now. The air was much cleaner and fresher than it was down in Los Angeles, even if he found himself blinking against blowing dust. A raven on a power pole peered down at him and made *gruk-gruk!* noises. Till it did, he took it for an extra-large crow. But he'd known crows in the Valley; they didn't talk like that.

He walked past a store that called itself Used Everything, and made a mental note of the address. If the guy who ran it couldn't sell him a bicycle, he might know somebody who could.

257

Quite a few bikes rolled along the wide streets. Not many cars. He'd already noticed that. People who got sent to a place like this would also have got sent to the bottom of the automobile queue at least once, maybe three or four times.

A few blocks farther on, he found the produce store. His stomach knotted as he walked up to the door. He'd be assistant manager here, not manager. Who'd be telling him what to do? When he thought of bosses, he thought of people like Emmett Muldberg and Horton Wilder. What was a boss but a petty tyrant trying to be a big one?

Did he want to work for somebody like that? Did he want to take crap from somebody like that? Whether he wanted to or not, he had no choice right now.

Muttering under his breath, he went inside. A man who looked as if he'd spent a long time in camps and hadn't been out long was examining tomatoes with the care of a judge at a fair where kolkhozniks showed off the best from their private plots. He chose three and took them to the woman behind the counter.

"Forty-five cents, Dick," she said. She was somewhere in her fifties, short and chunky, with a mane of wavy, graying hair that fell almost to her waist. Dick gave her a half dollar, waited for his nickel change, and went off with it and the tomatoes. The woman looked Charlie's way. "Haven't seen you in here before, Comrade. What can I do for you?"

"I'm Charlie Simpkins. I just got sent up here from L.A. If this is your place, Comrade, I'm supposed to be your new assistant." He handed her the letter that now bore the Lancaster Police Department stamp.

She held it out at arm's length to read it, then gave it back to him. "At least they told me you were coming, Comrade Simpkins. Uh, is Charlie okay?"

He nodded. "Sure."

"Then I'm Amy. Amy Katz. Comrade This, Comrade That, it's all silly when we're working together, you ask me."

"Fine by me," Charlie said. This might not turn out as bad as he'd feared. The produce looked … not always great, because you didn't always get great vegetables at this kind of store, but well tended, anyhow. And Amy Katz wasn't starting out as if she wanted to bust his balls.

She said, "In a place like Lancaster, it's rude to ask somebody what he did to wind up here. So do you mind if I'm rude and ask you what you did to wind up here?"

He laughed. "Nah. It all started when I tossed a propaganda poster in the trash instead of sticking it in my front window, and it went downhill from there. Next thing you know, I started liking Alex Eichenlode and even letting people know I did. So when we got normalized ... ." He turned the last word into a curse.

"You're a troublemaker," she said.

"My wife sure thinks so," he said, and then, "You don't mind my asking, what are you doing here?" If she got huffy and didn't want to tell him because she was the boss, he'd know things at the store wouldn't be so terrific after all.

But she said, "Fair's fair. Dave—Dave's my husband—and me, we put out a little samizdat newsletter, writing by hand and carbon paper, trying to let people in Bakersfield know what was really going on. They caught us ten years ago, and we've been here ever since. I guess we're lucky. They gave us internal exile instead of throwing us into camps."

"Lucky. Yeah." Charlie said. Amy wasn't wrong, though. In Tony Newman's day, that had been good luck. And, now that Gus Goslin was Premier, it would be good luck again, if not something more like a miracle.

"It's not a bad town, once you get used to it," Amy said. "We understand each other. Most of us have been through the sausage machine one way or another."

"'Through the sausage machine.' I like that," Charlie said. "Tell me what you'll want me to do around here, why don't you?"

"What were you doing in ... Los Angeles, you said?"

He realized she didn't know. They hadn't bothered to tell her that. Grinning crookedly, he answered, "I ran a store just like this."

"Oh!" She turned pink. She had very fair skin; he could watch it happen. "Will it bother you, working under someone else?"

"Not under you," Charlie said. "Even with a rotten boss, I'd try to take it. It's a job. I'm getting paid. I'm not busting rocks or chopping down trees or digging canals. I'm not eating dandelion soup and sleeping in a bunk with a burlap pillow full of sawdust and no mattress. Everybody knows the stories, and everybody knows they're true."

"Except maybe for the little while when Eichenlode was on top, this whole country's been a labor camp longer than anybody can remember. The whole world has," Amy said.

"You don't even know me," Charlie said. "If you talk that way to strangers, no wonder you got sent here."

"No wonder at all," Amy agreed. "Dave says the same thing. But they came for him first, not for me, so you never know, do you? And there aren't many people here in Lancaster who like the way things are. Except the ones who tell us what to do, I mean. So it's not too bad, really. And we never saw any Russians here, not one."

She didn't worry about informers, she'd never heard of them, or she was one herself. Those all seemed unlikely to Charlie. Not wanting to try to figure it out, he asked, "What does, uh, Dave do?"

"He runs a little hardware store a couple of blocks from here. Whatever you need to fix something, chances are he's got it."

Charlie wondered whether Dave still put out the tiny little newsletter and handed copies to customers he trusted. He wondered whether Amy did, too. That, he didn't ask; he was afraid she might tell him. Instead, he said, "Okay, thanks. I'll remember that. Give me his address before I go."

She nodded. "I will." Then she got back to what he'd asked her a little while before: "When you start, let's just play it by ear. Whatever needs doing, one of us can do it. Pretty soon, we'll figure out who does what best."

"That's fine," Charlie said. If somebody'd foisted an experienced assistant manager on him, he thought he would have said the same thing. That had to be part of why both Amy Katz and he'd wound up in a place like Lancaster. The West Coast People's Democratic Republic ran on precise plans, from the Four-Year Plans that defined the national economy on down to state, regional, county, city, and local plans.

Of course, the people who made all those plans didn't know the problems the people who had to fulfill them faced. The people who had to fulfill them did know they'd get in trouble if they failed. So they fudged, invented, and sometimes flat-out lied to keep the planners happy, or at least off their backs.

Everybody knew that kind of thing happened. Everybody was in the middle of it. When the goals were impossible and you had to meet them, what could you do but lie? The system ran on lies. Lies were part of what kept it going.

Like the lie that one of these days we'll get to true Communism and the state will wither away? Thinking that might not be true still rocked Charlie. It went dead against everything he'd always been told.

"Something on your mind?" Amy asked. "You looked like you were worried there."

"People who plan. People who play it by ear, like you said. Whether any of it makes a difference." Charlie spread his hands. "Sorry. Nothing real important."

"People who plan live in L.A. or San Diego or Sacramento. They have cars and big flats and dachas in the mountains or on the beach. People who play it by ear? We're in Lancaster." Amy grinned. "But the company's better here."

The company was bound to be better inside labor camps, too. That didn't mean you wanted to spend twenty-five years in one. He didn't argue with Amy. Life was too short, especially when they were on the same side. All he said was, "Will you let me have that address now, please? I want to wander around a little, see what kind of stuff there is in this exciting place."

"Exciting! That's what it is, all right!" Her grin got wider. She wrote down the address and gave it to Charlie. Lieutenant Peterson had neater handwriting, but he liked Amy Katz's better. It seemed more ... more human. And she sure as hell wasn't Horton Wilder or Emmett Muldberg. That was something, a big something.

He found the hardware store without any trouble. Lancaster was built on a grid, even more than Los Angeles was. It had no inconvenient mountains or rivers to break up the pattern. Only Sierra Highway, which didn't run straight north and south, and the train tracks next to it slightly spoiled the checkerboard.

He also found a movie theater, a secondhand book store, and half a dozen class-four taverns. He had the feeling he hadn't found anything like all of them. This looked to be a hard-drinking town. Well, what else was there to do here? Watch the tumbleweeds blow down the street? When the winds rose in the fall, you could do that in the Valley.

Lucille looked up from taking silverware out of a box when he got back. "What's he like? How horrible is he?" she asked.

"He's a she, and honest to God, I think it may work out." Charlie told his wife what he knew about Amy Katz, and what he thought. He finished, "She's not one of those people who enjoy telling other people what to do, that's the big thing. I'm pretty sure she's not, anyhow."

"That's good," Lucille said.

He went on as if she hadn't spoken: "Of course, she may just save all that stuff up for her husband, like somebody else I know."

Lucille threw a tablespoon at him. It caught him in the ribs, bowl end first. He decided he was damn lucky she hadn't been holding a knife.

On Saturday, he went to Used Everything. "Don't got any bikes right now," said the thin, grizzled man who ran the place. "Sorry. Folks snap 'em up soon as they come in. I'll put you on my list, though."

"How is this any different from the government?" Charlie was kidding, and then again he wasn't.

"You'll be number four with me, not number 5,271,009," the fellow answered. He had a far-side-of-the-mountains accent, like Alex Eichenlode's or Gus Goslin's. Charlie wondered what he'd done to wind up here. He didn't ask.

He did say, "Good point! Put me on." He gave the man his name and address.

He found a drugstore not far from his building that sold the *Times* and *The Daily Worker*. He got the papers on Saturday and Sunday. He wasn't so sure he'd keep doing it during the week. He'd used to read them on the bus then. You couldn't do that while you were walking, not unless you wanted to walk into poles or fall on your face because you hadn't noticed you were stepping off a curb.

Besides, under normalization all they printed was what Sacramento and Moscow wanted people to see. He thought they were even worse than they'd been while Tony Newman was Premier. Then, at least, you could read between the lines and get some idea of what was really going on.

Now? Now it was all praise for Gus Goslin and Yuri Zhuravlev, all overfulfillment of plans, all the glorious advance of Marxism-Leninism-Stalinism. The only things the *Times* didn't lie about, as far as he could see, were the sports scores. And the Stars, whose season was winding down, were having a rotten year. *Just like everybody else*, Charlie thought.

He did spot an item in *The Worker* noting that Vyacheslav Martillo had been sent to the People's Democratic Socialist Republic of Chungking as a member of the embassy staff. The story didn't say that Martillo had been Alex Eichenlode's Foreign Commissar. You had to remember, if you could. The purge went on, but quietly, discreetly.

Lancaster had one radio station of its own. The announcers bragged that Palmdale could hear it, too. Charlie wondered why Palmdale would bother tuning in. It was all propaganda all the time. Los Angeles stations came in fitfully, through waterfalls of static. They were a little better when they did—not much these days, but a little.

Monday morning, Charlie headed for the produce store. Lucille kissed him good-bye; he couldn't remember the last time she'd done that. "Luck," she said.

"Thanks, babe," he answered, and headed out.

He got there as Amy Katz was unlocking the front door. She waved to him as he came up. "Morning, Charlie!" she said. "You can't be late if I'm not inside yet."

"That sounds good," he said. "What kind of a routine do you have for starting the day—for starting the week, today?"

"I just do whatever looks like it needs doing," Amy answered. "And if it doesn't all get done exactly the way it's supposed to, you know what? The world's not gonna end. Not because of anything in Lancaster, it's not."

"You've probably got that right," Charlie said as she opened the door. He waved her in ahead of him.

Together, they filled the bins from stock in the back room. The quality left a lot to be desired; it was what he might have had in the Valley if Horton Wilder hated him worse than usual. As gently as he could, he remarked on that. Amy looked at him as if he wasn't very smart. "This town's full of zeks and politicals in internal exile. What do you expect me to get?"

"Oh." He thumped his forehead with the heel of his hand. If she thought him dim, she had good reason to. He tried a different tack: "When do you do the orders and the accounts?"

"When I have to." She looked as if she smelled something nasty.

He sympathized. Even so, it was always better not to give them an obvious paper trail if they were after something to land you in trouble. "Do you, um, want me to take a look at what you've got?"

"If you're crazy enough to do it, sure," Amy said. The bell above the door jingled as a gray-haired man with big, bushy sideburns came in. She smiled at him. "How are you today, Stan? Is your wife feeling any better?"

"Little bit, thanks," he answered.

"Good! I'm glad to hear it. Oh—and this is Comrade Simpkins. Charlie. He'll be working here with me from now on."

"Hello," Charlie said.

"How do?" Stan answered. He got some onions and apples and peas, then took them over to the counter so he could pay Amy.

She gave him his change and sent him on his way with a, "Give her my best, will you?"

"Thanks. Sure will," Stan said as he went out the door.

"You're good with people," Charlie remarked.

"I like 'em," she said simply. That had to make a difference, sure enough. Charlie mostly saved liking people for his wife and children. He wasn't rude or nasty to anybody else, but he'd never reached out to his customers the way Amy did. He didn't seem to have that in him. Till now, he'd never thought of it as a lack.

"You want to show me your stuff?" he asked so he didn't have to dwell on that.

"Sure." She pulled open a drawer behind the counter. "Remember, you volunteered, you old Stakhanovite, you. See what you can do, that's all."

He started looking. Every so often, somebody would come in. Amy knew people by name. She'd always introduce Charlie to them, so he glanced up to say hello every few minutes. After a while, when he was alone in the store with her, he said, "This is kind of a mess, you know."

Amy made a surprised face, an overacted one. "Really? I never would have guessed!" Then she got serious again. "Can you do anything about it?"

"I think so. I can lie like a son of a gun, is what I can do," Charlie said. "I'll try to do it so whoever supervises produce stores here—"

"His name is Lertxundi, Enrique Lertxundi. He's a nice man. Not the brightest bulb in the sign, but nice."

"Okay. That may even help. I'll try and lie so Comrade, uh, Lertxundi either doesn't notice anything's fishy or he does notice but doesn't care because the books look the way he'd want them to if they were on the level."

"Can you do that?" She sounded impressed.

"Probably. It'll take a while, 'cause I'll have to go back a ways and make your inventory and your expenditures and your income and coupons line up better than it looks like they do now. It won't be perfect, but it won't have to be. They just want it so they can believe it and not need to look real close. Doesn't seem like you were even trying to keep 'em happy."

He started playing with numbers and forms. He paused late in the morning, when a shipment came in. He was bigger and stronger than Amy, so he helped the driver lug crates and sacks into the storeroom, then stocked up the bins that needed it. After that, he got back to the books.

Amy handled most of the customers. Whenever she'd introduce him to somebody, he'd look up, smile, say hello, and go back to what he was doing. He didn't need long to see a pattern. When they had the store to themselves, he said, "I know what you've been up to."

"Me? What could that be?" Amy sounded demure and innocent.

"You've been giving a bunch of stuff away, or else this place would bring in a lot more cabbage," Charlie said. The other choice was that she was stealing food and selling it on the left, but he didn't believe it. She wasn't that kind of person. And he couldn't see her making all that much doing it, either, not here.

She echoed that thought: "This is Lancaster. People in internal exile don't have much money. They still need to eat, though."

"I did some of that down in the Valley—pitching produce that was still okay, not collecting coupons, things like that. I never thought I could get away with what you've been doing, though. I wouldn't've had the nerve to try."

"Chutzpah," she said. It wasn't a word he used himself, though he'd heard it before. He liked the sound of it. Amy went on, "You do whatever you can get away with, that's all."

Charlie laughed. "There you go! It's normalization! And lying to the sons of guns in the Party's been normal forever. I'll put a smiling face on your lies, like on the ones on the walls and the fences and the overpasses. Even more of them here than down in L.A., I think. I like it."

Amy Katz studied him, her head cocked to one side. "It's no wonder they sent you here, is it?"

"Comrade, it's no wonder at all," he answered, and went back to work.

When he got off for the day, he walked over to the hardware store Dave Katz ran. As he'd hoped, it was still open. He bought some stout screws so he could fix the family's shelves to the walls. The last thing you wanted was a bookcase falling on you if an earthquake hit.

He guessed the short, graying man who took his money was Amy's husband. When he asked, he found he was right. He gave his own name, adding, "Your wife is stuck with me at the produce place."

Dave Katz nodded. "Yeah, she told me about you. She said you were a born pest. If she's right, the two of you should get along fine."

"So far, so good," Charlie said. He grinned half the way home.

chapter

Charlie settled in at the produce store more easily than he'd dreamt he could. Before too long, his name came up on the bicycle list at Used Everything, so he started pedaling to work instead of walking. He also pedaled to the hardware store, where Dave Katz sold him a heavy chain and the best lock he could afford. He knew the bike would disappear if he gave it half a chance; he did his best not to let it.

About that same time, he got the books into a state that seemed orderly even if it wasn't. Amy told him Enrique Lertxundi seemed happy, too. "He's says he's never seen the accounts looking so good," she reported.

"'Looking' is the word, all right," Charlie said. He hadn't met Comrade Lertxundi yet, and didn't particularly want to.

"That's all he worries about. As long as his boss doesn't get sore at him, he doesn't care about anything else," she said.

They talked about kids. She had a son called Josh who'd got married and moved away just before the Nibbies came down on her and her husband. Somehow, the security organs hadn't swept him up, too, maybe because his wife's family had Party members in it. "He was lucky," Charlie said.

"I know it," Amy agreed. "And this past spring, Josh and Diana could finally visit and let us see the twins. It was wonderful!" Her face fell. "It was wonderful then. God only knows when we'll be able to do it again."

"I'm sorry. That must be rough as anything," Charlie said. "How old are the twins?"

"They're eight," she said. He made a fist and brought it down on the counter. You could find stories like that all over the world. This one hurt more because he knew and liked the person telling it—and because it had a little, happy interlude that got snuffed out. That made the pain of separation on either side all the worse.

A small story in the *Times* said that a former member of the West Valley Central Committee, a certain Nelson Yang, had been removed from the Party and sentenced to two years in prison on corruption charges. Charlie shook his head when he happened to notice it. Yang had lived well, yes, and enjoyed living well. Was he more corrupt than any other apparatchik, though? Not by anything Charlie'd seen. What he was really guilty of, of course, was backing Alex Eichenlode and his policies. Under normalization in the WCPDR, that kind of crime couldn't go unpunished.

All things considered, Charlie'd come off lucky himself. He hadn't thought so when he got the order to tear up his life by the roots and move from the big city to the High Desert. But, even in internal exile here, he was freer than most people who'd thought the way he did. Sure as hell, being a minnow had its advantages.

He didn't say anything to Amy about Nelson Yang. He'd got better at keeping his mouth shut once more. He'd done it for years; getting back in the habit wasn't too hard. That small bright segment of time when he hadn't had to? Something to remember and cherish and grieve over, the way she did about her son and daughter-in-law and grandkids.

A few days after he read about Yang's fall from official grace, Amy handed him a sheet of paper folded in quarters. "You might want to be careful with this," she said lightly. As if to underscore her words, the uppermost quarter showed a big eye, wide open, with THEY'RE ALWAYS WATCHING! under it in capital letters.

"I guess I will, then," he said, and stuck it in the back pocket of his work pants.

He remembered why Amy and Dave had got sent to Lancaster to begin with. If they internally exiled you for writing a little newsletter, what would happen if they caught you doing it again while you were in internal exile?

Some people, of course, couldn't keep their mouths shut no matter what. Charlie thought of Ervin along with Amy and Dave. Sadly, he shook his head. People like that were why Mary Ann Hannegan had said there would always be camps, even under true Communism.

He waited till he needed to go back to the storeroom before he pulled out the paper and opened it up. He didn't want to take the chance in the front part of the store. An informer or a disguised Nibbie might walk in at just the wrong time.

She and Dave called the newsletter *How It Looks to Us*. It looked to them as if the WCPDR was going to hell in a handbasket, and the handbasket's name was normalization. Charlie hadn't seen stories about all the horrors they mentioned, but he had seen pieces on several of them. He felt the same way about them they did. As far as he was concerned, anybody with an ounce of sense would.

Which didn't mean Gus Goslin's regime would let them get away with saying things like that. You had to be brave to try it. You also had to be a little bit nuts. He clicked his tongue between his teeth, refolded *How It Looks to Us*, and put it in his pocket again.

Then he noticed he had bluish smudges on his fingertips from the carbon paper she'd used to make copies. When he went back out to the front of the store, he sprayed his hands with a vegetable mister and got them mostly dry on a burlap sack they used as a wipe-up rag.

As he tossed the sorry sack behind the counter, Amy smiled and said, "You *are* careful."

"Well, you told me to be," he answered. A little while later, more or less out of the blue, he added, "Pretty good stuff."

She smiled again. When she did, he could see her as a little girl. "Thanks, Charlie. Dave and I do our best."

Having read her sheet, he had to figure out how to get rid of it. His first thought was to leave it someplace where other people would find it. But other people included the police and the Nibbies. They'd be able to trace it back to her and her husband. They were bound to have samples of the couple's earlier efforts to compare to it, too. It wasn't as if the organs of state security ever threw out anything like that.

Instead, he tore *How It Looks to Me* into tiny pieces. That evening, he rode home by a route different from the one he usually used. On his way, he dropped paper scraps into four trash cans. He made damn sure he didn't leave a single one in his back pocket. "Careful," he muttered. "Yeah." It was chilly out there. His breath smoked even when he didn't have a Progress in his mouth.

While he was waiting to cross Sierra Highway, a northbound bus rumbled past him. The destination placard above the front window said MOJAVE. If he wanted to go up there, he could. Mojave lay in the internal-exile area, too.

If he tried to go down to Los Angeles, though .... Before he got on a southbound bus, they'd check his destination and his internal passport. They'd see the stamp Lieutenant Peterson had put in the passport. If he was lucky, they'd only tell him he couldn't go. If he wasn't, all the other possibilities were worse.

When he walked into the apartment, the first thing he did was wash his hands with dishwashing soap at the kitchen sink. "What's that all about?" Lucille asked.

"I was reading whatsitsname, *Macbeth*, during lunch," he answered, for all the world as if he meant it.

"And then you wake up," she said, knowing as well as he did that he hadn't looked at Shakespeare since he'd had to in school.

He leaned close and whispered in her ear: "Destroying evidence." She didn't look as if she believed that any more than the other.

Late that night, they had one of those under-the-bedclothes conversations. Charlie thought the kids were asleep. If they weren't, he wouldn't worry; Lucille and he didn't talk loud enough for them to overhear. And the bedroom was so cold, it made disappearing under the covers seem reasonable.

Lucille picked up as if he'd just come in, asking, "What do you mean, destroying evidence?"

"What I said," he told her, and explained about *How It Looks to Us*.

"Oh." She didn't say anything else for a while. He wondered whether she'd go to sleep now that she had her answer, but she didn't. She asked, "Doing that was why they made them come to Lancaster to begin with?"

He nodded. Lucille would feel the motion even if she couldn't see it. "Uh-huh."

After another pause, she said, "They like living dangerously, don't they?"

"Yeah. I don't think they can help themselves."

"Mm. Well, I know about that," Lucille said.

Charlie grunted. As if it were yesterday, he remembered unrolling the WORKERS OF THE WORLD, UNITE! poster and thinking, *Oh, God, not this one!* Everything else had flowed from that: not everything in the country, but everything in his own life. If only they'd given him something new and halfway interesting …. *I'd be a different guy right now.*

But he liked the one he was better than the one he had been. That was crazy, but there it was. And here he was.

His wife hadn't finished yet. "They'll catch her again, you know, or Doug."

"Dave." He sighed. "You're bound to be right. All I can do is try and make the Nibbies believe me when I tell 'em I didn't know thing one about it." Now he paused. "It's a pretty good little newsletter, though. Let's sack out, okay?"

"Okay," Lucille said. Eventually, they did.

Saturday, Charlie said to Amy Katz, "Hey, Comrade Boss, can I ask a favor from you today?"

"Sure," she answered at once. "You ask for so little, it scares me sometimes. What do you need?"

"Can you turn me loose fifteen, twenty minutes early? I want to get up to your husband's place and buy a little tool kit before he closes. The one I had disappeared in the move. I swear we packed it, but we're mostly out of boxes now, and it hasn't turned up."

"Moves are like that, especially when you have to do it in a hurry. Something always gets lost," Amy said. "Go ahead. You'll even be putting money in our pockets."

"There you go, exploiting the downtrodden proletariat," he said. She made a face at him. They both laughed. He'd imagined laughing at his boss, but never with her. In a place like Lancaster, though, a boss was way more likely to think the way he did.

She waved when he went out the door at twenty to one. He lifted his own hand in reply as he swung onto his bicycle. Then he rode up to Dave Katz's hardware store. The sun shone brightly, but it was still bloody cold. He wore a jacket, and sometimes a sweater under the jacket, a lot more often than he had down in the Valley.

"Hey, Charlie! How's it going?" Dave said when he walked in.

"Pretty good. How are you? Your wife turned me loose so I could come spend some money up here." Charlie explained what he was after.

Dave Katz pointed. "Aisle Four, right-hand side, not quite halfway down. I've got four or five different styles. Pick the one you like best, then pay up. Amy and me, we'll eat caviar and drink champagne off what we make from you."

"Right." Charlie wondered whether even somebody like Nelson Yang (Nelson Yang before his fall, that is), who enjoyed the good life, ate caviar. He doubted it. Champagne might be a different story.

He found the tool kits without any trouble. Some were a little bigger, some a little smaller. Some had metal cases, others plastic. Some had a few more tools than others. Did he want Robertson screwdrivers, which he might use once in five years? After muttering to himself, he picked a kit—metal case, no Robertson screwdrivers—and took it to the counter.

Another man, taller than he was and a few years older, was there ahead of him, buying a wrench large and heavy enough to make a good murder weapon. "Here you go, Comrade," Dave said, dropping change into his hand.

"Thanks very much," the customer said, and turned to leave.

Brown hair receding at the temples, combed straight back. A nose a bit longer and sharper than most. That voice .... Charlie stiffened. "You're—you're him!" he exclaimed.

Alex Eichenlode's smile suggested he'd heard that, or something like that, more often than he wished he had. "I used to be him, anyhow," he answered.

"Can I shake your hand, please, uh, Comrade?" Charlie came closer to calling the fallen Premier *sir* than he ever had with anyone in his life. "You helped me when I was in trouble, before—before all this stuff happened."

"Ah? Tell me about that, will you?" Eichenlode held out his hand. As if in a dream, Charlie took it. The handshake was brief and firm, a professional politician's clasp.

Charlie told the story as quickly as he could, finishing, "I've still got the letter you sent back to me. I never figured I'd be able to say thanks in person."

"You're Comrade Simpkins?" Alex Eichenlode said. Charlie nodded. Eichenlode went on, "I remember you! I remember thinking that what happened to you happened to too many people, up and down the country, and that it never should happen at all."

"You fixed it so it might as well not've happened to me. That's what I wanted to thank you for," Charlie said.

"You're welcome, of course." Something in the ex-Premier's eyes glinted. They were as blue as Mary Ann Hannegan's, but not nearly so cold. "But here you are in Lancaster just the same. How did that happen?"

"About the way you'd guess. I liked what you were doing, and I let people know I did. I try to keep my big trap shut, but I'm not always as good at it as I oughta be," Charlie answered.

"Okay. We shouldn't have to keep quiet about what we think, or it seems that way to me, but nobody cares any more about how things seem to me. I'm in Lancaster, too, after all—in Mojave most of the time, but Mojave's such a small town, I had to come down here to get the tool I needed." The ex-Premier hefted the wrench. "This isn't the first time that's happened, either."

"Glad to help. My pleasure to help," Dave Katz said. "Everybody feels that way."

"People have been nicer to me since I left the Premiership than they were while I held it," Eichenlode said. "That must say something, but I'm not sure I want to know what."

"Could you, uh, would you give me your address in Mojave?" Charlie asked. "If I can, I'd like to visit you next Saturday after I get off work. I won't stay long, promise. I won't make a damn nuisance of myself, either."

The ex-Premier hesitated, considering. Charlie realized one of the things going through his head had to be *Is this an assassin?* Charlie stood there, looking as harmless as he could. Then Eichenlode pulled a pen from his breast pocket. He turned to Dave. "Let me have a piece of paper, please."

Katz pulled one off a pad and handed it to him. "Here y'go."

"Thanks." Eichenlode bent a little to write. He handed Charlie the small sheet. "Here. Just my address. Without my name, this will be less interesting to the security organs."

The same thing had crossed Charlie's mind. Finding that Alex Eichenlode thought about, needed to think about, the Nibbies and maybe the NKVD, too, saddened him almost to the point of tears. "Thank you very much," he said. "You don't know what this means to me."

Eichenlode's eyes glinted again. Since the Politburo and the Russians forced him into internal exile, how many people had told him that whenever he did something for them, no matter how small? If the line didn't stretch from Lancaster to Mojave, it would only be because they were both little towns.

But the former Premier said, "It's a good feeling to find out some people appreciate what I was trying to do, anyhow."

"Everybody does," Dave said. Charlie nodded.

"I wish that were true, but we all know it isn't," Eichenlode answered. "If everybody did, I'd still be trying. Instead .... Now, at least, I can fix a leaky water main." He lifted the wrench again. With half a wave to Charlie and the same small gesture aimed at Dave, he walked out of the hardware store.

"Wow," Charlie said, staring after him. "I never expected *that*, not in a million years."

"Neither did I, first time he came in here," Dave said. "I almost plotzed, I tell you. I didn't want to take his money when he bought something. He made me do it. I get the feeling that happens a lot, too."

"I believe it," Charlie said. Anywhere in the West Coast People's Democratic Republic, ordinary folks would treat Alex Eichenlode like a king. A king in exile, perhaps, but still a king. Here in a place like this, where so many were exiled themselves? All the more so.

He had to remind himself he was still holding the tool kit he'd chosen. Dave Katz took his money without hesitation. And why wouldn't he? Charlie was no king in exile. He was nothing but a guy, a guy who'd suddenly found one day that he'd had a bellyful of nonsense. He'd done what he could do to fight it, he'd lost, and now he was paying the price.

So was Eichenlode. So was the whole country.

As he turned to leave, he remarked, "Lucille's not gonna believe this when I tell her."

"Amy didn't want to," Dave said. "Next time *he* came in, I told him so. He walked into the produce store to say hello."

"There's a guy with class," Charlie said, and then, "She never said boo about it to me."

"Maybe she hoped he'd come in there again so you could drop your teeth, too."

"Could be, yeah. Say hi for me." Out Charlie went.

Dave would have told Amy the story over the weekend. Charlie knew that. He told it to her on Monday even so.

The way she smiled and nodded along said that, yes, she'd already heard it. "Isn't he something?" she said.

"Oh, you might say so," he answered.

She started to get angry, then realized he was trying to make her mad. She sniffed. "He's a handsome man, too."

"If you say so." This time, Charlie wasn't joking. He noticed good-looking women. Even if they were cops, he noticed them. Men? Men were just men to him. Amy sniffed again.

"When you compare him to what we've got there now .... When you compare what he was trying to do with all the stupid stuff they're up to these days ... ." Amy kept starting sentences without finishing them, which might have been just as well.

"Yeah," Charlie said. The policies Gus Goslin was following at Moscow's command made Tony Newman's seem enlightened by comparison. Charlie couldn't imagine anything worse to say about them. Goslin's answer to *What is to be done now?* was *Whatever Yuri Zhuravlev wants, and whatever shows the people who backed Eichenlode what a mistake they made.*

Most of the people hated the government of their people's democratic republic. Charlie's view of that might have been jaundiced, because he lived in a place where a lot of folks had hated the government long before anyone ever heard of Gus Goslin. Hating it was one thing. Being altogether unable to change it or resist it was something else again.

Bitter jokes abounded. Amy told one about a housewife in Sacramento who got sick of standing in an endless line for rutabagas. *To hell with this!* she screamed. *It's all Gus Goslin's fault. I'm gonna go kill him!* She left the queue and stormed off toward the Premier's residence.

Four hours later, she came back. Her place in line had moved forward about ten feet. As she slipped back into it, somebody asked her, *So, did you kill Goslin?* She laughed in the other woman's face. *Are you out of your mind?* she said. *The line for that's even longer than this one!*

Charlie countered with one he'd heard at the drugstore where he bought the papers on the weekend: "Did you know the West Coast People's Democratic Republic is now the most progressive socialist state in the world?"

"Oh, yeah?" Amy sounded as disbelieving as she should have.

"Sure," he answered. "Life was already better yesterday than it's gonna be tomorrow."

That one took a second to sink in. Then Amy winced and said, "Ouch!" In the WCPDR, yesterday *had* been better than tomorrow would be, at least for a few months of yesterdays. The Soviet invasion made sure of that.

When he got home that evening, Charlie told Amy's joke to Lucille—in a whisper, so any microphones that might be in the flat wouldn't pick it up. She snorted. "The only thing wrong with it is, it's true."

"I know." As soon as Charlie'd heard the punchline, he'd imagined a queue a hundred miles long, everybody moving forward slowly and patiently, some people holding guns, some knives, some pellets of rat poison, some axes, some firebombs like the ones that had burned up Russian tanks, some baseball bats, all with at least one murderous tool. Somewhere near the front of the line would be Alex Eichenlode, waiting to use the wrench he'd bought from Dave Katz.

After dinner, he turned on the radio. None of the Los Angeles radio stations wanted to come in for beans. Swearing under his breath, he tuned in to the Lancaster channel, the one that insisted life under Gus Goslin was beautiful all the time.

"Why are you wasting your time with that crap?" Sally rolled her eyes to show what an idiot her father was.

Charlie shrugged. "I'm a glutton for punishment?" he suggested.

She rewarded him with another eyeroll. "We're *already* in Lancaster," she said, winning the exchange without breaking a sweat. Having won, though, she left him alone after that.

There was a story about the Stakhanovite competition between shipyards in Oakland and Seattle, with both yards building freighters twice as fast as construction norms decreed. If the account wasn't pure invention, Charlie didn't think he'd want to put any cargo in those ships. How many seams weren't welded, how many rivets weren't put in, how many wires weren't connected? Those were the kinds of things you did, or didn't do, when you were going for speed.

Another story told of progress in building a major irrigation canal in California's Central Valley. It didn't say a word about the canal workforce. Because he lived in a place like Lancaster, Charlie'd heard it was all zeks. He'd also heard a joke about it. The people digging on the left wall of the canal had told jokes about the government. The people digging on the right wall had listened to them.

Then the announcer said, "Congratulations to Los Angeles County Commissar Sergei van Houten, who's been named a cadet member of the California state Politburo. Comrade van Houten, as I'm sure you know, serves the seventh district, which includes the San Fernando Valley and our own High Desert. No doubt he'll do a great job!"

How anybody could get excited about a promotion to the state Politburo was beyond Charlie. If it wanted to wipe its nose after it sneezed, the national government had to countersign the order first. But the announcer didn't seem to have any trouble.

Then she said, "Replacing van Houten on the County Board of Commissars will be Mary Ann Hannegan, of West Hills. Comrade Hannegan has been active in Party affairs for more than twenty years, and has been heavily involved in the ongoing process of normalization, so she'll bring the Board valuable experience. She—"

Charlie turned off the radio. He turned it off so hard, he was amazed he didn't break the knob. "Oh, my back!" he said. "Oh, my aching back!"

"What's the matter?" Lucille hadn't been listening. She was lucky.

Since Charlie had, he had to repeat the news he'd just heard. "I only hope she doesn't come after me now that she can reach me again," he said. "That'd be all we need, wouldn't it?"

He hoped his wife would tell him *She wouldn't do that!* But Lucille knew as well as he did that Mary Ann Hannegan might. "One more thing to worry about, like we don't have enough already," she said.

"Nothing to do but roll with it, whatever it is." Charlie shook his head. Here he'd been thinking internal exile in Lancaster wasn't so bad. If he had to have a boss, he couldn't have asked for a better one than Amy Katz. Getting around wasn't so bad now that he had the bike.

He wondered if a County Commissar had the clout to throw somebody into a corrective-labor camp. He wondered if Comrade Hannegan cared enough, or was vindictive enough, to find out. He also wondered if he'd see Ervin again if they decided to send him to a gulag after all.

Nothing to do but roll with it, as he'd said. He kept trying to find some happiness no matter what happened. The whole world kept trying to stop him. Well, almost the whole world. Not quite, though.

Nice as having the bicycle was, Saturday morning Charlie walked to work. Amy gave him a quizzical look. "I've got some stuff I need to take care of after I get off," he not-quite-explained. She shrugged and didn't push him. She was good people, Amy was.

He didn't walk home when his half-day ended. He walked to the bus station on Sierra Highway instead. It wasn't exactly busy and bustling in there. Glancing at the schedule board, he saw the next northbound bus was due in half an hour.

A bored clerk behind the counter took a minute or two to deign to notice he was there. "What do you need, Comrade?" the man asked at last.

"A ticket to Mojave," Charlie said.

"One-way or round trip? If it's one-way, I have to see a travel authorization before I can issue it."

"No, round trip. I'll be back later today."

"Okay." The clerk took out a ticket. He used a rubber stamp and a punch on it. Before plying the punch one last time, he looked up. "Return is today, you said?"

"That's right."

The punch clicked. The clerk told Charlie what the ticket cost. Charlie paid. As the clerk handed him the ticket, he pointed. "Waiting benches are over there."

"Thanks." Charlie went over to them. A woman sat on one; he parked himself on the other. They ignored each other. The benches had no roof or awning to keep off the sun. That didn't matter today. When summer came, they'd be bake ovens.

Naturally, the bus rolled in twenty minutes late. Charlie only sighed; it wasn't as if he were surprised. He waved the woman on ahead of him. She nodded her thanks. The driver added a punch mark of his own to her ticket and then to Charlie's. His punch made a hole shaped differently from the station clerk's.

Charlie found a seat. The bus wasn't crowded. After five or ten minutes waiting for late arrivals, the driver closed the doors. The bus pulled out onto the road.

When Charlie thought they were about halfway there, the bus stopped at a passport-control station on the border between Los Angeles and Kern Counties. Lancaster was in one, Mojave in the other. Alex Eichenlode had got rid of county-line internal passport checks. If Charlie'd ever known the normalized WCPDR had brought them back, he'd forgotten.

Two men in dark green uniforms went down the aisle. "Show me your ticket and your passport, Comrade," one said.

"Here you go." Charlie handed them over, hoping they'd satisfy the official.

The passport-control man examined them, then gave them back. "Purpose of your travel?"

"I'm seeing a friend," Charlie said, thinking, *Don't ask who!*

"Have a nice visit, then." The man wrote on a form he'd trapped in a clipboard. He took two steps down the aisle and asked the old woman sitting behind Charlie for her travel documents.

After twenty-five minutes, the bus chugged north again. Pretty soon, it stopped in Rosamond. The woman who'd got on with Charlie got off there. Nobody boarded. The bus started up.

Ten minutes later, the driver called, "Mojave!" The bus stopped at a station that made the one in Lancaster seem like the grand train station in downtown Los Angeles by comparison. Charlie and three other people got off there. He went into the sad little building and asked the clerk, "How do I get to Belshaw Street, Comrade?"

"One block up. You can't miss it." The woman seemed glad to have something to do, if only for a moment.

For once, somebody who said that proved right. Having found Belshaw, Charlie turned right—the only way he could turn, since the street dead-ended at Sierra Highway—and walked east, looking for the number Alex Eichenlode had given him.

There it was! The tiny clapboard house looked weatherbeaten and tired. It had a post office behind it and a graveyard across the street. Eichenlode had lived in the Premier's residence. He'd hobnobbed with big shots from the WCPDR and with foreign heads of state. What did he think of having to stay in a dump like this?

Heart pounding, Charlie climbed the three wooden steps to the front porch and knocked on the door. A suntanned blond woman in her mid-forties opened it. "Yes?" she asked, her voice polite but wary.

"Uh, hello," Charlie said. "My name's Charlie Simpkins. I met Alex Eichenlode down in Lancaster a week ago. I asked if I could come visit him for a little while today, and he was nice enough to say yes. So, well, here I am."

"Oh, you're Comrade Simpkins!" Her face cleared. She held out her hand. As Charlie shook it, she went on, "I'm Anne Eichenlode. Yes, Alex told me you'd be coming." Turning, she called into the house: "Alex! Comrade Simpkins is here!"

A moment later, Alex Eichenlode stood next to his wife. "Come in, Charlie—may I?" he said.

"Um, sure." Charlie couldn't imagine calling the ex-Premier Alex.

"Come in, like Anne said. Can I fix you a drink? What would you like?"

"Bourbon, if you've got it. If you don't, a beer'd be fine."

"I have bourbon. Straight up or on the rocks?"

"Rocks, please," Charlie said as he stepped inside.

Alex Eichenlode fixed drinks himself. Anne introduced Charlie to their three sons: Mike, Pete, and Paul. They ranged from sixteen or so to early twenties, and were all blond like her. None of them said much. Charlie could tell they were keeping an eye on him.

Eichenlode came back with a tray with four glasses on it: bourbon for Charlie and him, beer for Anne and for Paul, the oldest boy. "Your health!" he said, raising his glass to Charlie.

"Yours and your family's!" Charlie said. They all drank. He didn't think the bourbon was Jim Beam, but it was good. He knew it wasn't anything you'd get at a place like the Valley Relic.

They stood in the crowded front room—crowded, but neat and clean—making small talk till the drinks were gone. Then Eichenlode said, "Maybe you'd like to talk outside, where we have more space?"

Charlie heard *Maybe you'd like to talk outside, where the Nibbies can't listen?* "Sure," he said. "It's a nice day."

Paul Eichenlode came out with his father and Charlie. *Watching me, yeah*, Charlie thought. Alex Eichenlode lit a cigarette. As soon as he did, Charlie did, too. The soil behind the house was sandy; not much grass grew there. Eichenlode blew out a stream of smoke. "Now," he said, "what can I do for you?" *Cut to the chase.*

"I wanted to give you something." Charlie reached into his pocket. Almost casually, Paul stepped between his father and the stranger. But Charlie didn't pull out a pistol or a knife or a grenade. In his right hand, when he opened it, lay two gold coins, one round, the other eight-sided. He held them out to Alex Eichenlode. "They're for you. You may need 'em worse'n I ever will."

Whatever the ex-Premier and his son had expected, that wasn't it. Eichenlode didn't take the gold right away. "Where in the world did you get these?" he asked slowly.

So Charlie told the story: the Russian soldiers, the oranges, the five-ruble note, the drunk officers from the Southeastern Confederate People's Republic who were plundering the vault at the WCPDR Bank branch on De Soto, all of it. He finished, "I figured *something* good oughta come to you from the goddamn invasion, anyhow. So I brought you these. And who knows? Gold can get you out of bad trouble sometimes."

"And I might land in bad trouble?" Eichenlode said.

Charlie stuck out his chin. "You know you might."

"He's right, Dad," Paul said, and stepped away from his father and Charlie.

Alex Eichenlode sighed. "Yes. He is. I wish he weren't, but he is." He studied Charlie. "I'll take them in the spirit you offer them. Thank you. Thanks from the bottom of my heart. I hope I never have to use them the way you said. And if you ever need them yourself, get in touch with me and I'll give them back." He put the gold pieces in his own pocket.

"Don't worry about it. I'll be fine. Take care of yourself, okay?" Charlie said.

Eichenlode turned to his son. "Know what, Paul? When something like this happens, it makes me think true Communism may come one day after all. It makes me hope so, anyhow."

"Don't hold your breath waiting," Paul said. Charlie felt the same way. But Alex Eichenlode, plainly, was a man who always saw the best in other people. That made him a rare politician. It made him a pretty rare human being, too.

"Can I ask you something?" Charlie said.

"Right now, Charlie, you can ask me anything."

"Did you really think you could get away with what you were doing?"

"I thought I had a chance, or I wouldn't have tried. We *are* a small country."

"Powerless," Charlie murmured.

"Powerless, yes," Eichenlode agreed. "That's probably why Comrade Zhuravlev was willing, at first, to see how things here worked out. But we frightened our neighbors, and pretty soon we frightened the Russians, too. I didn't think that would happen—not as fast as it did, for sure."

"Okay. That's a fair answer. Thanks." Charlie nodded. "And thanks for trying. I've taken up enough of your time, I guess. I'll head on back to Lancaster now." He started to turn away, then stopped. "Sooner or later, somebody somewhere *will* do it."

"I feel the same way," Eichenlode said. By Paul's expression, he didn't believe it. The world as it was argued he was right. But you never could tell, could you? Charlie started back toward the sad little bus station.

END

www.ingramcontent.com/pod-product-compliance
Lightning Source LLC
Jackson TN
JSHW080235180525
83580JS00003B/3/J